Kind OF

Pete Townsend

Kind of Misbehavin'

Pete Townsend

Matador
9 Priory Business Park
Kibworth Beauchamp
Leicestershire LE8 0RX, UK
Tel: (+44) 116 279 2299
Fax: (+44) 116 279 2277
Email: books@troubador.co.uk
Web: www.troubador.co.uk/matador

ISBN 978 1780882 062

British Library Cataloguing in Publication Data.
A catalogue record for this book is available from the British Library.

Typeset in 10.5 ITC Giovanni Std Book by Troubador Publishing Ltd, Leicester, UK

Matador is an imprint of Troubador Publishing Ltd

Printed in Great Britain by the MPG Books Group, Bodmin and King's Lynn

For Erin and Noah

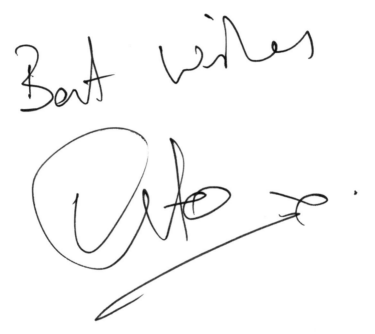

ACKNOWLEDGEMENTS

A huge round of applause to all those people that, unwittingly, provided much inspiration for this novel! And, to those who wittingly contributed, massive thanks to Liz for her editing skills, to Steve for his sterling effort in reading through an early draft and providing sage advice. In particular, thanks to Billy for his amazing artwork – yet again! To my family, thank you so much for making my life so rich. And, finally, to the love of my life, Ruth – you're wonderful!

CHAPTER 1

'You've done it again haven't you?' growled Mrs Baines, thrusting the repellent milk bottle towards her husband's face. 'If I've told you once, I must have told you a thousand times ...'

Mr Baines felt his eyes glaze. He swallowed noisily, much as he'd done on that fateful day when, under the shotgun stare of her father, he'd scrawled his signature on their marriage certificate. Since then he'd learned the secret art of servility and employed his hard-earned knowledge with a careful mix of cunning and eccentric logic. With a deftness that belied his age, Mr Baines glanced briefly at the assemblage of clothing draped around the rotund figure of his wife.

Instantly, Mrs Baines, seeing his surreptitious scrutiny of her figure, placed the milk bottle onto the kitchen table and began pulling at her cardigan.

'What do you think you're looking at?' she bristled. 'And don't,' she warned with a threatening wag of her finger, 'you dare get any funny ideas into that head of yours. I'm going over to our Edie's later while you clean that pig sty you call a shed.'

Mr Baines gave a defeatist shrug and nodded at the milk bottle.

'Do you want me to deal with that?' he asked obsequiously. Mrs Baines smartly hugged the bottle to her ample bosom.

'No,' she answered sharply, hugging the bottle even closer. 'I'll deal with it, just like I normally deal with things after you've gone about in your usual slovenly way.'

Making a feint towards the lounge door Mr Baines smiled to himself, knowing full well what would happen next.

'Don't even think about sulking in front of the television for the rest of the night,' cautioned Mrs Baines, waving the milk bottle. 'I've told you. Go and tidy that shed and don't be all night about it either.'

With apparent reluctance, Mr Baines slouched towards the backdoor triumphant in his temporary freedom for the next few hours.

The shed was the only sane environment in the life of George Henry Baines. It was the one space where he felt secure, safe from the viperous scrutiny of his wife and her incessant battle with cleanliness. Here he could enjoy blissful moments of fanciful indulgence, as he dozed in the creosote-tinged atmosphere of the wooden interior. It was also here that his alter ego, Group Captain, *Nipper* Baines, heroic fighter pilot, would swoop across the skies during the Battle of Britain in his battle-scarred Spitfire. At the end of each nightly revelry, he would arise from the deck chair, casually kick over a few rusting paints pots in the process, scatter a few sheets of newspaper carelessly over the floor in the certainty that Mrs Baines would inspect the shed the next day, mutter in dismay at the mess and tell herself that she would have to send her husband once again into his dishevelled domain to try and restore order.

As she watched the retreating figure of her husband, Mrs Baines turned to the altar of hygiene that was her kitchen sink. Turning the iniquitous milk-bottle upside down and, wiggling her podgy little finger inside the neck, she eventually retrieved the crumpled foil top that her husband habitually pushed inside. Firmly immersing the bottle into a cleansing bowl of detergent she washed away all traces of sinful bacteria.

With a final rinse she raised the bottle up to the fluorescent light of the kitchen and smiled, it was good. Satisfied with her act of ministration, Mrs Baines walked into the hallway, donned her favourite woollen coat, paused briefly to adjust her hat in the mirror, picked up her functional handbag and strode purposely towards her immaculately scrubbed front doorstep.

Outside, the Autumnal air hung cloyingly around the shrubbery while a nearby streetlamp cast an ineffectual aura into the darkness. Mrs Baines tugged at the collar of her coat as she felt the chilling fingers of the night pawing at her neck. She gave an involuntary shiver.

Lowering the freshly purged milk bottle towards the step, she paused. An almost imperceptible noise nudged at the edge of her hearing. Trance-like, she remained in a plump arc, framed in the light escaping from the confines of the hallway. Gradually, the throbbing, repetitive sound became louder, closer, indescribable according to the vocabulary of a female, whose command of language was limited to the verbs and adjectives contained within the washing instructions on a packet of detergent.

Mrs Baines listened intently for a moment and then sighed angrily. *'Typical'*, she thought to herself. *'Some young upstarts with a boombox, thumping music thing that's worth twice as much as the car disrupting a respectable, quiet neighbourhood like hers. There ought to be a law against it!'* She shut the door fiercely behind her and listened once again to the approaching, rhythmic pulse of noise. Fleetingly, she thought of rousing her husband from his ineffectual shed cleaning to make a complaint to someone in authority, but thought better of it. Knowing he'd be indulging in his nightly scuffle with the Scotch, she also knew he'd be good for nothing tonight … *thankfully*, she added as an afterthought.

Mrs Baines made a mental note to ring the appropriate people in the morning. With a sniff she walked along the path towards the geometric lines of her manicured privet hedge. At the gate, Mrs Baines stood perfectly still. The noise was gradually becoming louder but she couldn't discern from which direction the disquieting sounds were coming. A tingle of apprehension prickled the hairs on the back of her neck.

Clutching her handbag tightly to her chest, she peered anxiously into the opaque night. The noise was now almost deafening, pounding at her senses like a roaring tide. Then, as the crescendo of sound appeared to reach its peak, it stopped abruptly. Leaning forward her eyes carefully scanned the gloom, tracing every surface of the familiar surroundings. Everything appeared to be normal once again, as if the rhythmic pulse had been a figment of her imagination.

Just as she was about to unlatch the gate, a gentle waft of warm air caressed her face causing her to pause momentarily. Suddenly a loud snort pierced the night. Steaming vapour formed a shroud over her head as she came face-to-face with an apparition darker than the night itself. With a gut-wrenching scream, Mrs Baines, her eyes glistening with terror threw her hands across her face and promptly collapsed in an orderly faint to the ground, leaving the contents of her handbag scattered rebelliously over the ground.

Nipper Baines, meanwhile, celebrating a successful sortie over occupied France, was enveloped in a vapour originating from the stills of Skye. The scream barely penetrated the perimeter of his consciousness. With a vacant smile, *Nipper* raised his glass and saluted the night.

Unaware that the scourge of would-be invaders dwelt in a wooden hangar close by, the apparition gave a long, low-pitched whinny and thundered into the mist leaving a somnolent female figure sprawled death-like embraced in mist.

CHAPTER 2

Across town, where manicured privet hedges were the preserve of hired gardeners and milk was delivered direct from the supermarket, a mobile phone performed the first few bars from the *Blue Danube*.

'Hello?' responded the cautious tones of a prominent County Council Official.

'Bobcat, it's me, your little Popsicle,' replied the refined female voice.

Bobcat walked into the shadows of his hallway and whispered urgently into the phone. 'I thought I'd told you never to ring me at home,' he hissed.

'I rang your mobile,' said Popsicle emphatically.

'I realise that,' snapped Bobcat. 'But I'm still at home.'

'It's the papers,' replied Popsicle, her voice heavy with angst and ignoring Bobcat's annoyance. 'They're gone.'

'What do you mean, gone?'

'I'm not used to repeating myself,' returned Popsicle sharply. 'As I said, gone, missing, vanished, astray and not where I left them.'

The mobile phone company counted the cost of silence. Eventually, Bobcat sighed.

'That was careless,' he said heavily.

'Careless?' spat Popsicle. 'Carelessness is not in my nature,' she replied haughtily. 'Someone has removed the papers from a secure place.'

'Secure?' he replied with sarcasm. 'Obviously not as secure as you thought.'

Popsicle toyed nervously with her necklace. 'They were secure provided no-one intended to try and locate them,' she said.

'Do stop playing with your beads,' said Bobcat. 'You sound like a Nun at confession.'

Popsicle smiled into the phone. 'You should know I'm not a nun,' she breathed seductively.

Bobcat coughed. 'Yes, well, that's enough of that,' he replied hurriedly. 'Until next time anyway,' he added with a licentious smile of his own.

'There may not be a next time,' replied the Popsicle, 'if those papers fall into the wrong hands.'

'Council business,' called Bobcat over-loudly.

'What?' asked Popsicle sharply, her beads beginning to feel the strain.

'It's the wife,' whispered Bobcat. 'Look,' he said urgently. 'We must get those papers back at all costs.'

'I'll set things in motion,' replied Popsicle. 'There's too much at stake for the papers to become public.'

'Including our careers,' added Bobcat.

'And the rest,' said Popsicle. 'Let us hope that whoever has the papers is either an ignoramus or a complete fool.'

'Preferably both,' replied Bobcat hopefully. 'Coming Darling,' he added with finality.

Popsicle placed her phone and the table and picked at her beads erratically. With a sigh of determination she prodded another number into her mobile phone and mentally made a list of instructions as her phone made the necessary connection.

CHAPTER 3

Surveying the scene before him, Dick Hall, lecturer and ever the optimistic pessimist, sighed the sigh of academic malcontent. Confronted with the cerebral obstinacy of his part-time evening classes, he automatically assumed the jaded mantle of the long-suffering lecturer beloved by so many aged academics.

Dick, ever conscious of the law of diminishing returns, always endeavoured to ensure his evening class lasted no longer than was absolutely necessary. Rather than be a slavish follower of the functional clock on the rear wall of the classroom, Dick chose to take an active part in the passage of time by carrying six smooth pebbles in his trouser pocket. Every fifteen minutes during his class, he'd transfer a pebble from one trouser pocket to another until all six pebbles had found their way from his right hand pocket to the left, much as a cricket umpire would do while trying to idle their way through a yawn inducing stretch at the crease. At the precise moment that the last pebble hit the lining of his trouser pocket Dick would flick his folder of notes shut, smile a goodnight at the class and be the first through the door.

As Dick looked out over the landscape of indifference, that constituted his 'Introduction to the Principles of Marketing' class, he couldn't help but wonder what sort of convoluted logic had caused these students to choose a part-time course of study in retail persuasion. The students, representing every sort of business activity from a florist to a funeral parlour, also contained a mole. To the consternation of the academic staff, one Angie Browne, Personal Assistant to the Principal, had had the temerity to enrol on the part-time Business Studies course. Apart from the annoying fact that she was able to claim back the course fees from the College's Staff Development budget, she was also seen as an infiltrator sent to observe the supposedly nefarious activities of the lecturing staff.

Looking out once more at the learning collective, he gave an involuntary shudder and transferred a pebble between pockets.

'Not long now,' he quipped. Leaving the students bemused as to whether he was referring to the end of the lesson or some incurable medical condition. Walking briskly over to the whiteboard, he promptly withdrew a marker pen from his pocket and drew four circles onto the whiteboard.

'Now,' began Dick, tapping the whiteboard, 'just to emphasise the four points of the marketing mix, I'd like to … '

He glanced at the row of students nearest to him. Their attention seemed divided between the dark, misty night existing through the windows, and their assorted baggage, into which they were surreptitiously stuffing various items of note-taking paraphernalia. Dick allowed another sigh to escape. Clearing his throat and his mind, he tapped the whiteboard again.

'If you care to listen, you just might be the delighted recipients of a grain of knowledge which, given time, may grow,' Dick made an expansive gesture with his arms, 'into a pearl of wisdom, which if nurtured, cared for, guarded jealously, and only gazed upon in subdued lighting might allow you to enter your name correctly on your end of term revision test paper, which is a simple matter of a week away.'

Just as Dick completed his sarcastic monologue, one of the female students, usually reticent to respond to a question with words of more than one syllable, suddenly emitted an ear-piercing scream, which too only contained one syllable.

'What the Chicken Pâté?' exclaimed Dick, staring at the distraught female. 'What is it?' he asked, nervously toying with the two remaining pebbles in his pocket.

Given a direct question the girl flushed crimson and began to gesticulate at the little window in the classroom door. All eyes followed Dick as he walked towards the source of the girl's terror. He'd barely taken two steps before an inflated mouth and ill-fitting dentures appeared pressed against the glass. Dick flung the door open.

'Well good evening, Jim, and what can I do for you and your dentures on this dark and misty night?'

Jim, the guardian of the keys and all things of a care-taking nature grinned, allowing his dentures to wobble earthwards.

'Steady, Mr Hall' he mumbled. 'Ladies present you know.' Walking into the classroom, he squinted at the scrawl on the whiteboard. Ensuring that his gum enhancements were firmly in place, he nodded at the board. 'What's all this about then?'

Dick allowed another sigh to escape.

'This,' he indicated with a nod of the head. 'Is some abstract gibberish that I'm expected to colour with a hint of enthusiasm and a dash of enlightenment.' He gave a sardonic smile. 'Care to join us?'

Jim grinned again and stuck his hands deep into the pockets of his overalls. 'Not for me, Squire. Got all the education I need, thanks very much.'

Dick smiled and nodded towards the door.

'Have you been heavy breathing on every classroom window or have you selected us for some special purpose?' he enquired, casually wiping all traces of knowledge from the whiteboard.

'Don't know if you'd noticed,' sniffed Jim, rocking on the soles of his substantial Caretaker boots. 'Lot of the other staff have let their students go early,' he nodded towards the windows. 'On account of the fog,' he explained helpfully.

Dick was just about to formulate a sarcastic riposte when he noticed Jim grinning. Turning to face the once assembled class he saw the last of the students walking towards the door. Allowing a smile of resignation to decorate his face, he nodded to the student.

'I sometimes wonder why I bother,' said Dick, with a hint of dejection.

The student smiled.

'So do we Dick, so do we. See you next week.' And with a wave and hint of laughter the final student departed leaving Dick speechless. Jim followed the student through the door rattling his keys.

'Must be off,' he called over his shoulder. 'A few more jobs then I'm for home.' He disappeared down a labyrinth of corridors.

Placing his dog-eared notes into a folder, which served as his portable filing cabinet, Dick scanned the empty classroom. He began to speculate on what kind of life might exist outside of the universe that was known as East Bidding College of Further Education. Quickly shaking his head at such a fanciful notion, he dejectedly scooped up his filing cabinet and walked into the dim light of the corridor.

CHAPTER 4

In an effort to be seen as a responsible organisation, both to the community and environment, East Bidding College had implemented a series of cost-cutting procedures, which had resulted in a proliferation of posters around the College informing staff of their duty to follow the agreed guidelines for an eco-friendly learning environment. It was generally agreed that the 'eco' prefix to friendly was short for 'economic' and the guidelines were in place to save money and bolster the College's rapidly disappearing profit margin.

Feeling his way along the corridor wall, Dick peered into the eco-friendly gloom desperately attempting to negotiate his way out of the building without damaging his mental and physical health. Carefully following the vertical contours of the wall, he found his hand reach a section of the corridor, which provided him with several choices of direction. With a reluctant familiarity, he turned to his left and smiled. Before him a dull, orange glow lurked around the stairs, illuminating the exit to temporary freedom. Dick quickened his pace, confident that, short of a cataclysmic eruption of the College's heating system, he was nearing safety.

Adjusting his cardboard filing cabinet, Dick was just about to place his hand on the wooden rail that spiralled downwards when a voice cut through the darkness.

'Dick!' it rasped urgently.

'Aarrgh?' yelped Dick with fright as his nervous system imploded allowing his filing cabinet to navigate the stairs in solo flight.

'Ssssh,' urged the voice as an unseen hand gripped his elbow firmly and steered him through a doorway.

Trying desperately to adjust his eyes to the deeper gloom of the room, he shuffled cautiously forward stubbing his toes against an object that resisted his feeble attempts to nudge it out of his way.

'Stand still,' commanded the voice. A loud 'click' reverberated

11

in the darkness, swiftly followed by a regular churning sort of noise. Suddenly Dick found himself enveloped in a stark, bright light, leaving the rest of the room shrouded in shadows.

'Hey!' he blinked. 'What's so important about a little surreptitious photocopying of knitting patterns that requires my … '

'Please be quiet,' implored the voice.

Squinting against the light, Dick was reminded of the corny interrogation techniques depicted in all the second-rate films. He desperately tried to shield his eyes from the piercing glare while attempting to focus on the direction of the voice.

'Doesn't health and safety at work require the lid of the copier to be closed?' enquired Dick. 'And what is all this about anyway?'

'Something,' replied the voice, ignoring health and safety. 'That affects everyone.'

The deep, husky, female overtones of the voice would have been considered quite sexy, thought Dick, in other circumstances. The voice continued.

'In the photocopier tray, underneath a few sheets of un-copied paper, you'll find a document that I recommend you read carefully.'

'Look,' smiled Dick. 'Why don't you just hand in your assignment like any other abnormal student?'

'This isn't anything as trivial as a student's anal rambling,' insisted the voice. 'It's imperative that you keep the document safe and away from those in authority.'

'Are we talking MI5, CIA, FBI, DHSS, CSA, RSPCA?'

'Are you always this flippant?' questioned the voice irritably.

'Only on alternate weekdays, public holidays and during the Queen's speech,' replied Dick.

The voice growled with irritation. 'I thought you might be the best person to pass this document on to. Someone who would know what to do with the information and act accordingly.'

The voice paused with indecision.

'Well,' responded Dick, 'I consider that to be a totally irresponsible act of trust. You can't go around giving secret documents to any passing stranger. I could be an undercover agent for the Inland Revenue for all you know.'

'Most unlikely,' replied the voice with increasing agitation.

'Your tax code denotes a very average earner whom the Government can shackle with every possible financial regulation that exists officially and unofficially.'

'How the hell do you know what my tax code is?' growled Dick.

'That's trivia compared to the other things I know about you Dick. For instance, I know that you are overdrawn each month equivalent to your net salary, you buy a bottle of red wine every Friday evening which you consume in the company of a certain lady while listening to anything from Mingus to Monk.'

'You into the jazz stuff then?' asked Dick, eager to divert the conversation away from his economic behaviour.

'I sometimes indulge in Mahler or Mozart,' replied the voice, 'but I prefer Puccini to Prokofiev.'

'Classical buff then,' acknowledge Dick. He continued to shield his eyes from the fierce light issuing from the monotony of the photocopier. 'Look, is there any chance of putting the lid on that damn machine? Only it's giving me a cracking headache and I can't see a bloody thing.'

'That's the intention,' declared the voice. 'Well, the restricted vision, not the headache,' it said apologetically.

Dick emitted another sigh. Sighing seemed to be a feature of this evening he thought.

'Look,' said Dick with exasperation. 'What do you expect me to do with this document? It's not as if I'm senior management or anything.'

'That's exactly the reason for contacting you. When you've read the document I'm confident you'll know what to do.' The voice paused again. 'Well, sort of confident,' it added.

'I'm glad somebody is.' Dick shuffled his feet. 'But, just in case I haven't got a clue what to do, is there any way I can contact you?'

After a few quiet seconds, the voice produced a conclusive sniff. 'You know Regeneration Sounds in Wheelwright Lane don't you?'

'You seem confident that I do,' sighed Dick.

'Just leave a note for me in Duke Ellington's 'Money Jungle' CD. You'll find my reply in Charlie Parker's 'Yardbird Suite' later the same afternoon.'

'You seem to know your jazz,' congratulated Dick.

'I know a lot of things,' rasped the voice huskily, 'but some things need action, which is where you come in. Don't let me down.'

'Listen,' queried Dick, 'how do you know the shop will have these CD's in stock? And where shall I put the note if somebody has already bought Duke's CD?'

An expectant pause echoed as his words hung in the air. The photocopier continued to churn out its facsimiles. Dick reached forward and paused the copier mid-flow. The room reconstructed itself into silent darkness.

'Are you still here?' he asked the shadows. There was no reply. The only evidence of there being anyone else in the room was a stack of warm, blank paper and the faint smell of peppermint lingering in the air. Dick felt in the photocopier's tray and extracted a large paper folder. Concealing the document beneath his jacket, he left the room with a heady mixture of excitement and consternation. The thought that somebody might trust him to act responsibly and how a complete stranger knew so much about him was a complete, although not unpleasant surprise. Shaking his head, Dick went in search of his filing cabinet with which he'd parted company only a few minutes before.

CHAPTER 5

Dick threw his mobile filing cabinet onto the nearest table. The 'Bull & Gate', held all the allure of a public convenience at a railway station, but for most of the staff employed at the College, the pub was home. Inhaling the yeasty fug, he allowed his eyelids to draw a curtain over the indistinct images that formed the pub's clientele.

'Bright, full-bodied and ripe for consumption and I'll have a pint too,' called a friendly voice.

Dick opened his eyes and grinned; at least he could identify the owner of those masculine tones.

'Hi, Dubbya,' grinned Dick. 'Still got your eyes on the barmaid then?'

Dubbya smiled expansively.

'As always dear boy, as always.' He arched his back, allowing an expanse of indulged stomach to nudge the table. 'Life is far too short,' he continued, 'to pretend that we adhere to the protocol of an anally retentive, emotional fossil.'

Dick sauntered towards the bar, a broad grin spreading across his face. It felt good to be with other human beings who weren't trying to suck his brain dry in an attempt to pass meaningless exams, which qualified them to join the great farmyard of shared educational ineptitude. He ordered two pints and looked over to Dubbya. Acknowledging Dick, by raising his glass and nodding towards the barmaid, he yawned and gently caressed his abdominal bulge.

Dick grinned to himself, remembering the first time he'd met Dubbya. It had been during the obligatory induction meeting for all new staff at the College, which, with few flickers of recognition amongst the nervously mingling recruits, they'd found themselves sitting next to each other. After initial pleasantries, which ventured no further than exchanging the briefest of nods and a raised eyebrow at the assembled throng, Dick and Dubbya had quickly settled down to sleep cruise through the day. In an odd moment of consciousness, Dick had become dumbstruck at the Principle's vitriolic attack on the supposed elitism prevalent within the Education system. At the eagerly welcomed coffee break, Dick eagerly sought out Dubbya in the caffeine queue.

'Rather sulphurous monologue, don't you think?' commented Dubbya, acknowledging Dick.

'He lets you know what he thinks anyway,' grinned Dick in agreement.

Heaping three spoons of sugar into his caffeine and selecting as many custard cream biscuits as his spare hand could hold, Dubbya smiled.

'A trifle unhinged if I were to offer a professional opinion,' he replied, inserting a handful of biscuit into his mouth. 'Still,' he mumbled, 'at least we're getting paid to suffer this for a day. It beats teaching,' burbled Dubbya spraying the air with particles of custard cream.

Collecting his coffee and clutching the remaining custard cream, Dick sat on a tired plastic chair.

'He's got a point though,' replied Dick, licking the edges of his biscuit.

'Agreed' replied Dubbya, somewhat to Dick's surprise

'You really think so?'

'Two things strike me,' munched Dubbya. 'Firstly, is the abandonment of the notion that education should be about nurturing the individual and encouraging potential,' he said noisily drinking from his cup. 'And, secondly,' he slurped, 'is the inability of adults to correctly estimate the point of disintegration for the humble biscuit dunked in a hot liquid.'

Giving up the unfair challenge of rescuing sodden biscuit particles from his coffee, Dick sucked at his scalded fingertips and then offered Dubbya a damp handshake.

'My name's Dick.'

'Dick, I'm really pleased to meet you. People call me 'Dubbya''. He shook Dick's hand vigorously. 'And do not think of American political dynasties, think more of the multiple interpretation of phrases.' He smiled at Dick's cognitive discomfort. 'I'm an arch proponent of the à double entendre,' said Dubbya helpfully.'

Two years later and Dick fully appreciated Dubbya's propensity for the use of words with multiple interpretations closely followed by his capacity for beer. He placed the recently acquired pint in front of his colleague.

'Cheers, Dick,' frothed Dubbya. 'And how are you this dull and misty night?'

Dick took a deep draught of his beer.

'Bemused, confused, dazed, perplexed and other associated words normally confined to a thesaurus,' replied Dick.

'Life's a cryptic crossword, Dick. You need to appreciate the obscure to find the meaning.'

Dick, temporarily ignoring Dubbya's analysis of life, wiped the vestiges of brewery froth from his mouth, sighed one of his countless sighs of the evening and turned to Dubbya.

'I've just had a most disturbing experience with a female, well, I think it was a female,' frowned Dick.

Almost choking on his beer, Dubbya dabbed at the drops of escaped liquid on his chin and quickly placed his glass on the table.

'Dick,' he replied, 'there are two golden rules concerning amorous liaisons with students. One, don't, and two, if you must, don't get caught. Oh, and I suppose you should add a third, make sure it's got the appropriate equipment for whatever you have in mind.'

Dick shook his head.

'Nothing to do with a student, at least I don't think it was a student. It was far too dark to see and anyway, the light was in my face.'

This time, Dubbya did choke on his beer. In an act of masculine solidarity, Dick thumped his back until the choking had diminished to a feeble gurgle.

'OK, OK, already,' gasped Dubbya. 'Go easy on the framework.'

'Only trying to help,' smiled Dick. 'Can't have you expiring before you've finished your pint.'

'Such thoughtfulness,' coughed Dubbya, trying valiantly to restore some sense of normality to his speech. He rearranged the random creases of his fashion resistant cardigan and smiled benignly at Dick. The smile bestowed upon Dubbya all the characteristics of an elderly orang-utan who'd shed most of its hirsute exterior in favour of a bag of wrinkles. He nodded at Dick.

'Rewind would you and tell me from the beginning, slowly so that I can process the facts, digest the content and respond with an appropriate riposte.'

Inhaling sufficient breath, Dick launched into his tale.

'I'll skip over the banal bits shall I? You know, students, words thrown into the rarefied atmosphere to fall with a resounding thud on the floor, then trampled upon in the stampede of students exiting the hallowed halls of learning?'

Dubbya grimaced.

'Pass over the contemptible, get to the important part.'

Dick smiled and continued.

'After the visual treat of our beloved Jim encouraging us to leave the building indiscreetly early, I was navigating by radar through the darkened corridor, when I was summoned into the photocopying room by a husky female voice.'

'The stuff of dreams,' breathed Dubbya.

'It got really weird then,' said Dick thoughtfully.

'Weird? How?' demanded Dubbya, beads of sweat beginning to form on his top lip.

'Well, she had the photocopier going.'

'Appropriate, disguises noise,' interjected Dubbya excitedly.

'And she had the lid of the copier open so that the light shone directly into my eyes.'

'A simple act of demureness?'

'More like she didn't want to be recognised.'

'Incognito eh?' drooled Dubbya. 'An illicit liaison enacted against the industrial overtures of a reproductive object, how enthrallingly Freudian.'

'She said how that I was chosen as I would know what to do.'

'A discriminating seductress, superb,' enthused, Dubbya, his hands subconsciously stroking the edge of the table.

'And then she gave me a document to read,' concluded Dick.

A full-throttled chortle burst from Dubbya's mouth.

'She chose you because you could read simple instructions,' he said, struggling to control his lips. Taking another draught of beer and savouring both the liquid and the mental images formed from the narrative, he nudged Dick's arm.

'Go on, don't keep my voyeuristic thoughts waiting.'

'Didn't get a chance to read the document,' replied Dick, as Dubbya leaned back in his chair with fingers playing a thoughtful rhythm on his stomach.

'Acted on impulse and instinct,' he nodded encouragingly. 'Good man.'

Dick frowned. He wasn't at all sure whether he was being wound up or Dubbya really did think there had been some sort of sensual encounter. He shook his head.

'She disappeared before I could ask who she was, strange that.'

'Not at all,' pronounced Dubbya. 'Simply protecting her anonymity. Have you still got the document?' he asked, quickly abandoning his salacious thoughts for the more practical.

Dick took the document from its hiding place beneath his tired jacket and shrugged his shoulders.

'Nothing much to be secretive about,' observed Dick. 'Just columns of figures, copies of memos and what looks like a transcript of a meeting or something like it.'

Dubbya studied the document. In between turning pages he took alternate sips of his beer absentmindedly. Every now and again he would mumble a *'Mmm, ahah, tut* and *oh!'* Dick tried counting the number of dust-gathering books around the walls of the pub and gave up after two hundred and twelve. A sharp prod gained his attention.

'Better put that back under your jacket,' suggested Dubbya. He shoved the document across the table.

'Anything of interest?' enquired Dick.

Dubbya stared into space, prompting Dick to push a freshly acquired pint of beer towards Dubbya's hand. A millisecond later and the silence slurped into history as the beer disappeared quicker than it had been poured.

'Much appreciated,' thanked Dubbya with a lick of his lips. He prodded the surface of the document. 'Not the kind of thing to set your pulse racing and propel you on a flight of fancy,' he said looking yearningly at his empty beer glass. 'However,' he continued, his eyes flicking between his glass and the bar. 'I'm always suspicious of any document that contains rows of numbers and lots of abbreviations.' He sat back in his chair and rested his hands across an expanse of cardigan. He sniffed knowingly. 'Abbreviations, by their very nature, mean to shorten or,' he arched his eyebrows, 'to prune, cut back, to take a slice out of something.' Dubbya leaned forward and smacked the surface of the table with his hand. 'To make something less than what it once was!'

Several beer-laden eyes looked over at Dick and Dubbya. Ignoring the amused interest his actions had caused, he leaned towards Dick.

'How healthy is your bank balance?' he asked, his hop-tinged breath washing over Dick.

Moving his face discreetly away from the fusty odour, Dick shrugged.

'Well,' he replied thoughtfully. 'Fair to destitute, I'd say.'

'No wealthy crusties ready to ascend the stairway to heaven who might leave you a little farewell in their will?

Nibbling his top lip in thought, Dick slowly shook his head.

'Doubtful,' he replied. 'Doubtful that any of them will ascend and equally doubtful they'll bother to leave me anything.'

'Bit of a shame that,' sniffed Dubbya. 'But what I mean is,' he said with an emphatic tapping of the table with a soggy beer mat. 'What else would you do if you couldn't teach?'

Dick frowned. The evening was beginning to give him a headache.

'Always fancied playing the guitar in any sticky-floored dive that pays folding money,' he replied flippantly. 'Teaching is the nearest I ever get to performing before an audience.'

Dubbya closed his eyes and smiled. 'My dear boy,' he began. 'I've always subscribed to the view that teaching is twenty percent inspiration and seventy-five percent perspiration.'

With a wry chuckle, Dick arched a questioning eyebrow. Dubbya gave one of his non-committal shrugs.

'And five-percent for performing an act of human kindness,' he added with a droop of his eyelid. 'And allowing the students to escape academia with most of their senses intact.'

Dick nodded.

'One always has to suffer for their art.'

'Or make others suffer,' commented Dubbya with a crooked smile. 'Anyway, I suggest that after reading the document, suffering may form an ever increasing part of your existence.'

'Meaning?' asked Dick with an arch of his eyebrow.

Dubbya ran his finger slowly around the inside of his beer glass and sucked his finger noisily.

'My advice, such as it is,' he offered, licking his lips. 'Is to find out who or what those figures intend to prune. And,' he added with a flourish of his recently sucked finger. 'Discover who is going to benefit from our subsequent financial suffering.' He stared wistfully at his beer glass. 'Must be off,' he shivered. 'Need to put the milk bottles out before morning.'

With a casual wave Dubbya disappeared into the gut of the pub, leaving Dick staring at the document in a complete state of bewilderment. Disembodied voices were one thing, he thought, but when the very tangible form of Dubbya expressed concern, it was either a time for worry or action. A fleeting image of a certain lady flashed through his mind. It was time for the latter.

CHAPTER 6

The phone gave a sardonic trill as it disturbed the early morning fug that enveloped PC Ricketts's senses. With a slight hiss of exertion, she extended her arm and pulled the telephone towards her body. A series of vowels and consonants pummelled her eardrum until eventually she gave an imperceptible nod and equally inaudible grunt and replaced the receiver.

The physical effort of turning her body caused a brief spasm of consciousness to flutter her eyelids. Swallowing for effect, she managed a restrained coughed and waited for a glimmer of recognition to cast its shadow on Sergeant Cost's features.

'Sarge?' enquired PC Ricketts. 'Are we open for business?'

Sergeant Cost paused on three down of the daily paper's quick crossword. His eyes surveyed the uniformed features of PC Ricketts without interest. It wasn't the fact that her female form held no interest for him, far from it, but he'd developed a rabid distaste for anything in uniform.

'Sarge?' persisted PC Ricketts.

'Eh?' replied a particularly articulate Sarge.

'Do we want anything to do with hypothermia?' she asked.

"Hypo?' replied Sarge excitedly. 'Did you say "Hypo"?'

"Thermia" elaborated PC Ricketts.

'Grand,' smiled Sarge, 'just grand that.' His pen scribbled quickly on the paper. 'Real grand,' he reiterated.

'Sarge?' enquired an increasingly perplexed PC.

Sergeant Cost tapped his paper. 'Three down,' he grinned, "Medical prefix."

PC Ricketts shook her befuddled head slowly.

'Whatever,' she sighed.

Pausing on fourteen across, Sergeant Cost smiled benignly. 'Something to say Constable?' he asked with a syrupy slur to his voice.

PC Ricketts closed her eyes momentarily, took a deep breath and proceeded to relate the telephone message.

'Phone, ring, disrupt stupor, hospital, nurse, old lady taken in with hypothermia, rambling about ghostly apparition, husband drunk as a skunk in a shed.' She paused, took another breath and continued. 'Do we want to interview a somewhat less than lucid lady and her paralytic partner?'

Sergeant Cost smiled as his head moved negatively.

'Write it in the book,' he instructed the PC, 'and make us a cup of tea will you?'

PC Ricketts complied with the instruction and then sauntered towards the canteen, pausing briefly to wave an index finger at Sergeant Cost's back.

CHAPTER 7

On the other side of town, appearing as a sort of nondescript, geometric smudge on the landscape, sat East Bidding College of Further Education. Designed with architectural indifference, the origins of the College could be traced back to the early 1960's, as an establishment for the education of persons who wanted some form of elevation from the pit of the primary sector. A grand opening with local dignitaries and tactless journalists saw a ceremony planned with meticulous detail, albeit with one slight oversight: there were no students to welcome.

Not to be thwarted by a minor irrelevance, a council official snatched a rather bemused pensioner from the crowd of expectant onlookers and made a great show of handing the pensioner an enrolment form for the new College. The small band of journalists, eager to get back to the office for a mug of tea, quickly warmed their pencils on the pages of their notebooks. Unfortunately, the pensioner, a certain Mr Gresley, when asked what he thought of the new college responded in vernacular style.

'I've only come to walk me bloody dog, and what do I find? Someone's built a great sodding outhouse right across the fields where me dog dumps its load. Downright liberty taking I call it. I'll have you know I fought in the last war to protect fields like these so that dogs could crap in peace without ... '

Mr Gresley's final comments were lost amidst a choreographed orchestra of spontaneous applause from embarrassed dignitaries and council officials.

As the years slid by, the College, having never quite erased the demeaning sobriquet awarded by Mr Gresley, continued to labour under the colloquial *East Bidding's Outhouse*. It was as the *Outhouse* that the College's staff continually referred to their place of employment, a fact often used by local Head Teachers who would admonish their own staff with threats of being sent to work at the *Outhouse* if they didn't improve their results.

It was while Dick drove to the *Outhouse,* that he pondered on the previous night's encounter. Somehow, in the light of day, it all seemed surreal, a sort of close encounter of the imaginary kind. Dismissing the event by humming a few bars of Perry Como's version of 'Magic Moments', Dick nosed his ageing Peugeot, into the staff-parking arena and walked reluctantly into the main building.

Negotiating the all too familiar staircase, Dick manoeuvred his reluctant body between the expressionless figures decorating the stairs. He often wondered why students found perpendicular loitering so compulsive, especially on stepped inclines and so early in the day. Muttering the occasional 'excuse me', Dick's autopilot successfully navigated a course to the business studies staff-room.

With a barely audible 'Morning', Dick made his way toward the communal kettle. A quick snatch and grab informed Dick that no water lurked in the murky interior. 'Shit!' he announced to no one in particular.

'Wrong receptacle, wrong room,' declared a slightly muffled feminine voice.

'Hello, Tina,' replied Dick, as he watched her busily drain every last drop of caffeine from the mug her face explored so diligently.

'How are you?' he enquired.

'All the better for seeing you,' she smiled. 'However, that may be a caffeine fuelled response, so I'll reply in my usual style.' Clasping her hands to her face, Tina performed a silent replica of Edvard Munch's agonised figure from *The Scream.* Having completed her facial contortions, Tina swallowed noisily, brushed at her sleeves, and sat back at her desk.

Dick sniffed.

'That's what I like, a touch of normality on a day such as this.'

Fresh from her expressionist scream, Tina gave Dick a bemused stare.

'And what, pray, is a day such as this?' she queried.

'Nothing of note,' he replied. 'Suffice to say that we're here, not where we want to be but where we have to be given that this government is more adept at picking pockets than Fagin himself.'

'He's just a piece of fiction, much like the idea of democracy and freedom of speech,' remarked Tina.

'And that's just here in the College,' smirked Dick. 'I don't like to think about the outside world.'

Tina shrugged. She dragged her finger around the inside of her coffee mug and eagerly sucked on the resulting dregs.

'Don't worry your head with such thoughts,' she advised. 'Have a mug of coffee.'

'I would but there's no water.'

Tina raised both her eyebrows and shoulders in a synchronised action that celebrated the ingestion of caffeine.

'Since when has that stopped you?' she asked.

'True,' nodded Dick. Confidently walking over to a filing cabinet that had found a more satisfying role as a repository for digestive aids, he quickly prised the lid from the jar of instant coffee. Licking his finger, he stuck it deep into the granular recess. Satisfied that he'd acquired sufficient caffeine, Dick lifted his finger into his mouth, closed his eyes and sucked noisily.

'Better?' asked Tina, as she frowned at Dick's quirky behaviour.

'Mmm, just what I needed,' he said returning his finger into the jar. He lifted a granular finger and pointed it questioningly towards Tina.

Tina grinned. 'Thank you, but no.' She nodded at his hand. 'Look at the state of your fingers, they look like those of a tobacco fetishist.'

Dick examined his browned fingers.

'Smoking?' he asked. 'Disgusting habit,' he mused whilst examining his fingers. 'Much like trying to pronounce *fetishist* first thing in the morning, extremely anti-social.'

Placing the jar back on the top of the filing cabinet, Dick threw his carrier bag of academic paraphernalia under the desk, sat heavily in his chair and began licking the remnants of coffee from his lips. Tina, meanwhile, having thrown a student's essay into the waste bin in exasperation at the number of spelling errors and grammatical mistakes she'd read in the first sentence, blew out her cheeks noisily.

'If I never see another piece of student drivel,' she began.

'It'll be a moment too soon,' finished Dick with a grin. 'Usual standard?' he enquired airily.

'Standards!' rasped Tina. 'They went down the pan a long time ago.'

'Appropriate terminology,' smirked Dick. 'I suppose that's what happens when you've worked in the *Outhouse* for so long.'

Tina gave Dick a stare that would have frozen the assets on a polar bear had one been sufficiently reckless enough to amble into the staff room. She took a deep breath.

'If,' she began, 'by any chance you might be referring in any way, shape or form to my age.'

Dick held up a pair of apologetic hands.

'No, no,' he spluttered. 'I wouldn't be so insensitive. Besides,' he added with a gratuitous smile. 'Everybody knows that you were a child protégé eagerly conscripted to bestow your wisdom and knowledge upon an ungrateful hoard.'

A scrunched-up ball of newspaper hit Dick sharply on the forehead.

'Silver-tongue,' grinned Tina. 'You'd sell coal to an Eskimo,' she quipped.

Dick frowned. 'Isn't it supposed to be snow to the Eskimos and coals to Newcastle?' he asked. A second ball of newspaper hit his head.

'Don't try to be a smartass,' she warned. 'It doesn't suit you.'

'Well,' replied Dick brushing at his sleeve. "I'll tell you what else doesn't suit me.'

Tina sighed expectantly. Dick continued ministering to his sleeves, oblivious to Tina's need for salacious gossip. A third ball of newspaper flew towards Dick. Moving his head deftly out of the flight path, he smiled smugly.

'And neither does being a clever-dick suit you,' said Tina, fumbling with a fourth ball of newspaper.

Dick held both hands up in surrender.

'OK,' he grinned.

Tina rolled the newspaper ball around the desktop.

'Well?' she asked threateningly.

'I had an interesting encounter last night,' answered Dick casually.

Tina groaned and raised the palm of her hand towards Dick. 'I do not need to hear of your sordid exploits,' she said firmly. 'But,' she grinned mischievously. 'Should you so wish to appraise me of any regrettable behaviour, I might feel the urge to share my recently acquired knowledge with a certain female librarian.'

'Hey, there's no need for that,' said Dick, almost choking in his hurry to speak. 'It was simply a conversation that intrigued me, nothing salacious or life threatening,' he added hastily.

'Gotcha!' beamed Tina.

'That was uncalled for.'

'So was the age inference.'

'I never did,' replied Dick with a hint of indignation.

'That's as maybe,' breathed Tina. 'Now, you mentioned something about intrigue?'

'Oh, yes,' said Dick. 'Have you heard any hints on the rumour mill concerning the future of the College as we know it?'

Tina massaged her eyelids. 'Can't say that I have, but as you well know, there's forever talk of changing this and changing that,' she added with a shake of the head. 'Never gets done, it's always the same old same old.' She looked at Dick suspiciously. 'Do you know something that I don't?' she asked with a menacing twitch of her eyebrows.

'No, nothing at all,' soothed Dick. 'But, as they say, watch this space.'

'I will,' she warned. 'But should I ever find out that you've been holding out on me ... '

'God forbid,' smiled Dick with his hands held high. 'But should you come across anything just a little odd, you'll let me know?'

Tina cocked her head to one side. 'Come to think of it, there was an odd incident at the bottom of our street last night.'

'Odd?" asked Dick politely. 'How odd?'

'Well,' said Tina, mentally recalling the images and sounds of the previous night. 'An old lady was carried off in an ambulance with talk of a prowler or something equally nasty lurking in the undergrowth.'

'Different,' replied Dick. 'But I wouldn't have said it was odd.'

'Maybe not,' mused Tina. 'But some of the neighbours did mention hearing a funny noise, although it could have been the old bloke from the same house who was shouting *Tally Ho*, and *Up and at 'em boys*, as his wife was helped into the ambulance.'

'You do see life in your neck of the woods,' grinned Dick. 'Now,' he continued, rummaging in his carrier bag for a dog-eared copy of *Marketing for Dummies*. 'Just off to illuminate some Year Two students,' he informed Tina. 'But first I must see a woman about an ancient text, which has recently come to light.'

As Dick walked through the door into the bustle of the corridor, Tina heard him mutter something about it being a *'very bright light at that,'* leaving her feeling slightly confused, which was quite a normal situation for any conversation between Dick and herself. With the beginnings of guilt creeping into her consciousness, she rescued the binned essay and, with threats of vile torture, she continued to read the scribbled drivel assaulting her sanity.

Meanwhile, with arms wrapped around the bundle of papers, Dick carefully trod his way along the corridor towards the library.

Passing walls painted with every shade of a discontinued colour chart, Dick finally pushed open the double doors, revealing rows of shelves devoted to upholding learning at every level. He grinned as he caught sight of his quarry. Seated almost regally behind a well-groomed desk, Tracey dealt speedily and efficiently with the queue of students standing orderly in front of her desk.

Walking towards the quasi-monarch, Dick recalled the time a student, revered for his ability to intimidate teaching staff, had ignored Tracey's orderly regime, leant heavily on her desk, smiled at the assembled throng of students and promptly fell to the floor as the crushing force of the 2nd March made its impression on the back of his hand.

Returning the out-dated, date stamp to its revered position on her desk, Tracey gave him a beatific smile and asked for his full name as she filled out the necessary information in the accident book. The student, known from that date as *two-stroke-three*, had since become a familiar sight in the library, helping to return books to their appropriate shelves, collect magazines recklessly strewn around the tables and, whenever Tracey was engaged elsewhere, deputised by leaning heavily on any would-be miscreant.

Bypassing the orderly queue, Dick sauntered across to Tracey and gave her his most winning smile. Several members of the queue visibly cowered at the display of such foolhardy behaviour, whilst an indignant few smouldered at the audacity of a member of staff jumping the queue. Without hesitation, Tracey returned his smile and suggested, most courteously, that he would find it more suitable for his health if he were to go to the back of the queue and wait patiently like everyone else. To a chorus of grins, Dick made his way to the rear of the waiting figures.

Finally, after fifteen minutes of patient shuffling, he stood at the head of the queue. Before he could mouth a single consonant, Tracey placed a small, but effective sign on the desk. Dick frowned.

'What do you mean, you're closed?'

Tracey tapped the sign.

'It does exactly what it says on the desk. I'm closed.'

'To everyone?' enquired Dick.

'To everyone,' confirmed Tracey. 'Unless, that is, you are offering to buy me coffee and a stale bun from the canteen?'

CHAPTER 8

Seated in the canteen of East Bidding College of Further Evasion, Dick and Tracey slurped their coffee against a backdrop of indiscernible chatter, indefinable eating habits and indiscriminate embraces.

Tracey inhaled the noxious fumes that steamed from her coffee.

'To what do I owe the pleasure of your company whilst drinking ... ,' Tracey took a quick look into the mug cradled in her hands. 'This brown fluid and,' she continued, prodding the exceptionally stale bun in front of her, 'this reject from the brickyard?'

Dick shrugged. He began where he thought it most expedient.

'I met this woman last night, I think. Anyway ... ouch!' Dick clambered under the table to rub his recently damaged shin. 'What was that for?'

Tracey produced a look that would have withered a bunch of flowers at thirty paces.

'You have the temerity to ask such a question?' she spat. 'What else did you expect?' she asked, waving the piece of stale pastry in front of him. 'I could have force fed you this bun thing, but even I'm not that cruel.'

Dick's head appeared above the table. His face revealed the amount of acute pain that was currently playing havoc with his pride.

'At least let me finish what I'm saying before you hand out corporal punishment.' His head disappeared back under the table. 'I thought the birch and other methods of torture had been banned in educational establishments. Couldn't have read the small print, obviously,' he muttered.

'Stop grumbling and make yourself visible, I need something to aim at,' demanded Tracey.

'I'm not coming up until you promise not to inflict grievous mental damage or any other form of pain,' replied his muffled voice from under the table.

'OK, a truce,' agreed Tracey, 'but only until I hear the full sordid details of your female encounter and I think of some suitable retribution.'

Dick gradually forced himself into an upright position. After a cautious sip of his coffee, he studied the indignant face of his female antagonist. It was her hair that had first drawn his attention. He'd always been a real sucker for long hair, regardless of colour, frizz, curls or the silky straight kind. Tracey Barton's hair was of the dusky brown, fairly curly with a hint of frizz variety. Dick had awarded her seven out of ten before he'd seen her face or heard her voice. She'd been stacking recently returned books onto their respective shelves when he'd coughed politely and enquired whether she had anything on Charles Handy. At hearing his voice, she'd casually glanced over her shoulder and smiled.

'Nothing that the police would be interested in,' she'd replied. 'But I did hear that he was the son of an archdeacon, not that you can hold that against him.'

Dick had swallowed involuntarily.

'I didn't quite mean that kind of "anything on", but ... '

Tracey had turned around to give Dick the full force of her personality.

'I know,' she replied grinning. 'I was just responding to a cliché.'

Unfortunately, clichés were now the least of Dick's concerns.

'Well?' snapped Tracey, bringing Dick back to the present with a deft tap on the head with the stale bun.

'Well, what?' he replied, brushing crumbs off his forehead.

'Pussy's in it, and you too if you don't explain yourself.'

Dick searched the inner confines of his brain in an attempt to extricate himself from a sticky situation. He realised that anything he said now would be scrutinised, analysed and queried irrespective of his attempts to make it all sound believable. The difficulty was that even he found the whole episode to be unbelievable so what chance had he trying to explain the event to Tracey? He shuddered.

Deciding to forego the delights of tortuous interrogation, for the moment, Tracey took pity on the poor, unfortunate man opposite her.

'Why don't you start from the beginning and end at the point where I impale you on something sharp and painful looking?'

'You wouldn't go that far, would you,' mumbled Dick.

'There's always that possibility,' replied Tracey smiling, 'Start talking and don't leave out any of the sordid details.'

Dick then recounted the events of that bizarre evening, occasionally flinching whenever he mentioned words, which vaguely referred to the possible feminine bits of the encounter. When he'd finished, a silence, if it were possible to call a lapse in conversation amidst the surrounding cacophony of guttural exclamations a silence, existed.

Dick raised his eyebrows.

'Well?'

'Don't start me on wells,' said Tracey thoughtfully. She stared at the grime stained windows adorning the outer walls of the canteen. 'I presume you've read the document thoroughly?'

Dick allowed his face to crease in displeasure.

'I've read and re-read it but it just seems like a load of incomprehensible drivel to me.' He cocked his head to one side. 'Although Dubbya thinks it's important, I've no idea why anyone should want to give me a pile of cryptic refuse.'

Tracey ran her finger around the rim of her coffee mug thoughtfully.

'It all sounds rather intriguing,' she mused.

Dick rubbed his rapidly bruising shin.

'What kind of intriguing?'

Tracey thought for a moment. What kind of intriguing did she mean? Was she intrigued because Dick had been accosted by a voice that appeared to belong to a female? Was she intrigued because the whole story sounded so implausible that it had to be true? Or was she simply intrigued at the strength of her feelings? She certainly wasn't intrigued by the thought of a relationship that, in her experience, had all the longevity of a date stamp where, sooner or later, the item had to be returned for someone else to go through the introduction, become embroiled in the plot, explore the sub text and, finally reach a conclusion. Dick, despite his rapacious appetite for all things jazz, had provided a new chapter in her life, which she was loath to close. He certainly added a touch of eccentricity to what could otherwise be a dull existence with all the possibility of her being left on, what Tracey referred to as her self-inflicted pun, the notorious *shelf*. She wanted Dick to be part of her world and she his, regardless of his tendency to be grammatically incorrect during moments of passion.

'Don't worry,' smiled Tracey, stroking his hand. 'Do you still have this mysterious document in your possession?'

'Not on me at present,' replied Dick, 'it's in a safe place.'

'How safe's safe?' she queried.

'It's under the bed.'

'How on earth did you find room for it under there?' she enquired almost innocently.

'Cheek,' snorted Dick. 'I cleaned the entire bedroom fairly recently,' he added feigning injured pride.

'Really?' asked Tracey, trying to recall the state of the bedroom the last time she'd seen it.

'Yes, really,' replied Dick. 'I always like to have clean sheets and a tidy bedroom on my birthday.'

'That was six months ago,' growled Tracey with a threatening wave of the bun.

'Soon be time to do it again then,' replied Dick with a smile, which quickly turned into a grimace as Tracey brought the stale bun down hard on his knuckles.

'What the ... ' winced Dick.

'You might well ask,' said Tracey with the bun still hovering dangerously in the air. 'Six months is a long time to wait for a lot of things.'

'Things?' asked Dick as he gently massaged his knuckles.

'Do I need to elaborate?'

Dick did his best to smile.

'Look, why don't you come around to my place and share a bottle of Côtes-du-Rhône and have a look at this damn document, which is causing me more grief than I care to suffer.'

Tracey gave a chuckle, and twirled the stale bun between her fingers thoughtfully. 'Maybe,' she replied casually. 'Or maybe not,'

34

she continued. 'It depends on whether you have something worth offering besides a glass or two of liquid velvet?'

'Any something in particular?' asked Dick with a broad smile.

Tracey sat back in her chair. 'I was thinking along the lines of something tasty and sensual,' she said provocatively.

'Will I do?'

'I very much doubt it,' answered Tracey with a twitch of a grin. 'Unless you come accompanied by a rather large box of chocolates.'

Dick sighed.

'Your wish is my command, my dear one.'

Tracey stood up and nodded towards the exit. 'Duty calls,' she said with a shrug of resignation. 'Don't forget,' she called walking towards the doors, 'Something tasty and sensual.'

Dick watched the doors swing shut behind Tracey as a significant number of winks and knowing smiles emanated from the people at adjacent tables. Nervously sipping at his cooling coffee he began chipping at the extra-stale bun with his fingers. Leaning back and chewing at the bits of bun stuck under his fingernails, he surveyed the sea of munching heads around him. 'Weird,' he thought, 'right bloody weird.'

CHAPTER 9

Having completed his 11 o'clock obligation to a bunch of reluctant second year students, Dick sat in the staff room with his feet at a forty-five degree angle, munching an apple. Tina was the first to comment that Dick looked most uncomfortable with his legs sticking out unsupported.

'Isn't there supposed to be a desk under there somewhere?' she queried. 'Or even a subservient student?'

Ron, whose forte was supposed to be in Accounts but had still to decipher the intricacies of a solar-powered calculator, scratched his crotch and belched with aplomb.

'Making the place look untidy if you ask me,' he commented.

'Nobody asked you,' chorused Dick and Tina.

Ron belched again and ducked just in time as the remnants of an apple core flew within millimetres of his head, to land alongside a compost heap of rotting fruit that had accumulated on the shelf below the window.

Dick lowered his legs with relief.

'Good for the stomach muscles but bad for someone with a low pain threshold,' he mused.

'Don't do it then you daft bugger,' said Tina, busily shuffling a stack of unmarked essays into some semblance of order.

'Tokenism,' replied Dick, with his feet now firmly embedded on the desk.

'Just being here is tokenism,' offered Ron, 'we make a token effort to educate the massed hordes of those who aspire to nothing more than the ability to breathe, fornicate, sleep and eat,' he belched again for emphasis, 'and not always in that order.'

He rearranged his trousers, which had somehow become embroiled in a wrestling match with his braces and continued.

'We make a token effort to achieve the targets set for us by those that God has deemed unfit to empty dustbins and instead installed as paragons of inefficiency and ineffectiveness.' At this point, Ron stood up, gave a regal flourish with his right hand and took an exaggerated bow. 'To our senior management, we salute you.'

The staff-room door shuddered as it yielded to the force of Dubbya's entry.

'Rise and shine everyone,' he yelled. 'Time for a strange tale of life, the universe and all things of a dubious nature.' He took in the scene in front of him and frowned. 'Talking of things of a dubious nature, what's the matter with you Ron? Suppository stuck again?'

Ron sat down forcibly and mumbled incoherently.

'My dear boy,' cooed Dubbya, 'haven't I told you before, you don't swallow them you ... '

'Up yours,' thundered Ron angrily.

'And yours, my son,' replied Dubbya, happy to have rattled Ron's proverbial cage, again. He patted his rear cheeks. 'All is well at the Khyber Pass although I guess your rubble chute could do with a bit of fibrous content.'

Ron grabbed his briefcase and stormed out of the room, muttering furiously about constipated gorillas. Tina, having stifled a rumbling laugh, suddenly exploded. Wiping away a trickle of tears from her eyes, she shook her head slowly.

'Dubbya, you shouldn't bait the man so. It's too easy and far from fair.'

He shrugged nonchalantly.

'I can't help it, he's habit forming, irresistible, and so gratifyingly easy to wind-up.'

Tina shuddered.

'The idea of anyone finding Ron habit-forming is absolutely appalling. Haven't you got anything better to waste your dubious talents on?'

Dubbya spread his hands out innocently.

'What, and leave the poor boy thinking nobody loved him, cared about him or even bothered to recognise his existence?'

'Nobody else bothers,' commented Dick, 'not even his students.'

Eager to change the subject for something suitable for daytime viewing, Tina looked questioningly at Dubbya.

'You know that your visits are almost as welcome as an over-ripe pear, so what the heck do you want?'

Dubbya, smiled at Tina. Being unsure whether the over-ripe pear was a compliment or not, he decided that the smile could be interpreted as either one of thanks or condescension. He nodded towards the door.

'Thought you might like to grab the back row seats before they're snapped up by the obsequious hordes.'

Dick rubbed at the remains of sleep in his eyes. Blearily examining the gritty substance on his fingertip, he arched his back and yawned.

'Please don't use big words, Dubbya,' exhaled Dick. 'You know it makes us lower mortals feel a desperate urge to eat a can of alphabet soup. Anyway, what are you on about?'

Dubbya raised his shoulders ambivalently.

'Thought you might want to sit next to a friendly face at the Principal's emergency meeting, or were you planning to sharpen a few pencils instead?'

Tina slapped the desk in agitation.

'Damn, blast and fireworks, I'd forgotten all about it. Is it important?'

Dubbya blew out his already enlarged cheeks.

'What's an emergency for one person may constitute a pain in the arse for someone else. However, the Principal has cancelled all afternoon teaching sessions so that every Faculty could attend with no other distractions. It must be worth a few waking moments of anyone's time surely?'

Without further hesitation, both Dick and Tina placed a copy of the day's tabloid into a cardboard folder and, together with Dubbya, marched purposefully down an empty corridor.

CHAPTER 10

The Principal's emergency meeting was due to take place in the College's drama studio. Apart from adding a touch of the theatrical to the proceedings, the studio was also the only place large enough to accommodate all the staff where the Principal could monitor the effectiveness of his speech by the number of eyelids browbeaten into obedience.

Standing just outside of the entrance, Dick, Tina and Dubbya surveyed the assembled throng of staff with a mixture of antipathy and surprise. Neither of them realised just how many people the College employed and, more pertinently, what did all of these people do? Dick, scouring the sea of bobbing heads neatly arranged according to either their length of service or their desperation for promotion, noticed that the more recent additions to the payroll sat excitedly at the front of the studio, eager to impress or too naïve to realise the foolishness of their actions.

From their vantage point, the trio of truants could hear the funereal strains of Faure's 'Requiem' drifting over the combined aural receptors of the staff. Standing, sombrely on a raised dais in front of his subjects, stood the Principal, his willowy frame betraying his many years of service as an educational leader. The weight of responsibility had caused his shoulders to sag slightly, which emphasised the expanse of gnarled neck leading to a mop of wiry grey hair sitting on his head like a startled hamster.

Behind the Principal sat the combined might of the Senior Management Team along with rather stern looking female whose collective wrinkles and necklaces suggested someone accustomed to rich food and limited exertion.

Dick nudged Dubbya.

'I can't be doing with all this,' he said indicating the staged staff meeting. 'I'm going to do a bit of surreptitious reconnaissance.'

'My dear boy,' whispered Dubbya in alarm. 'That sounds most

39

painful. Do be careful!' He laid a hand on Dick's arm. 'To reconnoitre what precisely?'

Dick gave an awkward grin.

'Abbreviations,' he replied. Without waiting for any further comment or question, Dick promptly dashed behind the open door as the Head of Science loomed into view. Placing a hand on both Dubbya and Tina's back, the Scientific Head ushered them towards the academic gathering.

'Come along,' he said brusquely. 'No loitering.'

Dick waited a few moments before emerging from his short-stay behind the door. Keeping close to the wall, he quickly made his way along the corridor to put as much distance between himself and the Principal's latest diatribe.

Pausing briefly at the first flight of stairs leading to the upper echelons of learning, Dick made an instinctive decision to head for the offices of the Estates Manager, located close to the basement and netherworld of the maintenance department.

With a tentative knock at the office door, Dick listened for a couple of seconds and, when no voice of reply responded, he crept into the room and stood perfectly still.

When he'd left Dubbya and Tina a short while ago, Dick had no discernable plan other than to avoid a prolonged period of boredom listening to the Principal's latest hare-brained schemes. The only convoluted logic that had brought him to the Estates office was a tenuous link between the implied property development of the recently acquired document and the Estate Manager's role in anything connected to buildings. With no plan and little time, Dick did the only thing that seemed remotely sensible he began tugging at every locked drawer and cupboard within sight. After being thwarted by a mixture of limited strength and recalcitrant locks, Dick sat heavily in the Estate manager's padded chair.

From his comfortable position, Dick swivelled the chair from side-to-side trying desperately to identify anywhere that looked a likely hiding place for documents of a dubious nature. As was his custom when faced with a seat of a superior nature, Dick began playing with the adjustable controls on the chair. After several pneumatically enhanced ascensions in the chair, Dick went for the ultimate with a flick of the *tilt* lever whilst moving towards the ceiling.

'Houston, we have lift off,' drawled Dick in his best pseudo-Texan voice. Unfortunately for Dick, without the combined brainpower at NASA's disposal, he miscalculated his ascent velocity and at full-tilt his feet made earth-shattering contact with the underside of the desk.

'Damn,' muttered Dick as he hastily reassembled the paraphernalia cluttering the desk.

With all but a couple of items left to return to their previous jumbled state, Dick noticed a small key stuck to the bottom of a miniature darts trophy.

'Gotcha,' thought Dick as he quickly pulled the key away from the bottom of the trophy and immediately began inserting the key into each desk drawer in turn.

Finally, the key yielded results on the large bottom drawer of the desk. Triumphantly, Dick snatched open the drawer to be faced with a nondescript cardboard box. Eagerly pulling the lid open he was greeted with a collection of brightly coloured plastic building bricks.

Sorting through the box of bricks, Dick came across small sections still partially assembled. Portions of wall, the odd doorway and a couple of curved sections of wall were all that remained of the Estate Manager's last playtime. Shaking his head, Dick hurriedly closed the drawer and was just replacing the key when the door opened.

'I thought I heard a noise,' declared Jim the Caretaker. 'What you doing here Mr Hall?'

Dick, caught with his head just about to disappear beneath the desk, sat upright and smiled wanly.

'Ah, a good question,' he mumbled in reply. Shuffling a couple of objects on the desktop, he grinned at Jim.

'Needed a replacement barrier key for the car park,' said Dick, smiling hopefully that Jim would believe his feeble excuse for being in the office. He held both palms upwards. 'You know how it is, easily lost and not so easy to get a replacement.'

Jim frowned.

'Wouldn't the Reception desk be the best place to ask whether a barrier key has been handed in?' he asked suspiciously.

'Normally, yes,' replied Dick. 'But what with everybody occupied with the Principal's chat and no one to ask, I thought I'd come along and see if I could borrow one.'

Jim scratched at the stubble adorning his chin.

'Can't say as I like people helping themselves to things,' he said thoughtfully. 'But I suppose needs must.' Jim dug around in his trouser pocket and emerged with a rather worn barrier key. 'Found this a few days ago,' he announced. 'Been ran over a few times but it still works.' He hand the key to Dick. 'Best take it quick before his Nibs gets back. He hates people messing around with his things.'

Eagerly accepting the offer of a plausible way out, Dick took the key with a nod of thanks, leaving a bemused caretaker watching him walk along the basement corridor and back into the world of academia.

CHAPTER 11

Later that evening, as he gently stroked Tracey's unruly hair, Dick paused, kissed her neck and let out a protracted sigh.

'I just can't believe it,' he said thoughtfully.

'Mmm,' replied a Tracey from her semi-soporific state.

'Mmm, what?' asked Dick, laying his hand gently on her head.

'Mmm, soothing,' mumbled Tracey.

'Soothing?' queried Dick.

'Definitely. What else could it be?' asked Tracey, her head resting heavily on Dick's shoulder.

'Well,' said Dick, with a hint of irritation. 'I ask you, kiddies building blocks!'

Tracey, extracting her hair from between Dick's fingers, sat upright and stared directly at him.

'I can't believe you,' she said sternly.

Dick, sitting in the lounge of his typical 1930's 'Dunroamin' property and his feet nudging at the collection of drinking vessels on his coffee table, gave a tired smile. Taking a sip of his Côtes-du-Rhône, he glanced at Tracey, seated by his side, a glass of the same downtrodden grape held demurely in front of her.

'Believe it or not,' he replied. 'That's what was in the box.'

Tracey continued to stare at Dick, as if contemplating whether to hit him or hug him. She took a sip of her wine. Nodding slowly, Tracey pursed her lips and allowed them to slip into a grimace.

'I can't believe,' she said purposefully, 'that you'd ruin a perfectly pleasant moment by talking about the contents of some imbecile's draw. Nor,' she continued, becoming increasingly irate, 'can I believe you had the stupidity to go off on some infantile escapade that had as much forethought as one of your lesson plans.'

Dick winced at the personal attack on his academic professionalism.

'That was uncalled for,' he replied tersely.

43

'And so was your rummage in the Estate Manager's office,' she retorted.

'I'll remind you, that I was personally asked to investigate this case,' said Dick defensively. 'It's what she wanted me to do.'

'Case? What case?' asked Tracey angrily. 'And I don't need reminding of your tardy tête-à-tête with some noxious female.'

In her agitation, Tracey's wine glass, which had been balanced precariously on her knee now succumbed to a higher force and spewed its contents onto her jeans. 'Blast!' snarled Tracey mopping furiously at her wet clothing.

'Here, let me help,' offered Dick, pulling a partially shredded tissue out of his pocket.

Tracey pushed his helping hand away.

'If I need your help, I'll ask for it.'

'Well,' smiled Dick. 'You wouldn't be the first female this week to … '

The last words were completely muffled by the cushion that Tracey thoughtfully pushed into his face. When Dick finally managed to remove the offending fabric from his face it was to see Tracey holding up a warning finger.

'Don't,' she warned, 'even think about telling me once more about the puerile rambling of another woman.'

Dick took a deep breath.

'Look,' he began.

'No!' said Tracey still holding her finger in the air. 'Enough. This isn't some fictional bit of drama to pick up and put down at your leisure.'

'That's what I'm trying to tell you,' explained Dick. 'This could impact on our future.'

'Too damn right it could!'

Tracey paused for breath. She wasn't used to articulating her emotions quite so forcefully. The speed at which she had spoken concerned her. Had she become involved in a form of reality literature in which the story developed according to the interaction of the principle characters? She hadn't realised that being a librarian could be so dangerous for the soul. She noticed Dick's face layered with bewilderment.

'All I'm saying,' said Tracey more calmly than she felt, 'is that I'm not happy with you fantasising about some other woman, that's all.'

Dick sat back, his mind becoming a blur of thoughts and emotions.

'Are you,' he stuttered, 'Are we?'

'Are we anything?' asked Tracey softly.

'Are we talking about the same thing?'

Dick felt the full force of the cushion make contact with his face once again.

'Was that necessary?' asked Dick when Tracey condescended to remove the cushion.

'You tell me,' replied Tracey glaring at him.

Dick glanced at the cushion.

'Must I?'

Without waiting for an answer, Dick gave an almost imperceptible nod.

'Right, you are,' answered Dick, impersonating Yoda.

Tracey lifted the cushion threateningly. With his hands in front of his face, Dick grinned.

'The Force is with you, always.'

Despite herself, Tracey laughed. Grabbing the cushion, Dick leaned forward.

'A Jedi uses the cushion for knowledge and defence, never for attack.'

Wrestling the cushion from Dick's grasp, she hugged it to her chest.

'Enough with the quotes, Woebegone Bonobo or else.'

Dick grinned broadly. 'Well, that last one was more Yoda but … '

Tracey grabbed Dick's hands.

'But nothing,' she grinned back.

'Precisely,' replied Dick. 'There is nothing to be concerned about regarding this disembodied female voice, real or otherwise.'

Tracey gave a relieved smile.

'Then show me the evidence.'

'It's still under the bed,' smirked Dick. 'Fancy coming and helping me look for it?'

Dick scurried towards the door as a cushion followed his progress.

For the next twenty minutes, Tracey consumed the contents of the document avidly while Dick watched a Channel Four documentary about huge chunks of the polar ice cap becoming detached and making a bit of a splash. He'd turned the volume off, partly out of consideration for Tracey and partly because he couldn't stand the patronising tones of the commentator who sounded as if he knew far too much for his own good.

'Strewth!' exclaimed Dick as another large slab of glacier separated itself and fell into the sea. 'That'll make a damn big wave.'

Tracey looked up at the sudden interruption, she snapped the document shut and placed it on the coffee table.

'And so will that,' she concluded, sitting back and taking a long overdue sip from her refilled wineglass.

Dick waited while Tracey slowly drained the wineglass dry. Carefully drying her lips on a tissue, she stared at the wall in front of her.

'Mmm,' she murmured.

The minutes passed and Dick's patience crumbled. But, rather than ask a direct question, he decided to use a more devious route to elicit an appropriate response.

'Who was that woman at the Principal's meeting with the appalling sense of fashion?' he asked, fully aware that Tracey would instantly know whom he was referring to.

'That woman,' replied Tracey, momentarily losing her train of thought. 'Is Lady Faulkner, Chair of Governors at the College and quite influential amongst the local, political fraternity.'

Tracey gave Dick a calculating look as she tried to determine what precisely his sudden fixation with other women was all about. It was now her turn to change tack and bring the conversation back to something they could mutually share. She tapped the document, which still sat on the table.

'Do you want to know what's in this document?'

'I already know,' said Dick, 'it's full of numbers and pages of words amounting to a load of waffle. There!' he said triumphantly, 'I know enough to understand that it all amounts to trouble.'

Dick sat back on the settee with a smug look on his face. Tracey picked up the document and waved it at him.

'Trouble it may be,' she said angrily, 'but we can't just ignore the few facts it does contain.'

Dick grabbed the document, his face showing dangerous signs of annoyance. He flicked through the pages randomly and stopped at a page full of figures.

'There!' he said pointedly. 'Here we go, look.' His fingers traced the words as he spoke. 'Refurbishment: £112,008, Capital projects: £314,794, Marketing: £227,774, Expenses: £82,306, Miscellaneous: £69,736.' He closed the document. 'Good old miscellaneous, always the cheapest but a great way to tidy up the bits and bobs that tend to clutter a balance sheet and make it look untidy.'

'Ignore miscellaneous,' nagged Tracey, 'and take a look at the marketing expenditure again.'

'It doesn't say what it's been spent on,' stated Dick. 'Just that £227,774 is accounted for as marketing.'

'Precisely,' replied Tracey, 'and how much marketing have you seen recently?'

'Well now you come to mention it, not a lot really. There's the course leaflets and stuff and the adverts in the local free paper and the occasional reminder stuck on the back of a bus, but apart from that … '

'Don't forget the awful booklet that gets shoved in the free paper once a year advertising short courses for the cerebrally challenged,' interrupted Tracey.

'How could I?' said Dick.

'And does that little lot add up to £227,774?' questioned Tracey.

'Paper isn't cheap.'

'It isn't that expensive either,' replied Tracey. 'And another thing … ' She opened the document and thrust a page of text under Dick's nose. 'What's all that about "evaluation reports, feasibility studies and enhanced gratuities for services rendered"?'

Dick examined the page closely. There were several comments about events, sub-committee meetings, and discrete references to extraneous expenses. He looked up at Tracey.

'Bit of malpractice?'

'£227,774 of malpractice, if you ask me,' she said.

'Anything else I should take note of?' asked Dick.

Tracey shuffled a few pages and then produced a sheet of writing that contained numerous comments by faceless voices.

'This seems to be a transcript of a meeting between persons unknown concerning unknown amounts of money for an unknown project, along with a map, which appears to be something to do with the College's football pitch and car park.'

Dick looked closely at the page. A quick flick through others pages of figures and text and he looked thoughtfully at Tracey.

'Dirty tricks, dirty money and dishonest people,' he said flippantly. 'The sort of everyday tabloid fodder that keeps the nation happy.'

Tracey snatched the document from him.

'So?' she queried, 'and what are we going to do about it?'

'What do you mean, *"do about it"*' asked Dick. 'A few moments ago you were giving me grief for doing something about it!' He stared at her. 'I was doing something about it but what I was doing was obviously not what you thought I was supposed to be doing.'

He fell back into the sofa once more and allowed his pulse to regain some semblance of normality.

'I'm retiring from this investigation on health grounds,' he announced.

Tracey pummelled her head in exasperation.

'You are so damned annoying at times.' She prodded the document. 'We can't just sit here knowing that unknown people are collaborating on a project that is designed to make them a small fortune and us virtually destitute.'

'No,' said Dick licking his top lip. 'So what's the plan, providing,' he said with a twitch of his eyebrow, 'that it's worth coming out of retirement for.' He glanced at Tracey's smiling mouth. 'So what are you plotting?'

Tracey smiled.

'I don't know precisely,' she admitted. 'But this document suggests that we should be doing something.'

Dick raised his eyebrows.

'Do you want to discuss tactics?'

Tracy grinned and stood up.

'I think we need to consider our next move,' she grinned, as Dick nodded enthusiastically. 'And develop a strategy.'

Dick looked slightly bemused.

'Mine's usually to sleep,' he admitted.

'Nothing *usually* about it,' replied Tracey. 'That's guaranteed!' Collecting the document from the table, Tracey walked over to Dick, hooked her arm through his and nodded up the stairs.

'So what are we going to do?' she asked with an immodest smile.

Dick replied with another raised eyebrow.

'And I thought you were the spontaneous type.'

Tracey pushed her finger into Dick's ribs.

'We could just go to the police.'

'And say what precisely?' queried Dick. 'That we have a document that looks a bit suspicious and,' he continued, 'contains minutes of meetings and details expenses that we don't understand?'

'Tell them what we know,' replied Tracey, impatiently.

Dick paused as they reached the top of the stairs.

'Which isn't much,' he said coolly. 'I think we may have to give the police a bit more to go on before we get them involved. Anyway,' he smiled, nodding towards the bedroom door. 'Talking about getting involved.'

Tracey arched her eyebrows. 'A job for Dick and Tracey?' she quipped.

Dick couldn't help but laugh. It was inevitable that their names would always suggest references to Chester Gould's 1930's comic strip creation of a Chicago police detective.

'Away you go then,' he ordered, nudging the door open with his foot.

Obediently, Tracey allowed herself to be led through the doorway as Dick threw the document onto an almost empty chair. Within moments all thoughts of financial irregularities and fraudulent schemes were forgotten as other, more important procedures took precedence.

CHAPTER 12

The car bumped along the rutted track and finally came to a halt beneath a large Willow tree. Momentarily the fading headlights lit up the drooping branches before plunging the scenery into darkness once more. Frank Byers turned to his passenger and smiled hopefully.

'We're here then,' he whispered huskily.

His passenger stared immediately ahead into the impenetrable gloom, her hands toying nervously with the wrapper from the toffee she'd only recently placed in her mouth. Frank's hand wandered over to her knee.

'Happy days eh?' he chuckled.

Struggling to contain the still solid toffee, Frank's passenger demurely pushed his hand away and straightened her skirt. With the toffee firmly wedged against the inside of her cheek, she turned to face him. Her mouth bulging from the pressure of the caramel-centre, she smiled over-sweetly and nodded. Never one to avoid a sticky situation, Frank began a replay of the hand and knee connection, whilst kissing her earlobe as seductively as he could given the proximity of the toffee and the faint sucking noises.

'It's been a long time,' mumbled Frank between nuzzles. 'Years in fact.' Caught between the competing sensations of Frank's hand, mouth and the toffee, his companion shivered involuntarily. Frank, taking her bodily movement as confirmation that he was making all the right moves, allowed his lips to move downwards towards her neck. Buried in the pleasure of her scent, he sighed.

'There was a time when I could think of nothing else but you, the moon and Queen's Park Rangers Football Club.' He paused, allowing his eyes to adjust to the darkness. 'And then we had the kids and it's not been the same since!'

Frank sat upright and tugged at the sleeve of his coat.

'Damn! What time is it? We'll need to get back to the babysitter before long.'

Unable to discern the time in the pallid moonlight, he stabbed at the car's interior light. Both Frank and his wife blinked in the harsh reality of the yellow glow. With a smile Frank smoothed the sleeve of his jacket.

'Another thirty minutes yet, Pet. What do you say?'

Before she could form a reply, Frank made a quick move for a slither of naked flesh he'd caught sight of between her blouse and the waistband of her skirt. His sudden movement startled her, causing an involuntary intake of breath, which immediately loosened the toffee from its temporary confinement and began a rapid descent of her throat. Half choking and laughing she flung the car door open and began to point frantically at her back, hoping that Frank would have sufficient blood circulating around the top-half of his body for his brain to function. Caught between his physical desire and his wife's physical needs, he opted to massage her back vigorously, concluding that it would satisfy both of their needs.

Half sitting and half leaning out of the car, Frank's wife coughed several times and then spat the offending toffee into the undergrowth.

'Frank, you nut,' she hiccupped over her shoulder.

'Hazel, my sweet,' he burbled.

Just as she was about to sit up, a loud snorting sound filled the air followed by hot, moist air blowing onto her neck.

'Frank,' she shrieked. 'You absolute beast.'

Frank, attempting to fend off his wife's flailing arms, caught a brief glimpse of a large pair of dark nostrils looming out of the darkness.

'Oh my God,' groaned Frank.

'He's about the only one who can save you now, you animal,' growled Hazel, continuing to rain blows on her husband's head.

The last thing to register on Frank's senses was the sound of hooves thundering over wet grass and his wife's unruly hair silhouetted in the glimmer of the courtesy light, before darkness enveloped him completely.

CHAPTER 13

Somewhere, amongst the files and papers accumulated during a hectic night of administration, a phone shrilled its presence. Sergeant Cost groaned inwardly.

'Make yourself useful and answer that, Ricketts.'

PC Ricketts, mentally adding to the lengthening list of torture she'd planned for the Sergeant, gave a servile smile and searched for the phone.

Sergeant Cost, ignorant to the various forms of pain awaiting him, barely glanced in the direction of PC Ricketts and continued picking at the fluff and other bits of debris that had collected in the lining of his trouser pocket.

'It's the hospital,' she called over her shoulder.

Sergeant Cost grunted something indecipherable and wiped the fluff from a congealed lump of indiscernible origin. Carefully placing the rediscovered toffee in an old yoghurt pot, he turned to face PC Ricketts.

'What do they want at this time of the morning?'

Still with the phone to her ear, PC Ricketts repeated the information she'd just heard.

'Do we still want to interview that old woman who collapsed in her garden and,' she sighed tiredly. 'And are we interested in a battered husband?' She held up a warning finger. 'And don't say, "yes, with chips", will you.'

Sergeant Cost allowed himself the glimmer of a smile and brushed at an errant hair on his sleeve.

'As if I would,' he replied. His forehead wrinkled slightly, usually an indication that a thought had stirred a neuron. 'Why are they calling us, anyway? It sounds more like a job for a social worker.'

PC Ricketts mumbled something into the phone and then submerged the whole thing under a pile of paperwork once again.

The Sergeant, lost in concentration, continued with the examination of his other trouser pocket.

'Funny that,' observed PC Ricketts thoughtfully.

Sergeant Cost looked up momentarily. 'Not really,' he replied, with a fluffy lump stuck to his index finger. 'I think it's a bit of liquorice.' He held the small bead of black substance up for her inspection. PC Ricketts resigned herself to a sigh. She hated the night shift with Sergeant Cost. Not only was he totally oblivious to everything around him, he was also boring. She'd recently taken to reorganising the filing system, which in itself was equally boring but it was so satisfying when Sergeant Cost couldn't find a document he needed. She nodded in the general direction of the phone.

'I meant,' she said, ignoring Cost's recent discovery. 'It's a funny that the fainting woman and battered husband aren't related and yet both of these hospital cases reported seeing some sort of apparition.'

Cost paused in his fluffy exploration and looked hard at PC Ricketts. He was wary of any form of independent thought, particularly from someone whose understanding of the criminal world appeared to be gleaned from the Sunday papers.

'Just a coincidence,' he informed her. 'Doubt there's anything in it worth troubling yourself with.' Cost nudged his empty mug towards her. 'Make us a cup of tea, there's a good girl.'

Cost was completely oblivious to the sudden increase in the severity of pain that PC Ricketts had just added to his account. Picking up his tea mug she walked briskly towards the little alcove that housed the kettle and other drink related paraphernalia. Spooning several heaps of refined sugar into Cost's mug, she couldn't help but think how her revenge would be far sweeter.

CHAPTER 14

Regeneration Sounds found itself architecturally squeezed between a crumbling bakery and a grubby launderette. Most of the other shops on Wheelwright Lane were the usual assembly of newsagents, hairdressers, charity shops and chemists. Directly opposite Regeneration Sounds sat a jaded coffee shop whose motley collection of plastic topped tables and old pine chairs acted as a magnet for maudlin shoppers, aspiring musicians and writers.

As Dick approached the music shop, he felt apprehensive. Normally, he'd be eager to spend a couple of happy hours sifting through the combined works of the World's great Jazz and Blues artists. But today was different. Today he was to be denied the pleasure of browsing wherever his eyes led him. Instead, he was to act casually, nonchalantly flick through a couple of CD's and then, somehow, surreptitiously insert a note into a copy of a Duke Ellington's 'Money Jungle' CD.

Over breakfast, Dick had attempted to scribble several notes to his disembodied female informant with little success. He didn't know what to write and the more he thought about the whole business, the less inclined he was to do anything about it.

Eventually, Dick had managed to write a few questions and ideas for further action onto a piece of Tracey's mauve, scented writing paper. While she gently blew the hovering steam from her porridge, Tracey had read the note, made several disparaging clicks of her tongue and promptly scrunched the paper into a ball. Dick decided to finish his Frosties before making a comment. As he tipped the last dregs of milk into his mouth from the bowl, Dick nodded at the screwed-up piece of paper.

'Grammar?' he asked.

Tracey slowly dragged her finger across the bottom of her bowl and sucked at the porridge remnants. When she was satisfied that her breakfast was complete, she looked coolly at Dick.

'You weren't going to leave this,' she prodded the ball of paper, 'in a public place?'

Dick frowned. He wasn't sure whether this was a rhetorical question or a slice of buttered sarcasm. He opted for safety and shrugged.

'Because,' Tracey continued, ignoring his lack of response. 'You've included names, dates, places and even given precise details of every possible course of action we might take.' She shook her head. 'No wonder the Cold War lasted so long.' Lapsing into silence, Tracey absentmindedly pushed her spoon around the bowl.

'Hadn't it crossed your mind,' she asked, starring Dick in the face. 'That maybe there's a little too much detail?'

Deciding that another shrug was possibly a shrug too far, Dick blew out his cheeks.

'I thought a full report made it look like we've sort of done something,' he replied. He removed Tracey's bowl before she chipped the rim. 'At least it shows we've given the whole thing some thought and made a couple of enquiries.'

'Enquiries!' laughed Tracey. 'You've done nothing of the sort, apart from ask for a couple of opinions and get caught playing with kiddies building blocks!' She pushed a scrap of paper across the table. 'Try again,' she instructed Dick. 'But this time don't give all our secrets away. You never know who might pick up that CD and come across the note.' She rolled a pen towards the scrap of paper. 'Come on, write something.'

Dick picked up the pen and allowed it to hover over the scrap of paper while Tracey collected the breakfast pots and placed them in the sink.

'What shall I write then?' he asked Tracey as she disappeared out of the kitchen.

'What next?' she called over her shoulder. 'That's always a good question.'

Dick stood in front of the window of Regeneration Sounds. His stomach was complaining with embarrassingly loud grumbles. Although it was dinnertime, he'd not had the chance to delve into his lunch box before dashing across town and his appointment with Duke Ellington.

The front of the shop looked tired, as if it'd been involved in an all night dance contest and was on its last legs. Behind the grime-tinged window was a motley collection of faded posters, apparently thrown at the glass in an act of spontaneity. Behind the free-form posters, at an oblique angle, hung a large replica human ear. With his apprehension intact, Dick pushed at the door.

A large bell clattered above his head as Dick made his entrance into the shop. Allowing his eyes to adjust to the subdued light of the interior, he could just about pick out a faded picture of Miles Davis and his trumpert, sketching a melody of Spain. Dick shuffled further into the shop and began alphabetically browsing.

The interior of the shop could either have been called minimalist or, somewhat less charitably, cheap. Arranged around the single room stood a series of trestle tables supporting shoeboxes stuffed with CD's. Underneath each table stood a variety of larger boxes advertising breakfast cereals and soap powders, but containing vinyl albums rather than flakes of dubious origin.

Curiously, in the centre of the room sat a 1960's jukebox from where Miles & Co were performing. Dick paused for a moment and pondered on the shop's cataloguing system. Would Duke be under 'D', 'E' for Ellington or filed under 'M' for Money Jungle? Concluding that anything was possible, he made his way over to the 'D' section, based purely on the fact that it was the closest. He'd hardly managed to flick through a couple of CD's when a voice commanded his attention.

'Hang about, I'll be with you in a second.'

Dick looked over his shoulder towards the direction of the voice. To his amazement, a section of the rear wall appeared to move backwards and then slide to one side. In the newly created space stood a gangly bloke whose arms and legs appeared to be in a constant state of agitation. On top of this twitching mass sat an unruly crop of copper-red hair that radiated all the vibrancy of a fairground. Dick's schoolboy sense of humour quickly surfaced at his comic surroundings and the even more comical shop assistant. Before Dick could regain control of his mouth, the gangly bloke rushed forward.

Good morning, good morning,' he said, shaking Dick's hand.

'Welcome to Regeneration Sounds.' He took a step backwards, still holding Dick's hand. 'Are you looking for anything in particular or simply browsing our comprehensive selection of all things jazz?'

Thankfully, the gangly assistant released Dick's hand prior to making a sweeping gesture towards the shop's musical stock. Dick stood rooted to the spot. He couldn't think of a sensible word to say or put together a sentence that would explain his visit. He opted for a simple, straightforward response.

'Yes,' replied Dick, his mouth barely opening to allow the words to escape. With a condescending smile, the gangly bloke nodded.

'I understand.' He indicated the jukebox. 'You like Miles?'

Dick nodded.

'So do I,' enthused the bloke. 'My name's Malc, by the way.'

Before Malc could reignite the handshake, Dick pointed to a pile of CD's stacked by the door.

'Going out, or coming in?'

Malc laughed. 'Your guess is as good as mine. Haven't got around to sorting through them yet.' He walked over to the CD's and picked three from the top of the pile. 'Ah,' he breathed. 'Been wanting to listen to this one for a while now.' Malc waved a CD at Dick. 'The Marcin Wasilewski Trio, you know. They were formerly known as the Simple Acoustic Trio. Well worth listening to.' He glanced at the other two CD's. 'Pat Metheny, Chick Corea,' he muttered to himself. Without waiting for a response, he replaced the CD's on the pile and, turning to Dick, rubbed his hands together.

'If you like Miles, could I suggest something by Duke Ellington? The reissue of "A drum is a woman", "Black, brown and Beige", or,' mused Malc. 'Perhaps his "Money Jungle"?'

Dick felt as if he'd been prodded in the chest. His head reeled. Looking at Malc's face, he couldn't see a hint of amusement or complicity. Nothing. Malc simply stood there, fascinated at the discomfort his comments appeared to have caused. Recognising a purchasing dilemma, he decided to expedite matters by providing a little musical insight. He picked the Duke's 'Money Jungle' CD out of the shoebox.

'This 1962, jazz masterpiece,' he informed Dick. 'Has the Duke on piano, Charles Mingus on bass and Max Roach on drums, and,' he paused dramatically. 'Rumour has it that there was a great deal of tension between Mingus and Ellington. In fact, Mingus actually walked out of the recording session on the first day.'

Screwing his eyes shut, Dick fought to clear his head of the farcical events that threatened his sanity. Mistaking Dick's facial expressions as doubt, Malc placed a hand on his arm.

'I realise it's purely subjective,' he admitted. 'But I do believe that you can hear the tension on the title track.'

Dick shook his head and coughed.

'Just trying to work out which CD to buy,' he lied. He nodded at the pile of CD's on the floor. 'I think I'll try that Wasilewski thing.'

Malc smiled. Retrieving the CD from the pile, he walked towards the rear of the shop.

'I'll just find a bag for it,' he called over his shoulder.

While Malc was busy searching for a bag at the back of the shop, Dick quickly slipped his note into Duke's CD. Malc returned just as Dick was replacing the CD in the shoebox.

'Tempted?' he smiled. 'Thought you might be.' He hand Dick a small plastic bag containing his CD. 'I've always got Duke's stuff in stock so drop by any time.'

'Cheers,' said Dick, handing Malc a credit card.

Malc sighed.

'Sorry,' he apologised. 'Cash only I'm afraid.'

Dick mumbled a swift apology himself and, calling over his shoulder as the doorbell clattered above him, promised to call back after making a quick visit to the bank.

CHAPTER 15

Several minutes later, and with sufficient cash in his pocket, Dick walked back towards Regeneration Sounds. The whole situation had a surreal feeling to it, and Dick couldn't help wondering whether he was caught up in some elaborate charade or did people really act this way? In an attempt to gain a few minutes respite he wandered into the café opposite the music shop.

The café seemed to be full of people either taking refreshments prior to an onslaught on the local shopping emporium or simply recuperating after a hard fought battle against the retail brigade. Selecting a table close to the window, and with a clear view of the door to Regeneration Sounds, Dick placed his jacket on the back of the chair and sauntered over to the counter to order a drink.

'Coffee, please,' he said, picking a pack of bourbon biscuits out of a basket. After hesitating for a moment, he offered a smile to the woman behind the counter. 'On second thoughts, could you make that a latte, please,' he asked.

The woman, her face a cosmetically powdered indulgence, gave him a stern look.

'Latte?' she queried. 'You'll have milk in your coffee and be done with!' She busied herself with unscrewing a jar of instant coffee. 'Highfalutin ideas of some folk,' she muttered.

Dick thought better of making a comment and stood obediently while the woman completed his request. Taking his milky coffee over to the table, Dick sipped his drink slowly as he watched the lack of trade at Regeneration Sounds.

After a while, and realising that sipping at an empty mug was attracting attention, Dick left the café followed by a further stare from the woman behind the counter.

The door to Regeneration Sounds announced his arrival with a reassuring clatter. Malc was busy doing something to the rear of the jukebox and didn't look up as Dick entered.

'Be with you in a moment,' he called. 'Bit of a queue at the bank was there?'

Dick was startled at Malc's exhibition of extrasensory perception. The effect on Dick's vocal cords was such that all he could manage in response was a strangulated grunt.

'I know how you feel,' replied Malc, apparently oblivious to Dick's confusion. 'You get in a queue, try to wait patiently and, just as it looks like you're going to be the next to get served, the person in front of you off-loads several bags of coins.' Malc popped his head out from behind the jukebox. He gave Dick a broad smile. 'Don't worry. I'm still here to liberate your wallet!'

Dick quickly pulled his wallet from the inside of his jacket.

'Only got a £20 note I'm afraid.'

Relieving Dick of the banknote, Malc gestured towards the rear of the shop.

'Not a problem,' he laughed. 'I've plenty of change out the back. Have another browse. You never know,' he winked. 'You might find something of interest.'

As Malc disappeared, Dick nonchalantly flicked through a few CD's. His attempt to act casual only succeeded in him kicking over a stack of CD's that were half hidden under the table playing host to those artists filed under 'M'. Quickly shuffling the CD's back into a haphazard pile, Dick moved along to the shoebox that he hoped would contain Charlie Parker.

Ignoring *The Genius of Charlie Parker*, and *Charlie Parker with Strings*, Dick hurriedly bypassed, *The essential Charlie Parker* and Charlie Parker *In a soulful mood*, before lifting *Yardbird Suite* out of the box. A quick inspection of the CD case revealed nothing more than a neatly folded voucher offering a free, introductory health and toning session at the local health club. With no other obvious bits of paper, Dick shoved the voucher into his back pocket just as Malc returned.

'There we go,' he grinned, giving Dick the bagged CD and a handful of change. 'Sorry about the coins,' he apologised, 'had to raid the piggy bank.' Malc nodded towards the shoebox of Charlie Parker. 'Anything interesting?' he asked.

Dick shook his head. Malc's comments were not only

disconcerting, but also becoming tiresome. Deciding to be equally awkward, he gave a gentle shrug.

'Maybe,' he answered. 'Can't be sure. I'll give it some thought and, you never know, I might be back.'

Leaving Malc with a slightly confused expression on his face, Dick hurried out of the shop and began to assemble his thoughts and just how he was to relate his retail experience to Tracey and just what he was going to do with the voucher in his pocket.

CHAPTER 16

Dick winced as Tracey slapped a liberal dollop of moisturising cream onto his back.

'Steady,' groaned Dick, as he writhed under the cold pressure of her hands. 'I don't need any more pain inflicted on my fragile frame.'

Moving his shoulder blades slightly to reposition Tracey's hands, Dick swallowed noisily. 'It was awful,' he mumbled into the pillow. An almost imperceptible movement of the bed promptly turned into a continuous jiggle as Tracey's hands rhythmically pummelled his back. Dick sighed with pleasure. 'That's so nice,' he murmured.

Abruptly, the pummelling stopped as Tracey toppled from her position straddling Dick's back and fell onto the bed. Convulsed with laughter, she desperately tried to hide her face in the pillow. Intrigued by the sudden change in Tracey's ministrations, Dick lifted his head. The sight of Tracey's head buried in a pillow, with her shoulders rocking from side to side, disturbed him. Lifting a leaden arm, he tapped Tracey on the shoulder.

'What?' he enquired of her heaving shoulders.

Tracey turned to face him with a large portion of pillow stuffed in her mouth. Her muffled reply was quickly engulfed by another wave of laughter. Dick's already tense body stiffened further as he attempted to sit up. Giving up the struggle, he resigned himself to resting on an elbow. Trying not to join in with the laughter, he sniffed.

'It's not in the least funny,' he said, trying to sound annoyed. 'For all you know,' he continued. 'I could have been permanently injured or worse.'

Tracey's response was to draw her knees into her chest and totally convulse with laughter. With the need to breathe becoming increasingly urgent, she reluctantly released the pillow and lay on her back gasping for air. She turned to look at Dick, but his look of feigned injury only made her collapse once again into a convulsive wreck.

'Thanks a bundle,' grumbled Dick, falling onto his back. Within seconds, his mock annoyance gave way to a fit of giggles as he and Tracey embraced laughter.

Earlier in the evening, Dick had dashed home from College, grabbed his sports bag and driven across town to the health club named on the voucher.

The club echoed the half-lit, dingy side street that it occupied. A part brick and metal construction, the club sat squarely in the middle of an overworked industrial estate. Flanked by various enterprises, the club didn't seem out of place next to industrial units offering body repairs, servicing and complete re-sprays. Smiling at the oddly compatible nature of its business next to the automotive trades, Dick entered the building.

Walking into the club, he was welcomed by a blandly decorated room with a self-assembly desk positioned just to the left of the door. Seated at the desk was a young female whose features matched the décor and with a body that obviously didn't make use of the health club's facilities. Dick had handed her the now crumpled voucher and she'd simply nodded towards a beige door in the far wall and resumed the laboured examination of her manicured nails.

Beyond the door lay a brightly lit corridor whose walls boasted a variety of services and facilities available at prices designed to inflict pain on both the wallet and the body. Dick ignored the cost of torture and began to walk along the corridor.

Just as he reached the end of the corridor, Dick was saved the effort of deciding whether to turn left or right, when a large figure obstructed his progress. Apologising, Dick made to move around the figure but was stopped by a muscular arm making contact with his chest.

'Can I help you?' enquired the arm.

Dick's eyes traced the outline of the arm and continued upwards. Barring his way stood a prime example of an over indulgence in the use of free weights. Every muscle was so well defined that they wouldn't have been out of place in a dictionary of anatomy. Dick took a step back.

'Sorry,' he mumbled. He craned his neck to search the face of his enquirer. She stood, critically assessing his ill-toned physique, with both hands now on her hips.

'Well?' she asked.

Dick coughed. He realised that he'd left the voucher with the woman he took to be the receptionist. He tried to smile.

'I er, had a,' he jerked his head back towards the door he'd entered moments before. 'Sort of voucher thing,' he explained. The female form frowned.

'Voucher?' she queried.

'Health and toning,' grinned Dick.

Without a word, the female turned and opened a door to her right.

'Get undressed,' she instructed. 'And then make your way to the steam room.' She indicated the way he should go. Looking at his body, she gave a short sigh. 'Make sure you cover yourself with the complimentary robe, which you'll find hanging on the back of the door.' Pausing in the doorway, she turned back towards Dick. 'Don't get lost, will you?' she said in a stern tone.

Dick followed orders and duly emerged into the corridor wrapped in the voluminous drapes of the club gown. Following the directions she'd given him, he soon found his way into a small room decorated with identical robes to his own. Unwrapping his body, Dick opened the inner door and was promptly engulfed by steam.

Gasping for breath, he took a few faltering steps forward and stopped. The heat made his eyes sting and every pore of his body screamed at the assault. Waving his hands in front of his face, he could just about make out a number of misty figures seated around the outside of the room.

'First time?' called one of the figures.

Dick swallowed. He was finding it difficult enough to breathe without the added pressure of engaging his voice. With an effort to be polite, Dick grunted. A second figure laughed.

'Don't worry mate. You'll soon get used to it.'

Dick was certain that this was something he didn't want to get used to but nodded and smiled anyway. The first voice called out again.

'Room for one more over here.'

Dick edged his way towards the voice until his feet made contact with a bench. Cautiously he sat down and draped the small towel over his lap that he'd found in the pocket of his robe. He'd just settled his back against the wall when a hand on his knee made him jump with surprise.

'Sorry,' said the figure next to him. 'Just wanted to make certain that I wasn't talking to hot air.'

Dick lifted the hand from his knee.

'My name's Dick,' he informed the figure, reinforcing the fact by placing the errant hand firmly on its owner's knee.

'Pleased to meet you, Dick,' replied the figure. 'I'm Gerald. Health and toning?' he asked, as several of the figures began to snigger.

'Yes, as it happens,' replied Dick. 'Something I should know?'

Gerald nudged his elbow.

'To misquote a cliché,' he said with an exaggerated whispered. 'Their bark is as bad as their bite.' Gerald turned to the rest of the room. 'We've all been there haven't we fellas?'

The sniggers turned into outright laughter as Dick sat bemused at the merriment he'd caused. Gerald nudged his arm again.

'Don't worry, Tilly will look after you.'

'Tilly?' asked Dick. 'Was she the … '

'You've got it,' laughed Gerald. 'We call her Attilla, but it's safer for you if you just call her Tilly to her face, OK?'

'Safer for all of us,' said the other figure next to Dick.

A nervous bout of strained laughter breezed around the steam. Dick was beginning to feel apprehensive and had just started to calculate how soon he could leave without appearing suspicious, when the other voice next to him spoke.

'What made you choose this place?' it asked.

Dick decided that honesty was the safest answer.

'I was given a voucher, and you really can't ignore a freebie can you?' he replied.

For the second time, a hand grasped Dick's knee causing a more violent reaction than before.

'Ah, there you are,' confirmed the voice. 'Thought I'd better introduce myself too. My name's Ralph.' The hand left Dick's knee and hovered in the air waiting for a response. Shaking Ralph's hand, he politely placed it on its owner's knee. Dick pushed his back against the wall. He wanted to make his visit worthwhile, but he didn't want anyone to get suspicious about his motives or even touchier than they already were. He decided to initiate some conversation.

'Steamy in here,' he offered.

'Isn't it just,' replied Ralph, all too quickly.

Dick swallowed and coughed at the same time and choked on the result. Both Ralph and Gerald simultaneously tried to pat his back.

'It's OK, ' gasped, Dick. 'I'm fine. Gulped too much steam I think,' he explained. With an effort, he chose another line of enquiry. 'Popular place is it?'

'Fairly,' answered Ralph thoughtfully. 'I quite like Wednesdays myself. That's when you meet all the right kind of people.' He nudged Dick's arm suggestively. 'You know what I mean?'

Dick was beginning to think he knew too much about too little. With his face and neck prickling more from embarrassment than heat, he wrapped the far too small towel around his waist and made an apologetic exit.

Thankful for the protection of his robe and the coolness of the corridor, Dick was just beginning to walk back to the changing room when a hand gripped his shoulder firmly.

'Leaving so soon?' enquired the female recently identified as Tilly. Dick shook his head.

'Just looking for you, as it happens,' he lied.

'Liar,' grinned Tilly. 'You were about to leave without saying goodbye.' She winked at Dick. 'Don't want to miss out on the toning session, do you?' Without waiting for a response, she took his elbow and steered him through a doorway and into a room full of ambient sounds and smells.

Half and hour later, and with no part of his skeletal framework left unscathed from Tilly's firm grip on anatomy, Dick drove home agonisingly slowly.

Once the giggles had subsided, Tracey leaned over towards Dick and wiped the tears from his eyes. She wasn't sure whether the tears were a result of laughter or post-toning pain, but she thought drying his eyes was the least she could do. Dick, much preferring Tracey's more delicate ministrations to those he'd endured earlier, allowed the pillow to embrace his head. He sighed.

'What a day eh?' He smiled at Tracey. 'Something to tell the children about, don't you think'

Tracey's hand paused halfway across his forehead.

'Children?' she asked, pressing her index finger gently on his nose. 'What children?'

Dick closed his eyes thoughtfully. In his present physical condition, prolonging a reply might cause further discomfort, but the temptation to tease Tracey was too much. He let out a protracted sigh, which promptly turned into a sharp intake of breath as a finger jabbed him in the ribs.

'Answer the question,' demanded Tracey, her voice playful but with worrying overtones.

'Well, you know,' gasped Dick. 'If we ever get around to the whole family thing.'

Tracey sat upright, her hands resting on her hips. 'Get around to it,' she grinned. 'How much more practice to you want?'

Dick's head jerked up from the pillow, causing him to wince.

'What are you suggesting?'

Tracey's face smiled at him. She'd often found it difficult to determine just how serious Dick was about their relationship. Sometimes he'd be almost too flippant and seriously erode her confidence about their future together. At other times, Dick would talk enthusiastically about their moving to somewhere more rural, a place where they could indulge their love of walking and even keep a chicken or three. She looked at Dick's questioning face.

'What are you suggesting?' she retorted impishly.

Fearful of any further infliction of pain, Dick returned her smile.

'I thought it might be nice to have a idea of where we're going,' he replied. 'Who knows what the future might hold?'

Tracey sat back on her haunches. She looked intensely at Dick's face, looking for any trace of jest or teasing. Seeing nothing to be concerned about, she sighed and contented herself with the thought that this was possibly about the best she could expect. She stroked his arm.

'I look forward to where we might be going,' she smiled. 'But, for now, I suppose we should concern ourselves with where you've been.'

Dick blew out his cheeks and exhaled noisily.

'I'd rather not think about it, if you don't mind.' He closed his eyes and shuddered. 'Fondled knees and persecuted muscles are more than a man can bear in one evening.'

Tracey ran the back of her hand against his face in a motherly fashion.

'There, there, then,' she said soothingly. 'Did that nasty woman frighten you?'

Dick pushed her hand away.

'I'm not sure what I was meant to find out at the Club,' he snapped angrily. But what I did find was more than I'd bargained for.'

Tracey shrugged wearily.

'Hopefully, it'll make sense at some stage.' She brushed the tip of Dick's nose with her finger. 'Switching the light out?'

Dick duly obliged.

CHAPTER 17

The following morning, Dick cautiously negotiated the students littered around the stairwell and shuffled his way upwards towards the staffroom.

'Morning campers,' he chirruped, sounding far heartier than he felt. The hunched forms of Tina and Ron merely nodded in greeting. Both were busily perusing the local free paper rather than trying to keep one step ahead of their students by reading the next chapter of the prescribed textbook. Dick threw his rucksack under the table and walked over to the collection of grubby mugs decorating the top of the filing cabinet.

'Coffee, anyone?' he asked his colleagues heads. He interpreted the slight movement of their heads as a positive response and began to wipe the inside of three mugs with a paper towel.

Whistling in tune with the kettle, Dick dumped the required granular ingredients for caffeine consumption into the mugs. Placing the steaming brews in front of Tina and Ron, he sat at his desk and watched each of them reach out an unsighted arm. As knuckles came into contact with the hot mugs, a synchronised cry of pain filled the staffroom.

'Ow!' exclaimed both Tina and Ron, their arms quickly retracting followed by a sucking noise as they soothed their scorched fingers. Dick shook his head. He never failed to be amazed at the combined exhibition of intelligence on display every morning.

'A simple statement of gratitude would have sufficed,' he said.

'Thanks,' replied the injured pair.

Dick coughed for attention.

'Anything interesting?' he enquired.

Tina allowed her newspaper to fall onto the desk and swivelled her chair to face him.

'Sorry, Dick,' she grinned. 'But we're trying to read between the lines about this story that's appeared in the paper. She stabbed a finger at the open page and shoved the newspaper over to Dick. Quickly scanning the headline and the first couple of paragraphs, he sniffed and looked at Tina.

'Interesting,' he offered. 'What do you think of it?'

Tina laughed.

'Lazy git,' she chuckled. 'You haven't read it properly.'

Dick nodded in agreement.

'Not enough pictures,' he grinned. 'But I did manage to work out the big letters.'

Ron sucked at the still hot liquid in his mug. Without turning around, he lifted his head and spoke to the window.

'Wonder if the pay will be any better than here?' he mused.

Tina shook her head.

'Doubt it,' she said. 'Those places never pay above the minimum wage if they can help it.'

'You never know,' replied Ron. He turned to face Tina. 'A man of my experience and all that.'

'I wouldn't bother,' retorted Tina. 'They might ask you how you acquired your qualifications without leaving the comfort of your armchair.'

Noisily sucking the remaining contents from his mug, Ron ignored Tina's comments and winked at Dick.

'Nice coffee, cheers,' he quipped.

Dick, beginning to feel confused, tapped the newspaper.

'Care to enlighten me?' he asked.

Tina spread the newspaper in front of him. Pushing her glasses onto the top of her head, she ran her finger across the headline.

'Luxury hotel on your doorstep,' she read aloud. She looked at Dick. 'In the proverbial nutshell, we're to have an architect's carbuncle built somewhere in the town, with an accompanying leisure complex.' Leaning forward, Tina tapped Dick's knee. With memories of the previous night still fresh in his head, Dick recoiled at the touch.

'Steady,' said Tina, in a half-mocking tone. 'Didn't take you for the modest sort.'

Dick felt the temperature of his neck rise.

'Sorry,' he muttered. 'You startled me, that's all.'

'You should get out more,' laughed Tina.

'I did,' replied Dick cryptically. Without waiting for any form of response from either Tina or Ron, he nodded towards the newspaper.

'Why the sudden interest?' he asked them.

'Because,' said Ron in the voice he usually reserved for Parents Evenings. 'There are very few sites around here that could be used to build a large complex such as this.' He leaned back in his chair, pressing his fingertips together. ' So, that leaves us to conclude that a site will have to be made available.'

'And,' continued Tina. 'What derelict sites do you know of?'

Dick couldn't help a huge grin spread across his face.

'There's the Principal for a start.'

Ron groaned.

'Very droll, I'm sure.' He closed his eyes and shook his head. 'Think again, Einstein.'

Tina moved to tap Dick's knee once again but stopped herself with a giggle.

'Remember you asked me if I'd heard anything about the future of the College as we know it?'

Dick cocked his head to one side and looked from Tina to Ron and back again. Distractedly, he scratched an imaginary itch on the side of his face.

'I do recall,' replied Dick cagily. 'And is this,' he tapped the newspaper. 'Supposed to refer to the perennial rumour of the College and Sixth Form joining together as some superlative institution that will perform miracles amongst our teenage intelligentsia?'

'Don't knock it,' said Ron. 'Sooner or later it's going to happen. You mark my words.'

Dick grabbed a bright orange highlighter pen from his desk.

'Stick your tongue out then and I will.'

'Leave him be,' chided Tina. 'It makes sense to reduce costs by joining forces.' She waved a hand at the wall. 'This place is falling to bits anyway. If you sell off the land and use the profits to rebuild a joint College on the Sixth Form site, then everyone is better off.'

'Except those made redundant,' said Dick.

Ron wagged his finger at Dick.

'Natural wastage,' he replied. 'Some of the money from the sale of this site could also go towards easing the transition of some staff into retirement.' He rubbed his hands together. 'Might be tempted myself.'

Dick thought through the possibilities of what he'd just heard.

'We could always check on the County Council's web site to see what applications for planning permission have been made.' Dick nudged the mouse on the staff room computer causing the screen to light up.

'Done that,' said Ron, smugly. 'And no planning applications have been made relating to either the College or Sixth Form.'

'Which is rather sinister,' intoned Tina. 'Surely if a hotel and leisure complex were to be built locally, there'd be some form of planning application?'

'An oversight?' queried Ron.

'Hardly,' returned Dick. 'These things take forever to organise and process through the various stages of the planning system.' He thought for a moment and then nodded his head. 'Somebody somewhere is sitting on the evidence.'

'It'd need a big arse,' remarked Tina.

'And one with plenty of weight,' added Dick.

All three colleagues began to laugh at the images being conjured in their heads. Ron suddenly clicked his fingers together.

'That reminds me,' he said.

'Really?' asked Tina, her face collapsing into laughter.

Ron turned his attention to Dick.

'Have you heard the one about the two Chairs?'

Tina began to laugh again.

'Oh, that one,' she grinned. 'Wasn't sure it was common knowledge.'

Dick felt totally confused at this change in topic.

'What about the two Chairs?'

'Ask Tracey,' Tina replied, promptly returning to her study of the newspaper.

CHAPTER 18

The Church of St Aloysius was renowned locally for both its choral work and for the ability of its group of stalwart amateur florists to turn bunches of limp vegetation into a blooming display. The floral creations, manipulated by the dextrous hands of the dedicated group known as the 'Ladies of the Lily', frequently attracted the attention of the local newspapers, parish magazines and, on one auspicious occasion, a mention on 'Gardeners' Question Time', concerning Thrips on their Pelargoniums. Unfortunately, with such public recognition for their endeavours, the 'Ladies of the Lily' had fallen out of favour with the choral group, whose only claim to fame had been a brief mention in the Parish magazine thanking them for their endeavours on the cake stall during the summer fete. As a result, a certain amount of rivalry existed, much to the consternation of the vicar who suffered palpitations whenever the two groups were under the same roof.

The barely veiled enmity between the two groups had reached the state where, knowing that several unfortunate members of the choral group had numerous allergies, the 'Ladies of the Lily' would place blooms with an extremely high pollen count next to the choir stalls. The choral group, in turn, would insist on the Church's heating system being driven to the maximum in order to keep their vocal cords warm and the flowers wilting.

One night, during a particularly fractious choral practice, Barbara Earnshaw was having particular difficulty with the proximity of a vase of assorted blooms. She'd tried discreetly moving the vase to one side, only for it to be returned to its original position by a rather vexed floristry lady, and had even resorted to misting the flowers with hairspray. Unfortunately, her voice refused to cooperate with the rigours of Mozart's 'Requiem aeternam'.

Mr Bradley, choirmaster and local councillor, tugged at his sleeves and pointed his baton at the soprano section.

'What is it tonight with you ladies?' he asked, brushing his forehead with the back of his hand, and giving a pretentious sniff. 'The hours I've spent annotating your parts and giving you precise instructions, have simply amounted to nothing but discordant hot air!'

Several of the sopranos began to mutter in low voices. They were fully aware that Mr Bradley's annotations were badly written as an intentional ploy on his part. They knew that any request for assistance in deciphering his scrawl was tantamount to an invitation for him to press his body against theirs as he slowly explained what he'd written. Although Barbara Earnshaw was one of those who detested his demonstrative explanations, along with the entire male contingent of Jones the Elder, Jones and Jones the Younger, there were several female members of the group who delighted in his attention. In fact, some of the younger attention seekers would purposely misread Mr Bradley's annotations, much to his delight.

Mr Bradley tapped his baton on the back of a pew.

'Now, ladies, can we take it from the first bar at the top of the page. One, two,' he counted. But, just as the combined choral diaphragms began to vent their fury, a high-pitched snorting sound reverberated around the Church.

'Damn and blast,' yelled Mr Bradley, throwing his baton onto the floor. 'Are you trying to make a fool of … ' Before Mr Bradley could suggest who exactly was being made a fool of, a terrifying shriek assailed his ears. Florence Pettigrew, second soprano and local postmistress, pointed at something behind Mr Bradley. Her face was ashen as her finger shook in horror.

'The Horseman of the Apocalypse,' she managed to mutter before her eyes rolled upwards as she promptly fainted, knocking over a rather elaborate floral display in the process.

In the confusion, with most of the choral group fretting over Florence Pettigrew and the two remaining Ladies of the Lily in an agitated state over the floral decimation, hardly anyone noticed a pair of eyes glinting in the doorway of the Church. For the couple of people who did glimpse something strange, they witnessed nothing more than a vague shadow slowly merging into the night leaving little more than a memory behind.

CHAPTER 19

PC Ricketts ignored the burping phone for as long as she could. With a sigh of resignation, she responded to the chiming summons with a barely concealed yawn.

'Ricketts,' she announced.

The caller, caught off-guard by the supposed medical prognosis, was left speechless.

'PC Ricketts speaking. Can I help you?'

'Oh, hello,' spluttered the voice. 'I want to report seeing something.'

PC Ricketts held the phone in front of her and stared at it. With a frown she shook her head in disbelief and, rejecting several delightful ripostes, put on her most courteous voice.

'I'm sorry, but could you be a little more precise as to what you may have seen?'

The voice spluttered once again, but this time with indignation.

'It's not what I *may* have seen, young lady.' The voice coughed politely. 'I wish to report that a person or persons, unknown, have been making a nuisance of themselves at the Church this evening.'

PC Ricketts pulled the relevant sheet of paper towards her and stabbed her pen at the box requiring a date and time of the incident to be inserted.

'What time did the incident occur madam?'

'Approximately 9.35,' reported the voice. 'And I'm not a madam, thank you very much.'

PC Ricketts began to sketch a gallows outline on the sheet of paper in front of her.

'And you are?' enquired PC Ricketts.

'Earnshaw,' said the voice in clipped tones. 'Mrs Barbara Earnshaw.'

PC Ricketts added a short length of rope to the picture.

'And which Church are we talking about,' she asked, drawing a head dangling from the rope.

'St Aloysius,' replied Mrs Earnshaw. 'We were just about to

repeat part of Mozart's 'Requiem aeternam', when Florence Pettigrew pointed towards the doorway and shrieked.'

PC Ricketts added stray tufts of hair to the head.

'Did you see what she was pointing at?"

Barbara Earnshaw sniffed haughtily.

'Of course not,' she snapped. 'We were all too concerned with Florence.'

PC Ricketts added a stick body to the head.

'Did anyone see anything at all?' she asked patiently.

'It was too dark to see anything clearly,' answered Barbara. 'We'd just been having a particularly difficult time with Mr Bradley and everything happened at once, what with the baton, the flowers, Florence and something nasty in the in the doorway.'

PC Ricketts gave the body arms and legs.

'I'll just take your details, Mrs Earnshaw and then we'll get on to it straight away.'

A few minutes later, and with the stick figure freshly buried in an unmarked grave, PC Ricketts waved the correctly completed form at Sergeant Cost. Without looking up from his newspaper, Sergeant Cost pointed behind him towards a row of cabinets.

'File it,' he ordered, holding his empty tea mug aloft for a refill.

CHAPTER 20

The early morning sun shone through the kitchen window illuminating a plate of freshly microwaved croissants. Cuddling a mug of equally fresh coffee, Dick allowed his eyes to close, not so much to keep out the sun but simply a way to savour the aromas in comfort. Across the table, Tracey busily spread blackcurrant jam onto her croissant, occasionally looking at Dick thoughtfully. On one of the rare moments that Dick's eyes were not totally closed, he caught Tracey smiling.

'What?' he enquired, blearily.

Tracey continued to smile, her eyes sparkling in the sunlight. Taking a sip of coffee, she suddenly began to hiccup and cough alternately. Dick, his eyes forcing themselves partially open, frowned.

'Are you OK?' he asked, placing his own mug of coffee safely on the table. Tracey took another sip from her mug and nodded, her eyes now glistening with tears.

'Fine,' she eventually managed to splutter. Rubbing the palms of her hands across her eyes, Tracey sniffed and grinned at Dick.

'So, what?' he repeated.

'Bizarre,' laughed Tracey. 'Totally bizarre.'

A myriad of thoughts ambled through Dick's mind as he contemplated all the different variables that Tracey might consider bizarre. Breakfast was their usual Saturday morning feast, the previous night had been, well, nothing that either of them would consider bizarre. Dick looked around the kitchen. Everything seemed perfectly normal to him with nothing standing out as remotely comical.

'What?' he asked for a third time.

Tracey took a long draught of coffee and smiled at Dick.

'This whole business is bizarre,' she explained. 'I don't know what to think about disembodied female voices and eccentric music shop owners and,' she began to chuckle, 'tactile steamers and an over-zealous masseur.'

Dick winced at the memory. His back still felt painful, with muscles complaining at every opportunity. He smiled lamely at Tracey.

'Something I've been meaning to ask you,' he said.

Tracey raised her eyebrows.

'Really,' she asked with crumbs of croissant falling from her lips.

'Yes,' replied Dick leaning forward. 'Have *you* heard about the two chairs?'

A shower of crumbs percolated the air. Tracey hugged her dressing gown around her tightly as she convulsed with laughter. Dick watched her performance with a growing degree of annoyance. Try as he might, there was absolutely nothing funny about the comment that he could think of. He coughed angrily.

'Care to enlighten me?' he asked as the laughter began to subside.

'The two Chairs,' she emphasised, 'are exactly that. Two Chairs.' Before Dick could respond, Tracey's collapsed into a fit of giggles.

'OK,' said Dick, his face beginning to colour. 'Please explain before I do something mean and messy with the blackcurrant jam.'

Tracey stifled her laughter and gave Dick a broad grin.

'The two Chairs,' she coughed politely. 'Refer to the College's Chair of Governors, our Lady Faulkner and her somewhat less than secret liaison with the Chair of Planning and Development at the County Council.' After the vocal exertion, Tracey swallowed the remains of her coffee. She examined Dick's facial contortions as he wrestled with the information. After a few moments he seemed to have digested the details sufficiently to ask a question.

'How come you know about this liaison and I don't?'

Tracey winked at him. 'As a Librarian, I am in the information business.' She licked a croissant crumb from her finger. 'Besides, I'm expected to know the answers to a myriad of questions should anyone care to ask.'

'OK,' offered Dick. 'Correct me if I'm wrong, but doesn't she have some influence over matters relating to the College and her amour having influence over matters pertaining to building stuff?'

Tracey clapped her hands together.

'*Exactement!*' she declared using her best French accent, in keeping with the continental breakfast.

Dick waved his hands in front of his face.

'It's too early to go all French and Hercule Poirot on me,' moaned Dick.

'Belgian,' corrected Tracey. 'Poirot was a Belgian detective.' She raised her eyebrows along with a slight smirk.

'Whatever,' muttered Dick, his eye lids beginning to lose their ability to stay in the open position.

'The point is,' continued Tracey, ignoring Dick's apparent loss of interest. 'Is that together they make quite a formidable couple. A couple who are able to influence much more than their combined heart rates.'

Dick screwed his eyes tight as he contemplated the facts and examined them in the light of other bits of information he'd heard during the last couple of days.

'Influential enough to bury planning applications and suchlike?' he asked.

'Easy,' said Tracey. 'And powerful enough to make sure lots of things are hidden from prying eyes until it's too late.'

Dick sucked at a cold croissant for several minutes and then, having reached a cerebral conclusion, pushed the entire crescent-shape into his mouth. Tracey watched with fascination as her partner demolished his breakfast. Dick, brushing any loose crumbs from his mouth grinned at Tracey.

'Well,' he said thoughtfully, 'that explains the absence of any planning applications, but it doesn't explain how the paper got hold of the hotel and leisure complex story.'

'Somebody either talking out of turn,' replied Tracey. 'Or there's a mole within the County Council.'

'Hmm,' murmured Dick, his finger idly pushing croissant crumbs around his plate. 'So, we have potentially sensitive documents indicating spurious expenditure, an illicit liaison between two chairs and an unfounded story in the local rag. Not quite on a par with Watergate, Blairgate or the garden gate.'

'Better than nothing,' grinned Tracey.

Dick gently rubbed his aching limbs as thoughts of the masseur's administrations flicked through his mind.

'At this moment in time,' he said with a slight wince, 'I'd take the *nothing* right now.'

'Wuss,' laughed Tracey unkindly.

'If you say so,' replied Dick. 'Anyway,' he added desperately attempting to change the subject, 'you never did tell me what happened at the Staff meeting?'

'Ugh!' snarled Tracey. 'His Royal Principalship simply wanted an audience to witness his latest Powerpoint creation.'

'A visual extravaganza for the hard of hearing?' enquired Dick cynically.

'In one,' grinned Tracey. 'More bells and whistles than Easter Mass in Saint Peter's Square.'

'But anything that we should be interested in?' asked Dick with a brief examination of his coffee mug.

'Now you come to mention it,' replied Tracey thoughtfully. 'He did go on a bit about the possibility of the College and the Sixth Form amalgamating for what he termed *"Effectiveness and Efficiency"*, or something like that.'

Dick smiled.

'Didn't there used to be a magazine of the same title with pictures of people in various states of undress playing racket sports and such like?'

Tracey gave him a cold stare.

'In your pubescent dreams, no doubt,' she said. 'But this is more to do with the very real possibility of redundancies or so our beloved union representative would have us believe.'

'I suppose the Union are calling for us to work to rule?'

'I very much doubt that,' laughed Tracey. 'Nobody wants to increase their workload.'

Dick allowed a laugh to escape.

'Predictable,' he chortled.

'As ever,' agreed Tracey, 'but always an interesting topic of conversation at parties and supermarket checkouts.

Dick frowned and decided that it was better to focus on more positive things than Tracey's indecipherable thought processes.

'We might have a lead or two, of sorts,' he said, rubbing his hands together. '

'Well,' replied Tracey. 'We do have a number of interesting coincidences, agreed.'

'Coincidences?' spluttered Dick. 'Look,' he said sitting upright for emphasis. 'We have His Royal Principalship wittering on about a merger with the Sixth Form College, we have the Union moaning about possible redundancies, we have the local rag regaling us with rumours of a Hotel complex and we have a sheaf of incriminating documents. How many more coincidences do you want?'

Tracey waited patiently while Dick recovered his breath and composure and then smiled.

'And don't forget about the two chairs.'

Dick leaned back in his chair and rubbed his eyes.

'Please don't,' he replied in a quiet voice. 'The thought of any form of amorous interaction between those two overweight luminaries makes me feel quite ill.'

'OK,' smirked Tracey, enjoying Dick's discomfort. 'There are a few chance occurrences, but the connections are pretty tenuous.' She sucked her bottom lip for a few moments and then gave a slight nod. 'Worth exploring though.'

'So,' grinned Dick, 'what next?'

Tracey winked at him. 'Regeneration Sounds,' she replied with a twinkle in her eye.

A dull thud and a prolonged groan greeted her suggestion. She waited for a few seconds until Dick lifted his head from the table.

'Better?' she asked him.

'Not really,' he mumbled. 'But if I'm going to get a headache, I'd prefer it to be from my own actions rather than inflicted upon me by some freak of nature.' He began to massage the ache slowly developing across his forehead. He squinted at Tracey. 'Anyway, do I have a choice?'

'Not really,' she replied, leaning across the table and gently touching his forehead.

'That's good,' he murmured. 'Thought you'd lost your touch.'

'So?' she ventured.

Dick stood up, wiping a few clinging crumbs from his sleeves as he did so. 'I'd better make myself presentable for the Mad Professor,' he grinned, picking up the mugs and plates and placing them in the dishwasher.

Tracey began to gather up the remaining breakfast things from the table. 'Hang on,' she called after Dick. 'I'll come with you.'

'Why don't you give Two-stroke three a ring and ask him to come along too?' shouted Dick from the top of the stairs. 'We can leave him watching the record shop for us while we go and do whatever it is we're supposed to do.'

Tracey pressed the dishwasher into action and went in search of her phone book. She felt pleased that they were going to involve someone else in this palaver if only to have a witness when things turned really odd.

CHAPTER 21

Two-stroke three sat in the back of Dick's car with what looked like a huge grin on his face. It was difficult to see exactly what his face was doing under the tatty Trilby hat, dark glasses and theatrical moustache. Occasionally, catching sight of Two-stroke three in the rear view mirror, Dick couldn't hide the wince of embarrassment at each glimpse of the farcical figure occupying the rear space.

Earlier, as they'd driven along to collect Two-stroke three, Dick and Tracey had been chatting about various possible suspects for the as yet unknown crime, when, suddenly a large figure clad in a threadbare mackintosh had walked straight into the road with both hands held up intimating that it would be provident to stop their car. Given no choice but to avoid making a very large dent in his car, Dick had stamped on the brakes stopping a thumb-width away from the figure. With one hand holding the front of the car on the tarmac, the other hand lifted the Trilby in a gesture of greeting. Without waiting for an invitation, the almost mysterious figure clambered into the back of the car.

'Wotcha, Two-stroke three,' chorused Dick and Tracey.

The rear of the car bounced in response.

'Brilliant, don't you think,' asked Two-stroke three, his bulk continuing to cause severe stress on the car's suspension.

'Yes, brilliant,' laughed Tracey. 'Now, please sit still so that Dick can concentrate on his driving.'

Replacing the Trilby, Two-stroke three turned the collar up on the mackintosh and sat back in the seat, occasionally waving or pointing a finger at people. One or two people had waved back but, on the whole, most people ignored the comical figure grinning inanely at them from the back seat of a Peugeot 205.

Parking the car at the top of Wheelwright Lane, a distance away from Regeneration Sounds, Dick spoke to the rear of the car.

'I realise that it may be a futile request, but could you try and make yourself a little less conspicuous and blend in with the scenery?'

Two-stroke three nodded.

'Gotcha,' he replied in a hoarse whisper. With an exaggerated look either side of him he tapped Dick unnecessarily on the shoulder. 'I've been giving it some thought,' he declared. 'As I'm under cover like, I reckon I should have one of those suede things.'

Panic gripped Dick as a host of suede-clad images rumbled through his mind. Trying to ignore everything from an enormous leather truncheon to a leather gun holster, Dick desperately shook the thoughts from his head and turned to Tracey, whose mouth puckered in the attempt to restrain a giggle. Looking at Two-stroke three, she patted his arm affectionately.

'You mean a pseudonym?' she asked.

'Yeah, one of them,' he grinned. 'And I've thought of a good one too.'

Tracey cocked her head to one side while Dick waited nervously for the result of Two-stroke three's thought processes.

'And?' asked Tracey.

'Two-stroke,' he announced proudly.

Dick gained control of his facial features. He nodded encouragingly.

'Good choice,' he said sagely, 'industrious, efficient and cheap to run. I like it.'

Tracey turned and patted Two-stroke's hand.

'That's not quite a pseudonym,' she smiled. 'It's more of an abbreviation.'

The newly named Two-stroke looked slightly bemused and shrugged his shoulders.

'I just thought it was easy to remember,' he muttered with a nonchalant flick at the brim of his trilby. 'Anyway,' he added. 'I can't be doing with fancy, double-barrelled names in this business. I want to be taken seriously,' he said with a nod towards Dick.

'Ignore him,' said Tracey, encouragingly. 'He's just jealous he didn't think of it first.' Two-stroke's face broke out in a broad grin causing part of his fake moustache to become unstuck and droop alarmingly.

Standing by the side of the car, and with Two-stroke busily fiddling with his disguise, Dick and Tracey quickly decided on a plan of action.

'So, a note for Duke Ellington?' enquired Tracey, extracting a piece of paper from her bag. Dick's hand automatically began to massage his back.

'Can we add a post-script asking for no more physical stuff?' he asked ruefully. Tracey grinned while Two-stroke, his mouth slightly open, looked at them both with raised eyebrows. Noticing the confusion, Dick placed a finger under Two-stroke's chin and gently closed his mouth.

'Nothing to concern you,' said Dick reassuringly. He leant forward, adding a touch of theatrical conspiracy. 'I want you to keep a look out,' he explained in a loud whisper. 'We need to know who goes into Regeneration Sounds and who comes out.' Two-stroke nodded, his eyes fixed firmly on the shop, which squatted complacently several metres away. Dick tapped Two-stroke on the arm. 'It's really important that we find out who's involved with the shop. Understand?'

Two-stroke beamed with pleasure. Pulling the collar of his mackintosh towards the Trilby, he gripped Dick's wrist.

'Gotcha, Boss,' he breathed loudly.

Leaving Two-stroke leaning heavily against an aged lamppost, Dick and Tracey ventured into Regeneration Sounds.

The shop door announced their arrival as it barged into the large bell placed inconveniently above it. Tracey immediately jumped at the noise, grabbing Dick's arm in alarm. Dick grinned and wondered whether he'd get the proverbial 'ticking off' from Tracey for not warning her about the bell.

At the sound of the tolling bell, Malc's head appeared from under a table.

'For whom the bell tolls,' he said, and then muttered a brief apology at his own inane joke.

'Hello, again,' answered Dick. He smiled towards Tracey. 'This is Tracey.'

Malc wiped both hands down the side of his jeans and placed them over Tracey's hand.

'Pleased to meet you,' he said, pumping her hand warmly. 'Hope the bell didn't startle you too much,' he said with a smile of apology. 'But I was trying to sort out some old stock that's been under the table for absolutely ages, and half of the time I couldn't have told you if the shop was empty or hosting a Baroque Orchestra,' Malc explained with a grin.

Tracey smiled graciously as she removed her hand from the continued pummelling. 'I don't think,' she said with a nod at the assorted CD's, 'that this is the sort of place you'd find a Baroque Orchestra performing a homage to Hoagy Carmichael.'

'Ah,' mused Malc, '*Georgia on my mind*, what a wonderful composition by Hoagy. Did you know,' he added enthusiastically, 'that the term *baroque*, is derived from the Portuguese word "barroco", meaning an imperfect pearl. What a wonderful term to describe jazz.'

'Is that really necessary?' interjected Dick before Malc could provide further insights into all things of a baroque nature. 'The bell, I mean,' said Dick with a gesture towards the offending object.

'Can't be doing with buzzers and things,' explained Malc. He cocked his head to one side. 'Funny, though, the Baroque style was initially encouraged by the Catholic Church, as a response to the Protestant Reformation ... '

'OK if we just have a quick browse?' asked Dick hastily interrupting the flow of unnecessary information.

'Browse away,' replied Malc apparently unperturbed by the interruption. 'Feel free to take another look at Charlie Parker's *Yardbird Suite*.'

Promptly dropping onto all fours, Malc crawled back under the table. 'It was in response to the Protestant Reformation you know,' came Malc's muffled voice. 'Something to do with conveying religious themes in ... '

Tracey took Dick by the arm and moved him away from Malc's monologue.

Have you got the note?' she asked.

'What was that?' coughed Malc from the dusty atmosphere under the table.

'Nothing,' shouted Dick ushering Tracey's towards the shoebox containing all the jazzy 'P's'. As he flicked through the CD's, Tracey nudged him.

'Aren't we supposed to leave the note with the Duke Ellington CD?'

Dick cautiously looked over to where Malc was still under the table sifting through various boxes.

'I don't think we were meant to wait for a response,' he offered. 'Seems to me our movements are being pre-empted.' He lifted Charlie Parker's *Money Jungle* out of the box. 'Just as I thought,' he muttered, lifting a slip of paper from between the pages of the CD notes. Replacing the CD, Dick put the slip of paper in his pocket and walked towards the door.

'Still not sure,' he said over loudly, 'even with a second opinion.'

'Not a problem,' replied Malc from under the table. 'Anytime.'

Once outside and clear of the raucous peel of the shop's bell, Dick glanced at the slip of paper and handed it over to Tracey.

'Seems like we want to do golf,' he said, as Tracey scrutinised the instructions. She turned the paper over and, satisfied that there were no other words of advice, returned it to Dick.

'What's your handicap?' she enquired teasingly.

With a smile, Dick looked from Tracey to Two-stroke.

'Guess,' he replied.

CHAPTER 22

While Two-stroke continued to put a strain on the lamppost opposite Regeneration Sounds, Dick and Tracey drove across town to the local golf club.

Built reassuringly in the 1930's, the golf club retained the exclusivity of a *Member's Only* club while desperately trying not to appear too discriminatory where money was concerned. The precise extent to which the club succumbed to monetary temptation was discretely screened by a large, manicured privet hedge, which obscured the fact that the Club's coffers could barely stand a round of drinks at the nineteenth hole.

Walking past the hedge and towards the clubhouse, Dick and Tracey couldn't help feeling that they were being observed. Gripping Dick's arm tightly, Tracey put on a beatific smile as they climbed the short flight of stairs leading to the main door. As she took a quick glance at Dick, Tracey noticed that he wore a sanctimonious grin making him appear slightly demented. She dug her fingers into his wrist. Still maintaining his smile, Dick's pain-filled eyes looked questioningly at her.

Tracey paused briefly in front of the door. 'You're enjoying this aren't you?' she said.

Dick gave a slight shake of his head and wriggled his arm free on the pretext of opening the door for her.

'After you, my sweet,' he murmured. Leaning towards her ear, he added, 'It makes a change to see a librarian at a loss for words.'

'Make the most of it,' she replied. 'I'll be exacting my revenge later.'

Before Dick could express his thanks, a dishevelled figure appeared before them.

'Good afternoon,' spoke the figure in clipped tones. 'How can I help you?'

Dick stepped forward confidently and offered his hand.

'Good afternoon to you, I'm Dick Hall and this,' He gestured with an incline of his head. 'Is Tracey Barton.'

The figure, with hands firmly clasped behind his back, nodded to Dick and Tracey in turn.

'My name is Blanchard, Richard Blanchard, and I am Chair of the Committee. Can I be of service?'

Dick removed his floating hand and smiled courteously.

'Tracey and I,' he intoned. 'Have been considering a number of Clubs with a view to our becoming members.'

'Members, eh?' snapped Mr Blanchard. 'And what do you suppose I'm to make of someone who comes along to us as a sort of last resort.'

Forestalling any further comments, Tracey swiftly took Mr Blanchard's arm and began to lead him towards the bar.

'It wasn't quite like that Richard. I may call you Richard? Good. Now, can I get you a drink? Good. Now, about this *last resort* nonsense ... '

Dick, amazed at Tracey's sudden loss of earlier reticence, stood in admiration. Her words and any response from Mr Richard Blanchard became inaudible as they moved further towards the drinks dispenser. With the freedom that Tracey's intervention had brought, Dick took the opportunity to visually digest his surroundings.

The front doors of the Clubhouse led straight into a reception area that held an air of ambivalence, neither appearing to welcome or deter visitors. The noticeboard, which lay to the right of the reception area, displayed the usual plethora of fading bits of paper and adverts for events that everyone ignored until the occasion had slipped into history. The carpeted area in front of Dick wore a well-trod pathway directly to the bar. Either side of the pathway sat an assortment of tables and chairs supporting a variety of arms, legs, glasses and the sporadic dozing head. Recognising the fact that he didn't know any of the assembled faces, Dick drifted towards Tracey and Mr Blanchard.

Tracey, her hand still on the Blanchard's arm, was just offering to buy him a drink when Dick approached.

'A most agreeable Clubhouse,' observed Dick, trying desperately to sound sincere. With cursory a look of disdain, Mr Blanchard ignored Dick and treated Tracey to a wrinkled smile.

'If you don't mind,' he drooled. 'I'll take you up on that offer of a drink after I've shown you and,' he indicated Dick with a slight movement of his head, 'your partner, the facilities.' Taking Tracey by the arm, he led her through a set of veneered doors into the depths of the clubhouse. With a shrug, Dick followed them at a discrete distance.

A little while later, and teetering on the verge of slumber, Dick and Tracey left their host at the bar while they ventured outside to explore the 'verdant pastures', as Mr Blanchard had described the various lumps and bumps that comprised the golf course. Tracey let out a deep sigh.

'My goodness,' she breathed. 'More hot air than Prime Minister's Question Time.'

'Oh dear,' yawned Dick in mock surprise. 'And I thought you two were getting on so well.'

'Some things need all the guile and cunning that only a woman can bring,' replied Tracey. 'Besides, you never know what interesting things I might have picked up during my aural suffering.'

'And did you,' asked Dick with an expressive yawn, 'pick up anything interesting that is?'

'No,' snapped Tracey sharply.

Dick squinted at Tracey.

'I've not been as bored as that outside of a classroom.'

Tracey jabbed him in the ribs.

'Fine talk for a lecturer,' she grinned. Linking arms with Dick she began to follow the directions for the first hole.

The neatly gravelled pathway, edged by a manicured lawn that implied a regular visit from a horticultural stylist was an absolute priority, meandered leisurely away from the buildings. The blended colours of soporific shrubbery followed the curves and lines of the path in its unerring journey to the golf course. Interspersed with birdsong and the occasional whine from a stray dog, a muted hubbub drifted across the turf. At first, Dick and Tracey were oblivious to the background sounds until they both suddenly stopped and looked at each other. Tracey, her head leaning slightly to one side, nudged Dick.

'Listen,' she whispered.

Dick frowned. The exterior of the clubhouse was as sleep inducing as the interior. The sights and sounds seemed to combine in creating a drowsy atmosphere. Realising that if he stood still too long he'd succumb to sleep, Dick shuffled forward.

'Listen!' hissed Tracey, her hand holding firmly to Dick's sleeve. 'Stand still for a moment and use your ears.'

Dick obliged. After a few seconds of feeling like a stuffed olive, he shrugged.

'What am I supposed to be listening for?' he asked, plunging his hands into his pockets truculently.

Tracey sighed. 'It's a golf course, right?'

Dick's almost imperceptible nod was taken for granted as she continued.

'And they play golf here, correct?' She paused politely. Dick nodded, confident so far that his limited knowledge of golf wasn't being stretched. 'So,' asked Tracey, her eyebrows rising. 'Can you hear golf?'

Dick listened obediently. He hadn't really noticed anything out of the ordinary, but then again, with his limited understanding of all things pertaining to golf, he hadn't a clue what was supposed to be ordinary. He looked quizzically at Tracey.

'What's golf supposed to sound like?'

Her shoulders sagged with exasperation. With a withering glare she moved her head from left to right.

'There's supposed to be,' she elongated each word to allow Dick time to catch up, 'the occasional Neanderthal grunt of exertion, along with a dose of unintelligible language that usually indicates a loss of composure as well as direction.' She caught hold of Dick's elbow and manoeuvred him into a dense patch of shrubbery. Without even looking in his direction, Tracey continued with a whisper. 'And you can take that silly grin off of your face too.'

Suitably chastened, Dick allowed himself to be led through the foliage until Tracey motioned him to be quiet and kneel down. Following suit, she moved her lips towards his ear.

'Thought it best to try and be discrete,' she whispered. Her eyes sparkled as she allowed herself a broad grin. She gently nudged

Dick in the ribs. 'Observe,' she said, carefully parting some small branches in front of her.

Immediately in front of the amateur sleuths lay a broad area of grass flanked by shrubs and trees on either side. In the distance, a yellow flag sagged against a metal pole that protruded from a patch of dense green grass. In the opposite direction to the flag, a gaggle of male golfers stood admiring each other's trolleys and chatting busily. As they observed the golfers, Dick and Tracey noticed that they seemed to be getting quite animated in their discussion. In particular, two garishly decorated men appeared to be at odds with each other, with both of them agitatedly prodding the ground with their golf clubs, in an almost tribal manner. As Dick watched this apparent golfing ritual, he began to think that there was something vaguely familiar about the two figures. He closed his eyes momentarily, and tried to remember where he'd seen the two men before. After a few moments, he opened his eyes to see Tracey looking at him. He grinned.

'It's just come to me,' he announced to a perplexed Tracey. She arched her eyebrows.

'Remind me to build a shrine to enlightenment,' quipped Tracey sarcastically, as she brushed leaf mould from the knees of her jeans. 'So,' she asked, 'what's just come to you and don't wind me up, whatever you do,' she warned.

Not wanting to endanger life or limb, Dick decided to share his knowledge.

'Two of those fancy dressed blokes, over there,' he pointed at the gaggle of golfers. 'The two with ill-fitting jumpers and highly creased trousers are, I think, the same two blokes I met in the steam room, remember?'

'I wasn't there,' replied Tracey, prodding Dick's shoulder 'Remember?' Suddenly, the memory of Dick's experiences in the steam room came flooding back causing her to giggle. She stroked Dick's knee. 'It wasn't me caressing your leg if you recall.'

Dick pushed her hand away. 'I don't need reminding of that, thank you very much,' he growled. 'Anyway, if I'm not mistaken, those two blokes over there are Gerald and Ralph.' While Tracey fought to contain her laughter, Dick continued watching his recent acquaintances.

The small gaggle of golfers appeared to be discussing something of importance, as their conversation grew more animated by the minute. Dick turned around to Tracey who, still wrestling with her facial muscles, had crept deeper into the shrubbery. Carefully moving towards her, Dick indicated the golfers with a nod.

'Don't you think it's strange that Gerald and Ralph appear to spend so much of their leisure time together?'

Stroking his knee again, Tracey grinned. 'Not really, dear.'

Dick pushed her hand away angrily. 'Give over, woman.' Then, taking her hand, he led her out of the foliage and back onto the main pathway. 'Now,' he said, trying to control his own desire to laugh. 'We should try and get ourselves into a position that allows us to catch what they're talking about. You never know,' he continued. 'It might shed some light on this bizarre caper.'

Moving further along the pathway, Dick and Tracey skirted the edge of the fairway until they found a convenient gap in the various bits of shrub and trees. Tracey blew out her cheeks.

'We need to cross over the fairway and manoeuvre ourselves behind Gerald and Ralph if we're to get any chance of hearing what they're talking about.'

Before Dick could offer any strategic comment, his phone vibrated noisily in his back pocket. Fumbling with the phone he eventually managed to prod it into submission and listened to the hoarsely whispered tones of Two-stroke.

After a few seconds of head nodding and the occasional grunt, he cut the conversation short.

'Two-stroke, shut up and listen. Just make your way over to my house. We'll be there shortly. OK?'

Stroking the phone into silence, Dick shook his head.

'Two-stroke says that Malc locked up the shop straight after we visited. So faithful Two-stroke has been watching an empty shop for the last hour.'

Tracey gave a short laugh. 'They don't make them like that anymore, thankfully.'

Dick, with another shake of the head, took Tracey's hand and began a crouched jog across the grass towards the trees on the other side of the fairway. Halfway across the grass-covered strip of land, an angry voice announced their discovery.

'Hey, you two! Get off the fairway.'

Momentarily pausing, Dick raised his hand to acknowledge the voice. As he did so, Gerald and Ralph looked at each other then looked again at Dick. Nervously the pair half-heartedly raised their hands in partial recognition as both Dick and Tracey disappeared into the shrubbery.

Tracey squeezed Dick's hand. 'I think they recognised you, how nice.'

'So much for covert surveillance,' muttered Dick.

'If you'd have wanted to go *undercover*,' Tracey replied. 'Then we should have dressed in some gaudy patterned garb and waltzed around with a couple of shopping trolleys.'

'Look,' growled Dick in annoyance. 'We look stupid enough without theatre props.'

Tracey pursed her lips tightly together, hoping to retain the laughter welling up in her stomach. Dick shook his head and grinned. When Tracey was in this type of mood, there was nothing to do but sit tight while the gale of laughter rent the air. Just as he began to lean forward to place a finger against Tracey's lips, a tremendous *crack* sounded above his head. Dick looked around to see a golf ball falling to the ground having left a surprisingly deep indent in the tree behind him. Tracey's laughter subsided immediately while Dick, ashen faced, tried to work out which direction the golf ball had come from.

Fortunately for Dick, moving to see where the first ball had come from, saved him from being hit by a second ball, which cannoned off the tree and flew into the shrubbery behind Tracey. With an agility, that astonished even Dick, Tracey grabbed his shoulders and pushed him headfirst through the foliage and away from the fairway.

Ignoring the frequent attempts of the barbed twigs and branches to grab their attention, Dick and Tracey jogged determinedly through the shrubbery. After narrowly missing a raised tree root, Dick turned to warn Tracey of the obstacle and promptly fell over.

Tensing himself for a vicious attack from the undergrowth, he was surprised to hear a sharp expulsion of air sound in his ear. Looking down, Dick was shocked to see he'd tripped over two rotund figures locked in an embrace. Their facial expressions, which moments earlier had been caressed with passion, were now creased with pain. Anxious to make his escape, Dick muttered an apology and hobbled after the fast disappearing figure of Tracey.

Tracey slowed her pace to allow Dick the chance to catch up with her. As he approached, Dick frowned at the sight of Tracey trying desperately to suppress her laughter once again. Breathing heavily, Dick stood before Tracey and shook his head.

'You seem to be finding this whole escapade one continuous bundle of fun,' he gasped sarcastically. Tracey grabbed his arm and hurried him away from the scene.

After a few metres, Dick caught hold of Tracey's arm. 'Hold up, a moment,' he spluttered. He pointed back into the vegetation. 'What,' he wheezed, 'is so funny?'

Without explanation, Tracey took hold of Dick's face and kissed him fiercely on the lips. After Dick's flailing arms had signalled the fact that oxygen was in extremely short supply, Tracey released him and, still holding his face between her hands grinned happily. 'You're priceless,' she said with genuine admiration.

Thankful for the opportunity to exercise his lungs once more, Dick shrugged and smiled agreement. 'If you say so,' he grinned breathlessly.

Tracey allowed a small chirrup of laughter to escape.

'Didn't you recognise the two romantic forms you've just stumbled across?' she asked.

Dick shrugged again but left out the grin.

'Well,' he mumbled, 'I couldn't say who was more embarrassed, me or them.'

Tracey kissed his nose teasingly.

'It was the two Chairs,' she answered his bewildered stare.

Without waiting for Dick to respond or pausing to say goodbye to Mr Blanchard, Tracey led Dick back to their car and careered down the driveway leaving only a trace of disturbed gravel and wisps of dust to signal their departure.

Leaving the car parked at an awkward angle on his drive, Dick opened the front door of the house and immediately went into the kitchen to switch the kettle on. Tracey, following slowly behind, hit the play button on the answer phone and listened intently to the messages. The kettle was just beginning to generate a head of steam when she walked into the kitchen. Dick looked up and smiled.

'Everything OK, pet?' he asked.

Tracey blinked an emerging tear away.

'That was a message from Dubbya,' she ran a finger under her eye. 'Two-stroke's been arrested.'

CHAPTER 23

Two-stroke sat on the edge of the sofa, a hot mug of tea cradled in his ample hands. Both Dick and Tracey waited patiently for him to relax while Dubbya sat leisurely on the sofa, an empty mug lying against his stomach. Two-stroke looked at the expectant faces, his eyes twitching nervously.

'I'm sorry, Boss,' he mumbled into his drink.

Tracey patted his hands. 'Don't worry, Two-stroke. It's over now and your back safe and sound with us.'

Two-stroke took a comforting sip of his tea. Since returning from the Police station, he'd divested himself of his detective disguise and now looked quite forlorn in his pale yellow 'T' shirt and jeans. Dick coughed.

'So,' he asked. 'Do you feel up to telling us what happened?' He rubbed the still warm mug against his chin as he watched Two-stroke struggle to locate the explanatory words.

'Well,' began Two-stroke licking his lips. 'I did exactly what you told me, you know, watch the shop and all that.'

'Brilliant,' encouraged Tracey, eager to find out herself how Two-stroke had got himself arrested.

'Yeah,' he grinned. 'Wasn't easy standing around trying to watch what was going on, and keep an eye on the record shop and everything.'

Dick clicked his tongue in annoyance.

'You were supposed to be keeping an eye on what was going on at the record shop!'

Two-stroke shrugged. 'I did that as well,' he replied, beginning to sense a hint of reprimand in Dick's voice. Tracey patted Two-stroke's hands again.

'And you did really well, thank you. We couldn't have done it without you, could we?' she gave Dick a glare.

'Oh, right, yeah, no way,' agreed Dick.

Two-stroke looked questioningly at Dick, unsure whether he'd received approval or not. Finally, deciding that there wasn't any reproach in Dick's voice, he grinned.

'I made sure nothing escaped my attention,' he continued confidently. 'Moments after you both left that bloke came out, looked up and down the street and then locked the shop up.'

'Are you certain he didn't come back later?' asked Dick. 'He might have just popped out, you know, for a sandwich or something.'

Two-stroke shook his head vehemently. 'No way,' he said. 'I stood around for ages, even went and looked through the shop window forever but the bloke never returned. No way!'

'We believe you,' soothed Tracey. 'It's just that we need to be sure of events.' She nodded knowingly at Two-stroke. 'You understand how this detective business goes.'

Two-stroke positively beamed. He liked the idea of being an accomplice in whatever escapade Tracey and Dick were involved with. He brushed his hands up and down the legs of his jeans, grinning inanely at everyone.

'So,' nodded Dick. 'What happened next?'

'Like I said,' replied Two-stroke. 'Nothing!'

'After the *nothing* bit,' encouraged Tracey. 'What happened after you'd phoned Dick?'

Two-stroke's hands stilled on his legs, his face clouded at the memories.

'Well,' began Two-stroke slowly. 'I did as you told me to, like and then ... '

'And then, what?' interrupted Dubbya, keen to get involved in the conversation. 'Get to the interesting bit.'

Two-stroke sucked his top lip. He glanced nervously at the door, as if pondering on making a quick escape. 'I, er, got myself arrested, sort of,' he murmured.

'Sort of, nothing,' snorted Dubbya. 'I had to come down to the police station, vouch for you as not being a danger to the community or any other wildlife and then smuggle you into my car.'

Two-stroke contemplated his knees while Dubbya toyed with his distinctly cold mug. 'Any chance of a refill?' asked Dubbya hopefully. Tracey removed the mug and disappeared into the kitchen. Amid the various sounds of drink making, she called over her shoulder to Two-stroke.

'Ignore Dubbya,' she said, coldly. 'He's just jealous that he's not an integral part of the team.'

My dear lady,' replied Dubbya. 'Contrary to perceived wisdom I was involved in this intriguing puzzle from the very beginning. In fact,' he continued smugly. 'I was aware of the problem before you.'

Tracey returned with a tray laden with hot drinks and a plate of assorted biscuits.

'As is so often the case,' she addressed Dubbya, in measured tones. 'Being aware of a problem and knowing what to do about it are often two completely separate things. And,' she continued. 'Whilst you may have understood the odd word or two from the document, in between drooling over the bar maid and dribbling into your beer, an appropriate course of action would not have clawed its way easily through the murky depths of your thought processes.'

Carefully selecting a biscuit, Tracey silently went though the ritualistic dunking process. Dubbya, feeling suitably chastened and unsure whether a response wouldn't elicit another viperous comment, decided to make amends.

'Nice brew,' he said obsequiously. 'Very refreshing.'

Tracey smiled politely and turned her attention to Two-stroke.

'Why did the police mistakenly arrest an innocent citizen such as yourself,' she frowned at Two-stroke. 'And why did you telephone Dubbya to come and pick you up?'

'Well,' began Two-stroke, returning to rubbing his legs. 'I arrived here and waited, as instructed. But I got a bit bored just standing around, like I'd done at the shop, so I took a stroll.'

'You took a stroll,' mused Dick, stroking his chin. 'Very interesting, Two-stroke, but what exactly did you do during this stroll that made the police sit up and take notice?'

Two-stroke swallowed hard. 'Dunno.' He shook his head slightly. 'I walked up and down the street a few times, read the Council notice that was tied to one of the lamp posts, and then I peered into a few gardens. Neat lot around here aren't they.'

Tracey nodded knowingly.

'Proud of their Petunias,' she said. The quip was lost on Two-stroke who simply looked at her with bewilderment. Tracey smiled reassuringly. 'Don't fret yourself, Two-stroke. Now,' she paused and smiled at Two-stroke. 'What happened next?'

Two-stroke raised his shoulders. 'Dunno,' he replied. 'I was just looking at those daft gnome things opposite here when a police car pulled up and two uniforms got out.'

Dick sat back in his chair. 'So, you told them the truth?'

'Course I did,' said Two-stroke. 'Told them that I wasn't doing anything.'

'Helpful,' commented Dubbya. 'Very helpful that.'

'They kept on asking me what I was doing,' continued Two-stroke. 'And I kept telling them that I wasn't doing anything. At that point this old geezer came out and starts going on about seeing suspicious characters. I didn't realise he meant me. After that, the uniforms told me I was to come down to the station and tell them exactly what I was up to.'

'Ah,' smiled Dubbya. 'Now I understand why they were so insistent on me vouching for you. I didn't realise I was acting as a guarantor for a prowler!'

'Weren't my fault,' insisted Two-stroke. 'Just some busybody with nothing better to do that goes and gets me into trouble.' He slouched back into the chair. 'And then I rang Dubbya because I thought you'd be mad at me for getting into trouble.'

Tracey stroked his arm. 'As if we would,' she said soothingly. 'It's an occupational hazard.' She gave Two-stroke a smile. 'It's all sorted now anyway.' She looked at the three men in turn. 'What do we do next, that's the question?'

Dubbya grinned broadly. 'Easily answered,' he replied. 'There's a vote on strike action at the College tomorrow. That will give you something else to think about.' He waved his mug in the air. 'Any chance of another refreshing brew?'

CHAPTER 24

The odorous staffroom hummed with the sound of moaning.

'Stupid,' announced Ron, slamming his mug of coffee onto the desk and decorating his jacket with fresh stains.

'It's more than stupid,' declared Tina, who thought about slamming her mug onto the desk but decided to drink the contents first. 'It's puerile!'

'Look,' said Dick, interrupting the flow of vitriol. 'It's for your own good you understand.'

Ron slowly swivelled his chair to face Dick. Brushing at the newly formed damp patches on his jacket, he shook his head solemnly.

'You sound more like my dear departed mother everyday. Come to think of it,' he said, leaning towards Dick. 'You're even beginning to look like my mother everyday.'

'Thanks for that charming comparison,' replied Dick, stroking the recently mown stubble on his chin. 'But I suggest you put your thumb print on the ballot paper and support the call for strike action.'

Ron, still dabbing at his coffee stained jacket, drew a cross on the ballot paper and folded it in half.

'There,' he said triumphantly. 'Done and I hope you're satisfied. That's a day's pay down the pan.'

'More than that,' snapped Tina. 'They'll average it out over the academic year and include holiday pay. In the end, it's the best part of two days pay.'

Dick swung his legs off the table and stamped them onto the floor.

'It's no use quibbling over a couple of days pay when the future of your job is in the balance.'

Tina creased her ballot paper sharply. 'It's not so much quibbling over pay as quibbling over what it is we're supposed to be striking for,' she said.

'Exactly,' agreed Ron. 'What are we striking for?' He held his fist in the air. 'Is it about pay?' He raised his index finger. 'Is it about pensions?' A second finger was added to the first. 'Is it about conditions of service?' A third finger joined the other two. 'Is it about teaching load?' The fourth finger hit the air. 'Or,' he added with a touch of finality. 'About the future of education, whatever that might be?' His thumb made up the set.

'Let's face it,' sighed Dick. 'There's not enough money to go around, both our building and that of St George's Sixth Form are far from adequate for the demands of the Twenty-First Century, and,' he continued with a shake of his head. 'Staffing takes up about seventy-percent of the total budget. Need I say more?'

Tina, who during Ron's finger waving exercise, had been reading through a statement from the union.

'It says here,' she said, tapping her finger on the paper. 'That it's the implied threat of redundancies and the extent of the restructuring that should concern us.'

'Isn't that what I've just said?' queried Ron.

'No!' chorused Tina and Dick, both with a huge grin.

Ron, his pride injured and his jacket still feeling damp in places, screwed the ballot paper into a ball and threw it onto Dick's desk. 'For what it's worth,' he muttered.

'It's got to be worth something,' replied Tina, putting an extra crease in her ballot paper. 'I suppose a show of solidarity stops the management walking over us completely without thinking first.'

'That's an oxymoron,' laughed Ron, showing the fillings in his teeth. 'The management actually thinking first is about as likely as me becoming a member of the senior management itself.'

'Good grief!' exclaimed Tina. 'As unlikely as that?'

Ron grunted a response and then disappeared under the desk in search of his wayward lunchbox. 'Got it,' he called in a muffled voice. At the same moment the fire alarm began to snarl in earnest. A dull thud announced the spontaneous meeting of Ron's head with the underside of the desk.

'Blood and sawdust!' he spat as he emerged rubbing the top of his head. 'What dimwit set that off?'

Reluctantly, Tina left the comfort of her chair and started to walk towards the door.

'Hadn't we ought to make an orderly evacuation of the building?' she asked.

Ron sorted through the debris in his lunchbox, selected several pieces of what looked suspiciously like a sandwich and joined Tina by the door.

'I expect it's just a drill, as normal. Do you think there's time to pick up a cup of coffee from the machine on the way out? You know how long it takes to clear the building and go through the motions of counting heads.'

Dick peered at his desk and opened a couple of draws in search of his own lunchbox.

'Damn,' he muttered. 'I must have left my lunch in the car. No matter, I'll collect it after we've been ticked off.'

In the corridor, other members of staff and a few bedraggled students were shuffling their way out of the building. The only urgency in the proceedings was whether the process would last long enough to make it pointless returning to the classroom before lunch. To try and make this a certainty, many of the staff and students adopted impeccable manners and repeatedly requested other staff and students to go before them, even going to the extreme of holding the doors open for each other. Eventually, the whole shambolic mass that embodied the educational ethos of the College assembled itself on the playing fields. As the different classes dissolved into friendship groups, Mr Roberts, the member of senior management responsible for health and safety, prowled up and down the unruly lines of bodies clasping a megaphone to his chest. Occasionally muttering and gesticulating to individuals, *Megaphone Roberts* as he was affectionately known, finally appeared to succumb to the disorganised mess before him. Shaking his head in agitation, he lifted the megaphone to his mouth.

'You're all dead!' he announced with finality.

The chattering hubbub quietened slightly at the pronouncement. A few students prodded each other's shoulders, shrugged and began to laugh.

'Its no laughing matter,' bawled Mr Roberts, forgetting to use the megaphone. Suddenly aware of more laughter, he switched the implement on causing a mass of hands to cover ears as the squeal of the megaphone drowned out the laughter. Mr Roberts coughed into megaphone.

'As I said, this isn't a laughing matter.' Composing himself, he took a deep breath and addressed the crowd again.

'You all took so long to evacuate the building, if this had been a real fire, you'd have all burned to a cinder. Dead, crisped, charcoal, smoked, fried … ' The rest of his diatribe was lost as he threw the megaphone to the ground and stormed off into the building. Quite a number of students adopted zombie-like postures and ambled back towards the College in search of sustenance.

Taking advantage of the bustling confusion, Dick decided to grab the opportunity to retrieve his lunch from the car. Making sure that no member of the senior management appeared to be loitering with intent, he quickly moved behind a line of rambling students and escaped along the narrow path leading towards the staff car park.

Dick couldn't help smiling at the thought of him behaving like a student and sneaking out of class. Unfortunately, the smile evaporated immediately as he saw two men peering into his car.

'Oi!' yelled Dick, his voice tailing off into a high-pitched shriek.

Almost in slow motion, the two men paused, turned their heads and, seeing a screaming figure running towards them, stood up. As Dick approached the men, he could see that the rear door of his car was wide open with several bits of assorted paraphernalia strewn across the back seat. More out of annoyance than bravery, Dick started to point at each man in turn.

'What the hell do you think you're doing with my car?' he demanded.

The two men looked at each other uncertainly. It was as if getting caught in the act wasn't a part of their thinking. As Dick stepped forwards the largest of the two men, a brawny specimen with more hair than his hat knew what to do with, quickly reached into the car and pulled out a tatty sweatshirt that Dick used whenever the urge to exercise came upon him. Holding the sweatshirt at arms length the brawny bloke ran at Dick.

'Grab him,' he yelled at his accomplice, thrusting the sweatshirt over Dick's head and pinning his arms to his sides.

'Gerroff!' yelled Dick, muffled by the fabric of his sweatshirt. Kicking out indiscriminately, he heard the satisfying grunts of pain from his attackers until his shin made contact with the car's wheel arch. This time it was Dick who grunted with pain, as he hopped madly about. The sound of laughter filtered through the fabric. Turning to face the source of the mirth, Dick tried to shout for help. Unfortunately, his muffled yells only caused more laughter from the passing students. In one last desperate attempt to draw attention to his predicament, Dick began to jump up and down. The sight of someone behaving like an overgrown pogo stick only produced a spontaneous round of applause from a couple of bystanders.

Concerned at the unwanted attention, the brawny bloke back-heeled Dick in the shin causing him to bend double in pain. One of the students called out in concern.

'Is he OK?'

'Yeah, what's this all in aid of?' enquired a female voice.

'He's fine,' smiled the brawny bloke. 'Rehearsing a bit of a gag for rag week. Should be fun, look out for us.'

'Didn't know there was a rag week,' shrugged the female as she began to walk away.

Dick heard the metallic screech of doors being opened and then he felt a violent shove in the back as he fell forward, hitting his knees against a solid edge. Lying on the floor of the van, he heard a gruff voice asking someone called 'Jonesy' for keys and then he felt something that smelt similar to the carpet in his bedroom thrown on top of him. After that, Dick's senses became a blur as darkness cocooned him.

CHAPTER 25

With each groan of the canteen door opening, Tracey looked up from her still shut lunchbox to see if it was Dick entering the room. She'd looked up so often that the students around her joined her in anticipation of some potentially intriguing person making an entrance.

After twenty minutes of frustrating her hunger needs, Tracey removed a sausage roll from her lunchbox, popped it into her mouth, stood up and promptly left the canteen.

With an impatience that was beginning to colour into anger, she negotiated the student-strewn stairs and made her way to the Business Studies staffroom in search of her erstwhile partner. Deciding not to knock on the door, and allow Dick a millisecond warning, Tracey stormed through the door. Her prompt entrance caused Ron to immediately swallow a cherry tomato whole. She watched as his face began to imitate the colour of the tomato and then gave Ron a sharp thump on the back.

'That,' rasped a relieved Ron, 'was a dangerous thing to do.' He massaged his throat vigorously. 'Besides, you could have burst in on a private situation.'

Tina, who until now had sat busily chewing a cereal bar and watching the proceedings with interest, shook her head.

'Wouldn't have happened, Ron,' she chewed. 'Firstly, I'm in here and you're not getting into a private situation with me and,' she grinned. 'Secondly, you know what College policy is concerning a staff liaison with a student, or any other inanimate object.'

Ron began to choke once more.

'I meant no such thing,' he spluttered. 'Neither with you or any wretched individual in this College.'

Tracey, her anger still intact, stared at Ron.

'Wretched am I?' she blazed. 'That's just about all I need, thank you.' She nodded towards Dick's desk. 'So, where is he?'

Tina wiped any trace of discarded cereal from her mouth and smiled.

'He's dead,' she replied serenely.

Tracey's mouth gaped open, her eyes moved from Tina to Ron and back again.

'Dead?' she whispered. You mean ... '

Tina nodded.

'Yup, dead as in Dodo.' She jerked her head towards the window. 'We're all dead according to Megaphone Roberts and our reluctance to leave a burning building.'

Tracey sighed with relief.

'You mean metaphorically speaking, dead?'

Ron closed his eyes and turned his head towards the ceiling.

'Without getting into a metaphysical discussion, if we are trying to establish that Dick exists, well, when I last saw him he existed. However,' continued Ron. 'If we are trying to establish the precise nature of Dick's existence then that, my dear Tracey, is something you are far better placed to comment on than I.'

Tracey looked at Ron and shook her head slightly.

'They're right aren't they?' she asked him.

'What about?' he replied lazily.

'That you are,' said Tracey walking towards the door. 'An insufferable pain in the arse.' Without waiting to see or hear Ron's response, she left the staffroom and walked down the stairs and out of the building.

Ignoring the assorted beings that watched her march out of the building and along the path to the staff car park, Tracey busily thought of various acts of retribution she would inflict on Dick if she found his car missing. Walking passed the scruffy hawthorn hedge and into the car park, the first thing Tracey noticed was Dick's aging car sitting exactly where he'd left it earlier that morning. As she approached the car, it occurred to her that something wasn't quite how it should be. Tracey peered through the windscreen and then opened the driver's door. The interior of the car was a tip. The glove box was open and everything that had once been force-fed into the compartment was now strewn across the front passenger seat. The back seat was in the normal state of littered chaos that it always was. Tracey stood looking at the car, wondering what it was that made her feel uneasy. Then she suddenly realised what it was, or rather the two things that were wrong. On the front seat sat Dick's unopened lunchbox, something his stomach would never have allowed to remain intact for so long. Secondly, and the thought made Tracey swallow nervously, the car had already been open when she got to it. Again, something Dick would never have allowed to happen.

Tracey sat in the car as tears began to form. She picked up Dick's lunchbox and, placing it on her lap, held onto the steering wheel tightly. Tracey knew something had happened to Dick but she hadn't the slightest idea what it was. Her earlier anger resurfaced. The various acts of retribution she'd been contemplating before were now being honed for some, as yet, unknown bodies.

CHAPTER 26

Dick couldn't feel his feet. Apart from being bound to a metal chair with his hands tied behind his back, the ropes that secured his ankles were so tight they'd almost cut off the blood supply to his toes. It didn't help that he was virtually naked and a bitterly cold wind seemed to blow from each point of the compass.

The journey in the van had been traumatic. Feeling totally disorientated and bounced around continuously, Dick had no idea where he was being taken or why someone would bother kidnapping him. To make matters worse, the musty smell of his stale sweatshirt and the foul odour of the carpet were making him feel nauseous. After an indeterminable amount of time he'd been dragged unceremoniously from the van and made to stand in what sounded like a large, cavernous building. His captors had held a brief conversation. They quickly pulled the sweatshirt up and wrapped it around his head as a sort of extravagant blindfold. After another brief mutter they promptly stripped him of everything but his boxer shorts. Dick groaned. The thought of him being almost naked in front of two strangers, although far from pleasant, was not the reason for his audible response. Neither was it the fact that most of his body was exposed to the chilling elements the cause of his dismay. The one, simple fact that transcended every other was his boxer shorts. He knew as soon as his underwear saw the light of day that he was in for ridicule. His boxer shorts were clean with no visible tears or bits of thread hanging loose. Quite a lot of people would have shown admiration for his choice of underwear, but not his captors. As soon as Dick heard the partially smothered snorts of laughter, he knew he was about to be the object of their mockery.

'Minnie Mouse,' sniggered the brawny bloke. Jonesy was almost too convulsed with laughter to make a coherent comment. Eventually, he managed to speak.

'And Mickey,' he chortled. 'Holding hands.' The last two words shot out of his mouth before he succumbed to another bout of laughter.

Dick took a step forward, blindly waving his arms in front of him.

'OK,' he said, angrily. 'You've had your fun now just let me go and I'll say no more about the slight matter of being kidnapped.'

Dick's words immediately sobered his captors. All he heard was a scuff of boots on the floor before his hands were grasped and tied behind his back. Satisfied that he was secure, his captors quickly manoeuvred him across the concrete floor and forced him down onto a metal chair. Further ropes were placed around his chest and feet to fasten him to the chair.

Dick had no idea of the time or how long he'd been held captive. The only indication of time passing was the gradual loss of feeling in his hands and feet. This numbness only seemed to heighten the sensitivity of the rest of his body to the cold slowly creeping around him. He shivered involuntary. The slight noise had the effect of disturbing his captors sufficiently to remind them he was there. Jonesy sniffed.

'It is a bit parky in here, ain't it?'

His brawny mate shrugged.

'You get used to it after a while.' He nodded towards Dick. 'Should wrap up a bit better, don't you reckon?'

Dick ignored the jibe and swallowed hard.

'What do you want with me?' he asked, wriggling in an attempt to try and get some feeling back into his extremities.

'Depends,' replied Jonesy.

Dick had the distinct feeling that the conversation could go around in circles. He was right. Reluctantly, Dick continued the questioning.

'On what?' he asked.

'On what you've got to tell us,' snorted Jonesy.

'What would you like to know?' asked Dick, almost breezily.

'Hey!' growled Brawny bloke. 'We're supposed to ask the questions, not you.'

Dick shrugged as best he could under the rope restrictions. 'Only trying to be civil,' he replied. He felt hot breath on his neck and the aroma of cheese and onion crisps. 'Hmm,' murmured Dick hungrily. 'Cheese and onion, any going spare, I'm feeling quite peckish?'

The smell of cheese and onion grew stronger as Jonesy opened his mouth.

'Nope,' he said, licking his lips. 'Just had the last bag. Lovely they were.'

Dick's chair shuddered as the Brawny bloke kicked the steel leg viciously. Dick now felt breath on his face accompanied by the smell of strong coffee and stale tobacco.

'Who have you been talking to?' rasped the Brawny bloke.

'Well,' started Dick, trying to move his face away from the odours. 'How far back do you want me to go? I mean, I could begin with the very first words I remember hearing as a baby, or the welcome address the Headmaster gave us when we started Primary school, or … ' The chair shuddered so violently it moved slightly across the floor. Dick felt a fist against his cheek.

'Look here, smart arse,' warned Brawny. 'Don't give me a load of nonsense, just tell us what we want to know.'

Dick sighed expressively. 'You see,' he began. 'That's the crux of the matter. What is it you want to know precisely?'

The smell of cheese and onion wafted in front of his face. 'Ain't nothing to do with no crux,' grumbled Jonesy. 'We just need to know what you know so that we know how much you know.' He paused for a moment. 'Get what I mean?'

Dick smiled. His head was beginning to spin, but he was damn sure it wasn't going to be a solo ride.

'Do you?' he asked.

'What?' answered Jonesy, his voice betraying a hint of uncertainty.

'Understand what you mean?' replied Dick. He felt the fist pushed hard into his face again.

'I thought I warned you about trying to be clever,' rasped Brawny.

Dick tried to move his face away but the fist pressed even harder. 'Only trying to clarify the situation,' he mumbled through contorted lips. The pressure on his cheek relaxed a little as Brawny replied.

'What about the situation?' he growled.

'I'm simply trying to ascertain what it is you want to know so that I can provide you with the pertinent information,' answered Dick. His head suddenly jerked back as Brawny's fist hit his cheek.

'Them clever words will only get you in more trouble,' growled Brawny, his fist now pressing against Dick's other cheek. Dick moved his jaw around as he tried to manipulate the muscles in his cheek. He could feel the bruise beginning to form.

'I didn't realise I was in any trouble,' replied Dick, wincing with the pain. 'And, more to the point,' he continued. 'I certainly don't have any information that could possibly be of any interest to you.' His other cheek registered the impact of Brawny's fist. A groan escaped as the pain erupted in his head.

'We'll be the judge of that,' whispered Brawny, his voice full of menace.

Dick felt the unseen room swim. His thoughts seemed to collide with each other in confusion. Slowly the dull throb of his cheeks overwhelmed his senses. He tried to concentrate on his surroundings, hoping to focus on some thing other than the pain spreading across his face. Somewhere, in the distance, he heard the regular rhythm of a train passing close by. Outside of the building he heard a car door slam and muffled voices taking their leave of each other. More, indiscriminate sounds competed for his attention. As if aware of his attempts to identify his surroundings, a hand pushed his head forward. The sudden rush of pain caused Dick to groan once again.

'Pay attention,' laughed Jonesy. 'No daydreaming now, there's a good lad.' The sound of his self-congratulatory chuckles receded as he walked away from where Dick was seated. A pair of hands gripped his shoulders and forced him back into the chair.

'And sit up while you're about it,' said Brawny sternly. Dick moved his aching face towards the sound of Brawny's retreating footsteps.

'Leaving so soon,' Dick called. 'And just when we were having such fun.'

The footsteps stopped. A menacing silence filled the atmosphere. Dick heard the scuff of a shoe heel and sensed Brawny's eyes upon him. He waited for the sound of approaching pain. Holding his shoulders back against the chair, he turned his head sideways, hoping to restrict the amount of damage to his face. Another scuffed footstep sounded.

'Leave it,' shouted Jonesy. 'Can't you see he's trying to wind you up?'

Jonesy's voice echoed around the empty warehouse. Dick remained tense against the violence that never came. Slowly, he allowed his body to relax. His shoulders sagged and his breathing returned to something approaching normality. Dick listened carefully for any sound that might be threatening. Nothing came. After a while he allowed a sigh to escape that had been waiting nervously within his throat. The muscles in his arms and legs renewed their complaints of being constrained while he became ever more aware of the rapid drop in temperature.

Dick had allowed himself to doze for a while before a loud, metallic screech of an opening door startled him into consciousness. He became vaguely aware of a voice, insistent in its tone, that didn't belong to either Jonesy or the Brawny bloke. After a prolonged monologue, the insistent voice must have issued an instruction as two pairs of feet scuffed their way towards Dick. His chair shuddered with the impact of someone's boot.

'Rise and shine,' growled Jonesy. 'Need another little chat with you we do.'

Dick lifted his head towards the sound of Jonesy's voice.

'I think I've told you everything I don't know,' he replied hoarsely. 'Any chance of a drink?'

His chair received another shuddering jolt, accompanied by a snarl from Brawny.

'You ain't got a chance of anything mate. So just tell us what we want to know.'

Dick shook his head.

'Aren't you getting tired of asking me the same question over and over again and hearing the same response?' he asked wearily.

'Interrogation,' replied Jonesy, from somewhere to Dick's left side.

'That's right,' added Brawny, who now appeared to be standing behind Dick. 'Wearing you down until you cave in and tell us everything.'

'It makes sense you know,' said Jonesy, now from Dick's right-hand side.

Brawny's voice now sounded from Dick's left-hand side.

'So,' he snapped. 'Use your common-sense and talk.'

Shuffling feet announced a further change in his captor's positioning. Dick moved his head from side-to-side.

'What are you two playing at?' he asked the space in front of him. Jonesy laughed.

'Ring a- ring o' roses. That's what we're playing,' he replied.

'OK, OK,' said Dick, his body and voice betraying his tiredness. 'I can tell you everything I know. Not that it's much mind you, but something is better than nothing eh?'

Jonesy laughed again.

'That's a good boy,' he replied, ruffling Dick's hair. He walked slowly around Dick. 'Ring a-ring o' roses, a pocketful of posies. A-tishoo, a-tishoo! Dick falls down.'

'It all started a long time ago,' began Dick, ignoring Jonesy's rhyme. 'In fact,' he continued, 'there's various interpretations of the truth depending on how you look at it.'

Brawny prodded Dick's shoulder.

'That's better. Better for us and certainly better for you,' he said menacingly. 'Carry on.'

'The documentary evidence is inconclusive,' obliged Dick. 'There are various accounts all fairly similar but each having a slightly different perspective.'

While Dick was speaking, Jonesy continued singing the nursery rhyme quietly.

'Ring a-ring o' roses, a pocketful of posies.'

Brawny tapped Dick's chair, encouraging him to continue divulging the information they so desperately wanted.

'What other accounts?' asked he asked. 'Who's got them?'

'Oh, they're all quite freely available now,' replied Dick.

Jonesy paused briefly in his singing while Brawny stood towering over Dick.

'I want every last detail,' he spat. 'Now!'

Dick smiled. He needed to keep his composure and not give too much away all at once. He heard Jonesy softly singing.

'A-tishoo, a-tishoo.'

Dick ignored the eerie tune and tried to concentrate on his story.

114

'There's conflicting evidence relating to when the material first came to light.' Dick waited a moment before continuing. His audience appeared to be hanging on every word. He smiled again. 'The earliest details first appeared in a publication by Kate Greenaway, with variations appearing in Lancashire, Shropshire and possibly London.'

Brawny slammed his fist into Dick's shoulder.

'Who's this Greenaway woman and where can we find her?' he demanded. Dick shrugged.

'Dick falls down,' chuckled Jonesy.

'Long gone,' replied Dick, trying to flex his complaining shoulder. 'Beyond your reach,' he added.

Meanwhile, Jonesy continued singing softly, his footsteps moving in rhythm to the rhyme. Brawny brought his face close to Dick's.

'I want all of the details and I want them now,' he spat.

Dick squirmed, unable to wipe the spittle from his face.

'As far as I know,' continued Dick reluctantly. 'It's associated with the Great Plague of London in 1665. However, the earliest written account appeared in Kate Greenaway's 1881 edition of *Mother Goose*. Although a similar German rhyme was published in 1796.'

'What the hell are you on about?' growled Brawny. 'Get to the details.'

Dick raised his shoulders slightly. 'OK,' he replied. 'Well, a posy of herbs was carried as protection against the plague. The symptoms of the plague were a rosy rash followed by sneezing, which was the final, and more often than not, the fatal symptom. Of course, "all fall down" was exactly what happened after that.'

A gurgle sounded in Brawny's throat that would not have been out of place in a second-rate horror film. Dick felt a pair of hands grasp at his throat. Suddenly a peel of laughter rang out. The hands stilled around his throat. The laughter continued as Jonesy continued humming the nursery rhyme tune.

'What?' barked Brawny to the laughing voice.

'Very good,' replied the owner of the third voice. 'I must congratulate you on your knowledge of nursery rhymes.' The voice continued to laugh quietly to itself. The only clues to the laughter's owner lay in the masculine timbre of the voice. In the distant reaches of Dick's memory, something stirred. He was vaguely aware of something almost familiar about the voice, something about the slight inflection at the end of each sentence. He was certain it wasn't a voice belonging to anyone at the College, but somehow there was a connection. The more he tried to concentrate the more elusive the familiarity became.

'Of course,' responded Dick, attempting to get the voice to speak further and help him identify its owner. 'Scholars can't agree on the validity of the rhyme being associated with the bubonic plague. Some suggest that the rhyme didn't appear until one hundred and twenty-five years after the plague.' Dick allowed himself a smile. 'Still, you never know, further evidence may emerge that places it around about 1665.'

'Enough,' ordered the unidentified voice. 'You're either very clever, attempting to distract us from the truth of your involvement. Or,' he mused. 'You're very stupid. And I suppose the fact that you're working at that College discounts the former.'

Brawny coughed for attention.

'So what do we do with him?'

Jonesy began to sing once again.

'Ring a-ring o' roses,' he sang. 'A pocketful of posies. Atishoo, a-tishoo.'

The singing stopped momentarily. Dick heard a slight movement in front of him. He felt the force of Brawny's fist against the side of his head and everything went dark.

'Dick falls down,' grinned Jonesy, as Dick slumped forward in his chair.

CHAPTER 27

Tracey hovered by the phone. Nervously she lifted the handset, hoping to hear a voice reassuring her that everything was fine. The silence simply reaffirmed her fears. After a moments hesitation she stabbed the numbers that she hoped would allay her anxiety.

'Dubbya,' she asked as an almost primeval grunt announced contact. 'Dubbya, it's Tracey.'

'Oh, hi Tracey. And to what do I owe this pleasure?' A chuckle reverberated in her ear. 'Although I'm fairly certain it's not pleasure you're after or you wouldn't be ringing me.'

Tracey tried to form the words that had been swirling around her head, but her vocal cords couldn't cope.

'Tracey?' queried Dubbya.

'Dubbya,' she managed to burble.

'What's up pet?' replied Dubbya, concern colouring his voice.

'It's Dick,' she said, almost choking on the words.

Dubbya breathed heavily. 'Dick?' he repeated. 'If he's done anything untoward I'll crush his testicles in a garlic press.'

'He's not here,' sobbed Tracey. 'He's gone, disappeared.'

Dubbya snorted with rage. 'Make that a pasta machine.'

'You don't understand,' said Tracey between gulps of air. 'His car is still at the College, his lunch hasn't been eaten and I haven't heard anything all day.' She paused to look at her watch. 'It's almost midnight and I'm getting worried.' She could hear Dubbya sucking his lip. Eventually, he sighed.

'Curious,' he concluded. 'Have you tried ringing around his family and other assorted beings?'

'Everyone,' replied Tracey. 'I've even phoned the Principal's secretary, just in case they'd sent Dick on some urgent business, but she says they haven't seen or heard from him for weeks.'

'Nothing unusual there,' replied Dubbya. 'Look,' he said firmly, 'give it another couple of hours and then, if you haven't heard anything, ring the police.'

'OK,' replied Tracey.

'If you need anyone to keep you company, just let me know,' chuckled Dubbya.

'Thanks for the offer, but I'm reading an old Rupert Bear annual. It reminds me of being a child again when everything was simple and someone else could do the worrying.'

Tracey replaced the phone and settled down on the sofa with her annual. She tried reading about Rupert's antics but couldn't concentrate on the story. For the next couple of hours she dithered on the cusp of sleep while waiting for the phone to ring.

CHAPTER 28

PC Ricketts blew the air from her cheeks as the phone burped for attention. She reluctantly lifted the receiver and listened to the urgent tones. After listening impatiently for a few moments PC Ricketts introduced herself with as much authority as she could muster in the early hours of the morning.

'I fully understand,' she said. 'Now, could you supply me with a few details please?'

Again she listened as patiently as possible before interjecting politely.

'I agree, missing his lunch is a cause for concern but there could be a perfectly rational explanation ... '

PC Ricketts paused to allow her caller to vent their frustration. 'Yes, I do understand. But we need a little more information upon which to base our ... ' Again, PC Ricketts paused politely to listen. 'Fine, yes, I appreciate it is quite a long time, but have you considered the possibility that he may have gone for a drink with friends or perhaps met someone?'

PC Ricketts held the phone away from her ear as the verbal tirade increased in volume. Nodding, she took a deep breath before answering.

'Yes, I am now aware of your relationship to Mr Hall, but it is still rather soon to declare him missing.' She nodded again. 'Of course, I'll make a note and get someone to call you in the morning. Would you please inform us should Mr Hall return within the next few hours? Thank you.'

PC Ricketts put the phone down and sighed deeply. She looked towards Sergeant Cost, who just happened to be engrossed in yet another crossword, and smiled.

'Are we interested in a potential missing person?' she asked the top of his head. Sergeant Cost continued tapping the clue to twelve down.

'Is there a phantom or ghostly apparition involved?' he asked.

'Not as far as I could make out,' answered PC Ricketts with a shrug of her shoulders.

'Then leave it for the morning lot,' he said, continuing his mental wrangle with twelve down.

CHAPTER 29

Dick slowly became aware of a strange sound toying with his eardrums. Moving his head slightly, a dull explosion of pain suddenly erupted making him immediately wished he hadn't. Wincing audibly, Dick tried to open his mouth to articulate his feelings but nothing more than a strangulated gurgle escaped. Easing himself into a sitting position, he waited for the shooting pains to subside as he listened again for the peculiar noises that had earlier intruded into his semi-consciousness.

Somewhere above him, pigeons seemed to be content mooching around, with an occasional flutter of wings mocking him with their freedom of movement. Other noises, that hadn't been audible before were now beginning to penetrate his consciousness. In the distance, Dick could hear the grunt of lorry engines alongside the monotonous grind of machinery. The outside world had begun to stir itself after a time of enforced dormancy.

As much as he was mindful of the world awakening, he was also aware of how much his body hurt. Tentatively he felt the raised areas of his face that had been subject to Brawny's attentive fists. Touching the side of his face that had experienced the last blow of interrogation caused an immediate sharp intake of breath as his fingers traced the outline of his swollen cheekbone. Slowly, it dawned upon him. He'd been so engrossed in exploring the extent of his injuries that he hadn't realised that his hands had been free to move. He quickly stretched his legs, flexing his toes to increase the circulation of blood to his extremities. During his enforced slumber, somebody had loosened his bonds sufficiently to allow a semblance of circulation to percolate through his body.

Reaching for the blindfold, Dick's fingers tugged clumsily at the knot securing the sweatshirt to his head. His partially numb fingers struggled to prise the garment from his head, and the harder he tugged and pulled the tighter the knot seemed to get. Eventually, with a tortured tearing sound, the sweatshirt finally succumbed to his efforts allowing an overdose of light to strike his eyes.

Peering through his fingers, Dick took the first look around his confining space. He appeared to be sitting at the centre of a large, rundown warehouse. Shafts of sunlight cascaded through various broken panes of glass situated in the roof above him. He could see metal rafters lining the roof space that were obviously the favoured perching place for defecating pigeons. The whole interior space was empty apart from a couple of white plastic garden chairs and the metal chair that he had been bound to. In the far wall, to his right, Dick could just about see the outline of a door that stood inside a much larger framework. Hanging just to the right of the door was a crude picture of an arrow pointing towards the floor with writing that suggested that all waste should be deposited below. A large, dark bin sulked immediately beneath the sign. To Dick's horror, a pair of naked feet protruded from the bin. Panic gripped his body as the sudden urge to empty his bladder became almost overwhelming. Quickly scanning the rest of the wall, he saw a couple of battered cardboard boxes resting dejectedly against each other. Emerging from the bottom corner of the box furthest from him was a hand with a finger pointing accusingly. Dick's stomach lurched as the rest of his excretory system signalled its intention.

Shuffling his reluctant body towards the boxes, Dick paused in front of the bin. The protruding feet, covered in pigeon deposits, appeared rigid, consumed by rigor mortis. With his eyes slowly becoming accustomed to the dingy light, Dick peered at the feet. Something was wrong. It wasn't just that feet shouldn't point skywards from the inside of a bin, there was something peculiar about them. He sniffed the air, expecting the stench of decay to assail his nostrils. Nothing. Apart from there being the smell of what was virtually a giant aviary, there was no indication of decomposing flesh. The angle of the feet was also distinctly odd. One foot bared its sole to the roof, while the other lay at an acute angle more appropriate to a ballerina performing a *Tendu* pose.

Dick moved closer to the feet. Slowly he lifted his hand,

allowing a finger to fleetingly touch one of the feet before recoiling. The hardness of the surface mystified him. He shuffled over to the boxes. Stumbling slightly, he gripped hold of the nearest box for support. A brief tearing sound was quickly obliterated by a cry from Dick's throat. As the box came apart, a number of disarticulated arms, legs and feet tumbled out. Momentarily, Dick held his breath until he realised what lay before him. Shaking his head in disbelief, he picked up an arm from the floor. Examining it, he could see the way it would have once been attached to the main torso. He peered into the other box and grinned at the contents. Inside the mannequin bodies and heads, that would have adorned shop windows a few decades ago, lay in a jumbled heap.

Taking a step back, Dick placed his hands on his hips and allowed a broad grin to spread across his aching face. He nodded to himself. He was beginning to get the hang of this detective lark, he thought. Looking around the vacant warehouse, he wondered what Tracey would make of all this. Tracey! He'd barely given her a thought since being bundled into the van that seemed like an age ago. What could she be thinking? Had she been thinking of him? Had she notified the authorities? The thoughts made his head throb. He walked over to one of the plastic chairs and sat down heavily, causing the chair to screech alarmingly.

The coldness of the chair and the various draughts that breezed through the ramshackle building reminded Dick that he still only had a pair of boxer shorts for dignity. Impulsively, he placed his hands over the front of his boxer shorts, and just as quickly realised that there was nobody around to witness his predicament.

Scanning the warehouse, for any sign of his clothing or anything else that might cover his embarrassment, Dick quickly realised that apart from the mannequin parts, there was nothing that could be described as even resembling an item of clothing. The only garment, if it could still be called that, was the sweatshirt that had been his blindfold and which now sat shredded on the floor. Looking at the once familiar rag, a sigh of dejection escaped his lips as he sat once again on the chilly plastic chair and pondered on his plight.

Outside of the warehouse, the volume of noise increased as life continued its usual course of the day. Inside, Dick was still trying to think of a way to contact Tracey and return to the relative safety of his house. After a few moments he grinned, shook his head and muttered negatively under his breath. He grinned again. There didn't seem to be any alternative. Only one possible solution presented itself and, with a wry chuckle, Dick made his way over to the small door, twisted the handle and stepped out into the bright morning light.

CHAPTER 30

After Dick had finally managed to wrench open the warehouse door and cautiously step outside, he realised he hadn't a clue where he was. Lining the street on either side were similar buildings in various states of disrepair. A couple of the buildings close by were visibly occupied as bent figures ambled about their business, showing little or no interest in Dick. The heady concoction of noise and exhaust fumes threatened to engulf him as he started to make his way along the pavement.

The first couple of minutes after he emerged from the confines of the warehouse had proved to be the most difficult. Tentatively jogging along the street, his feet seemed to locate the sharpest stones and other bits of detritus that lay in his path. Adding to his predicament, Dick wasn't sure whether it was the sight of an almost naked man jogging that caused the cacophony of motorised horns or the images of Minnie and Mickey Mouse on his boxer shorts. Stoically ignoring the early morning attention he continued his way along the streets. After stopping a few times to brush the painful grit from his feet, he eventually arrived at a junction where the industrial premises gave way to a variety of shops and business established to cater for every whim of the passing worker.

Adopting a sort of hobbling jog, Dick passed by each shop until he found what he was looking for. A few metres away sat a small café, playing host to a motley collection of individuals. Before he'd left the warehouse, Dick had concocted an almost believable story to explain his state of undress. Without pausing in his stride, he left the gaze of pedestrians and entered into the warm fug of the café.

The interior displayed a well-worn and well-loved look that the customers were obviously accustomed to. It seemed that they were also used to seeing strange sights bursting into their morning ritual as hardly anyone looked up from their consuming business.

Conscious of his vulnerability to prying eyes, Dick strode up to the counter and leaned heavily against the lacquered wood. Behind the counter, a tall, slim woman eyed the early morning apparition. With a smile playing on her brightly coated lips and an arch of crisp, black eyebrows, she welcomed Dick.

'And to what do I owe this pleasure?' she asked, winking at a table of Council workers to her left.

Dick swallowed hard. He felt in need of a vast quantity of liquid to soothe his parched throat.

'Victim of a prank,' he explained hoarsely. 'What was supposed to be a quiet meal with my so called friends turned into a nightmare.'

The woman laughed in a sort of disbelieving way. She leaned over the counter and peered down at Dick's lack of clothing and the variegated bruising adorning his cheek.

'So, what happened, didn't you offer to buy a round?' she asked. Dick smiled more warmly than he felt.

'Stag night,' he said with a grimace. Behind him he could hear various chuckles and a few comments that he chose to ignore. He shook his head slightly. 'I think they popped something into my drink, stripped me and left me in some decrepit old warehouse with only pigeons for company.'

Dick felt a warm hand on his shoulder.

'Can't say I'm too keen on some of the antics you young blokes get up to,' commented the old man beside him.

Glancing at the stubbly chin, which hung underneath a faded military beret, Dick nodded in agreement. 'They've been watching too many of these comedy films where blokes get marooned on remote islands and stuff,' he remarked. He looked down at his virtually naked body. 'Don't think they could afford a helicopter, thank goodness,' breathed Dick.

The old man cocked his head to one side. 'Weren't ought so stupid when I was to be wed.' He grinned at the memory. 'Nowt worse than some silly beggar shoved horse manure in me best boots. They made me wear the boots and took me on a pub crawl.' A chuckle escaped from the old man's throat. 'Right pong it were. Mind you,' he tapped Dick on the arm. 'Gave me an inkling of what married life was going to be like.'

126

'Eric, you old dog,' scolded the woman from behind the counter. She placed a steaming mug of tea in front of Dick. 'Here, my love, get that inside of you and ignore handsome here.' She gave the old man a smile. 'You've got nothing to complain about.'

'Dare say I haven't at that,' nodded the old man. 'Dare say I haven't,' he agreed, shuffling towards the door. The woman looked at Dick and then pointed at the mug. 'On the house.' Indicating a table nearby, she handed Dick a mobile phone. 'Here,' she offered. 'Get someone to come and pick you up before you catch your death of cold, or worse.'

Muttering his thanks, Dick took the phone and quickly made contact with Tracey.

'Yes, yes,' he said, as a clearly concerned voice answered his call. 'I'm OK, just a bit cold that's all.' He nodded with the phone clamped to his ear. 'Yes, yes,' he said again. He offered the woman behind the counter a wan grin and raised his eyebrows. 'No, no,' he continued. 'I can't come straight home right now.'

The woman placed a plate in front of Dick. He took one look at the aromatic bacon sandwich and threw the woman a kiss.

'Get away with you,' she laughed. 'Eat your sandwich before it goes cold.'

Dick suddenly held the phone away from his ear as the volume of Tracey's voice increased by several decibels.

'I can't right now,' answered Dick, placing the phone against his ear once again. He shook his head. 'No, I don't know who she is but she's been very kind.' Dick promptly removed the phone from his ear as Tracey produced a response that most of the café occupants could hear. Dick waited patiently for the atmosphere to calm down. Slowly he brought the phone closer to his ear. He shook his head again.

'I've told you, I can't,' he replied to a further question. 'I haven't got any clothes on.'

Tracey's response hardly required the services of a communications company. Dick chewed on his bacon sandwich while Tracey informed the café just what she thought of him. During a momentary lull in Tracey's vitriolic tirade, the woman from behind the counter took the phone from Dick.

'Hello,' she cooed into the phone. 'Now, before you get yourself all worked up, let me explain.' She arched her eyebrows at Dick as the phone exploded once again. 'Now, now,' she clucked into the phone. 'There's no need for that kind of nonsense. Listen,' she ordered. 'Your man here has got into a bit of a predicament through no fault of his own.' She sighed at Tracey's response. 'And through no fault of mine I can assure you. More's the pity,' she added with a grin. Placing the phone next to an empty mug the woman proceeded to rattle a spoon around the inside of the mug. After a few seconds she replaced the phone to her ear and smiled. 'Glad I've got your attention,' she said politely. 'Right, this man of yours is sitting in a café full of people and is in need of a bit of help.' She nodded at Tracey's voice. 'Precisely. Now, why don't I give you our address and you can come along and,' she gave Dick a knowing stare. 'Take this handsome man of yours home before someone else does?'

CHAPTER 31

Tracey drove in stunned silence while Dick fidgeted with the folds of a voluminous cerise coloured nightgown.

'Couldn't you have brought me something a little more glamorous?' he asked sarcastically.

Tracey dug her fingers into the steering wheel and snorted by way of reply. Ever since she'd collected Dick from the café, and been cryptically wished "all the best for your future together," Tracey had struggled to keep her emotions in check. At first, she'd vacillated between feeling angry with Dick for getting into such a state in the first place and then being angry with herself for getting into a state about Dick. After hurtling through the little back streets and flinging the car into a queue of rush hour traffic, Tracey had reduced her anger to a gentle simmer and was now busily trying to understand why she'd become so angry in the first place.

The woman at the café had been so helpful and understanding that Tracey had found it difficult to give vent to her feelings. Thrusting the vibrant nightgown at Dick, she'd escorted him from the café accompanied by several ribald comments and a couple of suggestive winks from old dears who should have known better but didn't. Silently, she'd opened the car door for Dick and barely waited for him to put his seat belt on before she slammed the car into gear and stabbed at the accelerator.

Now, sitting in a queue of traffic that made the main street look like a car park, Tracey tried to piece together her thoughts and feelings in a logical way. After a few seconds she gave up, grabbed Dick's face in her hands and kissed him. At first, he'd been stunned by her sudden movement but then the pain took over. He gently prised her off his face.

'Steady,' he winced, delicately touching his bruised cheeks. 'Give the facial rearrangements time to settle down.' He looked at

Tracey, who was now staring straight ahead with tears crawling down her cheeks. 'Hey now,' he said, gently touching away a tear.

Tracey turned to him, her eyes still leaking. 'Have you any idea what I've been going through?' she said, her voice barely audible against the background hubbub. Dick's eyes opened widely.

'What you've been going through,' he replied incredulously. He pointed at the multicoloured skin around his eyes. 'This wasn't the result of a bad dream, you know.' He paused momentarily. 'I just wish it had been,' he added.

Tracey looked at him, blinking away more tears she placed a finger against his lips. 'I didn't know what to think. Nobody had seen you after the fire drill and all I could find was the car with your lunchbox on the front seat and...' She dabbed her eyes with a tissue. 'You hadn't eaten a thing.'

Dick kissed her finger and replaced her hand onto the steering wheel. 'We're supposed to be moving,' he grinned.

Going through the motions of driving, Tracey managed to move them a little further along the street as the traffic stalled to a halt once more. Dick stroked her hand.

'Would you like me to drive?' he asked with a smile spreading across his face. Tracey glanced at him and returned the smile.

'If your driving is as uncoordinated as you look, then no thank you,' she replied, edging the car forward.

Musing on their respective situations, Dick and Tracey became oblivious to the stares of pedestrians and the occasional gesture from other motorists. Finally leaving the heady bustle of the town centre, their car began its journey home. As familiar landmarks passed the car, Dick leaned over and stroked Tracey's face. Her features remained indifferent to his caress, apparently concentrating on the road ahead. Dick tugged the nightgown around him, carefully tucking the flamboyant collar out of sight. As they waited for a set of traffic lights to go through the required procedure, Tracey glanced quickly at Dick.

'This is all getting rather serious,' she said.

'I rather hoped it would,' replied Dick, his eyes watching the complacent red light. Tracey, still looking ahead, raised her eyebrows.

'But you never thought it'd go this far did you?' she asked as the lights completed their sequence.

'I'm hoping it'll go even further,' he grinned.

Tracey, fumbling with the gears, looked across at him and saw the humorous creases at the sides of his mouth. She returned the grin.

'If my hands weren't occupied I'd take that silly grin off of your face,' she threatened. The effect of her warning only served to broaden the grin on Dick's face. He ran the back of his hand along her thigh.

'Sounds promising,' he chuckled, continuing to caress her leg. Deftly pushing his hand away, Tracey allowed her face to break out into a grin too.

'I appreciate what you're trying to do,' she said. Dick arched an eyebrow.

'If you'd like to show your appreciation,' he started to say, but Tracey's swift glare stopped him from elaborating further.

'Stop it,' she ordered, her voice on the verge of collapsing into a sob. 'I realise that you're trying to make light of the situation, but you can't disguise the fact that I came so very close to losing you.' She sniffed and took the opportunity to wipe a sleeve across her eyes.

'Look,' replied Dick, the grin suddenly vanishing from his face.

'That's what I'm having a bit of a problem with,' she tentatively smiled, her eyes concentrating on the road ahead. With a pain-tinged grin Dick gently touched Tracey's cheek. She nodded in appreciation.

'I think it's your cheek that needs the gentle touch,' she said as the car came to a halt in front of Dick's house. 'Come on, let's get you inside and out of that silly nightgown.' Dick was just about to respond when Tracey's warning finger stilled his voice. 'No facetious remarks either,' she cautioned him. 'Medical attention first,' she winked.

Running quickly up the drive and away from the inquisitive stares of the neighbours, Dick and Tracey closed the front door behind them and immediately stood perfectly still. In front of them, the hallway was almost unrecognisable as assorted coats, scarves and various bits of furniture lay strewn across the floor. The partially open door to the lounge revealed further chaos. Dick looked at Tracy.

'Party?' he enquired.

Tracey took a deep breath. 'If there was,' she replied. 'I wasn't invited.'

CHAPTER 32

Tracey sat on the sofa cradling a rapidly cooling mug of coffee. Taking a sip of the liquid, she took one look at Dick and dissolved into tears.

'This is just all I need,' she sobbed, cooling her coffee even further. 'Why us, why me?'

Dick shrugged. He didn't know what to say. At first, Tracey had appeared to be quite stoic about the burglary, apparently accepting it as simply another facet to the already confusing state of affairs. But now, her tears revealed a side to her that Dick had rarely experienced. Usually, Tracey appeared to be so in control, able to assess a situation and catalogue it according to its importance to life or impact on her bank balance. Seeing her like this unnerved him. Somehow the events of the past few hours seemed to be removed from reality, as if they'd happened to someone else with Dick hearing about them during a Monday morning's verbal ramblings in the staffroom. Unfortunately, the sight of Tracey and the continued ache from his bruised face dispelled any lingering hopes that it was all a dream.

Tracey smiled at Dick through the tears.

'You're not used to seeing me like this are you?' she asked, a tentative smile slowly spreading across her face. Dick removed the coffee mug from her hands, placed it on the table and hugged her towards him. He flicked a hand at the mess of furniture and paper that littered the lounge.

'This doesn't mean a lot,' he said dismissively. 'But you mean everything to me.'

Tracey leant her head against Dick's shoulder, a handkerchief dabbing at her moist nostrils.

'So,' she sniffed. 'It takes a traumatic event to make you show your true feelings?'

Dick hugged her tightly.

'It means we've certainly rattled somebody's cage,' he said, with a voice that he hoped sounded far more confident than he felt.

Tracey sniffed loudly and raised her head slightly.

'If this is what happens when we rattle the cage,' she said, her own voice sounding far from confident. 'Then I'd hate to see what happens when we open it.'

Dick tried to laugh but the merriment got stuck in his throat. Instead, a gargled murmur slipped from his lips. Tracey half looked at him and smiled. She understood precisely what Dick had attempted to say. Tracey found his efforts to inject a bit of humour into a situation quite endearing. Although he often made a complete hash of what he was trying to say, she loved the way he wanted to derail her train of thought and stop her getting too wrapped up in a problem.

'This does mean something though, doesn't it?' she asked his neck.

Dick took a deep breath and let it out slowly. It was a tactic he usually employed when he hadn't a clue what to say. The long, drawn out wheeze gave the impression of him deliberating on what to say and then, with a calculated narrowing of the eyes, make a considered comment that, even if it were total garbage, would often appear as if it were of value. Unfortunately for Dick, Tracey had long since sussed out his ploy and jabbed him in the ribs.

Dick let out the remaining air in a rush. Rubbing his side, he looked at Tracey with a pained expression. 'Does it?' he said through pursed lips.

'Of course it does,' she replied, placing her hand on his and helping to caress poked ribs. 'It means,' soothed Tracey, 'that our investigations have provoked a response.' She reached up to kiss his bruised cheek. 'But not quite the type of response I would have hoped for.'

Dick luxuriated in the closeness of Tracey. The last twenty-four hours had been traumatic to say the least, but they were now history. He inhaled deeply.

'We'd better check there's nothing missing,' he said as a yawn stretched his face. Tracey paused in her caressing and looked at him with a half-smile.

'Missing?' she enquired.

'Around the house,' replied Dick, with a mixture of frustration and regret.

After a couple of hours spent returning the house to its normal state of disarray, Dick and Tracey sat at the breakfast table nursing mugs of hot chocolate and both staring at a mysterious jiffy bag in front of them. Dick washed a mouthful of chocolate around his mouth and nodded at the jiffy bag.

'Seems that we've gained something rather than our losing anything,' he said before taking another mouthful of liquid. Tracey shook her head thoughtfully.

'Why break into the house, turn everything upside down and then leave us a parcel?'

Dick picked up the unopened parcel. He turned it around between his fingers.

'It's not addressed to anyone,' he said, giving the parcel a tentative shake. Placing the parcel back onto the table, he prodded at the package. 'There's something in there,' he announced with a final prod at the parcel. Tracey drained her mug and looked at him.

'There usually is something in a parcel,' she replied tersely. 'Aren't you going to open it?'

Dick pushed the parcel across the table towards Tracey.

'Ladies first,' he said nervously. With a sigh, Tracey picked up the parcel and tore it open. After carefully peering inside, she extracted an envelope addressed to them both. Tracey slid the envelope towards Dick.

'Your turn,' she grinned.

Dick looked at the envelope and then at Tracey. 'What kind of burglar trashes a house and then leaves a letter addressed to the owners?'

'Obviously the very polite kind,' she replied, blowing him a kiss. 'Aren't you going to open it?'

Nudging the envelope with the tip of a chocolate-coated spoon, Dick frowned. 'Shouldn't we check it for finger prints?' he asked.

Snatching the envelope from the table with an exasperated sigh, Tracey slid her finger under the seal and took out a sheet of paper and a photograph. Glancing between the sheet of paper and the photograph, Tracey's face displayed a mixture of emotions. At first, she didn't appear to see any connection between the two and then, after a couple of nods, she slid the photograph across the table towards Dick.

Gingerly lifting the edge of the photograph, Dick could see a group of people smiling inanely at the camera. He let the photograph fall back to the table and folded his arms.

'So?' enquired Tracey, without looking up from the sheet of paper.

'Bunch of grinning idiots who look like they've just won a tin of baked beans on the Tombola,' he observed.

Tracey put the sheet of paper onto the table and looked sternly at Dick. 'Are you sure you don't recognise anyone?' she asked tapping the sheet of paper. 'Because according to this you should.'

Dick reluctantly picked up the photograph and went through the motions of scanning the faces once again. He was just about to toss the photo to Tracey when something stirred within the dark recesses of his memory. Squinting at the photo, Dick placed a finger on one of the faces. He looked at Tracy.

'Is that who I think it is?' he asked.

Tracey grinned. 'Looks like it,' she replied with an arch of her eyebrows. 'Although he doesn't look too happy with having his photo taken.'

Dick studied the photo intently. He could see what Tracey was referring to and, with a bit of imagination he could identify two of the other faces in the group. 'Looks like these two are my golfing buddies from the steam room.' He ran a finger across the other members of the group. 'Can't say I recognise any of these people, but it looks as if we have my so-called buddies associating with the College's Assistant Principal for External Affairs.'

A lop-sided grin formed on Tracey's face. Dick held up a finger in admonishment. 'Before you make any ribald comments about his tendency to take his role too seriously,' laughed Dick. 'We should perhaps consider why he's in the company of two people who we've been directed towards as possibly being involved in something possibly illegal, allegedly.' He pointed at the piece of paper that Tracey had been reading. 'Does that give us any clues?' he asked. Tracey shook her head.

'I think it's suggesting that we do something illegal,' she replied, pursing her lips. Dick took the piece of paper and studied it carefully. He looked up at Tracey with astonishment written across his face.

'Is this suggesting what I think it's suggesting,' he said, his hands nervously rubbing at the sheet of paper. Tracey nodded.

'Looks like it,' she answered with a sigh of finality. 'It seems we've got to do a bit of burglary of our own.'

CHAPTER 33

Akela paused, wiped the sleep-rubble from her eyes and yawned expansively. After twelve years of leading her cub-scout group on its annual camping weekend at Acre's Wood, she still couldn't get used to the sleep deprivation resulting from a combination of pubescent snores, a damp sleeping bag and the after effects of cub-scout haute cuisine.

Walking into the cooking tent, Akela's senses were overwhelmed by the culinary odours of baked beans, sausages and mashed potato. She closed her eyes and swallowed noisily. Before her lay another night of digestive cramps as her system fought against the tide of nausea and intestinal gases that would leave her, once again, a sleepless wreck in the morning.

Akela strode to where Baloo, one of her assistants, stood hunched over a cauldron of molten liquid. As she looked through the cooking steam at Baloo, she was glad that she'd ignored current trends to dismiss Baden-Powell's obsession with *Jungle Book* as outdated symbolism and retained the old-fashioned ethos of the cub-scout movement. Besides, she thought to herself, the name *Baloo* suited her large hairy assistant whose ability to create chaos out of order were always well intentioned. Baloo turned to greet her.

'Akela, the very person,' he declared, wiping his tomato stained hands down the front of his already discoloured apron. He pointed at the bubbling cauldron. 'Would you care to taste tonight's menu?'

Akela took two steps back in alarm. 'What?' she half-shouted nervously. 'And deprive our starving Cubs of their much needed nourishment?' With an almost smile on her face, she moved forward and touched Baloo's arm. 'I'm sure it's up to your usual culinary standard,' she said hurrying towards the exit before Baloo had the chance to inflict any other gastronomic delight upon her. As she left the cooking tent, her hand began to gently massage her stomach in anticipation of the assault to come.

Later that evening, and with Akela trying desperately to stifle the disturbing cacophony of noises emanating from her abdominal region, the cub-scout troop sat around the celebrated campfire. The backdrop of the dark evening sky emphasised the fire's glow radiating around the sea of excited young faces. Baloo sat with his back to the dense wood, beads of sweat forming on his face under the intense glare of the fire.

'Right!' he said, gaining the rapt attention of every pair of eyes and ears. 'Long ago, deep in a wood not too far away,' Baloo gave a slight nod of his head to indicate the trees behind him, 'lay Closham Manor.'

Akela yawned. She'd heard the same story year after year and, although Baloo made minor amendments to some of the details, the ending was always the same. She yawned again. Baloo, noticing Akela teetering on the edge of boredom, decided to make a few alterations to the story. He sat back and placed his hands across his chest.

'Now,' he continued. 'Closham Manor wasn't just any ordinary place, oh no, definitely not. It'd been the home of the Shorethrift family for centuries yet nobody had ever seen them, never,' he clapped his hands together to emphasise the point. 'Of course,' he said with a smile, 'everyone claimed to have met one of the family, but because no-one had ever stood up and said *"My name's Shorethrift!"* nobody could say for sure that they knew a Shorethrift when they saw one!

Looking at the eager eyes in front of him, he smiled. Leaning forward, he carried on with the tale.

'Stories of strange goings on at Closham Manor had been told down the ages.' Baloo held up his hand. 'Nobody had ever seen anything but,' he paused for effect, narrowing his eyes as he did so. 'There were noises, not just ordinary noises but sounds that would carry eerily through the woods. Mysterious, high-pitched voices chanting in a long forgotten language. At night, curious lights would flash and sizzle above Closham Manor.' Baloo flicked at imaginary stars in the air. 'Blues, greens, bright red, orange, and,' he said, sitting upright. 'It would all suddenly stop with a terrifying scream that sent a shiver down the spine of every mortal being for miles around.'

Several cub-scouts began twisting their woggles nervously. The whole group sat silently, thankful for the warmth and light provided by the fire.

'Each morning,' said Baloo, making sure all eyes were watching him. 'After that awful scream of the night before, a terrible discovery would be made.' He looked around the group once again and suddenly pointed a finger at a young cub. 'You!' he shouted, making everyone jump including Akela who hadn't really been listening to the tale. 'How many toes do you have?'

The young cub gulped. His eyes dilated and his mouth began to gape open. 'Eh, erm, eh,' the cub stuttered. Baloo smiled knowingly. 'I suspect you have ten?' he said with an encouraging nod of the head.

'Yes, please,' replied the cub. Nervous giggles sounded around the fire.

'Well,' said Baloo. 'The children of the village hoped so too, but on those mornings, one or two children would awake to find they'd grown an extra toe or,' he deliberately hesitated before finishing the sentence. 'They'd wake to find a toe missing!'

A few gasps were heard on the night air. Baloo nodded sagely. 'Shoes would hide any problems with toes, but that wasn't all.' He took a deep breath. 'When those particular children reached their thirteenth birthday … they disappeared!'

Akela smiled to herself. The disappearing children, was a new twist Baloo had added. She was curious to know how he was going to develop the story further.

Baloo had noticed Akela beginning to take an interest in his story and he hoped the rest of the tale would even have Akela looking over her shoulder as she walked back to her tent. He licked his lips and resumed his tale.

'There was one particular lad,' he said. 'A certain Thomas Bickerpole, who was approaching his thirteenth birthday, was one of those children who'd mysteriously grown another big toe on his left foot. Now,' he grinned. 'That caused a problem for his parents whenever he needed new shoes.' The cubs laughed as one, thankful for a touch of humour. Baloo rubbed his hands together.

'As well as the occasional difficulties Thomas had with his shoes,' chuckled Baloo. 'There was something else that set him apart from the other children, he was inquisitive.' He shook his head slightly. 'Always sticking his nose into other peoples business, never satisfied with a simple explanation, dear me no. Thomas had to know everything, no matter who he upset to find the information he wanted.' Baloo sighed. He was trying to pad out the story as much as he could and give himself time to think of other scary bits to add to the tale. An idea suddenly formed and he smiled. With a loud click of his fingers, Baloo began to draw the tale towards its sinister conclusion.

'Two nights before his birthday, Thomas and three of his closest friends decided to go up to the Manor and find out what secrets lay within its walls.'

The cubs leant forward as one.

'They crept into the dark woods, eyes and ears alert for any strange sounds or moving shadows.' Baloo lowered his voice and the cubs leaned forward a little more. 'Slowly but surely they made their way through the trees towards the Manor.' He held a finger in the air and moved it slowly from side to side. 'Nothing stirred, not a whisper. Even the wind had disappeared and the only noise to be heard was the beating of boys' hearts. Now as they made their way to the rear of the Manor, they began to wonder how to get into the building. The Manor was completely surrounded by a high wall with tiny spikes running along the top. Approaching the wall, one of the boys motioned for the others to stand still.'

Baloo grinned at his audience, who were eagerly waiting to hear what would happen next, something he was beginning to wonder too.

'With a jerk of his head, the boy indicated a wooden door that stood partially hidden behind a large Rhododendron bush. Quickly the boys ran over to the door and Thomas, being by far the most inquisitive amongst them, pulled open the rickety door and stepped through the gap.'

Baloo took a quick look at his audience. All eyes and ears were waiting for the story to continue. He gave a nod and rubbed his hands together.

'Once inside the walls, the three boys huddled together, their eyes searching shadows.' Baloo's eyes darted from left to right. 'Silence, not a sound, not a whisper of wind,' he said, injecting a sense of urgency into his voice. 'Nothing stirred. The boys moved forward, a little at a time until they stood in the centre of a huge courtyard. Up above them towered the Manor with its moonlit windows reflecting a pale light, like cold eyes watching them. Suddenly,' he exclaimed. 'A stable door burst open and a dark beast galloped towards them.'

The cubs gasped in unison, their eyes wide with hands clenching knees. Baloo rose up from his seat, his arms hold aloft.

'The beast snorted, its piercing white eyes looked directly at the boys. Sitting on the beast's back was a tall, hooded figure with what looked like burning coals for eyes. The beast reared up.' As Baloo raised his arms to mimic the beast, the cubs recoiled in fear. Satisfied that his audience were hanging on his every word, Baloo took two steps forward, his arms still held high.

'As one the boys turned and ran, terrified that the beast would consume their flesh. Running through the door in the wall, the boys dashed towards the woods hoping the beast wouldn't follow.' Baloo waved his arms in front of his face. 'Branches and brambles whipped their legs and faces as they ran through the woods. Behind them they could hear the sound of hooves drumming on the ground, follow their every turn.'

As if to add a touch of theatre to his tale, a distant rumble sounded somewhere in the wood. Baloo, half heard the repetitive beat but dismissed it as a distant train or an overloaded lorry struggling with an incline. He waved his arms.

'The drumming of the hooves got louder and louder,' he growled. Right on cue the rumbling from the wood increased in volume. Baloo looked towards the wood as several cub-scouts nudged each other nervously. 'Louder and louder still,' he continued. 'The boys, panic flowing through veins, ran in blind terror, ignoring the branches tearing and slashing at their bodies. No matter how fast they ran or which direction they took, the drumming hooves followed them, getting closer and closer.'

By this time, most of the cubs were beginning to look towards the woods behind them as a rhythmic throbbing echoed through the darkness. Akela nodded, half smiling to herself. She had to admit that Baloo had surpassed himself this year. The sound effects gave a neat theatrical touch. She watched intently, eager to witness Baloo's finale.

Anxious to take advantage of anything that might enhance his tale, Baloo motioned towards the wood with his arm.

'With burning lungs and heavy legs, the boys suddenly found themselves in a small clearing in the woods. All around them towered huge trees, their branches hanging down to form an impenetrable barrier. The boys were trapped.'

Baloo placed his hands against his face. 'What could they do?' he asked, but nobody answered, as the rhythmic beat from the woods appeared to be getting louder. Eager to recapture his audience, Baloo smacked his hands together.

'Into the clearing charged the beast with its hooded rider. Steam rose from the skin of the beast as it circled the boys. Then,' cried Baloo, 'without warning the beast reared up, its mouth wide open as it gave a heart piercing scream.'

At that precise moment a large, dark shape emerged from the woods, its head almost touching Akela as it emitted a resounding, high-pitched snort. Several cubs screamed and grabbed each other in fear. Akela, fully aware of something terrifyingly odd behind her, spun around and came face to face with a terrifying apparition breathing a foul smelling vapour around her head. Clutching at her stomach, a low rumble sounded in her throat as Akela fell to the floor with a loud belch.

CHAPTER 34

PC Ricketts groaned as the phone chirruped annoyingly. Her enthusiasm, which had recently lost its life under an avalanche of paperwork, had once been sufficient to support her when the tedium of the job threatened to grind her down. Unfortunately, with nothing left to alleviate the constant pressure, PC Ricketts resorted to the only thing left to her that provided any sort of temporary release, a fierce stab of her pen into the list of useful numbers on the notice board above the phone.

A *tut* of reprimand followed her action.

'Why not just answer the phone like a nice Police Constable, rather than deface Constabulary property?' enquired Sergeant Cost, a supercilious smile toying with his upper lip.

Ignoring the sarcasm, PC Ricketts extracted the pen from the list of *useful numbers* and smiled serenely to herself as she answered the phone. Her brief moment of happiness lay in the fact that hidden behind the list was a picture of Sergeant Cost wearing a tiara at the previous year's Christmas party. PC Ricketts latest pen attack had caused serious trauma to the symmetry of the Sergeant's nose, resulting in an enlarged left nostril looking more like something the 4.50 from Paddington would pass through rather than a facial orifice. Satisfied with the mental imagery of Sergeant Cost's pen-pocked face, P C Ricketts listened to the voice on the other end of the phone.

'I'm sorry,' said PC Ricketts politely. 'But could you please repeat that, slowly?' The phone gurgled with a mixture of syllables and belches. 'I do understand,' soothed PC Ricketts. 'Now, as calmly as possible, please go over the events of the evening in as much detail as possible.'

For the next few minutes, PC Ricketts listened intently to the caller, only adding the occasionally nod or murmur of acknowledgement. With a grin, she finally nodded.

'Yes, I see,' replied PC Ricketts. 'You were listening to Baloo and … '
She paused as the caller muttered a clarification. 'Yes, I do know
who Baloo is.'

The mention of Baloo's name caused Sergeant Cost to
absentmindedly scratch at his stomach. Trying to ignore the
comical movements of her Sergeant, PC Ricketts swallowed noisily.

'I see, madam,' she continued. 'No, I don't think it amusing at
all. I'm sorry, no, I am taking you seriously.' She moved the phone
away from her ear and held it against her uniformed chest. 'Sarge,'
she whispered urgently. 'I think this one might need your finely
honed diplomatic skills.'

Sergeant Cost lowered his newspaper and appraised PC
Ricketts. Her broad grin and smiling eyes made him feel uneasy.
He wasn't quite sure whether she was simply amused at the
nature of the call or taking pleasure at being sarcastic. Utilising
his many years' experience, Sergeant Cost smiled back and nodded
at the phone.

'Learning how to deal with crank calls is an important lesson
in your police education,' he said in a hoarse whisper. 'Just be
polite, take the details and file it under Miscellaneous.'

While PC Ricketts' eyebrows raised each other towards the
ceiling, she gave a sigh and returned the phone to her ear.

'Sorry about that Akela, now we have a certain Mr Baloo, cub
scouts, extra toes and a dark apparition with bad breath, I see.'

At the mention of a dark apparition, Sergeant Cost once again
lowered his newspaper and glowered at PC Ricketts.

'Good grief,' he exclaimed. 'Has everyone in this town gone
stark, raving bonkers?'

PC Ricketts held a warning finger to her mouth and then
pointed to the phone.

'I don't care whether she can hear me,' replied Sergeant Cost,
shaking his head with disbelief. 'This apparition business is the
just the figment of some maladjusted, HRT-addled females,' he
rasped. The sergeant threw a ball of paper towards the waste-bin.
Grabbing several other sheets of paper in preparation for his next
onslaught on the bin, he sniffed noisily and nodded towards the
phone, 'shouldn't be allowed.'

PC Ricketts, unsure whether he was referring to HRT or the apparition, turned her attention to the verbal explosion erupting from the phone.

CHAPTER 35

Dubbya took a long look around and shook his head slowly. A barely audible gasp escaped his lips as his eyelids momentarily hid the scene from view.

'They really did make a mess of this place didn't they?' he said, the corners of his mouth giving a slight twitch.

While Dick was busily working his mouth into a piqued riposte, Tracey thrust a scolding hot mug of tea into Dubbya's hand.

'Actually, Dubbya,' she replied, as he massaged his heat-treated hand against his thigh. 'This,' she indicated with a sweep of her arm, 'is the post-vandalised version.' Tracey took a swift sip of her tea. 'I admit, it's a work in progress,' she continued, 'but it did encourage us to get rid of some junk as we went about the tidying process.'

Dubbya smiled meekly. 'Simply a bit of joshing on my part,' he explained. 'Didn't mean to cause offence.'

Tracey, taking another sip of tea, gave Dubbya the benefit of the doubt and returned the smile. 'Tea to your liking?' she asked sweetly.

'The tea,' began Dubbya, 'is absolutely ... ' His analysis of the tea was loudly interrupted by the sound of crockery crashing to the floor of the kitchen. Thrusting her mug of hot tea into Dubbya's free hand, Tracey hurried towards the kitchen, leaving him nursing both mugs in a pair of scolded hands.

Inside the kitchen, broken crockery covered the floor. Standing sheepishly, with a partially upturned washing-up bowl in his hands stood Two-stroke. Tracey, with her back resting against the sink, looked enquiringly at him. He smiled.

'I was just about to ... ' he stuttered. Tracey inhaled deeply.

'I can see what you were about to,' she said angrily. 'But I'm more interested in why you were about to?'

Two-stroke swallowed. 'Wash up,' he replied, his voice barely audible.

Stepping carefully over the crockery shards, Tracey removed the bowl from Two-stroke's hands and placed it in the sink.

'Why?' she asked, pointing to the corner of the kitchen. 'Would you want to indulge in manual scrubbing, when there is a perfectly good dishwasher waiting patiently for your attention?'

Two-stroke shrugged. 'Trying to help,' he explained. 'But the bowl was wet and my hands slipped and ... '

Tracey ignored the rest of Two-stroke's rambling and nodded at the door behind him. 'If you can negotiate the complexities of twisting the door-knob in the appropriate direction,' she said, allowing a hint of sarcasm to enter her voice. 'You'll find a dustpan and brush.' She turned towards the lounge. 'I'll leave you to work out what to do with them,' she called over her shoulder. 'Just so long as one of your solutions includes cleaning up the mess you've made.'

Two-stroke grinned, happy to be thought useful once again. 'OK,' he replied. 'Shall I clear the broken crockery off the floor too?'

In the lounge, Dick and Dubbya were deep in conversation.

'Mind if I join you?' asked Tracey, sitting demurely on the edge of the sofa. Dick smiled and nodded towards the recently discovered jiffy bag on the coffee table.

'We were just discussing the contents of the mysterious jiffy bag and going over some of the strange events that have come to light.'

Dubbya brushed his nose with the tip of his index finger.

'A bit of light on the subject would be most helpful,' he observed sarcastically. 'Just what have a steam room, golf course, jazz, kidnapping and a jiffy bag of dubious origin got to do with a document full of numerical waffle?'

Tracey shook her head.

'Men!' she chuckled. 'You couldn't boil an egg without assistance from Delia.'

Before either Dick or Dubbya could retaliate in defence of the male species, Tracey got up and left the room. After a few moments, she returned to find Dick and Dubbya exchanging curious glances. Smiling, she placed a roll of wallpaper on the tabled next to the jiffy bag.

'Now,' she said with a grin, 'we can get started.'

Dick cleared his throat, which Tracey always found annoying, more so because she knew that Dick was fully aware of just how much it irritated her. She pursed her lips while Dick finished gyrating his larynx.

'Tracey,' he began. 'I fully appreciate that the lounge is in need of redecorating, but is it really necessary to start right now?' Dick took a quick glance around the room. ' I mean, well, the burglars made a mess but not that much,' he grumbled. 'And besides, one roll will never be enough.'

Ignoring his plaintive moaning, Tracey picked up the roll of wallpaper and began to unfurl it. Satisfied that she'd unrolled sufficient for her needs, she tore the length of wallpaper from the roll. Once again, Dick and Dubbya exchanged glances but thought it better not to interrupt and so let Tracey continue.

Holding the blank side of the wallpaper towards her, Tracey placed the top edge along the mantelshelf. Securing the wallpaper with her finger, she stretched over towards the coffee table and grabbed two mugs. With all the dexterity accumulated after years of grappling with books and shelving, she deftly placed a mug at either end of the mantelshelf, temporarily pinning the wallpaper down. Tracey held her hand out towards Dick.

'Pen!' she demanded.

Dick dutifully stuck his hands down either side of the armchair cushion and began searching for the requested implement. After a few seconds he smiled, extracted his left hand from under the cushion and proffered a partially crushed marker pen to Tracey. Giving the pen a cursory inspection, she started to draw the outline of what looked like a cloud onto the wallpaper.

'Bomb-burst,' she exclaimed.

Dubbya grinned. 'And I thought you'd had burglars,' he said looking around the room.

Tracey sighed patiently and began to write inside the cloud. "OK,' she said. 'Operation Duster!'

'What?' cried Dick and Dubbya.

Tracey smiled. She loved being abstract and slightly confusing, which is why she enjoyed the various cataloguing systems employed within a library. The idea of knowing what was going on and the need to explain it to other people never failed to bring a smile of satisfaction to her face. Tracey raised her eyebrows slightly.

'We have a bit of a mess to clear up,' she explained. 'What better name, particularly after the most recent event than to call our endeavours *Operation Duster*? It's obvious to us what it means but not so obvious to other people.'

'Couldn't we have called it *Operation Hoover*?' asked Dubbya. 'Can't say I like the labour implications of *Duster*.'

'Ah!' grinned Tracey, tapping the side of her nose. 'A duster provides a more hands on approach, delicately allowing you to search through the dust to see what lies beneath.' Ignoring the look of resignation on Dick's face, Tracey began to add more words to the outside of the cloud.

'These are the things we know,' she said, pointing to the added words. 'But,' she continued, 'there are still several things that we don't know.' Tracey drew a number of blank clouds around the larger cloud. 'What do you think?' she asked.

'Absolutely brilliant,' shouted Two-stroke emerging from the kitchen with a plate of biscuits. 'Just how neat is that!' he said excitedly, pointing at the sheet of wallpaper.

'Thank you, Two-stroke,' replied Tracey. 'I'm glad you like it.'

'Like it?' grinned Two-stroke. 'I think it's amazing. I've always wanted to be part of a Council of War.'

'Not quite a war,' said Dubbya, scratching his rippling midriff. 'Besides, we are not exactly sure who's the enemy.'

'I know, but ... ' replied Two-stroke.

'People get hurt in a war,' declared Tracey, looking at Dick's bruised face.

'Too damn right,' grumbled Dick, gently touching the still colourful bruising.

Two-stroke held the plate of biscuits towards Dick and Dubbya. 'Biscuit anyone,' he asked dejectedly.

'How considerate,' said Dubbya grabbing a handful of custard creams, 'my favourites.'

Tracey stabbed the marker pen against the wallpaper. 'There are still too many unknown factors,' she said with a hint of exasperation in her voice. She drew several question marks around the main cloud. 'Who, what, where?' she asked.

'I don't know who,' replied Dick. 'But I know where and what hurts,' he groaned.

'Don't be such a baby,' answered Tracey sharply. 'What if I'd gone to fetch your sandwiches, what if it were me that had been kidnapped, what if ... '

'Now, hang on,' replied Dick hurriedly. 'I didn't mean that. I was simply trying to clarify what we do know and ... '

Tracey drew a love-heart in the bottom corner of the wallpaper and blew Dick a kiss. 'So you do care,' she grinned.

Dick felt the temperature rise in the region of his collar. 'Well, yes, er, of course I do but ... '

'Could we step out of the mutual admiration zone and get on with deciding what we're going to do next,' asked Dubbya, animatedly pointing at the sheet of wallpaper. 'I'd like to know what part I'm to play in all of this and calculate my expenses.'

Tracey took the plate of biscuits, that Two-stroke still cradled in his hands, and offered the plate to Dubbya. 'Take some on account,' she said impishly.

For a few moments, Dubbya 's eyes flickered between the plate and Tracey. The custard creams proved too tempting. Dubbya scooped up the remaining biscuits with the dexterity normally associated with a croupier.

'Thank you,' he mumbled through a cloud of crumbs. 'Much appreciated.'

With an almost imperceptible shake of her head, Tracey began to underline each of the question marks on the sheet of wallpaper. "We need to identify the main players in this little game,' she said with a final underlined flourish.

'Yeah, then we could get them all together in the same room, just like Hercule Poirot,' said Two-stroke enthusiastically. 'Then we could go through the sordid details,' he continued. 'Until finally pointing the finger of accusation at the culprit.'

Dubbya swallowed the remaining morsels of biscuit too quickly and quickly dissolved into a paroxysm of crumb-strewn coughing. Dick immediately began slapping Dubbya's back, which only served to increase the severity of the coughs. Just when Dubbya's complexion began to take on a sunset-hue, Tracey arrived with a glass of water.

'Thank you, kind lady,' wheezed Dubbya, after draining the glass. 'An act of compassion that other folk,' he frowned sternly at Dick, 'could do well to imitate.'

'Just trying to help,' said Dick, with a shrug.

Dubbya smiled. 'Perhaps get in touch with your feminine side a little more when administering aid,' he suggested. 'Rather than resort to the overly masculine approach.'

'Whatever,' replied, Dick. 'But if you think I'm going to ... '

'Look,' snapped Tracey. 'Could we just get on with working out what we're going to do?'

Both Dick and Dubbya nodded meekly. Two-stroke, who had been watching the scene unfold with growing agitation, pointed to the question marks on the piece of wallpaper.

'What about Poirot?' he asked.

In between the impatient glances of Dick and Dubbya, Tracey leaned forward and patted Two-stroke's arm.

'I don't think we're quite at that stage yet,' she replied. 'But you're right,' she smiled. 'We do need to identify the people behind the scam and try to get them together at some point.'

Feeling the warmth of approval, Two-stroke folded his arms and sat back in the chair, a broad smile spreading across his face. Sucking at his top lip, Dick nodded towards the wallpaper.

'So it's a scam then?' he asked.

'What do you think?' responded Tracey with a twinkle.

Two-stroke tapped a rhythm on his knees. 'Why don't we go through the facts, what we know and see if we can fill in the missing pieces?' he asked. 'You know, just like Poirot does.'

'I think that's a really good idea,' said Tracey, a congratulatory smile on her lips. 'The most useful contribution from the male contingent to date.'

'Now just a minute,' said Dick, looking for some sort of support from Dubbya.

'Yes?' asked Tracey, holding the marker pen threateningly close to Dick's nose. With no apparent supportive gesture from Dubbya,

Dick batted his eyelids submissively. 'Sounds like a good idea,' he agreed.

Tracey settled into the armchair and closed her eyes. Dick smiled to himself. He knew this was just the sort of thing Tracey would do when she was unsure of what to do or say. It gave her a few moments to sift through her thoughts before she assembled a response.

'We could start with the document,' suggested Dick, his index finger resting against his chin. Tracey momentarily opened one eye and immediately closed it again. 'Well,' she said softly. 'It's where it all began.'

Placing the tips of his fingers together, Dick looked at the cartoon cloud on the wallpaper. 'To be precise,' he said. 'It really all began with this mysterious woman who ... '

Tracey's eyes shot open and she sat forward in the chair. 'Careful,' she said, the word carrying sufficient menace to make Dubbya swallow hard.

'All I meant was ... ' began Dick.

'I know full well what you meant,' replied Tracey edgily. 'Let's stick to tangible facts, OK?'

'Tangibility,' mused Dubbya, attempting to bring a little levity into the threatening atmosphere. 'Now there's an interesting word.'

'Not for me it ain't,' grumbled Two-stroke. 'I failed English Language, big time.'

Tracey allowed herself a brief smile. 'Dubbya's more the hands-on, practical linguist,' she explained to a rapidly bemused Two-stroke.

'That's as maybe,' responded Dubbya. 'But the tangible facts, as we know them ... ' He looked enquiringly at Tracey. 'Ready with the pen?' he asked. Tracey removed the pen cap and held the marker pen theatrically in the air.

'Ready wise one,' she laughed. 'Spout away.'

'Right,' grinned Dubbya. 'We have a document detailing large quantities of money being spent on unspecified activities,' he said. 'Next, we have a couple of steamed gentlemen with a large golfing handicap.' Dubbya ticked the two details off on his fingers. 'Thirdly,' he continued. 'There is the little matter of flying golf balls, a kidnapping with synthetic body parts thrown in.'

Dick shuddered. The memories of that evening and the discovery of what appeared to be mutilated bodies still made the hairs on his neck bristle. 'Go on,' he urged Dubbya. 'Next?'

'Well,' replied Dubbya thoughtfully. 'We know the College is struggling to keep the senior management in the manner to which they are accustomed.'

'You mean they're strapped for cash?' asked Two-stroke.

'On the one hand, yes,' said Dubbya. 'But on the other hand, when it comes to spending money for some unknown, devious venture, then no.'

Two-stroke shrugged. 'Just asking,' he said.

Dick nodded slowly. 'We also seem to have a link between the College's Chair of Governors and the Chair of the Planning and Development Committee.'

'So,' said Tracey, as the marker pen hovered menacingly over the question marks. 'We have the College's need to raise funds, a possible imposed restructuring or merger with the local Sixth Form College, certain senior members of the College's Management who are in danger of losing their designated parking spaces, amorous links between the College and County planning department and a few unscrupulous business people sniffing around.'

'Sounds like the scenario at any College of Further Education in the UK,' chuckled Dubbya.

'Precisely,' replied Tracey. 'So what's so special about this College and,' she continued, looking at Dick. 'Precisely why is my love interest accosted by a disembodied woman, given a mysterious document, steamed, used for golfing practice, and kidnapped by two thugs?'

Dick reached over and grasped Tracey's hand. 'Not all at the same time,' he whispered. 'And you forgot to mention the odious task of visiting Regeneration Sounds.'

Tracey looked directly at Dick. Once again the strength of her feelings for him seemed to overwhelm her. 'You know what I mean,' she replied softly. 'Anyway, I thought you liked all things of a jazz nature?'

Dick leaned forward and kissed her briefly. 'I do, but not when it comes bundled with a talking mop.' He kissed Tracey once more.

'Now then, you two,' warned Dubbya. 'Young person present.'

Two-stroke gave an annoyed click of his tongue. 'Poirot would have kissed the lady's hand,' he said.

Dick kissed Tracey once again. 'But there again,' he breathed. 'He wasn't in love with the hand of the lady he was kissing.'

'Love?' enquired Tracey, as Dick returned to his chair.

Dubbya held up his hand. 'Before we sink into the mire of endearment,' he warned. 'Can we at least decide what we are going to do with the assembled facts?'

Tracey, emotionally digesting Dick's comment, smiled. 'It seems, to make any sense of the facts, we must break the law ourselves.'

Dubbya shook his head. 'Is breaking into the place of your employment actually breaking the law?' he asked.

'I suppose it depends on when and where,' he replied. 'Does the end justify the means?'

Dubbya sighed. The dietary value of custard cream biscuits was woefully inadequate and his stomach was beginning to complain. 'I think we should adjourn the meeting,' he suggested, rising from the sofa. 'It might be wise to take some advice, in a roundabout way, of course.'

Tracey suddenly displayed a broad grin. Dick, fully appreciating what had caused her to grin, shook his head. 'Oh no,' he said. 'Definitely not.'

'What are you on about?' asked a bemused Two-stroke.

'Time for Dick to flick through a few jazz CD's and exchange notes,' she replied cryptically.

Dubbya and Two-stroke exchanged looks. Without waiting for any form of explanation, Dubbya made his way towards the front door. 'Keep me informed,' he called over his shoulder.

'Be seeing you then,' said Two-stroke, bumping into the edge of the sofa as he made his way out of the room. 'Let me know how I can be of further assistance.'

'Will do,' replied Dick with a wave. He turned to Tracey. 'Malcolm?'

'Yes,' smiled Tracey. 'Malcolm.'

CHAPTER 36

Dick hovered near the door to the bakery. He was tempted to ignore the frantic waving of Tracey, who was comfortably seated in the coffee shop across the road, and purchase comfort in the shape of a custard doughnut.

A few minutes earlier, he'd sat in the anonymity of the coffee shop, sipping a lukewarm mug of strong brown liquid and listening to Tracey's encouraging tones.

'Really, Dick,' she chided. 'All you have to do is go into the shop, act furtively, indulge in a bit of banal chatter and leave without buying anything.' She sat back and took a quick sip of her tea. 'Just up your street.'

Dick had been tempted to relieve her of the mistaken perception she had of him, but thought better of it. In the time it would take to identify her misunderstanding of his character, state the case for an alternative version of his abilities and then field a barrage of questions, he could have popped across the street, dropped the note in Duke Ellington's CD and dashed back to his cooling seat and avoid a headache.

It was the latter option that found Dick dithering between the bakery and the newly painted door of Regeneration Sounds. The longer he vacillated between the opposing doors, the more Tracey gestured for him to go into the music shop. Conscious that he was beginning to attract unwanted attention from the other coffee shop customers, he finally pushed open the bright mauve door of Regeneration Sounds.

The clang of the bell above his head startled him, even though he knew its less than ambient tones would be waiting for him the moment he pushed open the door. His resulting stumble caused a stack of CD's rising from the floor to wobble alarmingly. Dick quickly placed a steadying hand on them.

'For whom the bell tolls, eh?' chimed a voice.

'Hello?' called out Dick at the clichéd response to the bell. His eyes surveyed the refitted interior of the shop. Where before there had been tattered boxes of CD's, dog-eared labels and faded posters adorning the walls, there now sat rows of neat wooden racks, all meticulously annotated against a backdrop of various swirls of green hues that liberally coated the walls. The overall effect was eye-catching, to say the least. Dick closed his eyes as the green swirls on the walls began to gyrate.

'Too much to take in all at once eh?' asked Malc, emerging from behind the jukebox.

The sudden appearance of Malc only served to startle Dick once more. Several CD's clattered to the floor as Dick tried desperately to steady both his nerves and the plastic cases.

'Hold on, there,' burbled Malc. He swiftly retrieved the fallen CD's from the floor and dropped them into their appropriate slots in the newly acquired racks. 'Tad nervous today, aren't you?' he enquired of Dick.

Dick wiped his clammy hands together. His throat felt dry and he wasn't sure, now, whether it was the green swirls that were gyrating or Malc's eyeballs. Dick leant against one of the new racks and took a deep breath.

'Left Tracey having a refuel in the coffee shop before she starts another shopping shift.' Dick indicated the racks of CD's with his head. 'Just thought I'd pop in and have a quick browse.' So many words in such a short space of time left Dick breathless. He tried to regulate his breathing to a tempo a lot slower than his current heart rate. Malc stroked the curves of the jukebox lovingly.

'Once I get this old beauty working again, the place will be complete.' He waved majestically at the shop's interior. 'What do you think of the décor?' he asked, his eyes moving rapidly in their sockets.

'Well,' gulped Dick. 'It's rather different from what it was before,' he replied diplomatically.

Malc smiled. 'It's for my grand re-opening,' he explained. He briefly touched Dick's arm, causing him to flinch. Malc ignored the apparent comment on his action. 'Not that I've ever been closed, you understand,' he grinned. 'But it's good for business.'

Dick nodded lamely in agreement. As casually as he could

appear, Dick walked over to the jazz artists residing under the 'D, E, F' category. Almost nonchalantly, he lifted Duke Ellington's: Money Jungle CD out of the rack.

'Same as last time,' called Malc, who had once again disappeared behind the jukebox.

'What? Oh yes,' mumbled Dick. 'Wondered whether it might be one of those digitally remastered efforts,' he explained.

Malc stood upright and ran his hand through his hair. 'Not really sure what to make of those digital makeovers,' he said thoughtfully. 'I may be wrong,' he mused. 'But I tend to think that something is lost in the process, what do you think?' he asked, as Dick fumbled the CD, quickly inserted a note and then popped it back into the rack.

'If I were a purist,' began Dick.

'Ah!' Malc exclaimed. 'Then you wouldn't be in my shop in the first place.'

Dick scratched his chin. He'd told Tracey exactly how the conversation with Malc would go, from the courteous to the curious. He resigned himself to the fact that, however hard he tried to make things easy, Malc had a way of making the whole consumer process a cerebral-mire. Dick sighed quietly. 'And why would that be?' he asked patiently.

'Because,' explained Malc, with a grin. 'A purist is precisely that. They would expect a shop to be dedicated to the only aural format deemed worthy of being the sole repository of all things jazz.'

Dick pretended interest while he tried to peer through the shop window in the vain hope of seeing Tracey and a possible rescue. She was either ignoring him or couldn't see him through the filter of grime on the coffee shop windows. He sighed inwardly.

'Which is?' asked Dick, knowing what the answer would be. Malc replied as expected.

'Why, vinyl of course,' he said with an expansive gesture of his hands. Malc nodded towards the back of the shop. 'I've still got a few boxes of old vinyl out the back, you know,' he gave an exaggerated wink. 'For those punters who prefer discretion when contemplating a purchase.'

Edging towards the door, Dick wracked his brain for a quick

get out clause. Catching a glimpse of the piles of CD's that remained neatly stacked despite his best efforts to topple them, he gave a brief shrug of his shoulders.

'Any new releases that I can save money on by ignoring?' he quipped.

Malc returned the jest with a huge grin. 'Funny you should say that,' he replied. Bending down to the stack of CD's on the floor, Malc sifted through the top layer until he found what he was looking for. 'Now,' he smiled at Dick. 'You just might be interested in a certain Julian Edwin Adderley.'

Dick's lips started to form a question. Malc held a finger in the air.

'Ah,' he continued. 'Who, you may ask? Well,' said Malc, handing the CD case over to Dick. 'Cannonball Adderley, as he was better known, recorded *Something Else*,' he tapped the CD in Dick's hands. 'In March 1958, in between playing on a couple of seminal Miles Davis albums, *Milestones* and a *Kind of Blue*.'

Dick quickly scanned the sleeve notes that accompanied the CD. He raised an eyebrow. 'It says here,' grinned Dick. "That this is a 1999, digital reissue.'

Malc frowned critically. 'That, my friend, is an original recording that has been remastered.'

'Same thing?' suggested Dick.

'Not entirely,' replied Malc, neatly rearranging the CD's on the floor. 'The spelling is different.'

Dick allowed himself a quick chuckle. He returned the CD to Malc. 'I'm tempted,' he said. 'But I'm not sure Tracey shares my affinity for jazz.'

Malc clapped his hands together. 'Easily solved,' he laughed. Without further comment, he disappeared into the back room of the shop, reappearing moments later with a CD in his hand. 'This,' he declared, stroking the CD. 'Is sublime.' Malc's eyes closed momentarily. 'Echoes of Ella Fitzgerald and Billie Holiday,' he murmured dreamily.

Dick looked at the abstract outline of a female on the CD cover. '*Some lessons, the bedroom sessions?*' he queried.

Malc snatched the CD out of Dick's hand. 'Don't even think it,' he warned. 'Those songs were recorded while the woman was convalescing after being hit by a car.' Malc shook his head. 'Almost robbed the world of a wonderful voice.'

Dick shrugged. 'Sorry, but I've never heard of Melody Gardot.'

Malc returned the CD to Dick. 'Then listen and be amazed,' he said. 'And,' he continued, wagging his finger. 'There's no charge for that CD. Give it to Tracey and let her be impressed with your taste in jazz.' He handed Dick the other CD. 'And that'll be a fiver for Cannonball.'

'Erm,' said Dick, busily searching his pockets for money.

Malc shook his head in exasperation. 'Owe it,' he said.

Dick gave a slight shake of his head. 'I'll be back in a moment. Just need to blag the money from Tracey.'

The shop bell dismissively as Dick fled through the door, leaving Malc standing with hands on hips and a huge grin on his face.

CHAPTER 37

Safe in the confines of the coffee shop, Dick updated Tracey on his latest verbal juggling with Malc.

'I'm not sure my nerves can take much more,' he moaned. 'The bloke's a complete nutter, a menace to sanity.'

Tracey laughed loudly, causing more than a few eyebrows to rise in criticism. ''You exaggerate,' she chided him. 'I'm sure he's quite harmless.'

Dick almost choked on the coffee he'd just begun sipping. 'Harmless?' he coughed. 'You've met him, you can see he's a few crochets short of a full bar.'

It was Tracey's turn to splutter. She dabbed at the trickle of tea seeping down her chin.

'Is everything all right with your refreshments?' enquired a mature female voice. Dick looked over at the cosmetically indulged features of the woman who'd served them their drinks earlier.

'Fine, thank you,' he called back. 'Just sharing a joke.'

The woman busied herself with a tea towel. Vigorously rubbing at the inside of a mug, she nodded towards their table. 'Nothing to joke about in my establishment,' she said sternly. 'I maintain the highest standards of hygiene,' she continued, breathing heavily into the inside of the mug and rubbing once again.

'I assure you,' Tracey answered soothingly. 'It's absolutely nothing to do with your drinks. It's my partner here,' she said. 'He's so funny.'

'I'm sure he is, love,' sniffed the woman noisily. 'But not in my café.'

Suitably chastened, Dick blew gently at his lukewarm coffee while Tracey's eyes danced in merriment.

'Now look what you've gone and done,' she whispered. 'Your unfounded comments have upset the woman.'

'Upset!' gasped Dick. 'I wasn't talking about her in the first place and ... '

'Sssh,' hushed Tracey. 'You'll get us thrown out.'

Dick silently drained his mug. Carefully placing the empty mug on the table, he leant back in the chair and folded his arms. 'I'm not going back in that shop,' he announced.

Tracey quickly removed the mug away from her mouth. 'You daft brush,' she whispered laughing. 'Don't be such a child.'

'I'm not,' replied Dick, sticking his bottom lip out. 'And I'm not going across the road to have my senses addled by that gangly mop of hair.'

Tracey held her mug tightly to avoid any spillage. 'Dick,' she smiled. 'We need to see if there has been a reply to our note and,' she brushed his hand with her fingertips. 'You owe him money.'

Dick shook his head. 'I haven't got any money with me,' he replied. 'Besides, you've been sitting here for ages. It'll do you good to stretch your legs and walk over the road.'

Tracey grabbed her handbag and stood over Dick. 'Duke Ellington,' she asked. 'Money Jungle?'

Dick nodded. 'That's where the reply should be,' he answered. If there is one, it'll be Money Jungle, don't forget.'

As Tracey walked out of the café, a bloke at the next table shuffled his chair towards Dick. Carefully spreading the back pages of the local newspaper in front of Dick, the bloke nodded at the paper. 'Money Jungle, you reckon?' he asked with a conspiratorial wink. 'Is it running in the 2.30 at Newmarket?'

161

CHAPTER 38

Tracey stood hesitantly in front of Regeneration Sounds. Even through the fume filters of the café, she had thought that the shop looked as if it had received a bit of TLC, but now that she was close up, she could see that the whole shop had been embraced in colour. Admiring the freshly daubed paintwork, Tracey pushed the door open.

'Hello,' trilled Malc, competing with the doorbell chimes. 'I didn't expect to see you. Not,' he hastened to add, 'that you're unwelcome here at Regeneration Sounds.' He gave a sort of apologetic, welcome smile and ushered Tracey further into the interior of the shop.

Tracey nervously fiddled with the button on her jacket as both Malc and herself struggled for the next sentence in their conversation.

'Is Dick OK?' enquired Malc, clearing his throat in the process.

Tracey nodded, thankful that Dick's warning of cerebral meltdown resulting from any form conversation with Malc was completely unfounded. 'He's fine, thanks,' she replied. 'He's just finishing his coffee.'

Malc grinned at the news, his eyes flicking between Tracey and her handbag.

'Oh, yes,' she flustered. 'I gather Dick owes you for a CD?'

'That'll be a fiver to you,' said Malc.

While Malc, with banknote in hand, proceeded to reunite it with like-minded denominations, Tracey purposefully browsed through the racks of CD's. Surreptitiously, or so she thought, Tracey removed the note that had been secreted inside Duke Ellington's, *Money Jungle*. Quickly stuffing the folded note into her pocket, she looked up just as Malc spoke.

'Popular CD, that,' he said, handing Tracey a receipt. 'Duke always seems to get a lot of interest. Funny that,' he added looking at Tracey.

With years of librarian practice, she smiled sweetly and nodded.

162

'Always reliable,' she replied cryptically. 'You've made a nice job of it,' she said, quickly changing the topic of conversation.

'Yeah, cheers,' shrugged Malc nonchalantly. 'Thought I'd make the place more presentable, you know.'

'Well,' smiled Tracey. 'You've done a good job. Business must be picking up?'

'Funny you should say that,' replied Malc as he rummaged through a stack of paper littering a chair. 'It's here somewhere,' he muttered. 'Got it,' he announced almost immediately. Waving the sheet of paper in front of his face, he inclined his head towards Tracey. 'It's where you and Dick work isn't it?' he asked.

'What are you on about?' asked Tracey. She caught hold of the wafted paper and saw the familiar College logo. 'I'm not sure that work is the operative word in some cases,' she said indicating the café across the road. 'He sees it as an interruption to the lifestyle in which he'd like to become accustomed.'

Malc shook his head. 'Don't be too hard on the man,' he scolded mockingly. 'He's a delicate soul with a passion for the finer things in life, like your good self,' he added diplomatically as Tracey frowned sternly.

Ignoring Malc's poor attempt at flattery, Tracey rustled the College notepaper. 'Why have you been deemed worthy of receiving a communication from the institute for the managerially inept?' she asked.

Malc drew his shoulders back. 'I,' he said with emphasis. 'I have been asked to provide the soundtrack for the College's fashion show,' he preened.

Tracey returned the notepaper to Malc. "My,' she said, a smile broadening her face. 'How you've come down in the world.'

Malc responded by staring down his nose. 'Not at all,' he replied stiffly. 'Quite the opposite in fact.'

Feeling a little guilty at ruffling Malc's self-esteem, Tracey gave an affirming nod. 'I'm sure it is,' she said encouragingly. 'Ignore my slightly jaundiced response.' She gave a slight shrug. 'You have to work there to understand.'

'I'm sure you do,' replied Malc as he sorted through a pile of CD's on the floor. 'But I see the fashion show as my chance to educate the untutored ears of a new generation of potential jazz lovers.' Apparently satisfied with his perusal of the floored CD's, Malc stood with a selected handful. 'These,' he said indicating the CD's in his hand. 'Will provide a soundtrack that will make the night unforgettable.'

'That's a very optimistic statement,' said Tracey casually moving towards the door.

'Not optimism,' said Malc with a smile. 'Confidence.'

'Well,' shrugged Tracey. 'I'm sure you'll do your best to make the evening one to remember.'

'You mark my words,' winked Malc. 'It will be an evening to remember.'

Tracey, pausing in her slow shuffle towards the door, looked enquiringly at Malc. She wasn't quite sure what to make of his comment or whether she should probe a little more. Deciding to err on the side of caution, Tracey simply raised an eyebrow. 'Memorable?' she asked casually.

'In lots of ways,' replied Malc equally casual. 'There will be so much going on, so much to see and do.' He winked again at Tracey. 'It'll be one of those evenings that will surprise some people and,' he pursed his lips. 'Maybe a shock to some.'

Tracey was taken aback at Malc's words. She really didn't know how to react. Malc, sensing Tracey's discomfort, walked over to her and patted her arm. 'Don't look so worried,' he soothed. 'You know what these arty students can be like,' he said, waving his hand from side to side. 'One minute apparent paragons of lost virtue and the next, well, shockingly outrageous I suppose.'

With her hand on the door, Tracey offered a noncommittal smile. 'Quite possibly,' she said. 'I'm sure I'll see you on the night.'

'You'll certainly hear me,' grinned Malc.

Tracey pulled the door open and waited a few seconds for the jangling bell to quieten. 'Oh yes,' she said eventually. 'Thanks for the Melody Gardot CD. Saw her on the Jools Holland show once, amazing voice for one so young. But,' she added. 'Please don't let on to Dick that I've already heard her sing. He likes to think he's educating my aural palette by introducing me to artists I'm not supposed to have heard before.'

164

'No worries,' laughed Malc. 'Your secret is safe with me.'

Tracey allowed the door to close behind her with confused thoughts echoing in her head. Was Malc as daft and innocent as he appeared or was he somehow involved in this whole confused situation? She ambled across to the café where Dick gazed at her through the fug-tinted window. She acknowledged his wave with a smile. Talking of confused situations, she thought, here was another one that needed a bit of clarification.

CHAPTER 39

Dick scalded each of the tea bags that lay expectantly in the mugs. Gazing through the kitchen window, his thoughts swirled around his head as he lazily nudged the tea bags with the back of the spoon.

'Brewing, mashing or pummelling them into submission?' enquired a voice over his shoulder.

'Sorry,' he said absentmindedly, half to himself. 'Just thinking.'

Tracey kissed his neck while lifting his hand away from the mugs. 'Don't overdo it,' she advised.

'What, er, oh yeah, sorry,' he said again, using the spoon one last time to remove the giddy teabags. For a moment he stood with one foot on the pedal, which operated the waste bin lid, while his hand held a spoon supporting four damp tea bags.

Tracey shook her head. 'If you're expecting them to jump, you might have a long wait,' she said mockingly. Without waiting for Dick to respond, she took the spoon from his hand, dumped the tea bags into the bin and nudged his foot off the pedal so that the bin lid closed to conceal the kitchen debris inside.

Leaving Dick to follow behind with a plate of biscuits she'd thoughtfully prepared earlier, Tracey walked into the lounge with the tray of drinks.

Following the encounter with Malc, earlier that day, Dick and Tracey had decided to call a meeting of Operation Duster. Dubbya had been the first to arrive, his face revealing all the signs of being flustered. Despite numerous enquiries from both Dick and Tracey, Dubbya had refused to make any comments concerning his welfare. Saved from further interrogation by the bulk of Two-stroke ignoring the doorbell and beating a syncopated rhythm on the woodwork, Dubbya had subsided into an agitated mound on the sofa. Tracey, keen to know the cause of his disturbed appearance had removed the door from Two-stroke's attention and settled him next to Dubbya.

Placing equally hot mugs of tea into the hands of Dubbya and Two-stroke, Tracey smiled graciously. 'Drink up,' she encouraged. 'We've a lot to discuss, so better make a start.' She looked towards the kitchen where Dick was busily rearranging the biscuits on the plate. 'Dick,' called Tracey. 'Biscuits.'

'Coming right up,' replied Dick with a final flourish to the biscuit decoration.

Tracey took a gentle sip of her tea and smiled at Dubbya. 'So,' she said calmly. 'What's got you into such a state?' she asked.

Dubbya tapped the side of his mug of tea. 'It's just, well, this code name for our little get together,' he began. Tracey raised her eyebrows questioningly. 'Well,' he continued. 'Could I politely ask for a change of name?' Two-stroke turned his head towards Dubbya. Pre-empting the obvious, Dubbya gave an embarrassed cough. 'For the Operation not for me,' he clarified.

'I thought the name quite apt,' said Tracey, feeling slightly put out that her suggested name appeared to be receiving some criticism. 'I'm not sure that the idea of *Operation Hoover* was much better.'

Dubbya sipped at his tea. He seemed to be struggling for words until a grin erupted on his face. 'Sorry,' he offered. 'Now I'm here, it's all quite funny, but at the time it was a bit hairy.'

Wiping his mouth on the back of his hand, Two-stroke shook his head. 'You'll have to spell that one out for me,' he sighed. 'Can't make head or tail of what you've just said.'

'Sorry,' Dubbya repeated. 'You had to be there.' Quickly noticing the warning signs in Tracey's eyes, Dubbya began to explain. 'Dick left a message for me on the answer-phone,' he said. 'My cleaner, Mrs Hammond, a devout lady where cleanliness is definitely next to Godliness, heard me play the message.'

'Can't see anything wrong with that,' grumbled Two-stroke in between sips of tea. 'You're lucky to get an answer-phone message. At our house, my mum listens to all the messages, decides which she thinks are important, ignores those she doesn't understand, writes down what she thinks she heard and then passes the messages onto whoever comes through he door first.' He took a gulp of tea. 'Gave our Eric a heck of a fright when he got a message to go and get his results from the doctor.'

'And,' smiled Dubbya, half expecting the reply.

'It weren't for our Eric,' he said nonchalantly. 'It were for our Sheena, she's got herself pregnant.'

'An immaculate conception?' enquired Dubbya with a grin. 'Or simply an immoderate inception?'

Tracey moved quickly to deter Dubbya from any further wordplay. 'And the link between Dick's message, Mrs Hammond and your earlier agitated state?' she asked.

Dubbya smiled lamely. 'Ah, well,' he said. 'She heard Dick's attempt at humour and his falsetto voice screeching "Operation Duster", and then Dick's inability to terminate the telephone call before dissolving into laughter is a sure fire way of making her think that I was either mocking her cleaning efforts or I was into some sordid fetish activity.' Dubbya shuddered involuntarily. 'She threatened to walk out there and then. I wouldn't have minded but she hadn't finished polishing the toilet seat.'

Tracey tried desperately to suppress the rising tide of laughter. Two-stroke had no such inhibitions and immediately dissolved into a full-throttled laugh. Dubbya revisited his earlier state of agitation.

'It's not damn funny,' he complained. 'Finding another cleaner of Mrs Hammond's calibre would be nigh on impossible.' He closed his eyes and breathed heavily through his nose. 'If only Dick hadn't resorted to that inane laughing bout.'

Tracey wiped a jovial tear from her eye. 'Dick,' she hiccupped.

Dick, with a towel folded neatly over his arm suddenly appeared at her shoulder. 'You called M'lady?'

Tracey giggled. 'Dick, you nit, offer the biscuits around and make sure that Dubbya gets triple rations.'

Obligingly, Dick thrust the plate of biscuits at Dubbya and waited as a third of the assembled custard creams disappeared.

'So kind,' munched Dubbya.

Tracey, delicately wiping away a few stray crumbs from her mouth, coughed for attention. 'Shall we get down to business?' she asked.

Dubbya, happily munching on biscuits, and Two-stroke, equally happy licking the cream from inside his biscuit, nodded their approval whilst Dick, still looking slightly distracted, smiled his assent.

Tracey gave a brief account of her and Dick's experiences at Regeneration Sounds and then held up the note for everyone to see. 'I was hoping this would make things a little less murky,' she said. 'Unfortunately, it seems to make things somewhat opaque.'

'What do you make of this Malc character?' asked Dubbya with a final lick of his lips.

'Precisely what I've been thinking about,' replied Dick. 'I can't help feeling as if we're being manipulated. If someone else knows what's going on, why don't they leave us out of the loop and get on with the job themselves?'

'Because, dear boy,' answered Dubbya. 'They're not so foolish as to get themselves mixed up in this palaver.'

'What?' asked a bewildered Two-stroke, 'is a *palaver*?'

'Long, boring and complicated,' answered Tracey. 'Not unlike Dubbya's lectures, allegedly.'

'Thanks,' grinned Two-stroke. 'I understand now.'

The sound of Dubbya choking on the remains of his tea brought a smile to everyone's face. 'Look,' he gargled. 'Don't you think I've suffered enough today?' He dabbed furiously at his mouth with a handkerchief. 'Can we get on with the serious matter of finding out what we should do next?'

Tracey obligingly held up the note that she'd retrieved earlier. 'I'm not sure,' she said. 'That this is a help or a hindrance?'

Dubbya leaned forward and took the note from her hand. Quickly scanning the few lines scrawled on the note he handed it back to Tracey. 'See what you mean,' he said with a sigh.

Anticipating Two-stroke's question, Dick extracted the note from Tracey's grip. 'We have a riddle to solve,' he began. 'If you're sitting comfortably, I'll begin.' In his best storyteller's voice, Dick began to recite from the sheet of paper.

"When Mr Gibson took to wings,
he made rather a mess of things.
On the night the waters did flow,
being chastised was such a cruel blow.
What a debt of gratitude is owed,
For in that year there rests a code."

The expected silence lasted for almost ten seconds when Two-stoke suddenly smiled broadly and clicked his fingers.

'Air America,' he announced theatrically. 'You know, the one with Mel Gibson as the veteran flyer.'

Dubbya looked along his nose at Two-stroke. 'Dear boy, if you mean that poor excuse for a film purporting to be a mix of antiestablishment escapades and antiwar earnestness, then do enlighten me.'

'Don't know about that,' replied Two-stroke. 'But it's got lots of flying in the Laos jungle and explosions and stuff.'

Dubbya inhaled noisily. 'I don't see how an inept film about political corruption in 1969, can help us solve the riddle here.'

'Unless that's the code,' suggested Tracey.

'What?" asked Dick, who was struggling to see what Mel Gibson had to do with East Bidding Technical College and dodgy deals.

'1969,' replied Tracey. 'Air America was set in 1969, dealing with covert CIA operations, corruption and undercover deals that the general public weren't supposed to know about.'

Dick thought on Tracey's analysis for a few moments. Reading through the rhyme again he pointed a finger at the third line. 'Where does the water bit fit in?' he asked.

'And,' sighed Dubbya. 'More to the point, why do we need to solve the riddle and why do we need a code?'

Everyone sat silently for a few moments. They'd each become caught up in the idea of solving the riddle without giving a moment's thought to the most basic question of *Why?*

Tracey nodded towards Dubbya. 'A good point,' she admitted. 'Perhaps we need to remind ourselves why we asked for advice.'

Dick grunted. 'My advice would be to forget the whole shebang, safest way all round.'

'Interesting,' replied Tracey patiently. 'As *Shebang* is slang for an affair or situation and possibly derived from the use of *Shebeen*, in Ireland meaning an illicitly made alcohol. So, a situation operating outside of the law is quite an apt description for what we are faced with.'

Dick held the back of his hand against his forehead. 'Just my luck to be involved with a walking lexicon.'

'You don't know how fortunate you are,' said Tracey with a raise of her eyebrows.

'I'm learning,' replied Dick. 'But it may take a while.'

'To the matter in hand,' interrupted Dubbya, fearing that the conversation was beginning to take on romantic hues once again. 'Correct me if I'm wrong,' he continued. 'But it's been suggested that we break-in to the Assistant Principal's office with a view to obtaining evidence that points to those involved in a possible scam.'

'We don't know what the scam is though,' Two-stroke reminded them.

'Apart from the fact that it involves the College, politicians, Councillors and dodgy business people,' said Dick ticking four fingers in turn.

'And loads of dosh,' grinned Two-stroke.

'Possibly more than we'll ever see in a lifetime,' said Dubbya gruffly.

'So,' said Tracey hurriedly before Dubbya became maudlin. 'We've got to break-in to a place where we're not technically breaking-in.'

'Except that the Assistant Principal keeps his door locked at all times,' said Dick with a wink. 'Behind closed doors eh?'

'Behind closed doors,' added Dubbya. 'The Assistant Principal plays computer games most of the day.'

'How do you know that?' asked Tracey.

'Because,' replied Dubbya grinning broadly. 'He forgets that his office is at the end of an 'L' shaped building. You can see directly into his lair from any of the rooms along the main corridor.'

'Rather remiss of him,' said Dick. 'Let's hope that he's just as remiss in locking away incriminating evidence.'

'And talking of locked doors,' smiled Tracey. 'Have you noticed how his door is locked?'

'I have,' said Two-stroke. 'He's got one of those fancy keypad things.'

'Exactly,' said Tracey softly. 'And what do we need to open the door?'

'Numbers,' grinned Two-stroke.

'Back to 1969, then?' asked Dick.

Tracey looked at him thoughtfully. His comments about the water mentioned in the riddle had made her think.

'I'm not so sure about the Air America link now,' she said. 'There's the water bit and the odd line about being chastised as a cruel blow.'

'There is the Mekong River in Laos,' said Dubbya. 'But I've no idea who was being chastised or why.'

Two-stroke leaned forward. 'There's Mad Max, Mad Max 2 and Beyond the Thunderdome,' he said eagerly.

Dick gave a long sigh. 'I think we're missing the obvious.'

'A typical male trait,' murmured Tracey.

'I'll pretend I didn't hear that,' said Dubbya feigning hurt.

Dick grabbed the notepaper and began circling some of the words in the riddle. 'Look,' he began. 'If we concentrate on the main words, we have *Gibson, wings, waters, chastised, cruel blow, gratitude and year*.'

'Why don't you just *Google* them,' suggested Two-stroke.

'Sounds like a job for someone who knows what they're doing,' suggested Tracey looking at Two-stroke. 'The computer's in the study go and see what you can find out.'

As Two-stroke ambled towards the study, Dick slouched off to the kitchen. 'I'll go and put the kettle on then,' he mumbled.

A few minutes later, Two-stroke walked into the lounge carrying a folded piece of paper and a huge grin. Sitting down, he took a sip of recently brewed tea and smiled contentedly.

'Well?' asked Dick.

'Lovely cup of tea, thanks,' replied Two-stroke. 'Just what I needed.'

'What did you find out?' said Tracey before Dick made a comment that she'd later regret.

'A cinch when you think about it,' replied Two-stroke taking a further sip of tea.

'Before the *ci* is replaced with *ly*, and used in the manner suggested,' threatened Dubbya. 'Would you please be so kind as to inform us of the outcome of your investigative endeavour?'

While Two-stroke's face displayed all the symptoms of confusion, Tracey leaned forward and touched his arm. 'What's on the paper?' she asked encouragingly.

'Ah, yes,' said Two-stroke. 'It wasn't anything to do with Mel, in the first place.'

'Glad we've got that sorted out,' said Dick with a hint of sarcasm.

'OK,' replied Two-stroke. He hesitated for a moment and then looked at his notes. 'It were Guy, not Mel.'

Dubbya nodded knowingly. 'I'm with you now.'

Dick looked to Tracey for some hint of explanation. Unfortunately, her face looked just as blank as his mind felt. 'Carry on, Two-stroke' said Dick with a little wave of his hand. 'Don't stop just when you were doing so well.'

Two-stroke wasn't at all sure whether he'd just experienced another sarcastic line or genuine encouragement. Deciding on the latter, he tapped the piece of paper. "What have the Sorpe, Möhne and Eder got in common?'

'I'm definitely with you,' declared Dubbya.

Dick gave a sigh of exasperation. 'OK, I'm not with you. So, could you please put me out of my misery and fill in the gaps for me.'

'All right,' relented Two-stroke. 'Wing Commander Guy Gibson commanded the dam busters raid on the three dams. That takes care of the Gibson and wings bit of the riddle.'

Both Tracey and Dick nodded encouragingly. Two-stroke smiled and read from his notes. 'The raid was called Operation Chastise and was meant to strike at the industrial Ruhr region of Germany. It sort of succeeded but the cruel blow was that over twelve hundred people drowned in the floods after the dams burst.'

Tracey smiled. 'Well done, Two-stroke, that gives us the year of?

'The 17 May,' replied Two-stroke. He paused for a moment. 'In the year 1943,' he said with a wave of the paper.

'We don't have to break-in after all,' said Dick with a smile. 'We just tap in the numbers and walk in.'

'Tracey shook her head. 'Aren't you forgetting something?' she asked.

'Sorry,' apologised Dick. 'I should have remembered. Ladies first.'

Tracey didn't say a word. She simply looked at Dick and gave a slight shake of the head. Dick, who thought a touch of chivalry was vastly underrated, swallowed noisily. 'And I've forgotten?' he asked nervously.

'You can't very well just walk in whenever you want to,' she said. 'Some sort of discretion is needed.'

'True,' mused Dubbya. 'We would need to enter the room when the Assistant Principal for External Affairs was performing his duty.'

'Preferably not in his room,' grinned Dick.

'Such base humour at times,' replied Dubbya with a sniff.

'Why not break-in late at night,' suggested Two-stroke eagerly. 'We could black our faces and wear dark clothes, synchronise watches and all that stuff.'

'Hang on,' interrupted Dick. 'That would be breaking-in as we'd have to force the main door to get into the building. Besides,' he added. 'I don't like the idea of leaving a warm bed in the middle of the night.' He blew Tracey a kiss.

'Steady,' warned Dubbya. 'Children still present.' Ignoring Two-stroke's look of bemusement, Dubbya tapped his chin thoughtfully. 'We'd need to do it while the college was still open, so as not to attract attention, but we don't want any witnesses.'

'You need a distraction,' announced Two-stroke. 'What if I set the fire alarms off?'

'And how would that look,' said Dick caustically. 'Being forcibly rescued by the fire brigade from the Assistant Principal's office clutching armfuls of documents and claiming that we were trying to save the College's valuables?'

'I think,' said Tracey offering Two-stroke the plate of biscuits for comfort. 'That Malc gave us the answer to our problem.'

'Really?' said Dick. 'I'd sort of assumed that Malc *was* a problem.'

'The fashion show,' laughed Tracey. 'While Malc's treating everyone to a hefty does of jazz, we can do what we need to do and be gone before you can say *Duke Ellington*.'

'Hmm,' murmured Dubbya. 'Slight problem there.'

'Where?' asked Tracey and Dick in unison.

'You are forgetting the minor fact that the Principal expects a show of unity, and that means all staff, both the ambitious and the ambivalent.'

'The proverbial three-line whip,' sighed Dick.

'In one, dear boy,' agreed Dubbya tersely. 'Believe me, he'll get to know one way or another if you fail to appear.' He gave a slight shake of the head. 'I don't want to even think about the repercussions of your non-attendance.'

A silence descended on the lounge as the four occupants exercised their neurons. Two-stroke's face twitched a few times and then he smiled.

'It's a fashion show, right?' he asked them. Three nods affirmed his statement. 'That being the case,' he continued. 'There will be a few dummies about.'

Tracey dissolved into giggles as she saw Dick's eyes dilate. 'You are quite right,' grinned Dick. 'The whole senior management team will be there.'

The smile on Two-stroke's face disappeared momentarily. 'I meant real dummies,' he moaned.

Tracey leaned forward and patted Two-stroke on the arm. 'I know,' she said wiping her eyes. 'So did Dick!' She patted Two-stroke's arm again. 'Carry on, I'm intrigued.'

Dick raised an eyebrow in query but refrained from making any further comment. 'Yes, do carry on, Two-stroke,' added Dick with a hint of encouragement.

'Well, what I meant was,' replied Two-stroke looking uncertainly at Dick. 'Is that we could nick a couple of dummies from the fashion department and dress them up like Dick and Tracey.'

Tracey clicked her fingers. 'That's brilliant,' she said. 'They'll be good company for Dubbya.'

Dubbya sucked at his top lip. 'I suppose they'll be an adequate substitute. With a little attention to detail, you'd be hard pressed to notice the difference from the real thing,' he said with a twinkle in his eyes. 'And I'm sure the conversation will be equally as stimulating,' he added.

Dick gave a snort. 'Ha, ha, so much,' he said flatly. 'But I have to admit, Two-stroke that it's a great idea.' He paused for a moment. 'Thinking about it,' he continued. 'With the dimmed lighting over the audience and all the attention on the catwalk, I doubt anyone will pay any attention to two more dummies sitting in rapt attention.'

'That's settled then,' declared Tracey. She smiled at Two-stroke. 'We will need your expert lookout skills while Dick and I make a thorough search of the Assistant Principal's office. Is that OK?'

Two-stroke grinned. 'Consider it done,' he replied confidently.

CHAPTER 40

Over the years, the fashion show had developed into the College's premier event of the season. From its humble beginnings as a transient display in the College's foyer, the fashion show had been quickly recognised as the ideal event for those seeking their first tottering steps on the pathway to shabby stardom.

After performing several circuits of the College car park, two of the College's lesser-known luminaries finally managed to abandon their car adjacent to an overgrown hawthorn hedge. Ignoring Tracey's consternation at being faced with a gear stick and handbrake to negotiate before she could clamber unceremoniously out of the car, Dick jumped out of his seat and stooped at the rear of the car.

'Dick!' hissed Tracey urgently. 'What do you think you're doing?' The last couple of words being forced between clenched teeth as she busily rearranged her clothing. Dick, his head appearing just above the rear indicator light, smiled weakly.

'Trying to be inconspicuous,' he whispered with a grin.

Tracey sighed deeply. She wasn't at all comfortable with the plans for the evening and the last thing she wanted was a clown for company. 'Stand up, for goodness sake,' she hissed angrily.

Dick, recognising the irritation in her voice as potentially life threatening, stood up and walked towards Tracey. Without speaking, she forcibly linked arms with Dick and set off across the car park at a furious pace.

Once inside the College, Tracey made no attempt to look for recognition in any of the faces that she passed by in a blur. With an apologetic grin to a couple of puzzled staff, Dick allowed himself to be hurried along the corridors until they were both safely ensconced in the lift. 'OK, Tracey, I can understand you being a bit miffed with me but that doesn't justify ignoring some of the people we work with.'

Tracey closed her eyes and gave a slight shake of the head. 'What's the point of trying to be inconspicuous if you insist on announcing our presence at every available opportunity?' Her shoulders shuddered slightly. 'You exasperate me sometimes.'

'Only sometimes?' smirked Dick. 'I'll have to practice more.' The jab in his ribs gave him a strong indication that any further comments would prove injurious. He gestured at the lift doors. 'Are we going somewhere?' he asked.

Tracey jabbed at the lift controls and a monotonous rumble accompanied their ascent. 'We've arranged to meet Dubbya in his office, remember?'

Dick gave a slight nod. 'I remember,' he replied. 'I'll be glad when this is all over.'

'Tonight or this whole mysterious mess?'

'Everything, the whole caboodle.' Dick sniffed noisily. 'I object to being here when I'm paid to be,' he grumbled. 'I object even more when I'm here voluntarily.'

Tracey frowned. 'How can you object to being here voluntarily,' she asked.

'You volunteered me.'

'So you'd prefer to let me do all this on my own,' she said icily.

'Don't be daft,' Dick retorted. 'How could I let you go and take all the credit?' He smiled in an attempt to defrost the atmosphere that had developed between them.

The opening of the lift doors silenced any further comment. Skipping along the passageway that led to Dubbya's office, the pair took a quick look around and knocked quietly on the door. Taking the grunt that emanated from behind the door as a welcome gesture, Dick and Tracey looked along the dimly lit corridors once more and quietly entered the room.

Immediately before them were three figures sitting with their backs towards the door. The middle figure, instantly recognisable as Dubbya, was busily tapping away at a computer keyboard.

'Make yourselves at home,' he called over his shoulder. 'I'll be with you in a moment'.

Dick and Tracey propped themselves against a filing cabinet while Dubbya finished exercising his fingers. With a final flourish of taps, Dubbya turned around and welcomed his visitors. 'I do so hope you find my humble abode agreeable,' he said with a smile playing upon his lips. He touched the shoulders of the figures sitting next to him. 'Dick, may I introduce you to Tracey, and Tracey, may I introduce you to Dick?' He slowly rotated the two office chairs to reveal his companions.

Staring open mouthed at the figures, Dick and Tracey faced a pair of mannequins loosely made up to resemble their namesakes. The female mannequin 's head was partially obscured by a mop of dark curly tresses that fell over its shoulders. What was visible of the face appeared to be crudely embellished with a range of cosmetic colours that Tracey hoped were not representative of her own attempts at beautification. The clothing Tracey recognised as being the outfit she'd recently put to one side to pop in a charity bag the next time one became entangled with her letter box.

'Cheers, Dick,' she said indicating her mannequin outfit that he'd given to Dubbya.

'And cheers to you,' replied Dick as he took in the male mannequin dressed in Dick's one and only suit. It wasn't the suit that Dick minded about so much as the floral shirt that his Aunt Vi had given him at Christmas. 'I haven't worn that yet,' he moaned gesturing at the shirt.

'I hope you hadn't any intention of inflicting retinal damage by wearing it anyway,' said Tracey wondering whether she had time to nip home and find a smarter outfit for the mannequin.

'I take it you approve?' enquired Dubbya with arched eyebrows. 'Of course,' he went on. 'We had little time to tease out the finer points of your respective features. However, given the circumstances, I think we've achieved a passable resemblance.'

Dick scratched his chin as he pondered on a response. Tracey, interpreting Dick's delay in answering Dubbya as a possible prelude to an altercation, smiled sweetly.

'It's fine, Dubbya,' she said. 'Besides, we haven't time for any modifications or alterations now.' She took a quick look at her watch. 'We need to get a move on. Our facsimiles need to be in place before the show kicks off.' Tracey instinctively tidied the hair on her mannequin. 'How are you planning to deploy our inert selves?' she asked Dubbya.

'Any moment now,' replied Dubbya glancing at his watch. 'Our willing but less than able accomplice will arrive to put our part of the plan into operation.' Almost on cue, the office door resounded to a dull thump. 'Come in, Two-stroke,' said Dubbya raising his voice. Two-stroke walked into the office with a broad grin.

'Wotcha,' he beamed. He nodded at the mannequins. 'I didn't recognise them with their clothes on,' he quipped.

Dick, Tracey and Dubbya looked at each other and groaned at Two-strokes feeble joke.

'Very droll,' sighed Dubbya.

Tracey smiled encouragingly. 'Where did you acquire these two fine specimens?' she asked Two-stroke.

'Easy,' he shrugged. 'They were the bits left over after the Fashion department had taken all the complete dummies down to the show.'

Tracey wagged her finger at Dubbya. 'No comments about senior management please.'

'As if I would,' Dubbya replied.

Concerned that her duplicate was made up from an apparent random collection of pieces, Tracey began to examine her model self more closely. After a few prods and tugs, she looked at Two-stroke. 'Am I safe?' she asked.

'Erm,' coughed a disconcerted Two-stroke.

'What Tracey means,' said Dick helpfully. 'Is will she fall to pieces?'

'Erm,' repeated Two-stroke beginning to feel embarrassed.

'The dummies?' suggested Dubbya giving a gentle hint.

'Oh yeah, right,' said a relieved Two-stroke. 'They'll be fine. I've used loads of sticky-tape to keep everything together.' He frowned slightly and looked at Dick. 'Pity about your two left legs though.'

Struggling to contain her laughter, Tracey clapped her hands together. 'Time to get going,' she gurgled.

Two-stroke and Dubbya picked up the dummies and prepared to leave the office. 'After you,' said Two-stroke who was holding the male dummy clumsily under its arms. Dubbya, balancing the Tracey lookalike carefully, smiled and began to waltz down the corridor with the dummy.

'Very nice,' exclaimed Tracey.

'You should see us tango,' called Dubbya over his shoulder.

Dick looked sternly at Two-stroke. 'Don't even think about it,' he warned.

Suitably advised, Two-stroke hobbled down the corridor with his arm around the dummy's waist. Dick closed his eyes and shook his head. 'I can't think which is worse, the dance or the amorous arm.'

'Don't worry,' soothed Tracey. 'No one will notice.'

Dick grunted.

'I love it when you go all articulate on me,' grinned Tracey.

Dick returned her smile and switched the light out in the office. He leaned forward and kissed what he hoped was Tracey's ear. 'Time for action,' he whispered.

'Shouldn't we ransack the Assistant Principal's office first?' queried Tracey with a smirk on her face that Dick couldn't see but knew was there.

'And I thought bad jokes were my domain,' he laughed.

'Can't have it all your own way,' said Tracey as she grabbed Dick's hand and led him out into the subdued light of the corridor.

Dick placed his arm around her waist. 'A waltz or foxtrot?'

CHAPTER 41

Lady Faulkner peered down at her damp shoes. The gathering twilight caused her footwear to appear almost nondescript, an image she had never envisaged when she first caught sight of the shoes glistening in the shop window. As she always did, Lady Faulkner had imagined the shoes matching various outfits that hung expectantly in her vast wardrobe. When she had decided that the shoes were suitable for pairing with several of her favourite outfits, and with the added bonus of being sufficiently eye-catching with just a hint of functionality, her husband had done the gentlemanly thing and handed over his credit card. Now, as she felt the evening dew permeate her shoes and stockings, she did wonder whether functionality should have been given a slightly higher priority. Lady Faulkner made a mental note to discuss the purchase of more practical shoes over breakfast the next morning. Thinking of her husband caused a trickle of guilt to run down her spine.

'Bobcat,' she wheezed. 'Is it much further?'

Bobcat, or more commonly referred to as the Chair of the Planning and Development Committee at the County Council, placed a finger to his lips and motioned for quiet. 'Not far, Popsicle,' he trilled. He glanced around and once again placed a finger to his lips. 'Do try to be quiet my love, we really don't want to attract unwanted attention, do we?'

Lady Faulkner breathed heavily. Her regular assignations with Bobcat had not contributed to her physical fitness at all, but had increased the level of guilt she felt each time she made some plausible excuse to her husband explaining her frequent evenings away from the marital home. Taking a lungful of damp air, she plodded after her lover into the descending darkness.

At night, the golf course assumed an almost unearthly character. The neatly groomed greens of the day became wild, hostile areas that seemed to protest at the presence of human forms. Lady

Faulkner paused in the pursuit of her lover and looked around at the foreboding shadows. She shuddered involuntarily. The dampness, that coiled snake-like around her ankles, made each step leaden, causing her to breathe heavily with the effort of movement. As she listened to the various sounds of wildlife that emanated from the undergrowth, Lady Faulkner began to feel increasingly uncomfortable. Both she and Bobcat were due to attend the College's fashion show later that evening and his little off-road diversion was proving to be disastrous for her heavily lacquered hair, her costume and her nerves. She felt isolated, guilt and discomfort weighed heavy on her senses. Lady Faulkner gave a little sob.

Out of the night, a pair of arms wrapped themselves around Lady Faulkner from behind. Squeezing tightly, the arms pulled her towards a waiting body. A shrill scream rang out across the golf course.

'Steady, my little Popsicle,' breathed Bobcat. 'It's only me, nothing to be scared of.'

Lady Faulkner relaxed into her lover's arms. The warmth from his body made her feel less vulnerable to the night. Bobcat gently turned Lady Faulkner to face him. With the vegetation forming a discreet screen behind him, Bobcat began to nuzzle her neck while his hands caressed her ample hips.

'Ah, my succulent Popsicle,' he crooned. 'I love the feel of you beneath my hands.' Suddenly, he felt Lady Faulkner stiffen in his arms. Bobcat turned his face to gaze into his lover's eyes. Her face wore a mask of terror, the whites of her eyes glistened in the moonlight. 'What is it my love?' he asked urgently. 'What's wrong?'

Lady Faulkner was unable to speak. Her mouth opened and closed in quick succession. Bobcat felt the hairs on the back of his neck bristle. 'It's not your husband is it?' he said with panic filling his voice. Lady Faulkner's lips trembled as she shook her head from side to side. Suddenly, a loud snorting sound echoed around the green as a cloud of hot, moist vapour wrapped itself around Bobcat's neck. The lovers collapsed into a rigid heap on the green at the thirteenth hole. The dark apparition, ignoring the comatose pair, melted away into the night.

CHAPTER 42

Although the National fashion paparazzi had yet to discover East Bidding Technical College, the local free newspaper considered the annual fashion show to be a visual extravaganza that rivalled the catwalks of London, Paris or Milan. Ignorant of the local tabloid fashion sensibilities, Dubbya and Two-stroke surveyed the scene in front of them while their partners looked on impassively.

The gym, which had been on the receiving end of the fashion students' ministrations for most of the week, was bedecked in a motley collection of items that wouldn't have looked out of place at the local waste disposal site. In fact, most of the items had actually been sourced from the rubbish site, which had proven to be inspirational for the *Recycle* theme of the show.

Even with the dim lighting casting sufficient shadows to obscure many of the less savoury objects on display, the garish sight still managed to stop Dubbya and Two-stroke in their tracks.

'Great Scott of the Antarctic,' exclaimed Dubbya. 'It's a veritable dump.'

Struggling for words, Two-stroke resorted to a quick shake of his head in disbelief at the copious amount of rubbish littering the walls. Leaving Two-stroke to support both of the mannequins, Dubbya quickly looked around for three inconspicuous seats.

Most of the audience were sitting engrossed in conversation as snatches of jazz music wafted over their heads. Malc, from Regeneration Sounds, had compiled a broad selection of jazz music that complimented the discordant décor of the gym. Dubbya peered through the semi-darkness at the sea of heads, frantically searching for the relevant number of gaps to accommodate himself and his two inert accomplices. After a nerve-wracking few seconds, he caught sight of a suitable location towards the rear of the gym. Ambling towards the gap, Dubbya smiled at the generously endowed woman sitting next to the empty seats.

'Excuse me, madam,' said Dubbya. 'But might I impose on your company and have the pleasure of sitting next to you?'

The woman adjusted her glasses and squinted at the bulk of Dubbya. She retuned his smile. 'Of course,' she replied patting the adjacent seat. 'Do make yourself comfortable.'

Dubbya nodded his acceptance. 'I'll return in one moment,' he said with a slight bow. Hurrying over to the agitated form of Two-stroke, he placed an arm around each of the mannequins and hobbled back to the waiting seats.

Nearing his destination, Dubbya saw two figures suddenly appear out of the shadows. His heart skipped several beats as he recognised the Principal immersed in conversation with a tall, balding figure. As they approached, the Principal caught sight of Dubbya.

'Ah, Mr, hum, yes,' stumbled the Principal, pushing his spectacles towards his eyebrows. 'I wonder, have you seen our Chair of Governors, Lady Faulkner?' He indicated the tall figure next to him. 'Her husband appears to have mislaid her.'

Dubbay swallowed noisily. 'Er, I'm afraid not, Principal. Only just arrived, traffic you know,' he said quickly.

'Yes, quite,' replied the Principal. 'Well, should you happen to see her, would you please inform her that her presence is requested most urgently. Thank you.' He looked at Dubbya's companions. 'I do hope the three of you have a most enjoyable evening.'

As the two figures merged into the darkness, Dubbya patted his chest. 'Be still my beating heart,' he murmured. Breathing heavily, he manoeuvred the mannequins between the rows of seats until he stood next to the voluminous lady.

'Hello again,' she cooed. 'Your friends arrived safely then,' she observed.

'Hello,' smiled Dubbya, as he arranged the male mannequin on the seat next to the lady. 'All safe and sound.' His fragile confidence immediately vanished as, in his attempt to place the female mannequin on her seat, he stumbled on the feet of the male mannequin and sat in an undignified heap on the chair with Tracey's lookalike sitting on his lap. The large lady smirked.

'Now, now,' she grinned. 'Time and place you know.'

Dubbya fought the rising tide of embarrassment and hastily

rearranged the mannequin onto the seat next to him. Dick's counterpart appeared to be coping well with the enforced seating arrangement. Occasionally, the large lady leaned forward and gave the mannequin a wink from behind her glasses only to see her advances rebuffed as the figure stared stoically forward. Grateful that one of the mannequins was behaving, Dubbya glanced at Tracey's impersonator and was horrified to see that the wig had slipped dangerously to one side giving her a sort of 1980's New Romantic hairstyle. As discretely as possible, Dubbya slipped his hand behind the mannequin and adjusted the hairpiece.

For the next few minutes, Dubbya was completely occupied with pushing the recalcitrant wig back into place. Eventually, he gave up the unequal struggle and embraced the mannequin with his left arm, ensuring that his hand was strategically placed to hold the wig in position throughout the show. All around him the audience began to get restive. Each time the music began to fade, the audience would become quiet, expectantly awaiting the show to begin. Unfortunately, Malc's DJ abilities were not quite up to the demanding standards of a fashion show audience and the music would once again make itself heard over the hubbub of impatient fashion connoisseurs.

During these all too frequent pauses in sound, Dubbya noticed the large lady becoming increasingly familiar with the male mannequin. At first, she limited her activity to a surreptitious connection of thighs. When this didn't appear to have the effect she desired, she moved on to rubbing her foot up and down the mannequin's shin. Dubbya couldn't quite believe what was happening and he too began to get impatient with the delay in proceedings in the fashion department.

Despite the unsolicited attention of the large lady, Dick's counterpart smiled resolutely. There were one or two moments when Dubbya thought he might need to intervene but, on the whole, the mannequin seemed to be dealing admirably with the physical demands of the lady. Thankfully, just when she appeared to be on the verge of implementing a new strategy, by walking her fingers across the mannequin's shoulder, a thunderous roll of dustbin timpani reverberated around the room. The audience gasped and one or two hands were seen to cover their ears including, much to Dubbya's relief, the mannequin's lady friend.

The *Recycling* theme of the show had extended to the orchestral section where various items normally associated with a scrap-yard had been pressed into service. The dustbin timpani had, until two hours before the show, been happily employed in the catering department of the college and their return later in the evening would hopefully go unnoticed, apart from the musically imparted dents and dings that might, incorrectly, be attributed to the local feline scavenging pack the next morning.

Once the crescendo of drumming echoed into oblivion, the curtains rose on a fanfare of tuneless trumpets, to reveal a stage laden with refuse. As the clouds of dry ice made their entrance, a gentle hubbub of chatter began. The audience seemed unsure how to respond to the virtual tip that presented itself before them. A ripple of applause stuttered amongst a small section of the audience, which quickly transformed into a chorus of embarrassed coughs when nobody else seemed at all keen on approving of the rubbish in front of them. Sensing a perplexed audience, a stagehand hastily gestured towards the left side of the stage. Almost immediately, a low rumble rolled around the floor as the rear of an imitation dustcart crept into view. Once stationary, a small procession of fashion models appeared to emerge from the dustcart. This time the applause moved like a raging tide around the audience as any earlier anxiety was quickly forgotten at the sight of the eagerly anticipated models. Displaying an assortment of torn fabrics loosely held in place by plastic bows and string, the models began their parade along the catwalk.

The large lady patted the arm of the male mannequin excitedly. 'What's going on?' she squeaked. Pushing her glasses closer to her face, she squinted in the direction of the stage. 'Aren't you going to tell me?' The mannequin remained expressionless, unmoved by the procession littered in front of it. The large lady snuggled closer to the mannequin. 'I do so love the tall, silent type,' she murmured.

Dubbya, with his arm firmly around the female mannequin, checked that the wig was still in place and closed his eyes at the whole scenario developing on the stage and either side of him. All he could hope for now was that Dick and Tracey were making the most of the time available to them. He wasn't sure how long he could keep the pretence going, but one thing was certain, if the large lady made any further physical advances towards the male mannequin, she just might find less than she bargained for.

CHAPTER 43

Tracey tugged at Dick's sleeve. 'I'm getting cold feet,' she whispered urgently. Dick paused in his stride. 'This isn't the time or place to use my back for warming your feet on,' he growled. 'You'll have to wait.' Tracey jabbed him savagely in the ribs. 'That isn't what I meant and you know it,' she hissed.

Since leaving Dubbya's office, Dick and Tracey had remained silent, creeping amongst whatever shadows were left undisturbed by the minimalistic lighting of the College's eco-friendly policy. Normally, the journey to the floor where the Assistant Principal's office was located would have taken a few minutes. On this occasion, the couple seemed to have been walking for hours, barely drawing breath and treading as lightly as their bodies would allow along the corridors. Finally, they'd managed to negotiate the various twists and turns of the building to arrive at their destination.

Dick, bravely ignoring Tracey's venomous riposte, politely tapped on the door of the Assistant Principal's door.

Tracey gasped. 'What are you doing?' she whispered sharply. She took a quick glance along the corridor. 'Are you trying to draw attention to our little escapade?'

Dick shook his head. 'Of course not,' he replied. 'I just thought I'd better check that he wasn't using his office.'

Tracey nodded towards the little window in the door. 'There isn't a light on,' she said firmly. Dick smiled.

'He doesn't always conduct his business with the light on,' he grinned.

Tracey sighed knowingly. 'Point taken,' she breathed. 'Come on, let's get on with it.'

Dick rested his shoulder against the door and gently turned the handle. The door remained obstinately closed. He turned to Tracey and smiled. 'Worth a try,' he said. 'What was that Gibson number again?'

It was Tracey's turn to smile. 'Do I get to warm my feet later?' she asked.

Dick gave a gentle snort. 'There's always a catch,' he groaned. 'OK, warm feet, now tell me the number before I change my mind.'

'That'll be a first where physical contact is concerned,' she joked. Dick gave her a stern twitch of his eyebrows. '1943,' she grinned openly.

Dick tapped in the required numbers and tried the handle again. This time the door opened smoothly into the room. As he stepped to one side, allowing Tracey to explore the dark interior of the office, Dick's nostrils immediately picked up the musky aroma of aftershave tinged with the stale scent of feet. He breathed heavily.

'Terrible, isn't it,' Tracey replied in answer to his unspoken statement. 'How can anyone fancy someone who needs to bathe their feet in aftershave?'

Dick grinned in the darkness. 'Animal magnetism?' he suggested. Ignoring Tracey's grunt of disgust, he dug in his pocket for his car keys, which also held a small key fob light. Pressing the dull beam of light into action, Dick shuffled towards the Assistant Principal's desk. He sat down behind the desk and began to open the desk drawers in turn. He heard Tracey give a cough of annoyance.

'Sometimes I wonder about you,' she muttered.

'What?' asked Dick, preoccupied with sifting through the administrative detritus of the desk drawers.

Tracey gave a slight tut and switched on the desk lamp. A warm glow pushed the shadows against the office walls. Dick blinked in the aura of the lamp. This new light on the proceedings worried him. He had no intention of getting caught and having to explain his presence in the office or, worse still, he didn't want a repeat of his warehouse experience. He touched his cheek gingerly. It still felt tender from the overt physical attention it'd received a couple of days before. Dick frowned at Tracey.

'Isn't that risky?' he asked indicating the lamp. Tracey shook her head.

'I think it's riskier struggling under the sheer brilliance of your fob light,' she said cynically. 'At the rate you're going, we've more chance of being caught by the cleaners in the morning than we have of finding whatever it is we're supposed to find.'

'OK,' said Dick. 'Why don't you tackle the filing cabinets while I continue rummaging through the desk?'

Without a word, Tracey turned her attention to the wall of filing cabinets lining one side of the office.

Opposite the line of cabinets sat two leather chairs and a magazine-strewn coffee table. A small wooden bookcase stood behind one chair with various pristine books on its shelves that seemed more concerned with medieval history than modern education. Beneath the shelves rested two doors that hid a fine selection of malt whisky and several bottles of nondescript sparkling wine. Tracey knew precisely what the lay behind the doors from her one and only visit to the office two years before.

It was the Assistant Principal's custom to invite each new female employee for an introductory chat and informal welcome to the college. Although, during her time in the office, Tracey had insisted on drinking the cup of weak coffee provided, the Assistant Principal had equally insisted on showing her his drinks cupboard and peppered the conversation with frequent hints for her to enjoy a little tipple with him at a more mutually convenient time. If the sniggers of several students on her way to the office hadn't provided sufficient warning, the smug attitude of the Assistant Principal and his questionable taste in vibrant shirts and gaudy cufflinks were adequate warning of his unwelcome welcome. Tracey had left the office with her dignity and self-respect intact but her trust in senior management and hair gel completely shattered.

The filing cabinets had succumbed surprisingly easily to Tracey's persuasive touch. She quickly sorted through the plethora of files relating to numerous failed sponsorship strategies, business partnerships and implausible franchise arrangements. A rather large file, partially hidden behind several reams of committee minutes, proved to be quite a distraction for Tracey. However, the detailed personnel notes and ratings for the majority of female staff at the college, along with very revealing handwritten annotations by the Assistant Principal, failed to shed any real light on the business in hand. Reluctantly, Tracey returned the notes to their file and continued searching through the remaining filing cabinets.

Tracey dropped onto one of the leather chairs. 'Nothing,' she said flatly. 'Not a thing that would help us identify the miscreants behind whatever's going on.'

'Nothing at all?' asked Dick.

Tracey shook her head. 'Not unless you're interested in knowing what our illustrious Assistant Principal for External Affairs thinks about most of the women working at the college.'

'Really?' said Dick half rising from his chair.

'Don't even think about it,' warned Tracey with a threatening finger. 'It'd be more than your love life is worth.'

Dick sank back into the chair. He felt totally deflated. This whole affair seemed to be a complete waste of time. He looked over at Tracey who appeared to be equally dispirited. 'Any ideas?' he asked.

Tracey shook her head and then paused. She thought for a moment and then looked earnestly at Dick. 'Tell me again how everyone knows that the Assistant Principal plays computer games,' she said, a smile beginning to play on her lips.

Dick shrugged. 'Through the window,' he replied. He turned in his chair and pointed towards the building that ran at ninety-degrees to the office. 'From over there.'

'How?' asked Tracey.

'You can see his screen here,' replied Dick pointing to one side of the desk.

'How?' repeated Tracey.

'Precisely, how?' nodded Dick in agreement. Pulling open the bottom drawer of the desk, Dick extracted a lap-top and placed it on the table. Within seconds the screen displayed the college logo and a desktop full of animated icons. Tracey touched the edge of the screen.

'How can anyone see what he's doing on that screen?' she asked.

Dick grinned. 'Third set of windows on the left is the drama room. A casual exploration with opera glasses, word gets around and before you know it binoculars are an integral part of the curriculum offer.'

Tracey frowned. 'I think voyeurism is on the curriculum, not binoculars.' She tapped the lap-top. 'Shall we search?'

Dick deftly moved the cursor over the icons and explored their contents. After a few minutes, Dick and Tracey gave a mutual sigh of frustration.

'Simply a repetition of the stuff you've found in the filing cabinets,' he shrugged. 'It's his usual belt and braces approach.' He looked up and smiled at Tracey. 'He sent me an email once, followed by an internal memo, a phone call from his personal assistant and a visit from her an hour later wanting to know why I hadn't replied immediately to his email.' He gave a sarcastic laugh. 'They conveniently forget that we have students to teach.'

Tracey nudged his shoulder. 'Stop moaning and find something,' she insisted.

After a few more clicks of the mouse, Dick shook his head. 'There's only one file left.' He indicated a folder with an icon depicting a palm tree. 'Sun, sea and surf it's called.' He double-clicked the folder. 'Have we time to look at his holiday snaps?'

Tracey stared at the screen. 'This looks a bit stubborn,' she said indicating the still closed folder. Dick clicked again and a text-box appeared asking for a password.

'1943, again,' he suggested.

'Doubtful,' replied Tracey. 'But try it anyway.'

The screen displayed an *invalid password* warning. 'Any ideas,' asked Dick. Tracey shook her head. 'It must be something memorable,' she replied. 'He has a reputation for being unable to retain any information that doesn't relate to his particular interests.'

'Talking of his particular interests,' laughed Dick. 'Who is his latest love interest?'

Tracey thought for a moment and then walked over to the filing cabinet containing the female personnel details. She flicked through several small files before selecting one that appeared less dog-eared than the others. 'Just guessing,' she grinned.

Dick took the file from her and scanned the information. He smiled to himself and tapped six digits into the text box. The screen replied with an *invalid password* warning.

'Damn,' muttered Dick. 'I was pretty certain that would be the password.'

Tracey glanced at the screen. 'Are you sure he'd remember her vital statistics?' she asked.

Dick shrugged. 'It was worth a try.' He studied the file once more and tapped in another idea. The same *invalid password* invaded the screen. 'Double damn,' groaned Dick. 'If this system is anything like the one in our office, we have one try left before we're frozen out of the computer.'

Tracey sat on the edge of the desk. 'We could always take the computer and get Two-stroke to have a look at it,' she suggested.

Dick raised his eyebrows. 'Are you sure a hammer would work,' he asked.

Tracey smiled. 'No, but he is rather good at games and things and,' Dick smacked the desk with his hand. 'You're brilliant,' he said smiling. 'Remind me to kiss you later.'

Whatever you say,' grinned Tracey. She nodded at the computer. 'Although I'd never normally refuse your advances, it'd be nice to know why you desire to kiss me so urgently.'

'Games,' said Dick eagerly. 'It's a game.' He quickly tapped at the keyboard and the folder opened to reveal several sub-folders, each seemingly referring to details of meetings, finances, businesses and people. 'You beauty,' he laughed.

Tracey looked at him quizzically. Dick caught her face in his hands and kissed her nose. 'On account,' he grinned. He motioned towards the computer screen. 'Solitaire,' he said triumphantly. 'He plays it all the time.'

Dick quickly opened the meetings folder. Instantly, pages of minutes appeared detailing discussions held by a group of people, denoted by their initials, and describing a range of strategies that would result in a hotel and leisure complex being built on the College's playing fields. Skipping to the most recent notes, Dick read for a moment and then gave a low whistle.

'Strewth,' he breathed. 'This goes beyond petty pilfering.'

'What does?' asked Tracey excitedly.

Dick pointed to the computer screen. 'This is not just a scam to get a prime site location for a hotel on the cheap.' His eyes closed and groaned. Tracey nudged his shoulder.

'Tell me then.'

Dick opened his eyes and looked at her. 'The hotel is just phase one of their project.'

'And phase two is?' asked Tracey as she tried to see what was illuminated on the screen.

'Phase two,' answered Dick. 'Is to build a casino and theatre.'

Tracey grabbed the computer mouse and moved the document around the screen. 'Where do they plan to build that lot?' she asked.

'Here,' replied Dick. He placed his hand on hers and steadied the erratic movements of the mouse. He highlighted a section of text on the screen. 'As I told you,' he sighed. 'Here.'

Tracey looked at the screen and then at Dick. 'But how?' she asked. Dick rested his head in his hands and rubbed his eyes. Blearily he looked at Tracey.

'They plan to totally demolish the college, down to the last brick and satellite dish. Goodbye East Bidding Technical College and welcome Las Vegas, East Bidding style.'

'They can't do that,' said Tracey angrily. 'They'd be far too many complaints.'

'Not if you nobble every last person involved in the decision-making process.'

Tracey nodded. She was beginning to understand the enormity of the situation. 'From the Chair of Governors through to the County Council,' she said sighing.

'Correct,' said Dick tapping the desk agitatedly. 'Don't forget the local MP who, for a welcome donation to his pension fund will make sure that your interests are kept in your interest.'

Tracey double-clicked another sub-folder and began looking through the list of names that filled the computer screen. After a few seconds she walked over to the far wall and removed a framed photograph. Walking back to the desk she handed the picture to Dick. 'Recognise anyone?' she asked.

Dick held the picture closer to the comforting glow of the desk lamp. The picture had obviously been hanging around for quite some time, as some of the figures and faces appeared slightly washed-out. Despite the blanching effect of sunlight, Dick instantly recognised two of the figures as being erstwhile friends from the steam room and golf course. He indicated the figures to Tracey. 'They seem to get around,' he quipped.

Tracey forced a smile. 'Don't they just,' she replied. 'Recognise any other rogues from the gallery?'

He placed a finger on one of the female figures in the picture. 'I'm not sure,' he murmured. 'But that could be our Chair of Governors before she discovered the virtues of indolence.'

Tracey nodded in agreement. 'There's no mistaking that lack of dress sense,' she replied scathingly. She stabbed a finger at two of the male figures. 'And there's our Assistant Principal with our joke of an MP.'

Dick scanned the other faces in the picture but didn't recognise any of their features. 'Can't say I know who the rest are, but given their penchant for loud suits and heavyweight watches, they must be some other elements of the business underclass.'

'Whatever and whoever they are, I can't imagine our Assistant Principal associating with anyone that didn't have their own interest at heart.'

Dick smiled. 'You've become quite cynical lately,' he jested. Tracey shrugged and took a memory stick out of the top pocket of her jacket.

'You've thought of everything,' he said approvingly.

'Always be prepared,' replied Tracey as she inserted the memory stick into the computer. Dick frowned.

'I thought that was the boy-scout motto.'

Tracey grinned at him. 'You didn't think I was a girl guide do you?'

'Well ... ' mumbled Dick.

Tracey kissed his forehead. 'Camping was always more fun with the scouts.'

After making a few movements of the computer mouse, Tracey disappeared under the desk and started to crawl around the floor. Dick looked on in amazement.

'What on earth do you think you are doing?' he asked. Tracey made no response to his question but simply kept shuffling around under the desk. 'Please yourself,' grumbled Dick. He opened another sub-folder on the computer and looked at the architect's schematics filling the screen. 'It's all here,' said Dick to the desk. A grunt sounded from under the desk. Dick shrugged. 'Everything from the type of roofing material to the colour of the taps in the lavatory.' He opened another sub-folder and gasped in surprise. 'There's other plans here for what looks like a World War Two air-raid shelter made out of glass, but on a much larger scale,' he added.

'That'd be for the new college building in the centre of town,' explained Tracey emerging from her carpet crawl.

'Feminine intuition?' asked Dick with a grin.

'Hardly,' replied Tracey as she tapped busily at the computer keys. 'They'd never get away with demolishing the college and putting nothing in its place.' She tapped the keyboard with a final flourish. 'Done,' she said happily. She smiled at Dick. 'Bit of a smokescreen,' she explained. 'But the easiest way to make the whole scam work was to propose a brand new, purpose built college to replace the ageing monolith that currently exists.'

'I suppose so,' agreed Dick. 'But still plenty of room for the odd slip-up or two.'

'That's where the good old miscellaneous funds come into play,' explained Tracey. 'Lubricate a few important cogs and we have motion. Especially if you could pay for a lab report to suggest that the current building has traces of asbestos. Health and safety would have a field day, shut the place down before you could say myxomatosis.'

'That's to do with rabbits,' retorted Dick with a grin. 'Not an industrial disease.'

Tracey snorted. 'Pay the lab enough and you can have any 'tosis from the menu.'

Dick nodded in agreement. 'It also explains,' he added. 'Why the Principal keeps going on about restructuring and efficiency measures.'

Tracey scratched her nose, as if the conversation was beginning to irritate her. 'Precisely,' she replied. 'And I think he's also guessed that it's unlikely the powers that be would appoint him as the Chief Executive of the New Centre of Excellence.'

'I wouldn't appoint him to manage a bag of jelly babies,' said Dick. He removed the memory stick and replaced the computer into the desk drawer. 'Time we were away from here,' he said walking towards the door. Tracey switched the desk lamp off and began to follow Dick. He opened the door and turned to Tracey. 'We'd better go and relieve Dubbya from his chaperone duties,' he said smiling.

'Going somewhere?' asked a vaguely familiar voice.

Dick tried to identify the owner of the voice in the depressing gloom of the corridor. Suddenly, he felt a sickening pain between his eyes and the corridor became totally black.

CHAPTER 44

'It's another one Sarge,' called PC Ricketts lazily cradling the phone on her shoulder.

Sergeant Cost exhaled noisily. He wondered, after all these years, whether he was beginning to lose his grip on the job or whether the standard of police recruits were slowly deteriorating over time.

'PC Ricketts,' he said sternly. 'It's never *Sarge* or any other corruption of the correct form of address to a superior officer.'

PC Ricketts looked directly at the sergeant. There were plenty of other names, corrupt or not, that she'd like to call him but, on this occasion she resisted the temptation. 'Sorry, Sergeant,' she said meekly. 'But we have another incident involving the apparition.'

Sergeant Cost laid his newspaper and pen carefully on the table. He took a deep breath and looked equally carefully at PC Ricketts. He was now more convinced than ever that initiative was something that had been surgically removed at some stage during Rickett's formative years. He cleared his throat with a low rumble.

'The details, if you please,' he said acidly. 'Time, place, people involved, injuries, damage, and why can't it wait until morning?' Sergeant Cost lowered his gaze and examined his fingernails. 'Ascertain the facts, PC Ricketts, before you ignore the obvious with such enthusiasm.' He picked up his pen and resumed his battle with twelve across in the quick crossword.

PC Ricketts turned her back on the sergeant and began speaking into the phone. She made several notes responding with an affirming noise each time the caller gave her the relevant answers to her questions. Eventually, satisfied that she had all the information she required, PC Ricketts thanked her caller and pushed the phone under a pile of forms.

'Sergeant?' she crooned politely.

Sergeant Cost slowly raised his head from the study of twelve down. 'Yes, PC?'

PC Ricketts smiled. 'Are we interested in two chairs on a golf course?'

Sergeant Cost sighed. He placed the pen next to his newspaper and slowly stood up. He could feel a vein throbbing in his neck and his palms were beginning to sweat. 'PC Ricketts,' he began. 'This,' he gestured at their surroundings. 'May not be quite the salubrious form of accommodation that you're accustomed to. However,' he continued. 'It is warm, dry and protects us from the prevailing winds and the general public.' He ran a finger around the inside of his collar. 'I have no wish to exchange our austere shelter,' he banged his fist down on the table. 'For two bloody chairs on a golf course.'

PC Ricketts smiled infuriatingly. 'My apologies, Sergeant,' she said calmly. 'I didn't make myself clear. We have the local College's Chair of Governors and the County Council's Chair of the Planning and Development Committee unconscious on the green at the thirteenth hole.'

Sergeant Cost raised a questioning eyebrow. 'And?' he asked.

'They were discovered by a man walking his dog approximately forty minutes ago.'

'He is obviously sufficiently well acquainted with the said individuals to recognise them in their slumbers,' said the sergeant sarcastically.

'It appears he recognised them from pictures he'd seen in the local press,' replied PC Ricketts. 'I won't repeat the names he initially called them but Mr Gresley decided it was better that he rang from home as he wasn't supposed to be walking his dog on the golf course.'

'Did he ring for an ambulance while he was at it?' enquired the sergeant.

'No,' replied PC Ricketts with a shrug. 'He says he wasn't sure whether they were just slumbering after, you know, afterwards.'

'Afterwards?' asked the sergeant, keenly intent on any possibility of embarrassing the PC. 'After what precisely?'

PC Ricketts was fully prepared for the question. 'After whatever it was that caused their bodies to go into a state of temporary hibernation.'

Sergeant Cost loosened his collar once again. 'Stop being so bloody clever and get an ambulance out there straight away,' he ordered. 'And after you've done that make me a cup of tea.'

PC Ricketts smiled to herself as she recovered the phone from its hiding place. She wondered what the maximum heart rate was for a man of Sergeant Cost's age and whether an extra strong mug of coffee would significantly raise that level? With a smile she pressed the required digits on the phone and made a note to ring one of the many helpful doctors at the hospital.

CHAPTER 45

Dick became conscious of a small circle of extremely bright light searing his retina. He blinked, closed his eyes for a few moments, blinked again but still the light persisted. He couldn't believe what he was seeing. It was too corny, a cinematic cliché, something that you laughed at or ridiculed but definitely not something you ever thought you'd experience first-hand. He tried to raise a hand to rub his eyes but his arm felt heavy, impossible to lift. At the edge of his senses he could hear a voice calling his name, a gentle, soothing voice that repeated his name over and over again. He shook his head, or at least he thought he shook his head but he couldn't be certain. Everything seemed surreal, otherworldly and most certainly not where he wanted to be. The circle of light beckoned him and the voice called out once again.

'Dick,' said the voice softly. 'Dick, come on now.'

He felt a hand stroke his face, a warm hand that both comforted him and concerned him. Was he that close to death that he could feel its hand?

'Dick,' called the voice urgently. 'You can't stay there for ever.'

Dick felt his pulse racing. Pulse? Surely if he had a pulse he wasn't dead or even close to it. He forced his eyes open. The circle of light still shone in front of him. He groaned.

'For goodness sake, Dick,' urged the voice. 'Come on now.'

Dick groaned again and swallowed. 'Where am I?' he asked the voice.

'Where you shouldn't be,' growled a new voice.

'What?' cried Dick. He turned his head slightly to one side and could just about make out shadows in human form. 'Why am I here?'

'We thought you might like to tell us,' answered an almost recognisable voice.

Dick felt the gentle hand caress his cheek. The hand slowly moved over his head and settled on his forehead. 'Ouch!' he yelled. 'That hurts.'

The voice cackled. 'You walked into my fist just as I was about to knock on the door.'

'Thug,' spat the former gentle voice.

'Tracey?' enquired Dick, his head throbbing.

'Here, Dick,' she replied. 'It's OK, you blacked out for a moment that's all.'

'Tracey?'

'Yes, Dick?'

'Could you take that light out of my eyes now?'

Tracey immediately switched off the fob light and tucked it in her pocket. 'Sorry, Dick, I was just so concerned about you after that bait-breeder hit you.'

'Steady lass,' advised another voice that Dick thought sounded all too familiar. 'You don't want to go antagonising my friend here.'

Dick tried to identify the voice and face. He frowned slightly and then wished he hadn't as the pain came flooding back. The memory came flooding back too as he suddenly remembered where he'd heard that voice before. 'Jonesy?'

Jonesy chuckled. 'I was being to feel quite hurt that you hadn't recognised my dulcet tones.' He chuckled again. 'How have you been keeping?'

'Could be better,' replied Dick. 'And I suppose you've brought your pet ape along with you?'

He heard a chair make violent contact with a wall as Jonesy's pet ape took exception to Dick's taunt.

Jonesy laid a restraining hand on his mate.

'Steady both of you,' he commanded. 'This needn't get nasty.'

'What other scenario did you expect?' hissed Tracey. 'Where you're concerned it seems *nasty* is the only dish on the menu.'

'Such a sweet mouth too,' cooed Jonesy. 'No!' he said sternly, again laying a restraining hand on his mate. 'Not now.'

'What have you done to my hands?' demanded Dick in an attempt to distract attention away from Tracey.

'A temporary precaution,' said Jonesy without apology. 'We didn't want you walking into any more fists.'

Dick tried to pull his hands free from their bindings but realised that a piece of rope bound one wrist and then, passing under the leather chair, made an all too tight connection with his other wrist. He turned to Tracey.

'I gather we're still in the office?'

'We never left,' she answered. 'As soon as you fell to the floor these two bundled you onto the chair and tied you up.'

Dick leaned as far forward in the chair as he could. 'They haven't hurt you have they?'

Before Tracey could reply, Jonesy coughed. 'What do you take us for, Dick?' he asked. 'We may not get invited to afternoon tea at the Palace, but we do have some principles.'

Jonesy's mate began to laugh coarsely. 'Enjoyed searching her.'

Dick tried to kick out towards the voice but only managed to move air. Tracey placed a hand on his shoulder. 'Don't waste your effort on him. He got no further than my back pocket.'

'But where did he start from?' asked Dick angrily.

'Sssh,' soothed Tracey stroking his cheek. 'It doesn't matter now.'

Jonesy sighed happily. 'Just in case you were wondering, Dick. Yes, we've got the memory stick.' Dick heard a sharp crack and Jonesy chuckle. 'Whoops, silly me, I've gone and broken it.'

Dick sniffed. 'What a shame.'

Jonesy gave another infuriating chuckle. 'Before sarcasm gets the better of you, it might help you to know that we've also wiped the hard drive of the computer clean.'

Dick felt his shoulders sag. It felt like the proverbial so near yet so far. With no evidence what could they do now? Jonesy was thinking the same.

'All your evidence gone the minute you lay your hands on it.' Jonesy snorted with mirth. 'What are you going to do now?'

Tracey turned to Dick. 'Don't worry, we'll think of something.'

Jonesy's mate cracked his knuckles. 'Hardly worth your time,' he grunted. 'But please don't let me stop you, well, not until you try something and then I will have to stop you.' He cracked his knuckles again.

Dick winced. 'Don't do that.'

'Frightened are we?' asked Jonesy's mate. 'Just like at the warehouse?'

'Not at all,' replied Dick blithely. 'It's just that you might do your joints a permanent injury and we wouldn't want that to happen would we?' Dick coughed loudly. 'Besides, the sound makes me want to throw up.' He pretended to retch. 'I wouldn't sit too close if I were you.'

Jonesy's mate stepped back quickly. 'What we going to do with this pair?' he asked, giving Jonesy a look of irritation.

'Why should we do anything?' he replied. 'They can't do anything, they've no evidence now.'

Tracey looked at them coldly in the gloom of the office. 'The Assistant Principal will have a back-up somewhere. He wouldn't rely on the computer as his only form of insurance should anything go wrong with your scam.'

Jonesy chuckled annoyingly. 'He can have as many copies as he likes, but we'll have dealt with him well before he gets a chance to use his insurance.'

'Is that the only way you can deal with things,' spat Tracey. 'Violence and threats?'

'Oh we can be subtle at times,' replied Jonesy. 'But I find subtlety takes so long to work when you want things done in a hurry.'

'Can you hear that?' asked Jonesy's mate.

'Hear what?' said Jonesy.

'That scratching sound, listen.'

Everyone listened. Faintly, almost indistinguishable from the background noise of the fashion show came a gentle *miaow*.

'It's a cat,' said Jonesy dismissively. 'Nothing to bother about.'

'Cat?' said Tracey in Dick's ear. 'Since when did we have cats in the college?'

'Don't ask me,' replied Dick. 'I only work here.'

Jonesy nudged his mate. 'Go and make sure it's nothing more than a lousy moggy.'

His mate strolled over to the door and carefully opened the door. 'Here puss, puss,' he called gruffly into the darkness. 'Come to daddy you mangy cat.'

'Looking for someone?' asked a deep voice. Jonesy's mate managed to gargle a brief response before being doused with a fire extinguisher. Jonesy barely had time to rise from his chair before he too was engulfed in foam.

CHAPTER 46

Jonesy opened his eyes to see a crowd staring down at him. He shivered slightly and quickly realised that it wasn't just the sea of eyes that unnerved him, but the cold draught that wrapped itself around him where his clothes had once been. He tried to open his mouth in protest but the Gaffa-tape held firm.

'Why, hello there,' said Dick with a huge grin. He extended an arm to indicate the group of students standing around Jonesy and his mate. 'The welcome committee,' Dick jerked his head towards the group, 'would like to take this opportunity to thank you for visiting East Bidding College and hope that your stay is as short and uncomfortable as possible.'

Jonesy's eyes bulged in anger. He attempted to wriggle free of the Gaffa-tape that bound his hands and feet too, but only succeeded in ripping a crop of hairs from his legs. His scream of pain was virtually strangled by the sticky gag.

'I wouldn't struggle if you know what's good for you,' said Two-stroke gruffly. 'You'll only make matters worse.'

Dick tapped Jonesy on the shoulder. 'I hope you appreciate the gesture,' said Dick pointing to Jonesy's state of undress. 'But I thought you might like to experience being bound, gagged and stripped just as I was in that rather draughty warehouse you so thoughtfully abandoned me in.'

Jonesy's mate, who up until this point had remained quiet and motionless, suddenly began to nod towards Jonesy's waist. 'Ah, yes,' smiled Dick. 'I ought to mention that much as I would have left you with just your boxer shorts covering your modesty, it was thought that some of the younger elements of our student group shouldn't be exposed to such bad taste in the underwear department.' He nodded at both Jonesy and his mate's groin area. 'So we girthed your loins with the first thing that came to hand.' Dick stood up and started to sway. Tracey embraced him and stroked his forehead.

'Steady,' she whispered. 'That was a nasty blow you received earlier.'

Dick gingerly touched the emerging bruise on his head. 'Argh,' he groaned. 'That's really tender.' He looked down at Jonesy. 'Which reminds me. Sorry about the cling-film but adding several layers does appear opaque.'

A few of the students began to giggle at the sight of the two men naked apart from a swathe of cling-film around their hips and groins. Several areas of their bodies still bore the evidence of fire-extinguisher foam, which, under the layers of cling-film made it appear as if both men were being to dissolve. Jonesy and his mate made their objections known by wriggling and making guttural noises in their throats. Ignoring their complaints, Dick patted Two-stroke on the shoulder.

'Brilliant, Two-stroke, that was an absolutely first-class rescue.' Dick nodded towards the other students. 'And many thanks to all for your efforts, much appreciated.' He grinned 'Should be worth a few extra percentage points on your grades.'

Two-stroke beamed at the praise. 'Just thought you might be in need of a bit of help, that's all.' He gestured towards the other students. 'They saw these two characters prowling around the corridors and came to let me know.' He expanded his chest. 'Cos they knew I was keeping a look out.'

Tracey rubbed his shoulder. 'Really appreciated, Two-stroke,' she sighed. 'Don't know what we would have done without you all.' She pointed at Jonesy and his mate on the floor. 'And I don't know what we are going to do with these creatures.'

Two-stroke sniffed. 'All sorted,' he grinned. 'Amy, Donna,' he called. 'You're on.'

Amy and Donna moved from behind the other students and walked towards Jonesy and his mate. With two high-powered hair dryers in their hands, the girls smiled sadistically. 'We're ready, Two-stroke,' they purred.

Tracey, her eyes wide, looked at Dick. He grinned. 'I think we need some information.' He nodded at the hair dryers. 'Just a bit of encouragement.'

Both Jonesy and his mate began to squirm on the floor. 'Calm down,' urged Dick. He bent down and pulled part of the Gaffa-tape from Jonesy's mouth.

'Anything you want to tell me?

'Go to hell,' spat Jonesy.

Dick replaced the tape and inclined his head towards the two girls. 'See if you can persuade his mate to have a chat with us.'

Amy and Donna smiled sweetly, put the hair dryers on maximum heat and began to gently waft the hot air over the cling-film. Jonesy's mate desperately tried to avoid the searing heat, but the grip of four students held him firmly in place.

After a few moments, the cling-film behaved as predicted and clung tightly wherever the heat had been directed. Jonesy's mate wriggled frantically. His eyes bulged within his puce-coloured face. Dick signalled to the girls and the hair dryers fell silent. He leaned over and ripped the Gaffa-tape from the suffering guy's mouth.

'Aargh!' squealed Jonesy's mate.

Dick shrugged. 'Something you want to say?

Jonesy's mate nodded his head.

Jonesy banged his feet against the floor menacingly. Dick leaned over and partially removed his Gaffa-tape. 'Wimp,' yelled Jonesy at his mate.

It's not your manhood that's being pre-packed,' his mate yelled with contempt.

Dick grinned.

'Would you like to tell us a few pertinent facts or do I ask the girls to apply a little more persuasion?'

'Shut you mouth or else,' warned Jonesy.

'Go and boil yer head, Jonesy,' growled Jonesy's mate, his eyes narrowing in anger.

'I'm a bit incapacitated,' smirked Jonesy, 'or hadn't you noticed?'

'Sorry to interrupt this brief tête-à-tête,' smiled Dick. 'But time is pressing and all we're asking is a little co-operation. Surely that's not too much to ask?'

'All I'm saying,' growled Jonesy's mate, 'is that nothin' was my idea. I just did as I was told.'

'You got paid to do as you were told,' snarled Jonesy. 'You ain't clever enough to pour water out of your shoe even with the instructions written on the sole.'

Dick leaned forward and slowly pressed the Gaffa-tape back into place.

'That's enough,' said Dick sternly. 'You need to be more informative.' He turned to Jonesy's mate.

'Anything more to say,' he asked.

'Do your worst, but you'll get nothing out of me.'

'Oh well,' replied Dick calmly. 'You leave me no choice.' He smiled at Amy and Donna. 'Thanks girls, you did your best.'

Amy and Donna shrugged nonchalantly and walked away from the group.

'Vicky, Sam,' he called. 'We need your expertise.'

A tall girl with an equally tall lad walked confidently towards Jonesy and his mate. The two students each carried a small pouch. On opening the pouches, they took out a pair of latex gloves, which they slowly put on, finger by finger. Jonesy's eyes jerked nervously from one student to the other. Oblivious to the consternation they were causing, the two students then opened a long, cellophane packet and each extracted a waxing strip, which they lay on Jonesy's chest. Gently, the students pressed the strips in place and took hold of the bottom edge. Dick looked enquiringly at Jonesy, but saw nothing to stop the next stage of the treatment. He nodded at the students.

'On my mark,' he smiled.

Before Dick had a chance to make an utterance, Vicky and Sam simultaneously wrenched the wax strips from their resting place.

As Jonesy's body writhed in agony on the floor, his muffled screams hardly penetrated the combined conscience of the assembled students. Dick's hand suddenly clasped his mouth.

'Jonesy,' he said apologetically. 'I'm so sorry, the students were obviously so keen to demonstrate their skills.' He looked at the rapidly forming weals on Jonesy's chest. 'A little more streamlined now, I imagine,' he said absentmindedly.

A muted chuckle sounded. Dick looked around to see Jonesy's mate taking delight in seeing someone else in pain. Shaking his head in disgust, Dick nodded to Vicky and Sam who began to repeat their wax stripping actions on Jonesy's mate.

A couple of minutes later and the chuckles had been replaced with cries of agony as another two wax strips lay on the floor covered in dense hair. This time it was Jonesy's turn to find amusement in another person's pain. Dick shook his head sadly. 'You shouldn't enjoy suffering,' he said, slightly peeling away the Gaffa-tape from Jonesy's mouth. 'It's not right.'

Jonesy glared at him. 'It amuses me,' he said coldly.

Dick sighed. 'And you really wouldn't like to provide me with some interesting little snippets of information?'

'My travel directions still stand,' snarled Jonesy. 'Go to hell.'

'Dear, dear,' replied Dick, reapplying the tape. 'Your social skills do leave a lot to be desired. OK,' he nodded to Vicky and Sam. 'I think we'll do armpits next before we delve any further.'

Two students pulled Jonesy's arms above his head while Vicky examined the area to be waxed. She raised her eyebrows. 'Might need several waxings to do a really good job,' she advised. Jonesy began to throw his head from side-to-side while struggling to free his arms from the vice-like grip of the students.

Dick tilted his own head to one side.

'On second thoughts,' he mused. 'Why don't we combine talents?' He looked towards Amy and Donna. 'Waxing strips with appropriately applied heat?' he asked.

Amy and Donna nodded eagerly and walked over to where Vicky and Sam were busily applying the wax strips to Jonesy's underarms. Without any further consultation, they applied their heated talents to the wax strips. After a few moments, and with Jonesy becoming increasingly agitated, they nodded at Sam and Vicky. Again, without words, the pair deftly removed the molten strips. The muffled screams and bodily writhing were sufficient to indicate the level of discomfort.

'Ah, the ultimate beauty experience,' said Dick coldly. He looked at his former captor. 'Would you like to chat or go for a repeat performance?' he paused momentarily, 'on an area of our choosing of course,' he added with a casual glance at Jonesy's groin.

Jonesy nodded and shook his head frantically.

'Good,' smiled Dick. 'I take it that's an agreement to chat and forego the continued hair removal and not the other way around?'

Jonesy's head nodded furiously.

'Sensible choice,' said Dick casually. 'The gratuitous infliction of pain disturbs me. It puts me right off my food.' He removed the tape slowly from Jonesy's mouth. 'Sorry,' he said as Jonesy winced and his eyes watered. 'But I never know whether it's better to take sticky-stuff off slowly or just give it a quick tug.' He nodded at the students to release Jonesy's arms.

'How much do you want to know?' asked Jonesy, breathing heavily and tucking his arms tightly to his body to apply as much relief as possible. 'Anyway, what's it to you? No skin off your nose what happens is it?'

'I just don't like being abbreviated,' replied Dick recalling his conversation with Dubbya a few days before. 'Besides,' he continued ignoring Jonesy's look of bewilderment. 'It isn't right that a select few should benefit at the expense of the many.'

'Where have you been living these past few centuries,' replied Jonesy. 'There's always been a minority who will happily rip off the majority and there always will be, forever and ever, amen.'

Dick shook his head angrily. 'That doesn't mean we should sit idly by and do nothing.'

'And look what happened to you when you stuck your face where it wasn't wanted,' smirked Jonesy.

Dick touched the side of his face, which was still tender after the warehouse incident and the rapidly growing lump on his forehead. He looked at the recent wax impressions and shrugged.

'Not my idea of revenge,' he said simply. 'I'd much prefer to see those involved in the scam put behind bars.'

Jonesy shook his head. 'I'll not tell you anything that'll incriminate anybody, including him,' he said with a reluctant nod towards his mate.

Dick felt his anger colouring his neck and face. 'How do you expect to get away with the strong-arm tactics you've used on me and no doubt countless other people along the way?'

Jonesy gave a condescending smile. 'You mustn't get worked up. Think of your blood pressure. Anyway, it always pays to have a friendly uniform to sort out any misunderstandings.'

Tracey, who'd been listening passively al this time, stormed forward and placed the heel of her boot firmly into Jonesy's groin. She smiled at the satisfying sharp intake of breath as Jonesy winced in pain. Tracey applied a little more pressure.

'Gerrof,' gasped Jonesy. He looked pleadingly at Dick. 'For goodness sake, call your lunatic girlfriend off.'

'Ouch!' said Dick in mock annoyance. 'Wrong choice of word there my friend.'

'My apologies,' sniffed Jonesy. 'I should have said lunatic jam tart.'

Any further comments were obliterated by the scream of pain as Tracey moved her full weight onto her offending boot.

Dick leaned forward and gently lifted her boot from the injured area.

'No more,' he implored her. 'I really do need to eat soon and *jam tart* is rhyming slang for *sweetheart.* '

Tracey slowly removed her boot and stood looking down at the still writhing Jonesy.

'Do forgive me,' she said half-heartedly. 'I'm a simple librarian and my vocabulary is rather restricted.'

Jonesy nodded vigorously. With his hands still bound, he had great difficulty in nursing his injured accoutrements. Wriggling his hips from side-to-side was the limit of his ability to provide any form of comfort.

'So,' said Dick, 'just to confirm, you are implying that you have certain members of the police receiving remuneration for a lack of services rendered?'

Jonesy looked at Dick.

'Whatever,' he grunted. 'Anyway, it's not *Police* on the payroll, it's policeman, just the one.' He gave a shudder. 'We can't afford to fund the local constabulary's pension pot you know. Much like I can't afford any more injury to me family jewels.' He looked directly at Dick. 'So, what do you want to know?'

CHAPTER 47

The fashion show began preparing itself for the grand finale. During the previous scenes of decadence and decay, the models had been fittingly attired in costumes that depicted a world of consumerism and over-commercialisation. Unfortunately, not everyone at the show had appreciated the designers' satirical attempt at criticising the exclusive and expensive nature of fashion.

Throughout the penultimate scene, the large lady had snuggled ever closer to the male mannequin. Dubbya, preoccupied with the female mannequin's wig and posture, could only look on at the myopic woman with increasing alarm. The last fashion scene had concluded with the sound of water being sucked with force down a drain while the models had paraded in outfits comprised entirely of ragged imitation bank notes. The large lady had shuddered at the sound of water draining at volume and had taken the opportunity to affirm her intentions towards the male mannequin.

In the eerie silence that followed the watery demise, the audience began to fidget and little pockets of muttering could be heard. Gradually, the opening strains of *The Last Goodbye*, from *Metamorphosen* by Brandford Marsalis, crept around the room. A dull, orange glow began to seep upwards towards the stage. The curtains, which had been firmly closed at the end of the last scene, started to skulk slowly to either side of the stage.

Malc's use of *The Last Goodbye*, had been carefully chosen to convey a sense of expectation. He'd been given an outline script for the show and had selected the music, as he thought, to suit the scene. As the curtains reduced themselves to a slither of dark fabric outlining the stage, the music rose in volume and intensity. Vague images gradually came into focus against the backdrop of a city skyline. Emerging from the stage shadows stood two large, skeletal trees. Dangling from each tree hung what appeared to be a gigantic cocoon. Dubbya, in his haste to see what was happening on the stage, had dislodged the female mannequin's wig so that it completely obliterated her eyes and revealed an expanse of unadorned pate.

Suddenly, two spotlights each shone onto the cocooned forms hanging from the trees. In the harsh light, the cocoons began to wriggle violently until each form managed to turn to face the audience. Starkly outlined against the city skyline were Jonesy and his mate, both clad from head to foot in layers of shrink-wrapped cling-film with Gaffa-taped mouths intact and bulging eyes staring panic-stricken through thoughtfully constructed gaps in the synthetic wrappers.

A combined gasp came from the audience and one or two supposedly enlightened individuals managed a feeble clap. Jonesy and his mate continued to wriggle causing both trees to wobble alarmingly. While one or two stage-hands stood wondering what was happening and frantically searching their notes for inspiration, the large lady turned to Dubbya to ask him what was occurring on the stage. At that precise moment Dubbya, having seen the position of the female mannequins wig, was busily sliding the hairpiece around the mannequins head in a forlorn attempt to put it back in its correct place. The lady, seeing Dubbya apparently pulling the female's hair off her head, screamed with fright and nudged her male companion sharply in the ribs. The severity of the lady's action caused the male mannequin's head to wobble alarmingly. Taking his movement to be one of dismissal, the large lady smacked his arm sharply.

'Look,' she urged, pointing to Dubbya.

The male mannequin turned, looked at her for a moment and then his head fell off completely and landed on the lady's lap. For a moment she stared, transfixed at the site of the mannequin's head looking up at her with a steady smile. The lady looked at the body of the mannequin next to her and then again at the head in her lap. At that moment she began a series of ear-piercing screams.

The rest of the audience, unaware of the mannequin's beheading, reacted to the screams by adding their own motley collection of shrieks and squeals. Within seconds, like verbal wildfire, the room was filled with a raucous cacophony of screeching. As Dubbya hastily collected the various bits of the mannequins together, he couldn't help thinking that the noise was reminiscent of the sound of gulls on a rubbish dump. The large lady had, by this time, fainted with her head tilted backwards and her eyes staring through her unhelpful glasses at the ceiling.

Dragging his dummy companions towards the fire escape, Dubbya could see the college Principal desperately calling for calm from the stage. Negotiating the pandemonium, Dubbya managed to reach the fire escape doors just as Dick and Tracey walked into the uproar.

'Where the hell have you been?' shouted Dubbya above the din.

Dick and Tracey looked at each other and smiled. Dick cupped his hand over Dubby'a ear.

'Have you seen the Chief Constable? He's supposed to be here somewhere.'

Dubbya, struggling to keep the mannequins together, shrugged.

'No idea,' he yelled as he pulled the mannequins against his body. He jerked his head towards the front of the room. 'Posh seats are down there.' Abandoning any further attempts at conversation, Dubbya forced his way past Dick and Tracey and, dragging the two mannequins, escaped through the fire exit.

Tracey grabbed Dick's hand and together they went off in search of the Chief Constable.

The screaming commotion had finally subsided as Dick and Tracey searched the crowd of faces for the Chief Constable. The Principal's ineffectual gesticulating had only served to intensify the wave of panic that had struck the room the moment the cling-film cocoons appeared and the large lady's stoic toy-boy lost his head. The models and back-stage crew, on hearing the less than fashionable hysteria enveloping the audience had distributed themselves amongst the crowd and were busily mothering any of the audience who'd adopted the foetal position as a form of sensory defence.

The Principal, seeing that his calming influence was nothing of the sort, had stormed off the stage and was last seeing striding along the corridor to his office.

Tracey tugged at Dick's hand.

'Come on,' she urged. 'He's got to be here somewhere.'

Dick obliged by scanning the crowd for any sign of officialdom, but couldn't see any form of constable, chief or otherwise. He stopped and turned Tracey to face him.

'Look,' he said firmly. 'What's the point?' We haven't any evidence to give to anyone, let alone a Chief Constable. Everything we know is based upon some incomplete paperwork, tenuous connections and a confession gained under duress from a crook who'll deny having said anything.'

Tracey smiled. She kissed Dick on the cheek and continued with her search of the crowd.

Even though someone had thoughtfully turned on the stage lighting, the rest of the hall was still encased in a subdued halo. The two plastic wrapped cocoons, under the harsh stage lighting, were beginning to feel extremely uncomfortable as they began to cook under the glare.

Dick was just about to point out the plight of Jonesy and his mate to Tracey, when he felt a sharp tap on his shoulder.

'I was told to expect you,' said a deep, authoritative voice.

Both Dick and Tracey turned to see an uncapped, uniformed figure smiling at them. The figure nodded and made the necessary introduction.

'Chief Constable Hardly,' he winked at them. 'And yes, I've heard most of the jokes, such as *"Hardly ever catches a criminal," "Hardly ever works," "Hardly of the Yard,"* and so on. But do let me know if you think of an original pun won't you?'

Dick and Tracey were completely taken aback at both the fact that the Chief Constable had found them, that he was expecting them and his self-assured manner concerning his name.

'Well,' began Dick. 'Yes, we were looking for you but ... '

Tracey gripped the Chief Constable's hand and shook it vigorously. 'Pleased to meet you,' she said animatedly, ignoring Dick's hesitation. 'We need to give you some important information that will stop a dreadful scam dead in its tracks.'

The Chief Constable grinned. 'Anything that will make a substantial dent in my crime figures is always welcome.'

Dick took the Chief Constable by the elbow and indicated the perspiring forms of Jonesy and his mate still dangling from the trees.

'We really only have what they told us.' He shook his head. 'And I can't see them repeating what they know once they're unwrapped.'

The Chief Constable looked at the wriggling cocoons for a moment and then nodded to two uniformed blokes standing behind Tracey. 'Unpack them,' he said, indicating Jonesy and his mate. He held up a finger in caution. 'Slowly, mind,' he continued. 'And if they appear at all forgetful begin wrapping them up again and tell them you're simply trying to preserve the evidence.'

The uniforms began to walk leisurely towards the limp forms. Before they'd taken many steps, the Chief Constable called after them. 'Give my regards to Jonesy, won't you. It's been a while since we last spent an informative hour or two together.'

'You know them?' asked Tracey.

The Chief Constable nodded his head. 'We're acquaintances, yes.' He thrust his hands into his trousers pockets and seemed to be thinking. After a brief pause, he smiled. 'We used to see a lot of both Jonesy and his mate, Brown, but.' He shook his head sadly. 'They've not been quite so forthcoming of late.'

The Chief Constable appeared to be lost in thought again. Dick and Tracey fidgeted, neither of them wanted to interrupt the Chief Constable even if they had something to say. Dick looked over to the stage and saw Jonesy and Brown being unceremoniously dropped from the trees onto the floor, any cries of pain or indignation being totally muffled by the Gaffa-tape still firmly across their mouths. He suddenly became aware of Tracey and the Chief Constable deep in conversation.

'It was the only thing I could do under the circumstances,' said Tracey breezily.

The Chief Constable laughed. 'Good thinking all the same.'

Tracey nodded briefly. Dick frowned and felt vaguely disconcerted. His unease quickly evaporated as Tracey began twiddling her hair with her fingertips, in a way that Dick found really attractive. Tracey smiled as she caught Dick watching her.

'Sorry,' she said. 'Tell me, Chief Constable. Earlier you said you were expecting us, why?'

The Chief Constable shrugged knowingly. 'Let me just say that your foray into the world of detection hadn't gone unnoticed.'

'I object to that,' said Dick strongly.

'Steady,' said Tracey quickly, placing her hand on Dick's arm. 'At least we had someone watching over us.'

'Well,' replied Dick. 'We didn't foray and I've got the bruises to prove it.'

The Chief Constable stifled a chuckle. 'Ah, yes,' he grinned. 'We were watching Jonesy and company watching you. It seemed a shame to step in too soon before we could be certain who was involved.'

'Why didn't you step in when they kidnapped me,' said Dick angrily. 'I had to put up with a whole evening of Jonesy and his mate. Not to mention waking up next morning with a tender face and a load of dismembered bodies.'

The Chief Constable failed to stifle his next laugh. 'I'm sorry,' he spluttered. 'It was just a question of waiting to see who else turned up and we weren't disappointed.'

'So why did you leave me there all night?'

'We had to follow the three of them to see where they might lead us,' said the Chief Constable apologetically. 'We thought you'd be safe where you were and it was a mild evening after all.'

'Mild!' exclaimed Dick. 'I only had my boxer shorts for company.'

'Yes,' laughed the Chief Constable. 'I heard about that. You caused quite a stir in the café.'

'So,' enquired Dick. 'Was my sojourn in the warehouse worthwhile?'

'I should say so,' nodded the Chief Constable enthusiastically. 'We had our suspicions about Jonesy and company but it was the third person who intrigued us.'

'And that would be? asked Tracey raising her eyebrows slightly.

'That,' replied the Chief Constable, 'was none other than your Assistant Principal for External Affairs.' The Chief shook his head slightly. 'You just wouldn't credit that a bloke in his position could be so naïve when it comes to acting with subtlety.'

'You can believe it,' laughed Tracey. 'He has a reputation for flaunting the obvious without realising it. But,' she added with a tap on the Chief's hand. 'You still haven't told us why you were expecting us.'

'I know,' replied the Chief Constable. Before either Dick or Tracey could make a comment, he placed a finger against the side of this nose. 'Let me keep some things secret.' He gave an exaggerated wink. 'Must maintain a little bit of mystery.'

Dick sighed. 'But we still haven't got any real evidence for you.'

'Oh yes we have,' said Tracey giving him a huge smile.

Dick frowned. 'Have we?'

'I emailed it to myself,' she replied. 'That's what I was messing about for under the desk in the Assistant Principal's office.'

Dick pouted. 'And I thought it was because you liked my feet.'

Tracey blew him a kiss. 'Which reminds me,' she added thoughtfully. 'I need to go and retrieve my phone, which I'd taped to the underside of the desk after I'd sent the email. '

The Chief Constable nodded at each of them and began to walk towards the stage. 'Don't forget to email me,' he said to Tracey.

'Hang on,' shouted Dick.

The Chief Constable turned and took a few steps forward. 'What have I forgotten,' he asked.

'Oh, nothing,' replied Dick. 'It's just that I thought you might like to know that you have a runt in the Constabulary litter feeding from the criminal trough.'

'Do we now,' said the Chief Constable thoughtfully. 'Anyone I might know?'

Dick moved forward and whispered in his ear. The Chief Constable nodded, patted Dick on the shoulder and walked over to where Jonesy and Brown were being slowly unpacked. Tracey took Dick's hand.

'Anything you want to tell me?' she enquired sweetly.

Dick smiled, leant forward and kissed Tracey on the cheek. 'I'll tell you later,' he informed her.

The fashion conscious audience had slowly calmed down and the room was now practically empty, apart from the stagehands dismantling the various bits of scenery and Malc packing away his gear. Dick and Tracey sauntered across to where Malc was busily replacing his CD's in alphabetical order.

'Hiya,' he called, pausing briefly to try and recall where he usually stored *Jazz Sebastian Bach* by the *Swingle Singers*. He reflected for a moment and then shrugged. 'Dick, have you any idea where I should store this CD?' Malc handed the CD over to Dick. 'I rather think it's under 'S', but I can't be certain. Do you think I might have catalogued it under 'B' for Bach or 'M' for Miscellaneous?'

Dick looked at the back of the CD case and smiled. "Not one for the purists,' he mused. 'I read somewhere that it really upset people in both the jazz and classical worlds during the 60's'.

Malc snorted. 'Ingrates!'

Tracey winced at the ferocity of Malc's words. 'Steady on,' she said. 'Everyone's entitled to their opinion.'

Malc shook his head. 'Their opinions would create a narrow world where freedom of expression is by committee.'

'Too heavy for me at this time of night,' Dick joked. He waved the CD at Malc. 'Could I have a listen to this and if Tracey allows me any pocket money this month I might even buy it.'

Tracey gave Dick a playful jab in the ribs. 'Pocket money is only for good boys,' she grinned.

'If I promise to be good,' murmured Dick. Malc gave an embarrassed cough.

'Excuse me children,' he said with mock severity. 'But some of us still have work to do.' He quickly placed a few CD's in their respective positions and offered Dick and Tracey a smile. 'A very productive evening, wasn't it?'

Dick and Tracey exchanged glances. Neither of them was quite sure whether Malc references were general or vaguely pertinent. Tracey decided to try and find out whether Malc knew anything about their investigative escapades or not. She nodded encouragingly. 'In what way was the evening productive?' she asked as innocently as she could.

Malc shrugged in a noncommittal way. 'Just productive,' he replied casually.

Dick shook his head. 'Productive?" he asked. 'How could anything be productive when the highlight of the evening was two plastic grubs dangling from imitation trees?' Dick gestured towards the almost empty room. 'I don't see a queue of people desperate to buy your brand of jazz.'

Malc ignored the veiled criticism and threw his hands out

219

wide. 'Why, Dick,' he exclaimed. 'Sometimes I think you purposefully ignore the obvious to go in search of the obscure.'

'OK, so what was it that I so inadvertently overlooked?'

Malc indicated an empty box on the table next to a sign for *Regeneration Sounds*. Malc cocked his head to one side. 'Well?'

'Well, what?' replied Dick tersely. He tapped the box. 'So you haven't had any tips, how can that be productive?'

Malc sighed and looked appealingly at Tracey. 'Is he always this obtuse?'

Tracey laughed. 'This is one of his better days.'

'God help his students then,' replied Malc with a roll of the eyes. He picked up the box and waved it under Dick's nose. 'Business cards, dear boy, all gone.'

'Ah, yes,' grinned Dick. 'They do make exceedingly good book marks.'

It was Malc's turn to laugh. 'Agreed,' he admitted. 'But I have also had enquiries about providing the sounds for a birthday, two weddings, three anniversaries and a retirement. Now that's what I call productive.'

'*That* kind of productive,' said Tracey. 'I understand now.'

'Do you?' asked Malc raising his eyebrows.

Dick felt his eyes glaze. The whole evening was now fast taking on all the characteristics normally associated with a nightmare. 'Enough,' cried Dick holding his hands high in surrender. 'I'm off to embrace Morpheus and sleep the sleep of the just.'

Tracey jostled his arm. 'What's with this Morpheus? If there's any embracing to be done … '

Dick smiled and linked arms with Tracey. He waved the *Swingle Sisters* CD at Malc. 'Thanks.'

Malc dismissed them both with a wave. 'Goodnight, dear ones, see you soon.'

As they emerged into the coolness of the night, Tracey walked with her head resting on Dick's shoulder. 'Are you planning to buy any more CD's?' she asked dreamily.

'Not that I know of,' replied Dick. 'Apart from paying for the services of the *Swingle Sisters*.'

Tracey chuckled. 'I could make an interesting riposte there.'

'I'm sure you could,' smiled Dick. 'But I think it would be wasted on my tired mind.'

'Maybe,' whispered Tracey. 'But Malc seemed pretty certain about seeing us soon.'

Dick placed his arm around Tracey's shoulders. 'I think he lives in hope. I can't imagine he gets many customers with a jazz fetish.'

Tracey leaned into Dick's embrace. 'Possibly not, but you never know.'

Dick was just about to respond when a siren suddenly screeched through his thoughts. 'The police seem eager to be somewhere,' he observed as the noise faded into the distance.

'Perhaps they've just had a call to say the kettle's on back at the station,' chuckled Tracey.

Dick held the car door open for Tracey. 'Talking about kettles.'

They both looked at each other and grinned. 'Home.'

CHAPTER 48

All nocturnal activity at the Golf course had stopped under the harsh glare of the police car's headlights. Even the wildlife had decided to call it a night and slunk back to their various burrows, nests and bolt holes. The car had come to a turf-ripping halt on the edge of the thirteenth green, which was certain to cause apoplexy amongst the ground staff and members of the committee during the next period of daylight.

The two uniformed occupants sat for a moment, each oblivious to the impact of their arrival on the non-golfing fraternity. The sterile blue flashes created a hypnotic pattern that made the shrubbery appear almost alive with movement. PC James gripped the steering wheel.

'It's your turn to go out first.'

PC Wardle looked out at the ambiguous light and shuddered. 'What if there are dead bodies?' he asked in a whisper.

'Well, they're not going to do you any harm now are they,' replied PC James testily.

PC Wardle folded his arms. 'I'm not going out there on my own and that's final.'

'I went out last night.'

'So did I.'

'But you only had to deal with a drunk emptying his bladder in the graveyard.' PC Wardle shivered at the memory. 'Have you ever gone into a graveyard to be confronted by a wavering figure standing by a headstone with steam rising from the ground?'

'There was my Aunt Joan at Nan's funeral,' replied PC James. 'But she'd been at the cooking sherry since breakfast, so it was only to be expected really.'

'Ah!' said PC Wardle triumphantly. 'That was in daylight. You try it at night and you'll see what I mean.'

Both PC's sat silently for a few moments staring out at the eerie scene in front of them. Eventually, PC James inhaled deeply. 'After three?'

PC Wardle nodded. 'Right you are then.'

On the count of three, both PC's opened their respective doors and stood facing each other.

'What now?' whispered PC Wardle.

PC James shrugged. 'I suppose we'd better take a look around.'

Cautiously they flashed their torches into the shadows. 'Can you see anything?' asked PC Wardle, still standing next to the car.

In one swift movement, PC James opened his door and jumped into the car. 'Not a lot,' he called.

PC Wardle quickly copied his companion's movements until they were both feeling slightly more secure in the relative safety of the car.

'Best report back then,' said PC James gripping the steering wheel once again. He was just about to turn the key in the ignition when suddenly a grisly face appeared at the side window.

The interior of the car was instantly filled with a screaming duet. An angry tapping noise on the window only served to increase the intensity of the internal panic. A squawk from the radio caused the uniformed cacophony to stop as quickly as it started. PC James looked at the radio.

'Didn't catch what it said.'

'Hardly likely to the noise you were making,' replied PC Wardle.

PC James snorted.

'Speak for yourself.'

Before the altercation could delve further into the insecure nature of policing, the tapping started again. Swallowing noisily, PC James allowed the window to open slowly. The face forced its way into the emerging gap.

'You here for the bodies?' it rasped.

PC James nodded. 'We had a report,' he began but was interrupted by the face.

'Follow me then.'

Once more the PC's counted to three and simultaneously exited the car. The grisly face led them along the thirteenth green towards a sand bunker. 'Down there,' he said pointing towards the bunker. 'The pair of 'em, down there.'

Standing on the edge of the bunker, they shone their torches along the sloping sand. Almost instantly, the duel lights found the comatose forms of the two reported bodies.

'I'm not going down there,' said PC James as he played his torch along the edges of the bunker.

'Don't start that again or I'll ... ' PC Wardle's words were abruptly interrupted by the shrill yapping of a small dog. The startling noise caused the PC to lose his balance and slither into the bunker to join the immobile bodies below.

'Aaargh!' yelled PC Wardle. 'They're still warm.'

PC James looked at the old man with the grisly face. 'That your dog?' he asked sharply.

The old man shrugged. 'Could be, depends whose asking.'

'They're breathing,' observed PC Wardle from below.

PC James nodded at the dog.

'You should keep it on a lead at all times.'

'It's a free country,' said the old man stiffly. 'I fought in the last war to keep this country free you know.'

'A female and a male aged about sixty I'd say.'

'This is private property and, I think you'll find that you're trespassing.'

'I ain't then,' snapped the old man. 'I risked life and limb to keep the likes of your grandparents and parents safe so that they could bring up the likes of you.'

'No sign of foul play or other injury,' called PC Wardle from the depths of the bunker.

'I'll have to take a statement from you, sir.'

'Bloody liberty I calls it,' rasped the old man. 'I gets a string of medals fighting fascists and what happens, eh? I ask you, more bloody fascists.'

'Are you going to call an ambulance or what?'

'Name?'

'Gresley,' growled the old man. 'Mr Gresley to you.'

A barely audible female groan sounded from the bunker.

PC Wardle squeaked with fright. 'An ambulance and a change of underwear would be a good idea,' he called.

'And what precisely were you doing on the golf course?' asked PC James.

'Walking me dog so as he can do his business without the likes of you interrupting his endeavours.'

'Defacing private property, I see,' muttered PC James making relevant notes.

'I think you'll find it's defecating on private property,' corrected Mr Gresley.

'Ambulance, any ambulance would do.'

'Yer mate wants an ambulance.'

PC James stabbed his pencil against his notepad. 'Would you please refrain from interrupting an officer going about his duty. I'm trying to take a statement from you if you don't mind.'

'No skin off my nose,' said Mr Gresly gruffly. 'But yer mate seems pretty agitated.'

'999, anyone?' called PC Wardle feebly.

'Now,' said PC James steadily. 'You were walking your dog.'

'As I always do,' replied Mr Gresley. 'Ever since they built that monstrosity of a technical college right on the field where dogs have gone about their business since time immemorial.'

PC James gave an exasperated sigh. 'What has the technical college got to do with you walking your dog?'

'I can't that's what,' growled Mr Gresley. They built the damn thing precisely where I used to take old Bess. She were a grand lass she was.'

PC James felt his collar getting tighter as the temperature rose within his uniform. 'Bess?' he asked.

'An ambulance?' moaned PC Wardle. 'Before the end of my shift would be nice.'

'Springer spaniel,' answered Mr Gresley as a smile of fond memories played across his face.

'Mummy?' whimpered PC Wardle.

PC James strode over to the bunker and looked into the abyss. 'What the heck is the matter with you?' he asked angrily. 'Can't you do anything on your own?' He turned back towards the place where Mr Gresley had been standing. 'Now,' he began, but all he could see was the dim outline of the old man hurrying away with his dog in tow. PC James gave a cry of fright as he felt a sharp tap on his shoulder. He turned to see a wiry figure, dressed in an overly large raincoat facing him.

'Officer,' said the figure with the clipped tones reminiscent of someone used to being obeyed. 'Might I be so bold as to ask you why you've ploughed through the thirteenth green like a deranged boar and illuminating the course like some garish fairground?'

'Excuse me,' replied PC James as politely as his rising irritation would allow. 'And you are?'

'Blanchard,' snapped the man. 'Chair of the Committee here and Chairman of the local neighbourhood watch and I wish to know who that man was scurrying away with his filthy mongrel.'

PC James closed his notebook sharply. 'That man was helping us with our enquiries.'

'Enquiries?' spluttered Blanchard. 'What enquiries?' He waved a hand to indicate the entire golf course. 'If there are any enquiries to be made then I should be the first person to ask.'

PC James opened his notebook, 'Well,' he asked. 'What can you tell me about dead bodies?'

'Are you a raving lunatic, Officer,' growled Blanchard. 'Damn it, I'm a retired insurance salesman not some knife-wielding butcher.'

'That as may be the case,' replied PC James sharply. 'But we have reports of two dead bodies located here on the thirteenth green and,'

Blanchard's face froze and he pointed crazily at the edge of the bunker. 'Oh my giddy aunt,' he mumbled. For a second he wavered where he stood then staggered towards the edge of the bunker. He pointed once again, looked at PC James and then toppled over into the bunker with a loud groan.

PC James looked towards the bunker and saw the dim outline of PC Wardle's head bobbing up and down at the edge of the bunker. Taking his torch, PC James shone the light into the depths of the bunker to reveal Blanchard lying unconscious on top of the bodies of Lady Faulkner and the Chair of the Planning and development Committee. The three chairs lay oblivious to the world around them. An occasional groan escaped their lips as ghostly images slid through their dreams. PC James redirected his torch towards the face of PC Wardle.

'Now look what you've gone and done,' he shouted. 'We arrive on the scene and increase the body count.' He shook his head. 'Goodness knows what the Sarge will have to say about all this.'

'Nurse?' sobbed PC Wardle. 'Nurse, where are you?'

CHAPTER 49

The night seemed to be labouring under the misapprehension of being a favourite time of the day for those charged with working unsociable hours. Sergeant Cost looked at his watch for the umpteenth time, drummed his fingers irritatingly along the edge of the table and then threw his pencil at the uniformed figure of PC Ricketts.

PC Ricketts felt the pencil prod on her shoulder but chose to ignore it, fully aware that not responding to the Sergeant's request for attention was one of the most annoying things she could employ in her war of attrition against her superior officer. Busying herself with the tidal wave of forms arriving with increasing regularity, she could sense the temperature rising behind her. Smiling smugly to herself, happy in the knowledge that Sergeant Cost was quickly reaching boiling point, PC Ricketts continued her paper shuffle.

Sergeant Cost was fully aware that he was engaged in a form of cerebral snakes and ladders, where an unfortunate throw of the dice would see his self-esteem plummet. He smiled confidently, remembering fondly the number of recruits that had passed through his tutelage, most of them going on to become successful law enforcers, with just the odd one or two taking medical advice and finding alternative careers in the retail trade. Sergeant Cost smoothed his newspaper flat and licked his teeth.

'Anything to report on the golf course shenanigans?' he asked calmly.

'Not at the moment,' replied PC Ricketts without turning to face her tormentor. 'Still waiting.'

'Like my cup of tea then,' grinned Sergeant Cost.

PC Ricketts turned around slowly. She regulated her breathing to remain calm and controlled. 'I thought it better to try and keep on top of the paperwork,' she said.

'Thought!' exclaimed Sergeant Cost. 'Good grief, what nonsense are they stuffing your head with during initial training?' PC Ricketts was about to reply when he held up a warning finger. 'Careful now young lady, I haven't spent weeks nurturing you in the fine art of policing just to have you go and ruin my efforts by thinking.' He shook his head as if trying to rid himself of undesirable mental images. 'Go and make that cup of tea before I start thinking.'

PC Ricketts shuffled the forms meticulously, tapping the edges of the paper bundle sharply against the top of the desk as she did so. Gauging her actions to the second, she laid the forms out neatly in rows and, with a final nudge of an errant corner of paper, made her way to the designated brewing area of the office.

Staring at the newspaper in front of him, Sergeant Cost wrestled with the dilemma of whether to complete the day's quick crossword or attempt the cryptic challenge. A cool breeze played across his face as the outside door wheezed on its hinges. Without looking towards the source of his distraction, he delicately scratched the end of his nose and was just about to inform PC Ricketts that she had a customer when his finely tuned senses caused him to pause. Discretely sliding a sheaf of nondescript forms across his newspaper, Sergeant Cost turned his head towards the door. He stood up sharply, smoothing his uniform jacket as he did so.

'Chief Constable,' crooned Cost. 'This is an unexpected pleasure.'

The Chief Constable strolled leisurely towards the desk. 'Good evening, Cost.' He perused the office as he spoke. 'Are you on your own tonight?'

Sergeant Cost ran a finger around his collar. 'Ricketts!' shouted Cost towards the rear of the office. 'Get yourself out here pronto.' Sergeant Cost gave an ingratiating smile. 'My apologies, Sir, constantly brewing up she is.' He shook his head with derision. 'Leaving jobs half finished and forms left to fill themselves out.' He gave PC Ricketts a stern look as she approached the desk. 'Look sharp, Ricketts. Make yourself known to the Chief Constable.'

PC Ricketts walked smartly towards the Chief Constable and shook the hand he held out to her. 'Extremely pleased to meet you, Sir,' she said warmly.

The Chief Constable smiled. 'I've heard good things about

you, Ricketts.' He nodded towards the rear of the office. 'I don't suppose there's any chance of a cuppa is there?'

PC Ricketts nodded and walked smartly over to the cooling kettle. Flicking the kettle into action, she couldn't help wondering whether advancement within the police force was dependent upon the quality of tea, a sort of brew your way to the top. Allowing herself a gentle sigh, she successfully tossed three tea bags into their respective mugs, crossing her fingers and saving the mug with the hairline crack around the handle for Sergeant Cost. The Chief Constable placed his cap on the desk and relaxed against the nearest filing cabinet.

'How are the family, Cost?'

'Mustn't grumble,' replied Cost. 'Our Becky has just had her first brace fitted. Disgracefully expensive though,' he complained.

The Chief Constable smiled. 'Worth it in the end.'

'Reckon you're right there, Sir.'

'And Mrs Cost?' enquired the Chief.

'Doing nicely, thank you,' replied Cost. 'Got a nice little earner cleaning down at the Magistrate's court.'

'Keeping it in the family as it were,' grinned the Chief. 'Can't say I blame you.'

Sergeant Cost nodded and tidied the forms that PC Ricketts had adjusted moments earlier. His instinct told him that something was amiss, that the Chief Constable's visit was more than just a casual chat. In fact, he thought to himself, a visit by the Chief was unprecedented, it had never happened before and, as far as he knew, the Chief rarely went anywhere without a sycophantic entourage. He'd met the Chief several times at various functions and each time had been impressed with the Chief's knowledge of Cost's background and family. Nervously he filed a couple of blank forms and wracked his memory for anything that might possibly cause the Chief to make this unexpected appearance. Cost cleared his throat.

'Anything I can do for you, Sir, or were you just passing like?'

The Chief smiled. 'Ah, thank you Ricketts,' as the Constable proffered the requested cuppa. He took a cautious sip. 'Just what the doctor ordered.' Placing his mug on the desk, the Chief belched quietly and shrugged an apology towards PC Ricketts. 'I've just spent a very interesting evening at the College's Fashion Show,' he informed them. 'Not quite my cup of tea though,' he quipped taking another sip from his mug.

PC Ricketts turned her back, as if busying herself with some important task and allowed her eyes to roll towards the ceiling. *Good grief,* she thought, tea and clichés, what was the world coming to? The Chief took a long sip of his tea, his eyes firmly fixed on Sergeant Cost. With a sigh of satisfaction, the Chief reached into his jacket and took out a newspaper clipping. Laying the clipping on the desk, the Chief nodded towards the article marked with a yellow highlighter.

'What do you make of that, Cost?'

The Sergeant smoothed the piece of newspaper flat and read the indicated article. He paused a couple of times and glanced over at PC Ricketts but refrained from uttering any comments. After a few minutes, Sergeant Cost pushed the clipping back towards the Chief Constable.

'Interesting,' he said, in a sort of non-committal way. 'We've had a few instances of this apparition business.'

'What did you do about them?' enquired the Chief.

'All meticulously logged and filed, Sir. PC Ricketts is a stickler for procedure and systems she is.'

'You didn't think it worthwhile investigating then?' asked the Chief with a slight raise of an eyebrow.

Sergeant Cost felt a mixture of relief and discomfort. Relief that the Chief's visit seemed nothing more than a routine check-up but discomfort that it was actually the Chief making the enquiries. His feeling of unease deepened as the Chief appeared to be eager to pursue the issue.

'So, you didn't think a badly shaken member of the public and her petrified cub-scout pack worthy of investigation?'

Cost wiped his hands against his thighs. 'We're rather short staffed at night,' he explained nervously. 'There's more than enough to occupy the patrol lads in the town centre without asking them to enquire into the over stimulated imagination of some frustrated spinster.'

231

'I see,' replied the Chief calmly. 'And I suppose the reports of a comatose old lady, a terrified woman pummelling her husband and a church choir sprawled in the aisle are simply instances of over stimulated imaginations?'

Sergeant Cost swallowed hard. He didn't like the way the Chief's questions were going. He picked up a partially completed report sheet from the desk. 'We do have two lads out right now, Sir. Investigating reports of two dead bodies on a golf course.'

The Chief Constable nodded his head slowly. 'You have a policy of prioritising incidents?' he asked.

Cost responded with a series of nods. 'Yes, Sir, we have to deploy our resources according to what we consider the seriousness of the reported incident.'

'Hmm,' mused the Chief. He looked into the depths of his tea mug and drained the remaining cool liquid. He smiled at PC Ricketts. 'Have you got any holidays planned?' he asked.

'Nothing as yet, Sir,' she replied. 'I'll try and grab a last minute bargain. Failing that, I'll make an excuse to go and see my brother down in Exeter.'

'Nice part of the country,' said the Chief casually. 'Quite easy to catch some beach and do a bit of walking I presume?'

PC Ricketts nodded. 'Makes for a cheap holiday,' she grinned.

The Chief Constable licked the corner of his mouth. 'What about you, Cost, any holidays planned?'

Sergeant Cost was having difficulty following the meandering line of the Chief's enquiry. He shrugged. 'Not long got back from the Caribbean, Sir, although the wife constantly complained about the heat.' Cost sniffed. 'Might take her down to Bournemouth for a couple of weeks. She can sink an ice cream or three while cooling her feet in the Channel. Give her a break from being a domestic goddess.'

The Chief Constable sighed. 'I wish I could afford the Caribbean. What with University fees and the wife's health club fees, I'll be lucky to get a week in Clacton.' He tapped the newspaper clipping that still lay on the desk. 'Not the most positive comment on police efficiency.'

Sergeant Cost looked again at the article. 'I suppose they have a right to their opinion,' he offered.

232

The Chief Constable picked up the article. 'According to a certain Mr Richard Blanchard, Chair of the local neighbourhood watch committee, we are inept, incompetent and intransigent when it comes to matters of community safety.' He slapped the clipping onto the desk. 'Not the kind of comments I like to hear.'

Cost shrugged, an action that didn't go unnoticed by the Chief Constable. 'No comment, Sergeant?'

'Well,' began Cost. 'The public just don't understand the kind of constraints we operate within. How can they make a value judgement based upon the anal ramblings of some pubescent newspaper reporter? I mean,' he said, his voice taking on an agitated air. 'Are we expected to react to every bit of whimsical storytelling?'

The Chief Constable looked once more into his empty tea mug and smiled at PC Ricketts. Without a word, she picked up the mug and made her way towards the kettle. Nodding in approval, the Chief Constable turned his attention to the Sergeant.

'She'll go far,' he said casually.

Sergeant Cost let his eyes wander towards Ricketts and then back to the Chief Constable. 'As is often the way,' he said with a slight shake of his head.

'Meaning?'

Sergeant Cost lowered his voice. 'She's young, female, has something that passes for intelligence and makes a good brew.' He shrugged nonchalantly. 'As you say, she'll go far.'

'Quite a cynical viewpoint,' replied the Chief Constable raising an eyebrow. 'Do I detect a hint of resentment there?'

Cost gave a noncommittal shrug. 'Too late at my time of life to bother with resentment,' he said curtly.

The Chief Constable made no comment, encouraging Cost to carry on with an almost imperceptible nod of the head. Sergeant Cost didn't notice the slight inclination of the Chief's head as the years of frustration surged into his mind like a cerebral avalanche. He became oblivious to his surroundings as the resentment focussed his words.

'Years of dedicated service and what reward do I get? I'll tell you what I get, promoted to nursemaid some spotty sniffer who's being fast-tracked to affluence while I get a pension that will hardly keep me in tea bags.'

The Chief Constable shook his head in reply. 'Frequently, ours is a profession that gets taken for granted.' He inhaled deeply. 'Often it's simply a case of seeing a job well done and knowing that we've helped keep the rodent population down.' Reaching inside his jacket, the Chief withdrew his mobile phone. Pressing a few buttons, and adding the occasional click of tongue in annoyance, the Chief finally found what he was looking for and passed the phone to Sergeant Cost. Looking at the picture on the phone, Cost whistled noiselessly.

'They look rough,' he mumbled. 'I thought you went to a fashion show not to watch a pair of understudies for a Prom night at the local naturist club.' Cost took a closer look at the image on the phone. 'I can see why they're understudies though,' he grinned. 'Seems they've had quite a bit of hair removed.'

The Chief Constable allowed a smile to creep onto his face. 'The handiwork of some over enthusiastic students I'm afraid,' he said. 'I didn't know whether you might recognise these guys, even with their painful expressions?'

Cost peered at the images again. A nervous tick seemed to develop at the corner of his mouth. 'Vaguely familiar,' he admitted running his tongue across his top lip. 'But there again, they could be any number of the low life we have around here.'

The smile had disappeared from the Chief's face. 'Not just any old low life, I think,' he said calmly. 'It seems you must have made an impression on these gentlemen because they've been singing your praises.'

Sergeant Cost began to look rather ill. The colour had drained from his face as he began to develop an itch under his collar. 'I can't be expected to be on first-name terms with every half-baked criminal around here,' he blustered. 'Besides, it pays to keep tabs on some of the local villains. You never know where it might lead.'

'Well,' began the Chief. 'Keeping tabs, as you put it, certainly does seem to pay, and as for knowing where it might lead … ' He left the sentence incomplete as Cost staggered back to his desk and sank into the chair. He smiled weakly at PC Ricketts. 'A mug of strong, sweet tea for the Sergeant, if you please, Constable.'

CHAPTER 50

Apart from a mild outburst from Dick at a set of obstructive traffic lights, and an exasperated sigh from Tracey at his impatience, the journey home passed in silence.

Bringing the car to a grateful stop, Dick switched off the engine and began to flex his hands. He hadn't realised just how tense he'd become. His arms ached, his face ached, and his back ached. In fact, Dick had trouble locating a part of his body that didn't ache.

'How do you feel,' he said turning to Tracey, half hoping for some ribald comment from her. She sat staring at the house. 'Tracey?'

'The light's on,' she managed to mutter.

Dick laughed. 'And there's no one home, I know, but I still love you.'

Tracey slowly turned her head towards Dick. 'I mean it, the light's on.' She pointed towards the house. The first thing that Dick noticed was that the curtains were closed, which was something he hadn't bothered to do when they left the house earlier. Secondly, gently illuminating the curtains from behind was a light, which definitely hadn't been switched on when they left. Dick nodded.

'You're right,' replied Dick. 'The light is on and it's on in my house.'

'I was so looking forward to a cup of tea and a cuddle,' murmured Tracey.

'Well,' said Dick stroking her cheek. 'You never know, we might be in the process of being burgled by a more refined class of thief. The sort who put the kettle on for you, give you a reassuring hug and tell you that everything will turn out for the best before they abscond with all your worldly goods.'

Tracey jerked her head away from his touch. 'Trust you to be facetious at a time like this,' she said angrily. 'Can't you be a bit more constructive and phone the police or something?'

Dick shrugged 'I think we've had enough of dealing with

criminals for one day. I didn't particularly want to come home to find a welcoming party from the plunder world.'

'It could be some of Jonesy and Brown's mates,' said Tracey weakly. 'You know, a bit of revenge trashing.'

Dick swallowed noisily. 'I hadn't thought of that.'

The minutes passed as they sat staring at the subdued lighting emanating from the house. Eventually, Tracey touched Dick's hand. 'We need to do something,' she whispered. Dick looked first at her hand and then her eyes. Tracey sighed. 'Something practical relating to whatever's going on behind those curtains.'

Suddenly, Dick turned around in his seat and began rummaging through the miscellaneous items lodging behind the driver's seat.

'What on earth are you doing?' she asked, her voice heavy with annoyance.

Dick apparently didn't hear her question or decided to ignore her. Whichever the reason, Dick's lack of response caused Tracey to react angrily. Jabbing him in the ribs, she sat back and awaited his retort. She didn't have to wait long.

'Got it,' he exclaimed.

'Got what?' asked Tracey wondering whether another jab in the ribs might encourage Dick to be a little more lucid.

'This,' he said triumphantly holding up a pocket-sized folding umbrella. Tracey jabbed him in the ribs again.

'Ow,' he gasped. 'That was needless.'

'As is that,' replied Tracey pointing at the undersized umbrella.

'I may be a lapsed cub-scout,' said Dick. 'But I'm always prepared.'

'Definitely,' answered Tracey, her mouth broadening into a smile. 'But just what are you prepared to do with that thing?'

'I'm not sure yet,' said Dick thoughtfully. 'I just might need to be spontaneous,' he continued, thrusting the umbrella in front of him.

'That'll be a first,' grinned Tracey. 'Seriously, though,' she said giving his ear a stroke. 'Don't you think we should leave it to the police?'

Dick looked slowly at Tracey and smiled. 'The Police acting spontaneously?' he asked. 'Everything is by the book, in the book, written in triplicate and filed alphabetically.'

Tracey grinned. 'I know, and it's just the same for them when they're on duty.'

Dick returned her grin. 'I told you being associated with me would corrupt your sense of humour.' He took a deep breath and looked over at his house. 'Come on,' he said with mock bravery. 'Let's just take a quick peek anyway. If it looks like we might get more than we bargained for, we'll call the police.'

Quietly getting out of the car, the pair of tentative amateur sleuths crept along the drive to the house and stopped in the front of the door. Tracey pointed at the slightly ajar door. Theatrically, Dick held a finger to his lips and pushed the door open with his foot.

The hallway was in darkness apart from the dull, orange glow that seeped under the lounge door. Gingerly, Dick and Tracey moved forwards with Dick holding the umbrella defensively in front of him. The indistinct murmuring of voices could be heard beyond the door.

'They're in there,' whispered Tracey urgently.

Dick turned to look at her with his eyes wide in mock admiration. 'Really?' he mouthed. Tracey was just about to jab him in the ribs again but thought better of it, she didn't want to alert the burglars to their presence. Dick nodded at the door and held a finger in the air. 'After three,' he whispered. The second finger joined the first and Tracey raised her foot in anticipation of storming the door. The third finger rose and Dick thrust the door open with his arm extended holding the umbrella, which chose that moment to shoot forward forming a black canopy in front of them.

A stifled giggle echoed around the room. Slowly, Dick lowered the umbrella to reveal the occupants of the room. 'You!' he cried pointing to the first figure. 'You!' he gasped as he recognised the second person.

Sitting comfortably on the sofa, cradling a mug of tea sat Malc from Regeneration Sounds. Beside him sat Angie Brown, Dick's evening class student and PA to the Principal, holding her cup of tea rather more demurely than Malc. Dick looked from Malc to Angie and back again. His expression spoke more eloquently than his mouth.

'Eh?' he gargled.

'Surprised?' asked Angie taking a small sip of her tea.

'Told you I'd be seeing you soon,' quipped Malc.

Dick took a deep breath. Expecting to confront a burglar or two, in his home, had caused a surge of adrenaline to course through his body. Now, being faced by two acquaintances sitting on his sofa sipping tea had left him feeling confused. He was thankful he didn't need to display some sort of primal instinct and act in a bravely stupid fashion, but he was also disappointed that he had no opportunity to make even a half-hearted attempt at being heroic. Dick coughed loudly.

'So you two know each other?' he asked the pair on the sofa.

Malc laughed part way through taking another sip of tea. With the aid of Angie's ministering thumps on his back, Malc regained control of his breathing and narrowly avoid choking. He looked at Dick through moist eyes.

'And to think we had so much confidence in his powers of deduction!'

Angie grinned. 'He got there in the end though didn't he little brother?' she replied.

Dick's response was interrupted by the sound of a kettle being filled in the kitchen. Before he could make use of the remaining adrenaline in his body, Tracey rushed into the kitchen. He heard a few mumbled words and then the sound of laughter. He looked quizzically at Malc.

'What's going on?' he asked with an almost imperceptible shake of the head. Before Malc had a chance to answer, Dubbya walked into the lounge carrying a tray containing six mugs of tea and sufficient custard creams to satisfy his hunger.

'Evenin' all,' he grinned with a comical bending of the knees. The mugs of tea rattled alarmingly on the tray. 'Whoops,' laughed Dubbya. 'Nearly made a bit of a splash.'

Tracey diplomatically removed the tray from his grasp and placed the tea and biscuits onto the coffee table. 'Help yourselves,' she said with a jerk of her head at the tray. Malc and Angie eagerly exchanged their virtually empty mugs for the fresh brew. Dick, having helped himself to a handful of biscuits to accompany his tea, looked at the tray and then at Dubbya.

'You've miscounted.'

Tracey intervened with a shake of her head. 'No, he hasn't,' she said with a grin. 'Two-stroke's in the kitchen doing a bit of washing up for me.'

Dubbya, with a mouthful of biscuits he'd thoughtfully liberated earlier, raised his hands towards the ceiling. 'Dearly, beloved, we are gathered here today,' he intoned

'Dubbya!' said Tracey sharply.

'Sorry,' he said, popping another biscuit into his mouth. At that moment, Two-stroke walked into the lounge wiping his hands on a tea-towel.

'Wotcha,' he said with a smile at everyone. He sat down on the sofa next to Angie and tipped his mug of tea into his mouth. Dick took the weight off his feet and spread himself out on the armchair. He raised his mug towards Angie.

'So, he said with a quick gulp of tea. 'We're all here then?'

'All present and correct,' grinned Angie. 'I thought it only appropriate that Dubbya and Two-Stroke should be here for the finale.'

Dick shrugged. 'Saves me having to retell the story later,' he acknowledged. He nodded at Angie, 'So, you were a plant then.'

'Not quite how I'd put it,' she replied. 'But I did place myself in your evening class for a reason.'

'Pray, clarify your intentions for those amongst us lacking insight?' said Dubbya quickly wiping a few errant crumbs from his lips.

Angie waited a moment while Dubbya finished rescuing the biscuit remnants. 'Which was,' she smiled. 'To see if Dick had any particular feelings of loyalty to the senior management team or the College in general.'

Dick frowned. He was having difficulty making sense of who was supposed to be under scrutiny here and he certainly objected to any suggestion of harbouring managerial loyalty. 'Hang on a minute,' he began.

'No, you hang on a minute,' interrupted Tracey sharply. She turned to Angie and Malc. 'Before we ascertain Dick's feelings for those in positions of academic irresponsibility,' she paused briefly. Leaning forward she looked directly at Angie. 'How did you get in the house?' She didn't wait for a response before turning to Dubbya and Two-stroke. 'And are you two working with those two and leaving us two in the dark?'

Dubbya ingested a custard cream without the formality of crushing it first, while Two-stroke sat with a pained expression on his face desperately trying not to look guilty in his innocence. Dick, while slapping Dubbya on the back to aid his digestion, looked sternly at Malc and Angie.

'Was it you two who broke into here in the first time and trashed the place?'

Malc held his hands out as if trying to push back Dick's words. 'Hang on a minute,' he said firmly. 'We didn't trash the place, nor did we break in, well, not technically.'

Angie placed her hand on Malc's arm. 'Let me explain,' she offered.

'I think you'd better,' replied Tracey, her usual patience disappearing as quickly as the tea in her mug. Angie nodded and smiled.

'Your good friends Jonesy and his mate had already forced their way into your house and were making a frantic search for whatever evidence you may have gathered on the unscrupulous activities of their influential friends.'

'And I think we did you a little favour there,' continued Malc, clicking his fingers together excitedly.

Angie nodded eagerly. 'You should have seen Malc. He raced up the driveway, banged his fists against the front door and yelled, "It's the Police, open up". Well,' she laughed, 'you could hear the panic from inside. The next moment we heard the back door slam and the sound of someone clambering over the rear fence.'

'And then you were going to tidy up for us and leave us a little parcel?' enquired Tracey.

Angie shrugged. 'We were going to pop it through your letterbox, but decided it was safer to put it where it wouldn't get trodden on or missed in the jumble that Jonesy and company left behind.' She smiled apologetically. 'We didn't have time to tidy the place up. You might have caught us in the act as it were and it was far too soon to reveal our identities.'

The room was silent for a moment while various thoughts were processed. Dubbya broke the silence.

'I'm a little perturbed by your seemingly random choice of

assistance in this matter. Wouldn't it have been more prudent to inform the appropriate authorities?'

Angie fidgeted with the cuff of her jacket. 'Not quite so easy to decide who were the appropriate authorities,' she replied. 'There were no actual crimes, well, apart from the misappropriation of funds, but reporting that would have resulted in an audit of accounts and warned the main players that their devious scheme had been discovered.'

Dubbya clicked his tongue. 'That raises questions number two and three,' he mused. 'Secondly, why didn't you simply inform every official body going and put a stop to whole escapade once and for all.' He inclined his head toward Dick. 'Thirdly, why Dick and, by his literary association, why Tracey?'

Malc stifled a laugh. 'The answer to your third question was my doing I'm afraid,' he said trying to control his voice. 'When Angie told me about her concerns, she also mentioned some possible names of people she thought might be able to help without disclosing her identity and possibly alerting the culprits.'

'Ah,' said Dubbya with a satisfied smile. 'So you recognised Dick's anti-establishment stance aided by an analytical mind, in the form of our fair Tracey and formed the opinion that these were the ideal partners to assist you in your endeavour?'

'No,' declared Malc unable to suppress his laughter. 'It was their names.' He swallowed noisily. 'Think about it.' He pointed to Dick and Tracey. 'Whatever combination you choose, it points to the ideal investigative team. *Dick* and *Tracey*, *Dick* and Tracey *Barton*.'

Dubbya nodded. 'I understand.'

Two-stroke shook his head. 'Well, I don't.'

'Ah,' repeated Dubbya. 'How sweet is the ignorance of youth?'

'I ain't ignorant,' stormed Two-stroke. 'I just don't know what you're on about.' He pummelled the chair cushion in annoyance. 'And I ain't sweet either.'

Malc smiled kindly. 'Dick Tracy,' he explained. 'Was a comic-strip, sort of cartoon police detective in the 1930's.'

Two-stroke's eyebrows arched towards the ceiling. Malc grinned.

'And Dick Barton or, to give him his full name, ex-commando Captain Richard Barton, was a BBC radio series in the 1940's and

1950's. He solved all sort of crimes with the help of Jock Anderson and Snowy White.'

Two-stroke's eyebrows remained firmly raised. He breathed deeply and gave a slight shake of his head. 'I still don't ... '

Malc sighed. 'Indulge me,' he said. 'It was just one of those things, you know, almost too good to ignore.'

Angie decided to get the conversation back on track. 'Apart from the names, Malc also pointed out that the evidence we had was circumstantial.' She tapped the side of her head for emphasis. 'Think about it,' she continued. 'The amount of money apparently disappearing into the academic equivalent of a black-hole is pretty normal for education.' Angie grinned. 'And the somewhat less than discrete liaison between the College's Chair of Governors and the Council's Chair of Planning and Development was hardly a scandal. Thirdly,' she said with a shrug. 'Having a couple of large businesses interested in events at the College is something most educational establishments are eager to encourage.'

Dick let out the breath he'd been holding as Angie had been talking. 'So why not just inform the authorities and be done with?' he said shaking his head. 'You surely had enough bits and pieces of evidence to implicate somebody?'

'Hardly,' agreed Angie. 'Even the frequent visits of our MP could be explained as him being interested in those students who were nearing voting age, and as for the Assistant Principal for External Affairs, well ... '

Malc leaned forward. 'She's put out that he never made an improper advance towards her, but I happen to know...'

Angie interrupted him with a slap on the arm. 'Never crossed my mind,' she said crossly. In an attempt to create a little distance from Malc's remark, she reached into her pocket and removed a packet of mints. She quickly placed a mint into her mouth, smiled briefly and then looked surprised at Dick's pointing finger.

'It was you,' he said excitedly. 'You were the disembodied voice in the photocopying room.'

'Hmm,' smiled Dubbya, 'the female encounter of which, Dick so obligingly told me about in such tantalising detail. Delicious.'

Angie grinned sheepishly. 'I couldn't afford to give my identity away. It was important to see if Dick would take the bait and do whatever he could to uncover everyone involved in the scam.'

'Couldn't you have just told the Principal of your concerns?' asked Dick.

Angie shook her head firmly. 'You obviously have a misplaced sense of trust,' she said. 'The bloke's a nutter of the highest order. When he's not in his office watching DVD's of the Battle of Waterloo, he's reading biographies about Napoleon.' She closed her eyes and sighed. 'Ever since it was made clear by those in power, that any new venture involving the merging of the College with the local Sixth Form would require some young, energetic visionary and not some ageing traditionalist, the Principal has been a prime candidate for a sequined straight-jacket with matching slippers.'

Dick rubbed his eyes, as if the action would help him see how the puzzle fitted together. 'But how ... '

Tracey interrupted his question. Although she'd been listening to Angie's explanation of things, the seemingly random bits of information were now beginning to make sense.

'What we basically have,' began Tracey. 'Are two Colleges with insufficient funds to continue their current levels of expenditure.'

The room was silent. Two-stroke caressed his mug of tea with his lips and looked expectantly at the others, hoping for someone to lead him out of the dark recesses of his mind where he'd gone in search of understanding. Dubbya, his hands clasped tightly over the strained buttons of his cardigan, sat patiently waiting for the continuation of the story. Dick's shoulders sagged.

'I might have known a librarian would want to start at the beginning.' He looked at Tracey and blew her a gentle kiss. 'We're sitting comfortably.'

'Then I'll begin ... again,' ribbed Tracey, a smile receiving his kiss. She filled her lungs and launched into the next verse of the saga. 'The next, logical move was to be a merger of the two colleges to reduce costs, and staffing.'

Dick and Dubbya nodded strongly in agreement. The recent staff meeting had made it clear that cuts had to be made even though the Principal had avoided the actual word by using other fanciful expressions. Malc pressed his fingers together.

'The sweetener being a pristine, state-of-the-art building as the Town's new seat of learning,' he added.

'Precisely,' agreed Tracey. She took a sip of rapidly cooling tea. 'With the Sixth Form College being closest to the town centre, it made sense for that to be the location of the new building. That leaves an extremely valuable piece of land available for development to the highest bidder.'

Dubbya inhaled, putting an increased strain on his cardigan, which resulted in the middle button falling off and dropping into his empty mug. 'Whoops,' he mumbled. He held his mug up and rattled the contents. 'And that's where we come to the nub of the matter,' he declared.

Two-stroke looked quizzically at Dubbya's mug. He was still finding the unravelling of the evidence almost impossible to follow and hadn't a clue what Dubbya was referring to. 'Eh?' he asked.

Dubbya gave him a beatific smile. 'Why should the profit from that valuable piece of land, once the existing college has been dismantled brick by brick, simply be absorbed into the unappreciative coffers of the new college and the County Council, who still own a part of the current College's estate?'

'On the nail,' said Angie. 'That's where the potential for a redistribution of wealth became apparent to our Assistant Principal and the Chair of Governors.' Looking around at the assembled faces, it was difficult to ascertain whether everyone was following the plot. She noticed Tracey smile encouragingly at her.

'And that's when discrepancies began to appear in the accounts?'

'Exactly,' replied Angie. 'I can only assume, at that stage, the Assistant Principal and the Chair of Governors thought that they should be rewarded for the amount of time they'd invested in the College.'

'Along with the MP, a few local business people and some Councillors who also considered that they had a vested interest in the future of that land,' added Dick, thankful that he appeared to be keeping up with the storyline.

Two-stroke ran a hand through his hair. 'I still don't understand what they were trying to do,' he said, tapping the arm of his chair in exasperation.

Tracey leaned over and patted his arm. Two-stroke didn't consider her touch as being maternal or patronising. Instead, he thought her action a considerate move and one, which implied she wanted to make him feel a part of what was going on.

'If they could make sure that the land was made available to the *right* organisation, then *that* organisation might show its appreciation in a tangible manner,' explained Tracey rubbing her thumb and forefinger together.

'A bribe, you mean?' asked Two-stroke.

'More of a thank you for services rendered,' replied Tracey, hoping that Two-stroke wouldn't expand the analogy by discussing the World's oldest profession in detail.

'You mean like a ... ' began Two-stroke.

'Meaning,' interjected Dick to a thankful smile from Tracey. 'That providing the organisation could develop the site without hindrance from planning or political objections, then those who'd contributed to "easing the wheels of progress", would be rewarded accordingly.'

Two-stroke leaned back into his chair. 'I see,' he said. He thought for a moment and then shook his head. 'No I don't.' he said. 'What's the big deal? They don't own the land and a builder will only give them so much money for their help.'

'You're exactly right,' grinned Tracey. 'And that's where the beauty of their scheme comes to light.'

'I wish it would come to light,' moaned Two-stroke. 'It's giving me a headache.'

'There's definitely been a few headaches,' agreed Dick gingerly rubbing his face. 'As I understand, if the merger went ahead and the land was sold for development, then everything appears normal.'

'In the shell of a nut,' said Malc. 'But, if that organisation was not one that simply built and sold houses with a one-off profit ... '

'But one that produced a regular income from its activities,' continued Dick with a smile.

Tracey again laid a hand on Two-stroke's arm. A quick glance at his face suggested that he was on the verge of imploding. She rubbed his hand. 'Think about it, Two-stroke,' she soothed. 'What would you prefer? A single, small payment or a regular sum of money paid into your bank account and, if anyone asked where the money came from, you could say it was a consultation fee or profits from your investment in the organisation?'

Two-stroke grinned. 'A regular payment into my bank would take the heat off me. Dad's always saying it was about time I started to earn some money and contribute to the running of the house.' He patted his well-padded stomach. 'It's not as if I eat that much.'

Dick offered Two-stroke the plate containing the two remaining custard creams. Before Two-stroke could pick up both biscuits, Dubbya snatched the one nearest to him and popped it into his mouth. 'Appreciated,' he mumbled. Two–stroke took the plate and remaining biscuit. Holding the plate securely to his chest, he looked at Tracey.

'So why didn't the Assistant Principal and Chair of Governors just keep it to themselves? Why involve all those other plebs?'

Angie and Malc both tried to answer the question. 'Because ... ' they said simultaneously.

Dick clapped his hands together. 'It was in the local paper,' he said excitedly. 'They want to build a luxury hotel and leisure complex.'

'And,' added Malc. 'The proverbial icing on the cake, a casino.'

'Strewth,' whistled Dick. 'That really does make the idea of percentage payments worth twisting a few arms.'

Dubbya rattled the button in his empty mug. 'Any chance of a refill?' he asked the room.

'Just a minute, Dubbya,' said Tracey thoughtfully. 'I just want to get this straight in my head. Getting planning permission for a luxury hotel, leisure complex and a casino would prove quite problematic unless you had lubricated the appropriate political cogs, wouldn't it?'

Angie nodded. 'Virtually impossible,' she said emphatically. 'The proposed development would be right in the middle of a posh, residential area.'

'Definitely wouldn't happen,' said Malc with a flourish of his hand. 'If you hadn't got the major decision makers on the payroll.'

'Still a bit of a gamble though,' said Dick. 'It all depended upon the merger of the two Colleges going ahead.'

'What had they got to lose?' asked Angie. 'If they waited until the merger had been agreed, then it'd be too late to get everything in place, the right people and an agreeable developer. As it was, they'd got an eager developer and greedy politicians all ready to profit and nobody the wiser until it was too late.'

Dick held his chin in his hand for a few moments, deep in thought. 'Just a moment,' he said eventually. 'This is all conjecture, the possibility of some corrupt people making a lot of money and only a few abstract figures on a spreadsheet to indicate their intent?'

Both Malc and Angie nodded.

'So,' continued Dick. 'The agony I went through at the steam room, the near-death experience on the golf course, being stripped virtually naked and getting thumped for burgling the Assistant Principal's office was all just in case some corrupt gits got away with making a fortune, possibly?'

'Well,' replied Malc apologetically. 'If you put it like that, well ... '

'What he means,' said Angie, giving Malc a savage poke in the ribs. 'Is that we needed to identify the culprits behind the scam as discretely as possible. 'Think about it,' she said with a shrug. 'What real evidence did we have?'

Tracey smiled. 'We have plenty courtesy of the Assistant Principal's meticulous records and the confessions from Jonesy and his mate.'

Dick, who still appeared thoughtful, sighed. 'But why the notes in the jazz CD's and the daft rhyme for the code to unlock the AP's door?'

'I'll take the blame for that,' said Malc. 'We knew that a couple of County Councillors had dodgy connections and would resort to a bit of physical persuasion should the need arise.'

'And we needed to throw them off the scent if we could and not allow them to make the link between your enquiries and my job as PA to the Principal,' explained Angie.

Two-stroke belched loudly. 'So, what have we achieved apart from getting even with a couple of local hooligans?' he asked.

'I think,' grinned Angie. 'That we've put paid to any development of the old College site involving a casino and other questionable buildings and, in the process, terminated the careers of several

County Councillors and made it unlikely that a certain MP will stand at the next election.'

'And,' laughed Tracey. 'There are two Chairs who will most definitely not be sitting on any committees for the foreseeable future.'

'If that's the case,' said Dubbya raising his mug towards the kitchen. 'Do you think we could have that refill now?'

CHAPTER 51

The shrill chimes of the phone tore through the silence. Lazily, a hand stretched out and interrupted the noisy intrusion.

'Hello,' sighed a young male voice. 'PC Blencowe, speaking. How can I help?'

For a few moments, the PC listened intently to the caller, only pausing the flow of information to clarify a detail. Finally, satisfied that he had all the relevant facts, PC Blencowe thanked the caller and restored the phone to its usual state of preparedness. Picking up his notes, the PC turned to the rear of the room.

'Sarge?' he called. 'Something odd's going on in the centre of town.'

Acting Sergeant Ricketts smiled with a sense of satisfaction. It was only four weeks ago that the Chief Constable had made an unexpected visit to chat with Sergeant Cost. Within what seemed like minutes, the Chief and waiting enforcers had escorted the Sergeant out of the police station, out of her life and, hopefully, out of the Force for good. Sergeant Cost had been suspended pending an investigation into his alleged association with known criminals and his apparent ease at living well beyond his legal income. A cough interjected itself into her thoughts.

'Sorry, Sarge,' said PC Blencowe apologetically. 'But this does seem quite urgent.'

Ricketts nodded. 'I'm sorry, Blencowe,' she smiled. 'I was just thinking how circumstances suddenly change, even when you've got life down as being something to tolerate until something better comes along.'

PC Blencowe scratched his head. This was his first experience of life as a real PC after weeks of training and being placed in every out of the way police station serving tea to obnoxious sergeants who enjoyed nothing better than shining their boots on the trousers of a rookie PC. He'd warmed to Acting Sergeant Ricketts immediately. She had welcomed him cheerfully and even offered to make him a cup of tea when he first arrived. His only uncertainty lay in how to deal with her tendency to daydream while sitting at her desk with a huge smile on her face. He'd tried discretely to sniff her clothes for traces of exotic substances and even dipped his finger into the dregs of her tea mug to see if he could taste anything suspicious. Apart from Sergeant Ricketts predilection for something called *Lapsang Souchong,* he couldn't find anything to account for her bouts of happy silence. A polite cough sounded next to his ear.

'Sorry again, Blencowe. You seemed to be in a world of your own there.'

Acting Sergeant Ricketts took the notebook from his hand and quickly scanned top page.

'Good grief!' she exclaimed. 'You're damn right this is urgent.' Ricketts strode over to a bookcase and extracted a large book from the shelf. Running her thumb down the index of the Major Incident Procedure Manual, she made a series of scribbled notes. Apparently satisfied with her search, Ricketts turned to PC Blencowe. Her normal smile had given way to a look of steely determination. 'Action stations, Blencowe,' she snapped. 'Get a couple of patrol units over to the Town Hall immediately and then get an ambulance there pronto.' She took a quick glance at a list of telephone numbers on the wall. 'I'd better give the armed response unit a shout just to be on the safe side.'

While PC Blencowe busied himself with making the calls as instructed, Ricketts rubbed her hands together. 'Juicy,' she said with a smile. 'Real juicy.'

CHAPTER 52

Dick had lost count of the number of times Tracey had checked her hair and make-up in the mirror of the car's sun visor.

'Look,' he said, hardly disguising the irritation in his voice. 'I'm not driving recklessly, doing handbrake turns or indulging in emergency stops. Besides,' he continued, allowing himself a brief smile. 'You're safely cocooned inside the car, there are no windows open and I've turned the fan on the air conditioning off. There is absolutely nothing that is going to put a hair out of place or smudge your make-up.' He looked over at Tracey's pursed lips, a sure sign that she was annoyed and considering some sobering riposte. 'Anyway,' he said softly. 'I think you look beautiful.'

Tracey slowly looked towards Dick, her head tilted slightly. 'And if you think a titbit of flattery will disguise your large portion of moaning then think again.' She took a final look in the mirror and dabbed her little finger on a nonexistent mark on her chin. 'I've put myself out to make a real effort for tonight and now you're going to put yourself out.'

'Meaning?' asked Dick cautiously.

Tracey smiled at him. 'I'm going to choose the most expensive dish on the menu and not a word of admonishment or inappropriate reference shall be audible from your good self.'

The few short weeks since the auspicious evening of the fashion show had passed by in a blur of mediocrity. The normal hubbub of daily life had quickly reasserted itself as Dick and Tracey once more shared breakfasts uninterrupted by discussions concerning the unscrupulous activities of other people. At the College, things had quietened down after a brief flurry of reporters had made academic life almost interesting. The reporters had faithfully noted any comments made by anyone remotely connected to the events at the fashion show but had soon lost interest when news of someone dumping washing-up liquid in the municipal fountain and submerged the town centre in suds offered more opportunity for headline puns.

Finally, to celebrate a successful conclusion to their investigations, Dick had suggested they mark the occasion by dining at their favourite Italian restaurant. Tracey had readily agreed and, apart from a curt comment questioning the need for a reason to wine and dine a woman, she was looking forward to the evening out and Dick's plans for post-meal entertainment.

Tracey nervously checked her watch. They'd become stuck in a queue of traffic and there seemed to be no sign of movement.

'It's a good job you suggested leaving a bit earlier to have a drink before the meal,' she said with a second glance at her watch. 'As it is, we'll be cutting it fine.'

Dick drummed his fingers on the steering wheel. Traffic was notoriously bad on the approach to the town centre and it had become even worse recently after some demented planner had rerouted the outer ring road through the centre of town. Dick thought better of performing his usual rant at the lack of collective brain cells at County Hall and chose to imitate the timpani section for the 1812 Overture. Tracey coughed in annoyance.

'Before you think of any other ways of making percussive noises,' she said in the slightly clipped tone that Dick normally associated with trouble. 'Perhaps you could think of an alternative route to the restaurant.'

'Funny you should say that,' grinned Dick with a final flourish of timpani. 'I was just wondering whether it'd be worth going down the service road to the shopping mall and, if the barrier hasn't been put down, we could nip into the staff car park at the Town Hall.'

'As long as you don't expect me to run down the High Street in these heels,' she warned. 'They're killing me already and I'm sitting down.'

Dick performed a rapid three-point-turn and shot across the road and along the service road for the mall. After scattering a couple of cardboard boxes full of rubbish, and a cry of triumph as they sailed through the barrier-less gate, Dick turned smartly into the entrance to the Town Hall's staff car park and came to an abrupt stop before an armed police officer.

The officer walked purposefully towards the car. Dick felt his heart pounding and he tried to dry his sweating palms on the car seat as the officer leant down to the car and tapped sharply on the window. Dick lowered the glass.

'I'm so sorry officer,' he said in what he hoped was a subservient voice. 'But we're a bit late for a dinner and we took just the tiniest short cut and ... '

The officer ignored Dick's explanation and shook his head. 'I'm sorry, sir. But we have a bit of a situation on the steps of the Town Hall at the moment, and I need you to remove yourself and your vehicle from the immediate vicinity of the building.' The officer rapped his knuckle on the roof of the car. 'If you'd be so kind sir.'

Events at the front of the Town Hall were proving to be chaotic. In a small town such as East Bidding, any attempt at trying to stop people observing unsavoury scenes only served to increase their determination to decide for themselves whether they should witness events or not.

All the roads leading to the Town Hall were now successfully sealed off with small crowds anxiously waiting for something to happen. To the left of the Town Hall stood two ambulances with their rear doors expectantly open. Immediately in front of the building, a small cordon of police cars sat patiently while their occupants stared intently at the large wooden doors of the Town Hall. Several members of the armed response unit stood to the right of the building, their boots occasionally scuffing the tarmac in irritation at being called out on what seemed like the whim of an Acting Sergeant's overactive imagination.

The Chief Constable patted his leather-gloved hands together and cleared his throat with a polite cough.

'So, *Acting* Sergeant Ricketts,' he said with emphasis on the prefix to her newly promoted status. ' What have we got here?'

He was pleased to have been able to sanction the temporary promotion of PC Ricketts with the hope that, once the unfortunate situation regarding Sergeant Cost was resolved, the sergeant role would become permanent for her. Although the initial few weeks had been routine, the Chief Constable had begun to wonder whether this little party was a sign of Ricketts looking to prove herself worthy of Acting Sergeant.

Ricketts, aware that she could end up brewing tea again for some despotic sergeant, wanted her instincts to be right. 'It's those reports of a strange apparition terrorising the neighbourhood, Sir.' She shivered in the cool evening air. 'We had a report of a ghostly image and unusual noises somewhere over there.' Ricketts pointed towards the outline of trees that formed the perimeter where the park adjoined the Town Hall. 'A couple of witnesses thought the apparition was heading this way.'

The Chief Constable peered into the gloom that hung over the trees.

'Can't say I can see anything, Sergeant,' he observed coolly. 'I left a perfectly edible steak and kidney pie cooling to answer your summons.' He nodded towards the ambulances and armed response unit. 'Are you sure those were absolutely necessary? If all this turns out to be a wild goose chase then Acting Sergeant may prove to be the high point of your career.'

Ricketts shuddered involuntarily. She knew that the evidence was tenuous to say the least, but something told her that the precautions were essential.

'I'm aware of the possible repercussions should this be considered an over-reaction, Sir. But in each of the previous instances, the victims have required hospital treatment. And, as for the armed response unit, I've a feeling that any attempt at trying to apprehend the perpetrator of these crimes may require something a little more threatening than a truncheon.'

The Chief Constable smiled. He admired confidence and, in particular, a person who was willing to take a risk, as long as it didn't reflect negatively on him if things went a bit pear-shaped. 'Could I suggest that the armed response chappies make themselves less conspicuous. Hide behind a bush or something?'

Acting Sergeant Ricketts was just about to walk over to the bloke in charge of the armed response unit when a blast of hot, moist breath wrapped itself around her neck. She gave a startled gasp, which caught in her throat. A loud, echoing whinny almost deafened

254

her. Ricketts heard a woman scream somewhere behind her in the crowd. She tried to turn around but the weight of a comatose Chief Constable pinned her against the side of the squad car.

As she struggled to free herself, Ricketts became aware of a large black shadow brush past her. The dull, orange lights of the Town Hall outlined the figure of a wiry person sitting astride a magnificent dark horse. The rider urged the horse onto the steps of the Town Hall. All around a mixture of screams and gasps of admiration filled the air as the rider sat proudly observing the crowd of onlookers. The horse needed no embellishment to enhance its physical stature and elegance. The rider, conversely, had deemed it necessary to equip himself with the costume of a French cavalry officer from the Napoleonic wars.

Even in the murky light emanating from the Town Hall, it was possible to appreciate the splendour of the rider's costume. From the black boots to the gold-laced jacket, the detail on the clothing was outstanding. Across his left shoulder the rider had a red, fur-trimmed cape decorated with gold braid. On his head sat a tall, grey fur hat, or *Shako*, with an elegant, upright white plume. While one hand held the reins for the horse, the other hand, rather than holding a sabre held a lethal looking musket.

Momentarily caught napping, the armed response unit quickly clicked into operations mode and started to race towards the rider. Alert to the advancing police, the rider suddenly jerked the reins, causing the horse to rear up. At the sight of flailing hooves, the armed police stopped in their tracks. The College Principal smiled. At last he felt as if he was receiving the sort of attention he deserved. He felt resplendent in his French uniform, his horse obedient to his every wish and a sense of authority with a musket in his hand. Once more he jerked the reins of the horse. Waving the musket above his head the Principal shouted his final comments as a leader.

'*Liberté, Egalité, Fraternité!*'

Acting Sergeant Ricketts smiled triumphantly as she cradled the Chief Constable's head in her hands. She'd managed to solve the mystery of the ghostly apparition and done it within view of an appreciative public. Looking over towards the Town Hall, she saw the Principal walking beside his horse being led away by officers from the armed response unit. The Principal appeared to be enjoying the attention of the police and crowd, giving little regal waves as he passed the amused public.

The small matter of a senior officer fainting in full view of the crowd didn't concern Acting Sergeant Ricketts. She looked down at his vacant eyes. A muscle twitched in his cheek and his lips trembled.

'Any more gravy dear?' whimpered the Chief Constable.

CHAPTER 53

Forty-five minutes after their police encounter, and several circuits of the Town's one-way system, Dick and Tracey sat in their favourite Italian restaurant perusing the menu. As they drooled over the potential delights of *Bresaola Della Valtellina* or *Crema Di Porcini*, which Dick thought had more affect on the gastronomic senses than the mere translation of dried beef or mushroom soup, they were unaware of their Principal's escapade on the steps of the Town Hall. Instead they teased their taste buds and played footsie under the table in anticipation of a sensory satisfying evening.

'Here's to us,' grinned Dick lifting his glass of *Pinot Grigio* to Tracey.

"To us,' agreed Tracey. 'And to any other budding criminals who fancy their chances against us.'

Dick tried desperately not to choke on his wine. 'What,' he spluttered. 'What other villains?'

Tracey smiled. Although there had been a few moments where she'd feared for their safety, the whole episode had been quite enjoyable. 'I thought we did rather well, on the whole,' she said happily.

'What's with the *we* did rather well?' asked Dick wiping his mouth dry. 'I didn't see you offering to visit the steam rooms or sitting in a freezing warehouse in just your underwear.'

'Steady Rover,' laughed Tracey. 'Don't let your imagination run riot, we haven't eaten yet.'

Dick pondered on the image for a moment and then shook his head. 'You're right,' he agreed. 'I'm hungry.'

The first course hardly had time to register on their palate before it was swallowed to make way for the next portion. It wasn't until they were part way through the main course that their hunger gave way to curiosity. Tracey, pausing with a forkful of spaghetti, looked at Dick thoughtfully.

'Did you ever hear what happened to our less than delightful Chair of Governors and her Chair of Planning and Development?

'Relieved of duties, obviously,' replied Dick munching on a piece of baked artichoke. 'They disappeared off the scene pretty quickly after being rescued from the golf course.'

'The reports of their being found dead in the rough were a touch premature,' grinned Tracey. 'However, there were quite a few comments about Lady Faulkener's penchant for a bit of rough going around the college.'

'Dubbya's contribution to proceedings, I presume,' commented Dick. He sniffed. 'Dubbya has retold the story of his stalwart role with the mannequins over and over again to anyone willing to buy him a pint or three.' Taking a sip of wine, Dick nodded to Tracey. 'Is it true there's been a myopic lady of rather large proportions stalking the College reception area asking for Dubbya?'

Tracey quickly placed a hand over her mouth to stop the last few strands of spaghetti escaping. 'It's true,' she announced eventually. 'I think Dubbya's lost a bit of weight by continually taking the long way around the college to avoid going through the reception area.'

'The last I heard of the two Chairs,' said Dick carefully picking a piece of errant artichoke from between his teeth. 'Is that they were heading for an RSPB sanctuary somewhere north of Aviemore.'

Dick and Tracey's laughter generated a few raised eyebrows in the restaurant and resulted in one of the waiters coming across to their table to ask if anything were wrong with the food. Assuring him of their complete satisfaction with the contents of their plates, Dick and Tracey lubricated their throats with a generous amount of wine and tried to eat the remains of their main course in silence.

Tracey was the first to surrender to a further bout of curiosity. Mopping her plate with a piece of bread, she looked seriously at Dick.

'Whatever happened to Jonesy and his mate?' she asked.

Dick heard the concern in her voice and reached over to touch her hand. 'Secure in one of Her Majesty's finest establishments for those of a corrupt disposition.'

Tracey squeezed his hand. 'For how long?'

Dick shrugged. 'No idea,' he replied blithely. 'They're awaiting trial.' He fiddled with his napkin. After trying to fold it more than seven times he gave up and looked at Tracey. 'Don't worry,' he soothed. 'I gather the police are being helped by one of their own in the collection of evidence against that pair.'

'How do you mean?' asked Tracey as a frown creased her forehead.

'It appears,' grinned Dick. 'That a certain police sergeant had a blind spot where Jonesy and his mate were concerned. Apparently the sergeant was able to supplement his income by failing to monitor the odious activities of our two recent jailbirds and provide them with judicious bits of information regarding police activity.'

Tracey shivered. She was beginning to feel a little foolish for appearing so flippant earlier in the evening concerning their dealings with criminals. 'Sorry, Dick,' she said affectionately stroking his hand. 'I don't think I understood just how widespread the corruption had become.'

Dick returned the affection. 'At least we've helped reduce the crime wave a bit. Although,' he shrugged. 'I don't suppose for a moment that our efforts have had much of an impact on the local crime statistics.'

Tracey grinned. 'Talking of statistics, I gather the Assistant Principal for External Affairs has increased the unemployment figures this month.'

'The least he deserves,' replied Dick fiddling with his cutlery. 'External Affairs now appears to be an alternative analogy to gardening leave.'

'Angie reckons there will be a few County Councillors spending more time in their gardens soon,' added Tracey. 'If you fancy a change of career, there will be a few vacancies coming up at County Hall.'

Dick shook his head. 'I don't think I'd go down too well there,' he said taking hold of his knife. 'I imagine something nasty could happen to me in some dark, deserted photocopying room. You never know, one moment I'm whistling and the next ... ' Dick made a stabbing motion with his knife.

'Don't,' cried Tracey in alarm. 'That's a horrible thought.'

'Friends in high places,' joked Dick. 'You can run but you can't hide ... '

Tracey smacked his hand. 'Who said I wanted to run, or hide?' She winked at Dick. 'Did you want to order a desert or ... '

CHAPTER 54

A dark grey Ford KA crawled through the insipid light creeping out of the aged streetlamps. The air was heavily laden with an Autumnal mist that would soon take on a slightly more solid form as the night temperature descended towards freezing. Slowly the car edged forward, its headlights vainly trying to pierce the opaque vapour that clung to everything above ground level. Somewhere ahead, two cats fought for territorial dominance, the noise of their altercation more discernable than their forms. The grey body of the car continued its methodical progress along the street.

'Is this it?' asked the driver of the KA.

Mrs Baines rubbed the inside of the car window and squinted at the night outside. The vague outline of lights illuminating drawn curtains betrayed the presence of houses. With another rub of the window, Mrs Baines smiled.

'Just here, Becky love, I'd recognise that privet hedge anywhere.'

Becky, the teenage granddaughter of Mrs Baines, gently braked and applied the handbrake. 'Are you sure Gran,' she asked. Her voice was full of concern for the old lady who had only recently been discharged from hospital.

'I'm sure, dear,' replied Mrs Baines. She began prodding and pulling at anything she thought might open the car door and release her towards the familiarity of her own home.

'Hang on, Gran,' grinned Becky. 'I'll take your things in for you and make sure the heating is on,' She turned her face to the old lady. 'Are you certain you'll be OK here on your own? You know Granddad won't be able to get here until tomorrow afternoon.'

'I understand, Becky, love' said Mrs Baines with a smile. 'The old duffer is enjoying the company of your Dad's whisky too much to hurry home.'

'Gran!' exclaimed Becky. 'What a terrible thing to say.'

'It's true,' insisted Mrs Baines. 'He's using the excuse of needing the doctor to visit in the morning to give him the all clear so he can have another evening embracing the bottle.'

Becky laughed. 'Gran, you're a caution and no mistake.' She looked at her Gran's face. The car's courtesy light hardly flattered the old lady. What Becky often thought as laughter lines now seemed to emphasise the sunken hollows where her Gran's once sparkling eyes had stared out at the world. Becky sighed. 'I could stay over for the night, Gran,' she offered. 'It'd be no trouble and tomorrow's Saturday so I haven't got to get up early for work.'

Mrs Baines smiled. 'Getting rid of you young people is worse than getting muck off a shoe,' she said with mock severity. 'Anyway, you wouldn't want to spend an evening watching my type of programmes on the telly.' She tapped Becky's hand. 'And I definitely wouldn't want to watch the type of programmes you call entertainment either young lady.'

Becky laughed and got out of the car. 'I'll just get your things from the boot, Gran,' she called.

A few moments later Mrs Baines stood at the gate leading to her own front door. She stroked the gate, reacquainting herself with the wooden surface that had protected her domain all these years.

'Shall I pop the kettle on, Gran?' called Becky from the newly lit doorway.

'You do that, dear,' replied Mrs Baines. 'I'm just on my way.'

With a satisfied sigh, Mrs Baines began to make her way slowly along the well-worn path towards her sanctuary. She shivered as the cold mist crept around her ample figure. Tugging the collar of her coat tight to her neck, she shuffled towards the house. Surprised at the effort it seemed to take in walking the path that had served her so well, she stopped to take a deep breath before recommencing her short journey. The chill of the night air was unpleasant as it caressed the inside of her throat. Mrs Baines shuddered and then something out of place caused her to tilt her head to one side and listen. A throbbing, repetitive drumming sound began to emerge out of the mist. The sound seemed to envelope the air around her, pulsing with an almost deafening intensity. Mrs Baines stood still. Her eyes became dilated as her breath came out in short bursts.

Oh no,' she gasped. 'It can't be. Not again.'

The night suddenly returned to normality as the noise disappeared. Mrs Baines held her breath, almost knowing what was going to happen next. She wasn't to be disappointed. A dark apparition reared up out of the mist as a snorting, low-pitched whining battered her senses. With a gentle sigh, Mrs Baines collapsed neatly onto the path. Her torpid form oblivious to the shadow that melted into the embrace of the night.